B

D0385931

DISCARD

Jean Plaidy

A HEALTH UNTO HIS MAJESTY

G. P. Putnam's Sons
New York

AUTHOR'S NOTE

ANY NOVEL dealing with the days of the Restoration must inevitably be impregnated with one characteristic which was a feature of the times: licentiousness. Therefore I feel that, when presenting this middle period of Charles's life beginning with the Restoration, I must remind my readers that England had suddenly emerged from several years of drab Puritan rule. Bull-baiting and such sports had been suppressed, not from any consideration for the animals concerned, but solely because the people were known to enjoy those sports, and, in the opinion of their rulers, enjoyment and sin were synonymous; the taverns had been abolished; the great May Day festival was no more; Christmas festivities – even the Christmas services in the churches – were forbidden; the theatres were closed and their interiors broken up, and anyone caught play-acting was tied to a cart and whipped through the streets. It was therefore natural that, when the King returned, there should follow a turn-about, and it was only to be expected that the repressed population should swing violently in the opposite direction. Accordingly, no picture of Restoration days which ignores the fact would be a true one.

There may be some who will feel that my portrait of Charles is too flattering. I would say that excuses must be made for Charles's weaknesses as for those of his people. His fortunes had been subject to a similar abrupt change; he had grown cynical during his exile and was determined never to 'go a-travelling again'. He was the grandson of Henri Quatre, the greatest King the French had ever known, the man who had united France and put an end to the civil wars of religion when he had declared that 'Paris was worth a mass'. It was understandable that Charles should regard his grandfather as an example to be followed. Henri Quatre had the same good nature, the same indifference to religion; he was known to have declared that conquest in love pleased him more than conquest in war, and he had more mistresses than any King of France had ever had – or ever has had – including the notorious François Premier. I would say that Charles was unlucky in living when he did. The great plague and the great fire ruined the commerce of the country while it was engaged on a major war. If he appeared flippant and preoccupied with his mistresses, while his country was in danger, he was not really so. His demeanour of indifference had been acquired during the hardening years of exile when disappointments had quickly followed one another; he did not show his feelings, but the real man is to be seen when, during the fire, he worked as hard as any, standing with water up to his ankles, passing buckets, shouting orders and witty encouragement, so that it was said that what was left of the City owed its survival to Charles and his brother. Charles wins my sympathy as the man whose kindness makes him unique in his times, the man who declared he was weary of the hangings of those men who had killed his father and been responsible for his own exile, as the man who visited Frances Stuart to comfort her when he no longer desired her and her friends had deserted her, and again as the husband who held the basin when his wife was sick – the kind and tolerant King. For this King, careless and easygoing as he might be, and licentious as he certainly was, remains unique in his age on account of his kindness and tolerance.

In the research I have undertaken to write the book I have read a great number of works. I list below those which have been most helpful:

The National and Domestic History of England.
                    William Hickman Smith Aubrey.
Bishop Burnet's History of his Own Time.
King Charles II. Arthur Bryant.
Diary of John Evelyn. Edited by William Bray.
Diary and Correspondence of Samuel Pepys.
                    Edited by Henry B. Wheatley.
*The Diaries of Pepys, Evelyn, Clarendon
    and other Contemporary Writers.*
Personal History of Charles II. Rev C. J. Lyon.
Beauties of the Court of Charles II. Mrs Jameson.
Lives of the Queens of England. Agnes Strickland.
Great Villiers. Hester W. Chapman.
Titus Oates. Jane Lane.
Political History of England. F.C. Montague.
British History. John Wade.
The Gay King. Dorothy Senior.

                                        J.P.

A HEALTH UNTO HIS MAJESTY

ONE

IT WAS the month of May – the gayest and most glorious month, the people assured themselves, that England had ever known. This was the 29th, a day of great significance.

That morning, it seemed that the sun rose with more than its usual brilliance.

'A good omen!' people called to one another from the windows of houses, the overhanging gables of which almost met over the cobbled streets. 'It's going to be a fine day.'

In the country, as soon as the dawn showed in the sky, people were gathering on the village greens; there would be many to line the roads so that they should miss nothing when the time came.

'Listen!' one said to another. 'Even the birds are mad with joy. Have you ever heard a blackbird or chaffinch sing like that before? They know the good times are back.'

Others declared that the cherry trees had never borne such great masses of blossom in previous years. The flowers seemed more fragrant that spring. Children gathered buttercups and bluebells, celandines and lady's-smocks to strew along the road; they wore chains of daisies as necklaces and chaplets as they danced to the merry tunes of the fiddlers.

Now the bells were ringing from every tower and steeple between Rochester and London.

This was the happy month of May when the 'Black Boy' had come home to his people.

*

He rode in the midst of the cavalcade – tall, slim and elegant, his swarthy face prematurely lined, his dark eyes smiling, eager, alert, yet holding a hint of cynicism in their depth. He looked older than his years; he was thirty and this was not only the day of his entry into his capital, it was also his birthday. A meet and fitting day, all agreed, for his return.

With him came 20,000 horse and foot, swords held high, shouting to express their hilarious joy as they marched along.

7

The cavalcade had become swollen with every mile, for there had been a welcome for His Majesty at every point: Morris dancers had wished to show him by the abandoned joy of their performance that they rejoiced in his return which was a signal for the overthrow of solemnity; fiddlers had played the merriest jigs they knew till the sweat ran down their faces; even the dignified mayors in their robes of office were almost indecorously gay. Men and women of all conditions had come to add their loyal shouts to the general clamour.

At last they came into his capital, where the bells were making a merry peal and the streets were hung with tapestry, and the conduits flowing with wine instead of water. Citizens wept and embraced each other. 'The drab days are over,' they cried again and again. 'The King is restored to his own.'

There would be merry-making again; there would be pageants and ceremonies. On May Days the milkmaids would dance again in the streets, their pails flower-decked, while a fiddler led them along the Strand; the pleasure gardens would be thrown open; the theatres would flourish. Bartholomew and Southwark Fairs would be enjoyed once more; cock-fighting and bull-baiting would take place openly again; laughter would be considered a virtue instead of a sin; and when Christmas came it would be celebrated with the old gusto. The great days were here again for His Majesty King Charles II had come home.

What a brilliant sight this was, with the Lord Mayor and aldermen and members of City Companies in their various liveries and golden chains; coloured banners were held high; lines of brilliant tapestries were strung across the streets, while trumpet, fife and drum all sought to rival each other.

So great was the company that it took seven hours to pass any one spot. There had never been such pageantry in the City of London; and the citizens promised themselves that the revelry should continue for days to come. No one should be allowed to forget for a moment that the King had come home. It was eleven years since his father had been cruelly murdered; and for more years than that this dark young man had been a wandering exile on the continent of Europe. It was only fitting that he should know a right royal welcome was his.

He rode bareheaded, bowing this way and that, a faint smile about his mouth. He had remarked that it must surely have been his own fault that he had not returned before, as he had met no one, since he had stepped on English soil, who did not protest most fervently that he had always wished for the restoration of his King.

Now there were faint lines of weariness about his mouth. He had long dreamed of this day; he would never have believed that he could have come to it in this manner and that his restoration could have been brought about without the shedding of one drop of blood – and by that very army which had sent his father to the scaffold and rebelled against himself. This was to be compared with that miraculous escape after Worcester; it was the second miracle in his life.

But he was weary – weary, yet content.

'Od's Fish!' he murmured. 'I have learned to live on easy terms with Exile and Poverty, but Popularity is such a stranger to me that I am uneasy in his presence. Yet I trust ere long that he and I shall become boon companions.'

His eyes strayed again and again to the women, who waved flowers from the roadside as he passed or called a loyal welcome from their windows. Then the sombre eyes would lighten at the sight of a pretty face, and the smile he gave would be very charming, the regal bowing of the head most elegant.

The people looked at him with tears in their eyes. A young King – a King who, during his thirty years, had suffered hardship and frustration which must have made him sick at heart. Small wonder that rumours had reached England of his profligate habits; but if he was over-fond of the ladies the ladies would readily forgive him that, and the men would not hold it against him. He was such a romantic figure: a King returned to his country after years of exile. Charles Stuart on his thirtieth birthday, on entering his capital city, seemed to all beholders a King worthy to be loved.

The people grew hoarse with their shouting. Again and again the procession was delayed that yet another expression of loyal homage might be laid before the King, and it was seven o'clock before he came to his Palace of Whitehall.

Now the lights were springing up all over the city. Bonfires were raised in every open space, and lighted candles showed in all the windows.

'Let us welcome the King,' shouted a thousand voices. 'Let us cry "A Health unto His Majesty".'

9

The City was brilliant with thousands of candles which shone alike from the windows of great houses and the humblest dwellings.

In every window there must be candles to welcome His Majesty, for gangs roamed the streets ready to smash any window which was dark.

Everyone must join in the welcome, for the Merry Monarch had returned to make England merry.

*

In the Palace of Whitehall there was one who, with an impatience which she could not contain, waited to be presented to the King.

This was a tall young woman of nineteen, strikingly beautiful with rich, ripe colouring, bold flashing eyes that were almost startlingly blue; her rippling dark auburn hair was thick and vital; her features firm but beautifully moulded. There was in her evidence of a fierce passion which might have alarmed, but fascinated. Almost every man with whom she had come into contact had discovered her to be irresistible. Her rages came swiftly, and when they were upon her there was no knowing what turn they would take; she was beautiful and could be fierce as a tigress – an Amazon of incomparable beauty which was of a deep sensual kind. Barbara Villiers – now Barbara Palmer – was the most desirable young woman in London.

Now she fumed as she paced up and down the apartment in which she waited for audience with the King.

Her maids hovered some little distance from her. They were afraid to come too near, yet afraid to go too far from her. If they offended her, Barbara did not hesitate personally to apply corporal punishment. She would pick up the nearest article and fling it at the offender; and her aim was sure; all her life she had been throwing things at those who offended her.

She was not satisfied with the set of her dress at one moment; at the next her eyes glistened as she looked down at its smooth silken folds which fell seductively about her perfect figure. Her arms – very white and perfectly rounded – were bare from the elbow and the upper arm was visible here and there, for her wide sleeves were slit from the shoulder and loosely laced with blue ribbons. Her skirt was caught up to show a clinging satin petticoat. She was beautiful; and she wished to be more beautiful than she had ever been before. She patted those curls which had been arranged on her forehead and which were called, after the fashion of the day, 'favourites'. Those which rippled over her shoulders were 'heartbreakers', and those nestling against her cheeks 'confidants'. They were all lustrous natural curls, and she was proud of them.

Her husband, Roger Palmer, came to her then. His eyes shone with mixed pride and apprehension; he had been proud and apprehensive of Barbara ever since he had married her.

She gave him one of her disdainful looks. Never had he seemed to her more ineffectual than he did at that moment, but even as she glanced his way a smile curved her lips. He was her husband and that was how she would have him. She had strength and determination enough for them both.

Roger said: 'The press in the streets is growing worse.'

Barbara did not answer. She never bothered to state the obvious.

'The King is worn out with the journey,' went on Roger. 'All that bowing and smiling. . . . It must be wearying.'

Barbara still said nothing. All the bowing and smiling! she thought. Tired he might be, but he would be content. To think it had come at last. To think he was here in London!

But she was afraid. When she had last seen him he had been a King in exile, a very hopeful King it was true, but still an exile. Now that he had come into his own, her rivals would not be merely a few women at an exiled Court; they would be all the beauties of England. Moreover he himself would be a man courted and flattered by all. . . . It might well be that the man with whom she had to deal would be less malleable than that King who, briefly, had been her lover when she had gone with Roger to Holland.

That was but a few months ago, when Roger had been commissioned to carry money to the King who was then planning his restoration to the throne.

Charles had looked at Barbara and had been immediately attracted by those flamboyant charms.

Barbara too had been attracted – not only by his rank but by his personal charm. She had been sweetly subdued and loving during those two or three nights in Holland; she had kept that fierce passion for power in check; she had concealed it so successfully that it had appeared in the guise of a passion for the man. Yet he was no fool, that tall lean man; he was well versed in the ways of such as Barbara; and because he would never rave and rant at a woman, that did not mean that he did not understand her. Barbara was a little apprehensive of his tender cynical smile.

She had said: 'Tomorrow I shall have to leave for England with my husband.'

'Ere long,' he had answered, 'I shall be recalled to London. My people have been persuaded to clamour for my return, just as eleven years ago they were taught to demand my father's head. Ere long I too shall be in England.'

'Then . . . Sire, we shall both be there.'

'Aye . . . we shall both be there. . . .'

And that was all; it was characteristic of him.

She was faintly alarmed concerning the changes she might find in him; but when she held up her mirror, patted the 'favourites' which nestled on her brow, smiled at her animated and beautiful face, she was confident that she would succeed.

Roger, watching her, understood her thoughts. He said: 'I know what happened between you and the King in Holland.'

She laughed at him. 'I pray you do not think to play the outraged husband with me, sir!'

'*Play* the part! I have no need to *play* it, Barbara,' said the little man sadly. 'If you think to fool me with others as you did with Chesterfield . . .'

'Now that the King is returned it might be called treason to refer to his Majesty as "others". You are a fool, Roger. Are you so rich, is your rank so high that you can afford to ignore the advantages I might bring you?'

'I do not like the manner in which you would bring me these advantages. Am I a complaisant fool? Am I a husband to stand aside and smile with pleasure at his wife's wanton behaviour? Am I? Am I?'

Barbara spun round on him and cried: 'Yes . . . Yes, you are!'

'You must despise me. Why did you marry me?'

Barbara laughed aloud. 'Because mayhap I see virtues where others see faults. Mayhap I married you because you are ... what you are. Now I pray you do not be a fool. Do not disappoint me. Do not tell me I have made a mistake in the man I married, and I promise you that you shall not come badly out of your union with me.'

'Barbara, sometimes you frighten me.'

'I am not surprised. You are a man who is easily frightened ... Yes, woman?' shouted Barbara, for one of her women had appeared at the door.

'Madam, the King wishes to see you.'

Barbara gave a loud laugh of triumph. She had nothing to fear. He was the same man who had found her irresistible during that brief stay in Holland. The King was commanding that she be brought to his presence.

She took one last look at herself in her mirror, assured herself of her startling beauty and swept out of her apartment to the presence of the King.

*

Barbara had learned what she wanted at a very early age, and with that knowledge had come the determination to get it.

She never knew her father, for that noble and loyal gentleman had died before she was two years old; but when she was a little older her mother had talked to her of him, telling her how he had met his death at the siege of Bristol for the sake of the King's Cause, and that she, his only child, must never forget that she was a member of the noble family of Villiers and not do anything to stain the honour of that great name.

At that time Barbara was a vivacious little girl and, because she was a very pretty one, she was accustomed to hearing people comment on her lovely appearance. She was fascinated by the stories of her father's heroism and she determined that when she grew up she would be as heroic as he was. She promised herself that she would perform deeds of startling bravery; she would astonish all with her cleverness; she would become a Joan of Arc to lead the Royalists to victory. She was a fervent Royalist because her father had been. She thought of Cromwell and Fairfax as monsters, Charles, the King, as a saint. Even when she was but four years old her little face would grow scarlet with rage when anyone mentioned Cromwell's name.

'Curb that temper of yours, Barbara,' her mother often said. 'Control it. Never let it control you.'

Sometimes her relatives would visit her mother – those two dashing boys of another branch of the family, George and Francis Villiers. They teased her a good deal, which never failed to infuriate her so that she would forget the injunctions to curb her temper and fly at them, biting and scratching, using all the strength she possessed to fight them; this naturally only amused them and made them intensify their teasing.

George, the elder of the boys, had been the Duke of Buckingham since his father had died. He was more infuriating than his brother Lord Francis, and it became his special delight to see how fierce she could become. He told her she would die a spinster, because no man would marry such a termagant as she would undoubtedly become; he doubted not that she would spend her life in a convent, where they would have a padded cell into which she could be locked until she recovered from her rages.

Those boys gave her plenty of practice in control. Often she would hide from them because she was determined not to show her anger, but she soon discovered that she enjoyed her passions and, oddly enough, the company of her young relatives.

When Barbara was seven her mother married again and Barbara's stepfather was her father's cousin, Charles Villiers, Earl of Anglesey.

The marriage startled Barbara because, having always heard her father spoken of with reverence, it seemed strange that her mother could so far forget his perfections as to take another husband. Barbara's blue eyes were alert; she had always felt a great interest in the secret ways of adults. Now she remembered that her stepfather had for some time been a frequent visitor, and that he had seemed on each occasion always very affectionate towards her mother. She reasoned that her father, whom she had thought to be perfect, must after all have been merely foolish. He had become involved in the war and had met his death. The King's Cause had gained little by his sacrifice; and his reward was a tomb and the title of hero, while his cousin's was marriage with the widow.

Barbara told herself sagely that she would not have been as foolish as her father. When her time came she would know how to get what she wanted and live to enjoy it.

The result of this marriage was a move to London, and Barbara was enchanted by London as soon as she set eyes on it. It was Puritan London, she heard, and not to be compared with merry laughter-laden London of the old days; but still it was London. She would ride through Hyde Park with her mother or her governess in their carriage, and she would look wistfully at the gallery at the Royal Exchange which was full of stalls displaying silks and fans; she would notice the rendezvous of young men and women in the Mulberry Garden. 'London's a dull place,' she often heard it said, 'compared with the old city. Why, then there was dancing and revelry in the streets. A woman was not safe out after dark – not that she is now – but the King's Cavaliers had a dash about them that the Puritans lack.'

She was eager for knowledge of the world; she longed for fine clothes; she hated the dowdy garments she was forced to wear; she wished to grow up quickly that she might take her part in the exciting merry-go-round of life.

The servants were afraid of her, and she found it easy to get what she wanted from them. She could kick and scream, bite and scratch in a manner which terrified them.

Occasionally she saw George and Francis. George was haughty and had no time for little girls. Francis was gentler and told her stories of the royal household in which he and his brother had spent their childhood, because King Charles had loved their father dearly and when he had been killed in the Royalist Cause had taken the little Villiers boys into his household to be brought up with the little Princes and Princess. Francis told Barbara of Charles, the King's eldest son, the most easy-going boy he had ever known; and he talked of Mary who had been married to the Prince of Orange, after she was almost blind with weeping and hoarse with begging her parents not to send her away from Whitehall; he told her of young James, who had wanted to join in their games and from whom they had all run away because he was too young. She liked to hear of the games which had been played in the avenues and alleys of Hampton Court. Her eyes would glisten and she would declare that she wished she had been born a man, that she might be a king.

There came a time when Francis ceased to visit her and she knew, from the way in which people spoke of him, that some mystery surrounded him. She insisted on getting the story from the servants. Then she learned that Francis was yet another victim of the King's Cause.

Lord Francis had lost his life, and his brother the Duke, who had lost his estates, was forced to escape to Holland.

Seven-year-old Barbara, keeping her ears open, heard that Helmsley Castle and York House in the Strand, which had both been the property of the Villiers family, had passed to General Fairfax, and that New Hall had gone to Cromwell.

She was infuriated with those Roundhead soldiers. She would thump her fist on a table or stool. Her mother often warned her that she would do herself some injury if she persisted in giving way to the rage which boiled within her.

'Do we stand aside and allow these nobodies to rob our family?' she demanded.

'We stand aside,' said her mother.

'And,' added her stepfather, 'we keep quiet. We are thankful that the little we have is left to us.'

'Thankful, with Francis dead and George running away to hide in Holland!'

'You are but a child. You do not understand these things. You should not listen to what is not intended for your ears.'

It was a long time after that when she saw George again; but she heard of him from time to time. He fought at Worcester with Charles, the new King, for the old King had been murdered by his enemies. Barbara was ten years old at that time and she understood what was happening. She cursed the Roundhead soldiers whom she saw lounging in Paul's Walk, using the Cathedral and the city's churches as barracks or for stabling their horses, walking through the capital in their sombre garments, yet swaggering a little, as though to remind the citizens that they were the masters now. She understood George well, for he was very like herself – far more like her than gentle Lord Francis had been. George Duke of Buckingham wished to command the King's army, but the King, on the advice of Edward Hyde who had followed him to the continent, had refused to allow him to do so. Buckingham was furious – like Barbara he could never brook frustration – and was full of wild plans for bringing the King back to his throne. He was too young for the command, said Hyde; and at that time Charles had agreed with all that Edward Hyde advised. And Barbara heard how Buckingham would not attend council meetings in the exiled Court, that he scarcely spoke to the King; how his anger turned sour and he brooded perpetually; how he refused to clean himself or allow any of his servants to do this, and would not change his linen.

'Foolish, foolish George!' cried Barbara. 'If I were in his place . . .'

But George, it seemed, was not so foolish as she had thought him. He suddenly ceased to neglect himself, for the Princess of Orange, the King's sister Mary, had become a widow and George had offered himself as her second husband.

Barbara listened to the talk between her mother and her stepfather; moreover she demanded that the servants should tell her every scrap of gossip they heard.

Thus she discovered that Queen Henrietta Maria had declared herself incensed at Buckingham's daring to aspire to the hand of the Princess. She had been reported as saying that she would rather tear her daughter into tiny pieces than allow her to consider such a match.

Yes, George was a fool, decided Barbara. If he had wished to marry Mary of Orange he should have visited her in secret; he should have made her fall in love with him, perhaps married her in secret. She was sure he could have done that; he was possessed of the same determination as she was. And then he would have seen what that old fury, Queen Henrietta Maria (who, many said, was responsible for the terrible tragedy which had overtaken her husband King Charles I) would do!

Then for a time she ceased to think of George when she met Philip Stanhope, Earl of Chesterfield, who came on a visit to her stepfather's house. She had heard much talk of him before his arrival.

He was clever, it was said; he was one of the wise ones. He was not the sort to talk vaguely of what he would do when the King came home; he was not the sort to drink wistful toasts to the Black Boy across the water. No, Chesterfield would look at the new England and try to find a niche for himself there.

It seemed he was finding a very pleasant niche indeed, for he was betrothed to none other than Mary Fairfax, the daughter of the Parliamentarian General who, next to Cromwell himself, was the most important man in the Commonwealth.

Mary Fairfax was her father's darling and, good Parliamentarian though she might be, was bedazzled not only by the handsome looks and charming manners of the Earl, but by the prospect of becoming a Countess.

So this was one way in which a member of the aristocracy could live comfortably in the new England.

Barbara admired the man before she saw him, and he showed on the first day under her stepfather's roof that he was not indifferent to Barbara. She would look up to discover his eyes upon her, and to her surprise she found herself blushing. He seemed to sense her confusion. It amused him; and she, telling herself that she was furious with him for this, knew in her heart that she was far from displeased. His attention was reminding her that she was not a little girl any longer; she was a young woman; and she fancied that he was comparing her with Mary Fairfax.

She would ignore him. She shut herself into her own room; but she could not drive him from her thoughts. She saw the change in herself. She was like a bud which was opening to the warmth of the sun; but she was not a bud – she was a woman responding to the warmth of his glances.

He came upon her once on the staircase which led to her room. He said: 'Barbara, why do you always avoid me?'

'Avoid you!' she said. 'I was not aware of you.'

'You lie,' he answered.

Then she turned and tossed her long hair so that it brushed across his face, and would have darted up the stairs; but the contact seemed to arouse a determination within him, for he caught the hair and pulled her back by it; then he laid a hand on her breast and kissed her.

She twisted free and, as she did so, slapped his face so hard that he reeled backwards. She was free and she darted up the stairs to her room; when she reached it, she ran in and bolted the door.

She leaned against it; she could hear him on the other side of it as he beat on it with his fists.

'Open it,' he said. 'Open it, you vixen!'

'Never to you,' she cried. 'Take care you are not thrown out of this house, my lord earl.'

He went away after a while, and she ran to her mirror and looked at herself; her hair was wild, her eyes shining, and there was a red mark on her cheek where he had kissed her. There was no anger in her face at all; there was only delight.

She was happier than she had ever been, but she was haughty to him when they next met, and scarcely spoke to him; her mother reprimanded her for her ill-manners to their guest; but when had she taken any notice of her mother?

After that she began to study herself in the mirror; she loosened her curls; she unlaced her bodice that more of her rounded throat might be shown. She was tall, and her figure seemed to have matured since that first encounter. When she was near him she was aware of a tingling excitement such as she had never known before in the whole of her life. Feigning to avoid him she yet sought him. She was never happier than when she was near him, flashing scornful glances at him from under her heavy lids; it amused her in the presence of her mother and stepfather to ask artless questions concerning the beauty and talents of his betrothed.

She saw a responsive gleam in his eyes; she was wise enough to know that she was but a novice in the game she was playing; she knew that he stayed at her stepfather's house for only one reason, and that he would not leave it until he had captured her. This made her laugh. Not that she would avoid the capture; she had determined to be captured. She believed that she was on the point of making an important discovery. She was beautiful, and beauty meant power. She could take this man – the betrothed of Mary Fairfax – and drive everything from his mind but the desire for herself. That was power such as she longed to wield; and she had learnt from those moments when he had touched her or kissed her, that surrender would be made without the slightest reluctance.

Barbara was beginning to know herself.

So one day she allowed him to discover her stretched out on the grass in the lonely part of the nuttery.

There was a struggle; she was strong, but so was he; she was overpowered and, when she was seduced, she knew that

19

she would never find life dull while there were men to make love to her.

*

From that moment Barbara was aware that her first and most impelling need would always be the satisfaction of her now fully aroused sexual desires; but there was one other thing she wanted almost equally: Power. She wanted no opposition to any desire of hers, however trivial. She wanted to ride in her carriage through London and be admired and known as the most important person in the city. She wanted fine clothes and jewels – a chance to set this beauty of hers against a background which would enhance rather than minimize it. In the clothes she was obliged to wear, her fine already maturing figure was not displayed to advantage; the colour of her gown subdued the dazzling blue of her eyes and it did not suit the rich auburn of her hair. Clothes were meant to adorn beauty, yet she was so much more beautiful without hers; it would seem therefore that she wore the wrong clothes.

Clearly she must be free. She was sixteen and would be no longer treated as a child.

She thought of Chesterfield and wondered whether through him lay a means of escape. There had been more amorous encounters between them. Although there was little of tenderness in their relationship, both recognized in each other a passion which matched their own. Barbara at sixteen was wise enough to realize that her feelings for this man were based on appetite rather than emotion, and Barbara's appetite was beginning to be voracious.

Chesterfield was a rake and a reckless man. From an early age he had been obliged to fend for himself; he was not the man to sacrifice his life to an idea. He was as ambitious as Barbara, and almost as sensual. His father had died before he was two years old and he had received most of his education in Holland. He was some eight years older than Barbara and already a widower, for Anne Percy, his wife, had died three years ago and the seduction of females was no unusual sport of his.

Barbara often wondered what sort of husband he had been to Anne Percy. A disturbing one, she fancied, and of course an unfaithful one. He did not speak of Anne, though he found a malicious enjoyment in discussing his betrothed Mary Fairfax with Barbara.

He dallied at the house, delaying his departure; and it was all on account of Barbara.

That was why she began to contemplate marriage with him as a means of escape. They were of a kind, and therefore suited. She would not ask him to be faithful to her, for she was sure she would not wish to be so to him. Already she found herself watching others with eager speculation; so she and Philip would not be ill-matched.

He was betrothed to Mary Fairfax, but who was Mary Fairfax to marry with an Earl? Whereas Barbara, on the other hand, was a member of the noble family of Villiers.

She hinted that her family might not be averse to a match between them. He had visited her in her room – a daring procedure; but Barbara could be sure that none of the servants who might discover her escapade would dare mention it for fear of what might happen to them if their tattling reached their mistress's ears. Moreover she was growing careless.

So as they lay on her bed she talked of her family and his, and the possibility of a marriage between them.

Chesterfield rolled on to his back and burst out laughing.

'Barbara, my love,' he said, 'this is not the time to talk of marriage. It is not the custom, for marriages are not planned in bedchambers.'

'I care not for custom,' she retorted.

'That much is clear. It is a happy quality . . . in a mistress. In a wife, not so . . . ah, not so.'

Barbara sprang up and soundly slapped his face. But he was no frightened servant. His desire temporarily satiated, he laughed at her fury.

He went on: 'Had you intended to barter your virginity for marriage it should have been before our little adventure in the nuttery, not afterwards. Oh, Barbara, Barbara, you have much to learn.'

'You too, my lord,' she cried, 'if you think to treat me as you would treat a tavern girl.'

'You . . . a tavern girl! By God, you spit like one . . . you bite and scratch like one . . . and you are as ready to surrender . . .'

'Listen to me,' said Barbara. 'I'm a Villiers. My father was . . .'

'It is precisely because you are a Villiers, my dear Barbara, that you are a less attractive match than the one I am about to make.'

'You insult my family!'

That made him laugh more heartily. 'My dear girl, are you ignorant of the state of this country? There has been a turnabout; did you not know? Who are the great families today? The Villiers? The Stanhopes? The Percys? The Stuarts? No! The Cromwells! The Fairfaxes . . . Yet these newly made nobles have a certain respect for old families, providing we do not work against them. I'll tell you a secret. Oliver himself once offered me the command of his Army; and what do you think went with it? – the hand of one of his daughters.'

'And you would consider that, would you? You would take up arms against the King?'

'Who said I would consider it? I merely state the facts. No! I have declined the command of the Army, and with it the hand of either Mary or Frances Cromwell.'

'I see,' said Barbara, 'that you are telling me you are greatly desired in marriage by families which could be of greater use to you than mine.'

'How clearly you state the case, dear Barbara.'

Barbara leaped off the bed and, putting on her wrap, said with great disdain: 'That may be so at this time, but one day, my lord, you will see that the man who marries me will come to consider he has not made so bad a match. Now I pray you get out of my room.'

He dressed leisurely and left; it seemed that the talk of marriage had alarmed him; for the next day he left the house of Charles Villiers.

*

Buckingham came to London at this time; he was depressed, and on his arrival had shut himself up in his lodgings and had his servants explain that he was too low in health to receive visitors.

Barbara's imperious insistence fought a way through the barrier he had set about him. When she saw him she was surprised at the change in him. It was a matter of astonishment to her that a Villiers, a member of her noble family, could give way so easily to despair.

Buckingham was amused with his vehement young relative, and found no small pleasure in listening to her conversation.

'You forget, my cousin,' he said to her on one occasion when he had broken his seclusion by calling at her stepfather's house, 'that we live in a changing world. At your age you can have known no other, yet you cling to old Royalist traditions more fiercely than any.'

'Of course I cling. Are we not a noble family? What advantages can such as ourselves hope for in a country where upstarts rule us?'

'None, dear cousin. None. That is why I lie abed and turn my face to the wall.'

'Then you're a lily-livered spineless fool!'

'Barbara! Your language is not only vehement, it is offensive.'

'Then I am glad it rouses you to protest, for it is as well that you should be aroused to something. What of the King? He is your friend. He may be an exile, but he is still the King.'

'Barbara, the King and I have quarrelled. He no longer trusts me. He will have nothing to do with me, and in this he follows the advice of that Chancellor of his, Edward Hyde.'

'Edward Hyde! And what right has he to speak against a noble Villiers?'

'There you go again! It is all noble family with you. Cannot you see that nobility serves a man ill in a Commonwealth such as ours?'

'There are some who would attempt to find the best of both worlds.'

'And who are these?'

'My Lord Chesterfield, for one. He seeks to marry into the Fairfax family. He says that Oliver Cromwell offered him one of his daughters as well as a command in the Army. He refused the Protector's offer. He did not, I suspect, wish to set himself so blatantly on the side of the King's enemies. But a marriage with Fairfax's daughter is less conspicuous and brings him, he thinks, many advantages

'A marriage with Fairfax's daughter,' mused the Duke. 'H'm! Chesterfield is a wily one.'

'Why should not Buckingham be as wily?'

'Why not indeed!'

'George, you are the handsomest man in England, and could be the most attractive if you would but seek to make yourself so.'

'There speaks your family pride.'

'I'll wager Mary Fairfax would turn from Chesterfield if she thought there was a chance of marrying with one who is not only the handsomest man in England but a noble Villiers.'

'Barbara, you seem interested in this match. What is Chesterfield to you?'

Her eyes narrowed and she flushed faintly. Buckingham nodded his head sagely.

'By God, Barbara,' he said, 'you're growing up ... you're growing up fast. So Chesterfield preferred Fairfax's girl to Barbara Villiers!'

'He's welcome to her,' said Barbara. 'If he begged me on his knees to marry him I'd kick him in the face.'

'Yes, cousin, I doubt not that you would.'

They smiled at each other; both were thoughtful, and both were thinking of Mary Fairfax.

*

Barbara was amused and exhilarated by the manner in which events followed that interview of hers with Buckingham.

Certainly George was handsome; certainly he was the most attractive man in England when he cared to be. Poor plain little Mary Fairfax found him so.

It had not been difficult to obtain access to her. Abraham Cowley and Robert Harlow, friends of the Fairfaxes, were also friends of Buckingham. It was true that the lady was betrothed to Chesterfield, but Buckingham was not one to let such a thing stand in his way. Nor was Mary, once she set eyes on the handsome Duke.

Chesterfield was haughty; he was of medium height – neither tall nor possessed of grace; he was, it was true, unusually handsome of face; accomplished in social graces but very condescending to those whom he considered his social inferiors. Desirous as he was to bring about the match with Mary Fairfax, he could not hide from her the fact that he felt he was vastly superior in birth and breeding, and Mary, though shy and awkward in his presence, was unusually intelligent and fully aware of his feelings.

How different was the charming Duke of Buckingham who was so humble and eager to please! How such qualities became a gentleman of birth and breeding! He showed that he understood full well that the reversal of a way of life had altered their positions; yet, with a charming nonchalance he could suggest that such difference would have been unimportant to him in any age.

Mary had been well educated; she was, she knew, excessively plain. Neither her father's nor her mother's good looks had come to her; her gift was a calm shrewd intelligence. Yet as soon as she set eyes on the handsome Duke she fell in love with him; and nothing would satisfy her but the marriage which the Duke was soon demanding.

Barbara, in the privacy of her own room, laughed merrily when she heard of the marriage. This was her first real triumph, her first dabbling in diplomacy – and, as a result, her relative Buckingham had a bride, and her lover had lost one!

But when she next saw Chesterfield, although her sensuality got the better of her wish to remain aloof, and they were lovers again, she laughed at his desolate state and told him, although he made no such suggestion, that she would never marry him and one day he might regret the choice he had made.

*

In the next two years Barbara blossomed into her full beauty. At eighteen she was recognized as the loveliest girl in London. Suitors called at her stepfather's house and, although it was said that Barbara's virtue was suspect, this could not deter these young men from wishing to marry her.

Oddly enough Chesterfield remained her lover. She was completely fascinated by the man, even while she declared she would never marry him. Others were more humble, more adoring; but it was Chesterfield who, having first roused Barbara's desires, continued to do so.

There was one young man whom she singled out from the rest because in his quiet way he was so eager to marry her. His name was Roger Palmer and he was a student at the Inner Temple. He was a modest man and unlike Barbara's other admirers, for she had attracted to herself people of a temperament similar to her own.

It was not long before he declared his feelings and begged her to marry him.

Marry Roger Palmer! It seemed to Barbara at that time that he was the last man she would marry. She had no intention of marrying yet. She was enjoying life too much to wish to change it. She had all the pleasures, she assured herself, and none of the boredom of marriage. Certainly she would not marry Roger Palmer.

Her mother and her stepfather tried to persuade her to marry Roger. They were growing alarmed by the wild daughter whose reputation was already a little tarnished; they were hoping that Roger or someone would take out of their hands the responsibility for such a vital and unaccountable girl. But the more they persuaded her, the more Barbara determined not to marry.

Her appearance was so startling now that wherever she went she was noticed. People turned to stare at the tall and strikingly beautiful young woman, with the proud carriage and the abundant auburn hair. She was voted the most handsome woman in London; many declared there could not be one to match her in the world. But her temper did not improve. She would, when her rages were on her, almost kill a servant who displeased her. Her lovers were terrified of her tantrums, yet so great was her physical allure that they were unable to keep away from her. She was like a female spider – as deadly yet as irresistible.

When she heard that Sir James Palmer, Roger's father, had said that he would never give his consent to his son's marriage with Barbara Villiers, she laughed poor Roger to scorn. 'Go home to Papa!' she scolded. 'Go home and tell him Barbara Villiers would die rather than have you!'

Only for Chesterfield did she feel some tenderness; she would be mad with rage at his treatment of her, yet still she continued to receive him. He was so like herself that she understood him; she was furious when she heard that Lady

Elizabeth Howard shared the role of Chesterfield's mistress with her. His temper was as hot as hers. He had already been in trouble on two occasions for duelling. They quarrelled; she took other lovers; but back, again and again, she went to Chesterfield, and the chief gossip in London concerned the scandal of Lord Chesterfield and his mistress Barbara Villiers.

'Do you realize,' her parents pleaded with her, 'that if you go on in this way, soon there will not be a man in England who will marry you?'

'There are many men in England who would marry me,' she said.

'You think so. They say so. But what would their answers be if brought to the point of marriage, think you?'

Barbara rarely stopped to think; she allowed her emotions of the moment to govern all her actions.

'I could be married next week if I wished!' she declared.

But her parents shook their heads and begged her to reform her ways.

Barbara's answer to the challenge was to send for Roger Palmer. He came. His father had recently died and there was now no obstacle to their marriage; he was as eager to marry Barbara as he ever was.

Barbara studied him afresh. Roger Palmer, mild and meek, Roger Palmer, of no great importance, to be the husband of Barbara Villiers, the most handsome woman in London! It seemed incongruous, but Barbara would show them she was different from all other women. She would not look to her husband to provide her with honours; she would provide them for him and herself. How, she was not sure, but she would do it. Moreover, the more she studied him the more clear it became to her that Roger was just the husband for her. He would be dull and easy to handle. He would provide her with freedom – freedom to take her lovers where she wished. For Barbara needed lovers, a variety of lovers; she needed them even more than she needed power.

So she and Roger were married, to the astonishment of all, and then poor Roger realized how he had been used. The foolish man! He had believed that marriage would change her character, that a ceremony could change a passionate virago into a submissive wife!

He quickly learned his mistake and complained bitterly. But Chesterfield continued to be her lover until he was sent to the Tower during that year on suspicion of being involved in a Royalist plot; and after he was released at the beginning of the year 1660, he killed a man in a duel at Kensington and had to escape to France to avoid the consequences.

So at the beginning of the momentous year Barbara was missing her lover sorely when something happened which made their love affair seem of less importance.

Plans were afoot to bring the King back to England; Cromwell was dead, and the country was no more pleased with the Protectorate than it had been with Royalist rule. Cavaliers were disgruntled because of lost estates; the middle classes were groaning under heavy taxation and it was clear that the new Protector lacked the genius of his father; above all, the people were tired of the Puritans; they wanted the strict rules relaxed; they wanted to see pageantry in the streets; they wanted gaiety and laughter; they were weary of long sermons; they wanted singing, dancing, and fun.

General Monk was in favour of the King's return; Buckingham had been working for it with his father-in-law, Lord Fairfax; and Roger Palmer was entrusted with a sum of money which he was to take to the King's exiled Court in Holland; not only money did Roger take, but his wife, and there were many even at that time who said that it was the lady who pleased the young King more than the gold.

As for Barbara, she had never been so delighted in the whole of her life.

The tall dark man was a King and therefore worthy of her; he was as recklessly passionate as she was; in other ways his nature was completely opposed to hers, for he was tolerant, good tempered, the most easy-going person in the Court; yet while his eyes were upon her Barbara knew how to be sweetly yielding. She affected surprise that he could wish to seduce her; she reminded him that her husband would be most displeased; she hesitated and trembled, but made sure that there was plenty of time during her visit to Holland for the King not only to become her lover but to learn something of that immense satisfaction born out of her own great sensuality and complete abandonment to pleasure which she was fully aware she could give as few others could. Barbara was determined that the King should not only revel in a love affair which must necessarily be brief, that he should not forget her but look forward to repeating that experience as eagerly as he looked forward to wearing the crown.

Evidently she had succeeded, for on his first night in London the King had sent for her.

She went into his presence and knelt before him. She was fully aware that she had lost none of her beauty since they had last met. Rather had she gained in charm. She was magnificently dressed, and her wonderful auburn hair fell about her bare shoulders. The King's warm eyes glistened as he looked at her.

'It is a pleasure to see you here to greet us,' he said.

'The pleasure is that of Your Majesty's most loyal subject to see you here.'

'Rise, Mistress Palmer.' He turned to those who stood about him. 'The lady was responsible for great goodwill towards me during my exile ... great goodwill,' he repeated reminiscently.

'It is the utmost joy to me that Your Majesty should remember my humble service.'

'So well do I remember that I would have you sup with me this night.'

This night! thought Barbara. This very night when the whole of London was shouting its welcome; this first night when he had returned to his capital; this night when he had received the loyal addresses, the right royal welcome, the heartiest welcome that had ever been given to a King of England.

She could hear now the sounds of singing on the river, the shouts of joy.

Long live the King! A health unto His Majesty!

And here was His Majesty, his dark slumberous eyes urgent with passion, unable to think of anything but supping with Barbara Palmer.

'So,' said the King, 'you will sup with me this night?'

'It is a command, Your Majesty.'

'I would have it also a pleasure.'

'It will be the greatest pleasure that could befall a woman,' she murmured.

She lifted her eyes and saw one in the King's entourage

who, in spite of her triumph, made her heart-beats quicken.

There was Chesterfield. She hoped he had heard. She hoped he remembered now that he had once laughed at the idea of marrying Barbara Villiers. One day, thought Barbara then, and that day not far distant, Barbara Villiers would be the first lady in the land; for the King was half French by birth and all French in manners; and it was well known that the *maîtresse en titre* of a King of France was, more often than his Queen, the first lady in the land.

Chesterfield was going to regret and wonder at his stupidity. He was going to realize he had been a fool to think Mary Fairfax a better match. She wondered too how he was faring in his recent marriage, for he had had the temerity to marry again while he was in Holland – marry without consulting her! She wished him all that he deserved. She wondered how the simple little Lady Elizabeth Butler was going to satisfy a man like Chesterfield. If Lady Elizabeth, brought up in the affectionate home of her parents, the Duke and Duchess of Ormond, believed that all marriages were like those of her parents, she was about to be very surprised.

For, thought Barbara, even as she contemplated supping with the King, Chesterfield need not think that Barbara Villiers had finished with him.

The courtiers were looking at her boldly now. The King had brought French manners with him. They did not think it strange that he should openly claim her for his mistress before them all. In France the greatest honour that could befall a woman was to become the King's mistress.

Charles – and Barbara – would see that that French custom was forthwith adopted at the English Court.

*

Far into the night the revelry continued. Throughout the Palace of Whitehall, which sprawled for nearly half a mile along the river's edge, could be heard the shouts of citizens making merry. Music still came from the barges on the river; and the lights of bonfires were reflected in the windows. Ballad singers continued their singing; it was not every day that a monarch came home to his capital.

The King heard the sounds of rejoicing and was gratified. But he gave them no more than a passing thought. He remembered that some of those who were shouting their blessings on him had doubtless called for his father's blood. Charles did not put any great trust in the acclamations of the mob.

But he was glad to be home, to be a King once more, no longer a wandering exile.

He was in his own Palace of Whitehall, in his own bed; and with him was the most perfect woman to whom it had ever been his lot to make love. Barbara Palmer, beautiful and amorous, unstintingly passionate, the perfect mistress for a perfect homecoming.

From the park of St James's, beyond the Cockpit, he heard the shouting of midnight revellers.

'A health unto His Majesty. . . .'

But his smile was melancholy until he turned once more to Barbara.

TWO

IN HIS early morning walks through the grounds which surrounded his Palace of Whitehall the King was often a melancholy man during those first few months after his restoration.

He would rise early, for he enjoyed walking in the fresh morning air and at such times he was not averse to being alone, although at all others he liked best to be surrounded by jesting men and beautiful women.

He walked fast; it was a habit unless there was a woman with him; then he never failed to fit his steps to hers.

This was a January morning. There was hoar-frost on the grass and it sparkled on the Palace walls and the buildings which rose from the banks on either side of the river.

January – and seven months a restored King!

He had wandered into the privy gardens where in summer he would set his watch by the sundial; but this day the sheltered bowling green was perhaps more inviting. He would, as was his custom, look in at the small Physic Garden where he cultivated the herbs with which he and Le Febre, his chemist, and Tom Chaffinch, his most trusted servant, experimented.

He was in an unusually pensive mood on this day.

Perhaps it was due to the coming of the new year – his first as King in his own country. Those last months which should have been the happiest of his life were touched with tragedy.

He looked back at the Palace with its buildings of all sizes – past the banqueting hall to the Cockpit. Whitehall was not only his royal Palace, it was the residence of his ministers and servants, the ladies and gentlemen of his Court, for they all had their apartments here. And that was how he would have it. The bigger his Court the better; the more splendid, the more he liked it, for it reminded him sharply, whenever he contemplated it, of the change in his fortunes.

The stone gallery separated his royal apartments from those of his subjects; and his bedchamber – he had arranged this – had big windows which gave him a clear view of the river; it was one of his pleasures to stand at those windows and watch the ships go by, just as, when a small boy at Greenwich, he had lain on the bank and delighted in the ships sailing by.

In the little chamber known as the King's Closet, to which only he and Tom Chaffinch had keys, he kept the treasures that he had learned to love. He was deeply attracted by beauty in any form – pictures, ornaments and of course women, and now that he was no longer a penniless exile he was gathering together pictures by the great artists of his earlier days. He had works by Holbein, Titian, and Raphael in his closet; he had cabinets and jewel-encrusted boxes, maps, vases and, perhaps more cherished than any – except his models of ships – his collection of clocks and watches. These he wound himself and often took to pieces that he might have the joy of putting them together again. He loved art and artists, and he intended to make his Court a refuge for them.

He was already restoring his parks to a new magnificence. St James's Park was no longer to be the shabby waste ground it had become during the Commonwealth; he would plant new trees; there should be water works such as those he had seen in Fontainebleau and Versailles. He wished his Court to be as elegant as that of his cousin Louis Quatorze. And St James's Park should be a home for the animals he loved. He himself delighted to feed the ducks on his pond; he had begun to stock the park with deer; he would have goats and sheep there too, and strange animals such as antelopes and elks which would cause the people of London to pause and admire. And all these animals he loved dearly, as he loved the little dogs which followed him whenever they could and had even found their way into the Council Chamber. His melancholy face would soften when he fondled them, and when he spoke to them his voice was as tender and gentle as when he addressed a beautiful woman.

But on this January day, early in the morning, his melancholy thoughts pursued him, for those first months of his restoration had been overshadowed by tragedy.

The first trouble had been James's affair with Anne Hyde, the daughter of his Chancellor, the man who he had trusted more than any other during the years of exile. James had married the girl and then sprung the news on his brother at a most inconvenient time, falling on his knees before him, confessing that he had made this *mésalliance* and disobeyed the rule that one so near the throne should not marry without the consent of the monarch.

He should have been furious; he should have clapped them both into the Tower. That was what his ancestors – those worthy Tudors, Henry and Elizabeth – would have done; and they were considered the greatest King and Queen the country had ever had.

Clap his own brother into jail! And for marrying a girl who was so far gone in pregnancy that to delay longer would have meant her producing a bastard, when the child might well be heir to the throne!

Some might have done it. Not Charles. How could he, when he could understand so well the inclination which had first led James to dally with the Chancellor's daughter (though to Charles's mind she was no beauty, yet possessed of a shrewdness and intelligence which he feared far exceeded that of his brother) and, having got her with child, the impossibility of resisting her tears and entreaties.

Charles saw James's point of view and Anne's point of view too clearly even to feign anger.

'Get up, James,' he had said. 'Don't sprawl at my feet like that. Od's Fish, man, you're clumsy enough in less demanding poses. What's done is done. You're a fool, but alas, dear brother, that's no news to me.'

33

But others were not inclined to view the matter with the King's leniency. Charles sighed, contemplating the trouble which that marriage had caused. Why could they not take his view of life? Could they unmake the marriage by upbraiding James and making the girl's life miserable?

It was a sad thing that so few shared the tolerance of the King.

There was Chancellor Hyde, the girl's father, pretending to be distraught, declaring that he would have preferred to see his daughter the concubine rather than the wife of the Duke of York.

'A paternal sentiment which is scarcely worthy of a man of your high ideals, Chancellor,' Charles had said ironically.

He had begun to wonder about Hyde then. Was the man entirely sincere? Secretly he must be delighted that his daughter had managed to secure marriage into the royal house, that her heirs might possibly sit on the throne of England. There had been whispering about Hyde often enough; a man so high in the King's favour was bound to have his enemies. He had followed Charles in his exile and had always been at his side to give the young King his advice. Charles did not forget that when Hyde had left Jersey to come to him in Holland he had been taken prisoner by the corsairs of Ostend and robbed of his possessions, yet had not rested until he had effected his escape and joined his King. His one motive was, he had declared, to serve Charles and bring about his restoration; and Charles, believing him, had made the man his first adviser, had asked his counsel in all political matters, had made him Secretary of State in place of Nicholas, and later, when it seemed that one day Charles might have a country to rule, he had become Chancellor. The man had had many enemies who envied him his place in the King's counsels and affections; they had done all they could to poison the King's mind against him. But Charles had supported Hyde, believed him to be his most trusty servant because he never minced his words and was apt to reproach the King to his face concerning the profligate life he led. Charles would always listen gravely to what Hyde had to say, declaring that although he was ready to accept Hyde's advice on affairs of state he felt himself to be the better judge in matters of the heart.

Chief of Hyde's critics had been Henrietta Maria, the King's own mother, who traced all the disagreements – and they were many – which existed between herself and her son, to this man.

Still Charles supported Hyde; and only now, when the man declared himself to be so desolate because his daughter was the wife and not the mistress of the Duke of York, did Charles begin to doubt the sincerity of his Chancellor.

He made him Baron Hyde of Hindon, and had decided that at his coronation he would create him Viscount Cornbury and Earl of Clarendon, to compensate him for his years of loyal service; but he had decided he would not be quite so trusting as hitherto.

Poor James! Charles feared he was not the most courageous of men. He was afraid of his mother. Odd how one, so small and at such great distance, could inspire terror in the hearts of her grown-up children. Henrietta Maria had made a great noise in Paris concerning this marriage – weeping, assuring all those about her that here was another instance of the cruelty of fate which was determined to remind her that she was *la reine malheureuse*. Had she not suffered enough! Was not the whole world against her! Charles knew full well how these tirades had run, and who had borne the brunt of them – his beloved little sister Henrietta, his sweet Minette. So James had trembled in Whitehall although it was so far from the Palais-Royal or Colombes or Chaillot or the Louvre, wherever his mother had been when calling those about her to weep for her sorrows, and the saints to bring vengeance on those who persecuted her. Then there had been his sister, Mary of Orange, who was furious that James could so far forget himself, and who had blamed herself because it was while Anne Hyde was in her retinue that she had first met the Duke.

Poor James! Alas, no hero. Alas, possessing no true chivalry. Terrified at what he had done in bringing upon himself the wrath of his formidable mother and strong-minded sister, he had declared his mistake to the world; he had lent his ears to the calumnies which those who hated the Hyde family were only too ready to pour into them. Anne was a lewd woman, he declared; she had trapped him; the child for whose sake he had rushed into marriage was after all not his.

And so poor Anne, deserted by her family and by her husband, would have been in a sorry state but for one person.

Charles shrugged his shoulders. He did not believe the calumnies directed against the poor girl, but he suspected that if he had, his reaction would not have been very different, for he could never bear to see a woman in such distress.

So the one who had visited the Duchess at her lying-in, when all the world seemed against her, was the King himself; and it was the royal hand which had been laid upon her feverish brow with, as he said, the tenderness of a brother, and it was Charles who whispered to her to have no fear for all would come right for her, since it was the envious enemies of her family who, denigrating its special talents and good fortune, had sought to harm her.

Whither the King went so must the Court go too. How could the courtiers neglect one whom the King chose to honour? 'Come, man!' he cried to Hyde. 'This business is done with. 'Tis a fool who makes not the best of what cannot be mended!'

To James he said: 'You shame me! You shame our family. The Duchess is your wife. You cared enough for her to make her that. Is your love for her then less than the fear you have for our mother? You know she is innocent of these calumnies. For the love of God, be a man.'

Thus had that most unhappy matter been satisfactorily settled, and it was then that Charles had given Hyde his peerage to show where his sympathies lay.

The next disaster had been the death of his brother, Henry of Gloucester, the younger of his brothers, and the best loved. Death had come swiftly in the guise of the dreaded smallpox; and young Henry, strong and healthy one week, had been gone the next.

Such a tragedy coming so soon after his restoration – Henry had died in September, a few weeks after the trouble with James had blown up, and little more than three months after the King's return to England – dampened all pleasure, and even the sight of his beloved sisters could not entirely console him.

Minette he loved dearly – perhaps more dearly than any other person on Earth – and it was delightful and gratifying to receive her in his own country which had now acknowledged him its King, to do honour to the lovely and sprightly girl who had suffered such humiliation as a poor relation of the French Court for so long. But with Minette came her mother; Charles smiled now at the thought of Henrietta Maria, the diminutive virago, eyes flashing, hands gesticulating, longing to give James a piece of her mind and assuring everyone that she would only enter Whitehall when Anne Hyde was ordered to leave it.

And to Charles had fallen the task of placating his mother; this he did with grace and courtesy, and some cunning. For she was dependent upon his bounty for her pension, and she had been made to know that the obstinacy of her eldest son still existed beneath the easy-going manners, and that when he had made up his mind that something should be done, he could be as firmly fixed in his purpose as that little boy who had refused to take his physic and who had clung to the wooden billet which it had been his custom as a small boy to take to bed with him each night.

So he had triumphed over his mother as gently as he could. 'Poor Mam!' he told his little Minette. 'She has a genius for supporting lost causes and giving all her great energy to that which can only bring sorrow to herself.' He had insisted on her receiving James's wife in public.

And then almost immediately the dread smallpox, which had carried off his brother Henry, had smitten his sister Mary, and in the space of a few short months, though he had regained his throne, he had lost a beloved brother and sister.

How the family was depleted! There was now his mother – but they had never really loved each other – his brother James – and James was a fool and a coward, as was obvious from his treatment of Anne Hyde – and Minette, his youngest sister, the best loved of them all; yet she was rarely met and the water divided them. He had said farewell to her but a few days ago, but how did he know when he would see her again? He would have liked to bring her back to England, to have kept her with him. Dear Minette! But she had her destiny in another country; she had a brilliant marriage to make; he could not ask her to forsake her affianced husband and come to England merely to be the King's sister. There was scandal enough concerning them already. Trust the malicious tongues to see to that!

37

So it was small wonder that he felt melancholy at times, for he was a man who liked to surround himself with those he loved. He could remember happy days when he had been the member of a family; and it had been a happy family, for there was affection between his parents, and his father was a noble man and loving father; but that was before he had found it necessary to oppose his overbearing mother; he remembered her from then as ever demonstrative, quick to punish but full of an affection which was outwardly displayed by suffocating embraces and fond kisses. Yes, Charles was a man who needed love and affection; he longed to have his family about him. He suffered their loss deeply as one by one they left this life.

He remembered now, as he bent to examine a herb in his Physic Garden, the terrible anxiety he had suffered when he had believed that Minette herself was about to die. Stunned by the loss of a brother and sister he had thought that life was about to deal him the most brutal blow of all. But Minette had not died; she had lived to return to France, where she would marry the brother of the French King and every week there would be, as in the old days, loving letters from her to remind him of the bond between them.

Yes, he still had Minette, so life was not all melancholy; far from it. He had his crown and he had his beloved sister, and there was much merriment to be had in the Court of Whitehall. A man could not have pleasure all the time, for if he became too familiar with it he would be less appreciative of it. The loss of his dear brother Henry and sister Mary had made him all the more tender to his sweet Minette.

There were other matters which gave him some uneasiness. Were the people a little disappointed? Had they hoped for too much? Did they think that with the King's restoration all the old evils would be wiped out? Did they look upon the King as a magician, who could live in perpetual royal state and give his people pageants, restore estates, abolish taxes – and all because he had found some magic elixir in his laboratories? Oh, the many petitioners who hung about in the stone gallery of Whitehall which led to the royal apartments! How many there were to remind him that they had been loyal supporters during the years of exile! 'Sire, it was due to me . . . to me . . . to me . . . that Your Majesty has been restored.'

38

'Sire, I had a great house and lands, and these were taken from me by the Parliament....' 'Sire, I trust that Your Majesty's restoration may be our restoration. ...' It was easy – too easy – to promise. He understood their different points of view. Of course he understood them. He wished to give all they asked. It was true that they had been loyal; it was true that they had worked for his restoration and lost their estates to the Parliament. But what could he do? How could he confiscate estates which were now the property of those who called themselves his loyal subjects; how could he restore property which had been razed to the ground?

It was his habit almost to run through the stone gallery to avoid these petitioners. They would drop on their knees as he passed, and he would say quickly: 'God bless you! God bless you!' before he strode on, taking such great paces that none could overtake him unless they ran. He dared not pause; if he did, he knew he would be unable to stop himself making promises which he could not fulfil.

If they would but let him alone to enjoy his pleasures – ah, then he would forget his melancholy; then he would practise that delightful habit of sauntering through his parks followed by his spaniels and surrounded by gentlemen who must all be witty and ladies who need not be anything but beautiful. To listen to the sallies (and he had made it clear that they could disregard his royalty in the cause of wit) and to feast his eyes on the graceful figures of the ladies, whisper to them, catch their hands, suggest a meeting when there might not be quite so many about them to observe their little tendernesses – ah, that was all pleasure. He wished that he could indulge in sauntering more often.

In November the army had been disbanded at Hyde's wish. Charles was sorry to see that happen, but whence would come the money to keep it in existence? It seemed to the King that as a monarch he was almost as poor as he had been an exile, for, although he had a larger income, his commitments had multiplied in proportion. Monk kept his regiments – the Coldstream and another of horse; and that was all, apart from another regiment which was formed from the troops which had been brought from Dunkirk. Charles christened this regiment the Guards and from it planned to build a standing army.

But there was one other matter his ministers were determined on, as fiercely as on that of reducing expenses, and it was one which gave him as little pleasure; this was revenge.

Charles alone, it seemed, had no wish for revenge. The past was done with; his exile was over; he was restored; let all the country rejoice in that. But No! said his ministers. And No! said his people. Murder had been done. The King's father was Charles the Martyr, and his murder should not go unpunished. So there had been a trial, and those men who were judged guilty were sentenced to the terrible death which was accorded to traitors.

Charles shuddered now as he had then. If he had had his will he would have acquitted the lot. They had believed they were in the right; in their eyes they had committed no murder; they had carried out the demands of justice. So they saw it; and Charles, still remembering with great affection the father whom they had murdered, still very close to the years of beggary and exile, was the one who alone had desired that these men should remain unpunished.

Ten men died the terrible death that October, and there were others waiting to meet it. But the King could bear no more. He cried: 'I confess I am weary of hanging – let it sleep!'

So he prevailed upon the Convention to turn their attention away from humble men to those who had been his father's true enemies; those who were already dead. And so the bodies of Cromwell, Pride and Ireton were dug from their graves, beheaded, and their heads stuck on spikes outside Westminster Hall.

This was gruesome and horrible to a man of fastidious tastes, but at least their dead bodies could feel no pain. It was better to offend his fastidiousness than wound his tender nature.

Revenge, he had said, was enjoyed by the failures of this world. Those who achieved success spared little time for something which had become so trivial. He was now back in the heart of his country and the hearts of his people. He forgave those men who had worked against his family, as he trusted God would forgive him his many sins.

So with the King's indifference to revenge, the people satisfied themselves with gloating over the decaying remains of the great Protector and his followers, which were displayed exactly twelve years to the day after the death of Charles I.

There were difficulties still over religion. How his people discoursed one against the other on this subject! What hot words they exchanged, what angers were aroused; how they disputed this way and that! Why could they not, Charles asked them and himself, be easy in their minds? Why should not men who wished to worship in a certain way worship that way? What should another man's opinions matter to the next man, providing he was allowed to preserve his own?

Tolerance! It was a hateful word to these fierce combatants. They did not want tolerance. They wanted their mode of worship imposed on the country because, they declared, it was the right way.

The struggle continued between Presbyterians and Anglicans.

Charles exerted all his patience; he was charming to the Anglicans, he was suave to the Presbyterians; but at last he began to see that he could never make peace between them and because the Anglicans had supported him during his exile he shrugged his shoulders and went over to their side.

Had he been right? He did not know. He wanted peace . . . peace to enjoy his kingdom. He, who could see the fierce points of argument from both angles and many more, would have cried: 'Worship as you please – but leave each other and me in peace.'

But that was not the way of these earnest men of faith, and Charles's way was to take the easiest route out of a dispute which was growing tedious.

So now he had come to the end of those months, and the year was new, and who could say what fresh triumphs, what fresh pleasures and what fresh sorrows awaited him?

He must find a wife ere long. He was thirty-one, and a King should be married by that age if he were to provide his country with sons.

A wife? The thought pleased him. He was after all a man who loved his family. He pictured the wife he would have – gentle and loving and of course beautiful. He would discuss the matter with his ministers, and it might be well to discuss it now, while Barbara was less active than usual. She was expecting a child next month; his child, she said.

He lifted one side of his mouth in a half-smile.

It could be his, he supposed, though it might be Chesterfield's or even poor Roger Palmer's. None could be sure with Barbara.

It was time he grew tired of her. It astonished him that she had been almost his sole mistress since he had set foot in England. Yet he did not grow tired of her. Handsome she was – quite the most handsome woman he had ever known. Physically she was unique; the symmetry of her body was perfect and her person could not fail to delight such a connoisseur. Her face was the most beautiful he had ever beheld, and even her violent rages could only change it, not distort it. Her character was unaccountable; and thus there was nothing dull nor insipid about Barbara. He had tried others, but they had failed to interest him beyond the first few occasions. Always he must go back to Barbara, wild Barbara, cruel Barbara, the perfect animal, the most unaccountable and the most exciting creature in his kingdom.

He looked at his watch.

It was time the morning perambulation was ended.

He chided himself lightly for thinking of Barbara so early in the day.

*

Barbara sat up in bed in her husband's house in King Street, Westminster. In the cradle lay her few-days-old child, a girl. Barbara was a little sulky; she would have preferred her first-born to be a boy.

She smiled secretly. There should be three men who would come to visit her, and each would believe in his heart that the child was his. Let them have their secret thoughts; Barbara had long decided whom she would name as the little girl's father.

Roger, the first of the visitors, came early.

How insignificant he was! How could she have married such a man? people wondered. She smiled when she heard that. Her reasons were sound enough. Poor Roger, he should not suffer for his meekness. Unfortunately nowadays he was not inclined to be as meek as she could wish.

He stood at the foot of the bed and looked from her to the child in the cradle.

Barbara cried: 'For the love of God, do not stand there looking like a Christian about to be sent to the lions! Let me tell you, Roger Palmer, that if danger came within a mile of you you'd be squealing to me to protect you!'

'Barbara,' said Roger, 'you astonish me. I should not have thought any woman could be so blatant.'

'I have little time for subterfuge.'

'You deliberately deceive me with others.'

'I deceive you! When have I ever deceived you? I am not afraid to receive my lovers here . . . in your house.'

'Shame, Barbara, shame! You, a woman just delivered of a child! Why, there are many who wonder who the father of that child may be.'

'Then they need not wonder long. They shall know, when the titles due to this child are given to her.'

'You are quite shameless.'

'I am merely being truthful.'

'I suppose, when you married me you had your lovers.'

'You surely did not think, sir, that you could satisfy me?'

'Chesterfield . . .?'

'Yes, Chesterfield!' she spat at him.

'Then why did you not marry Chesterfield? He was free to marry at that time.'

'Because I had no wish to marry Chesterfield. Do you think I wished for a husband who was ready to draw his sword every time he thought his honour slighted?' She laughed the cruel laugh he had come to know so well. 'Nay! I wanted a meek man. A man who would look away at the right moment, a man without any great title . . . or hope of one, except that which *I* should bring to him.'

'You are a strange woman, Barbara.'

'I'm no fool, if that's what you mean.'

'Do you think that I should wish for any honours which you could bring me. Honours, did you say? They would be dishonour in disguise.'

'Honours are honours, no matter how they come. Ah! I see the look in your eyes, Roger Palmer. You are wondering what His Majesty will do for you if you quietly father his child, are you not?'

'Barbara, you are vulgar and cruel, and I wonder . . . I wonder I can stay under the same roof.'

43

'Then cease to wonder. Get out. Or shall I? Do you imagine that there are not other roofs under which I could shelter? Why do you not admit the truth yourself, Roger Palmer? You are jealous ... jealous of my lovers. And why? Because *you* wish to be my lover!' She laughed. 'My lover *en titre* ... You wish to exclude all others!'

'I am your husband.'

'My husband! What should I want of a husband except his complaisance.'

He strode towards the bed; his face was livid with fury.

Barbara called to her women, who hurried into the room.

'I am very fatigued,' she said. 'I wish to rest. Arrange the pillows more comfortably. Roger, you must leave me now.'

'You must not excite yourself at such a time, Madam,' said one of her women.

She lay back upon her pillows and watched Roger as he went quietly to the cradle and bent over the sleeping infant. She knew he was telling himself that the little nose, small though it was, was yet a Palmer nose; and the set of the eyes, that was Palmer too.

Let him go on thinking thus, she mused, for what harm is there in thinking?

And when he had gone, she sent one of her women with a message to Lord Chesterfield at Whitehall.

*

Barbara's messenger found the Earl of Chesterfield in his apartments at the Palace. The Countess was with him, and it was not the most propitious moment to deliver a message from Barbara; but all Barbara's servants knew that to disobey was quite out of the question, and she would be amused to know that Chesterfield's bride was present when he received his summons to call on his mistress.

Chesterfield still felt the power of her attraction, and he had not ceased to be her lover at intervals ever since their first encounter. There had been a time when Barbara had actually seemed to be in love with him; when she had so far subdued her personality as to write to him: 'I am ready and willing to go all over the world with you, and will obey your commands whilst I live.' That was after Barbara's own marriage but before the return of the King, before Chesterfield had fought

44

that duel which had necessitated his leaving the country. Then she had compared him with the meek Roger and when she knew there could never be marriage between them, she had felt he was the only man who could please her.

That mood had not lasted. The King had come home, and the occasions when Barbara had been at home to Chesterfield became less frequent, although she had wished to receive him more often when she had heard of the beauty of his wife.

Barbara was a wanton, Chesterfield told himself; Barbara was cruel; but that did not prevent her from being different from all other women and very desirable. His common sense told him to have no more to do with her; his senses refused to release him.

Now he looked at the quiet girl who was his wife. She was about twenty years of age – the same age as Barbara – but compared with his mistress she seemed but a child. There was no guile about Elizabeth; she was pleasant to look upon but seemed dull when he compared hers with the flamboyant charms of Barbara. And of course he must compare her with Barbara, for Barbara was constantly in his thoughts.

'A message?' she said now. 'From whom, Philip? I had hoped that you would spend an hour or so with me.'

'It matters not from whom the message comes,' he said coldly. 'Suffice it that it is for me, and that I must leave at once.'

Elizabeth came to him and put her arm through his. She was very much in love with him. He had seemed so handsome and romantic when he had come to Holland; she had heard the story of the duel; she did not know the cause, and she imagined that it was out of chivalry that he had fought and killed a man. He would not talk of it. That, she had told herself, is his natural modesty. He will not speak of it because he fears to appear boastful.

She had led a sheltered life with the Duchess her mother, who, horrified at the licentious exiled Court, had kept her daughter from it in an endeavour to preserve her innocence; she had succeeded in her task too well, for Elizabeth at the time of her marriage had no notion of the kind of man she had married, nor of the kind of world in which she would be expected to compete for his affections. The marriage had seemed a good one. The Earl was twenty-five years of age, the

Lady Elizabeth nineteen. Chesterfield, a young widower, needed a wife and it was time the Lady Elizabeth was married.

It was true that the Duchess, having heard rumours of the bridegroom's reputation, was a little hesitant; but those rumours were not so disturbing as they might have been, for at that time Barbara Palmer had not achieved the notoriety which she attained when she became the King's mistress; and, as the Duke pointed out to his Duchess, a young unmarried man must have a mistress; Chesterfield would settle down when he married.

So the marriage took place at The Hague a little while before the Restoration; and Lady Elizabeth who, having seen the affection between her parents, had expected to enjoy the same happy state with her husband, met with bitter disappointment.

The Earl made it quite clear that the marriage was one of convenience and Lady Elizabeth found that her naïve expressions of love were cruelly repulsed.

At first she was hurt; then she believed that he still thought of his first wife, Anne Percy. She asked questions about her of all who had known her; she tried to emulate what she heard of her rival, but her efforts seemed to win her husband's impatience rather than his kindness. He was brusque, cold, and avoided her as much as possible. He made it clear that any intercourse between them was undertaken by him because it was expected of him.

The naïve and gentle girl, being in every way different from Barbara, irritated him beyond all measure because, in everything she did, by the very contrast, she reminded him of Barbara, and set him longing to renew that tempestuous relationship.

Even now when they had returned to London she was kept in ignorance of the life he led. Her mother, unknown to her, had spoken to the Earl asking that he treat her daughter with the deference due to her; at which he became more aloof than ever, and Elizabeth, left much alone, continued to brood on the perfections of Anne Percy who she believed could charm from the grave.

But at this moment the Earl was beside himself with the desire to see Barbara – and not only Barbara. He was sure the child was his. He had visited Barbara at the time she became the King's mistress; he remembered the occasion when he had accused her of seeking royal favour; he remembered her mocking laughter, her immense provocation, her insatiable lust which demanded more than one lover at a time. Yes, the child could very possibly be his.

'Philip....' Elizabeth was smiling at him in a manner which she fondly imagined was alluring.

He threw her off, and the tears came to her eyes. If there was one thing that maddened him more than an attempt at coquetry, it was her weeping; and there had been much of that since her marriage – quiet, snuffling crying which he heard in the darkness.

'Why do you plague me?' he demanded.

'I ... plague you?'

'Why do you seek to detain me when you know full well I have no wish to be detained by you?'

'Philip, you talk as though you hate me.'

'Hate you I shall if you will insist on clinging to me thus. Is it not enough that you are my wife? What more do you want of me?'

'I want a chance, Philip, a chance for us to be happy. I want us to be as husband and wife....'

That made him laugh. The spell of Barbara was on him. He was sure she was a witch who could cast spells from a distance. It was almost as though she were there in the room, mocking him, scorning him for not telling this foolish little girl the truth.

'You wish us to be as husband and wife? To live, you mean, as do other wives and husbands of the Court? Then you should get yourself a lover. It is an appendage without which few wives of this Court find themselves.'

'A ... lover? You, Philip, my husband, can say that!'

He took her by the shoulders and shook her in exasperation. 'You are like a child,' he said. 'Grow up! For God's sake, grow up!'

She threw her arms about his neck. His exasperation turned to anger. He found her repulsive – this fresh and innocent young girl – because she was not Barbara on whose account he had suffered bitter jealousy ever since the King came home.

47

'Know the truth,' he cried. 'Know it once and for all. I cannot love you. My thoughts are with my mistress.'

'Your mistress, Philip!' Elizabeth was white to the lips. 'You mean . . . your dead . . . wife?'

He looked at her in astonishment and then burst into cruel laughter.

'Mrs Barbara Palmer,' he said. 'She is my mistress. . . .'

'But she . . . she is the King's mistress, they say.'

'So you have learned that? Then you are waking up, Elizabeth. You are becoming very knowledgeable. Now learn something else: the King's mistress she may be – but she is mine also. And the child she has just borne . . . it is mine, I tell you.'

Then he turned and hurried away.

Elizabeth stood like one of the stone statues in the Palace grounds.

Then she turned away and went to her apartment; she drew the curtains about her bed and lay there, while a numbness crept over her limbs, and it seemed that all feelings were merged in the misery which was sweeping over her.

*

Before Chesterfield arrived at the house in King Street, Barbara had another visitor.

This was her relative, George Villiers the Duke of Buckingham. He was now a gentleman of the King's bedchamber; his estates had been restored to him, and he was on the way to becoming one of the most important men in the country.

He did not look at the child in the cradle. Instead his eyes were warm with admiration for the mother.

'So Mrs Barbara,' he said, 'you flourish. I hear that the King continues to dote. This is a happy state of affairs for the family of Villiers, I'll swear.'

'Ah, George,' she said with a smile, 'we have come a long way from the days when you used to tease me for my hot temper.'

'I'll warrant the temper has not cooled, and were it not that I dare not tease such a great lady as Mistress Barbara, I would be tempted to put it to the test. Do you bite and scratch and kick with as much gusto as you did at seven, Barbara?'

'With as much gusto and greater force,' she assured him. 'But I'll not kick and scratch and bite you, George. There are times when the Villiers should stand together. You were a fool to get sent back from France.'

'It was that prancing ninny of a Monsieur. He feigned to be jealous of my attentions to the Princess Henrietta.'

'Well, you tried to make her sister Mary your wife and failed; then you tried to make Henrietta your mistress and failed in that.'

'I beg of you taunt me not with failing. Mayhap your success will not last.'

'Ah! Had I not married Roger mayhap I should have been Charles's wife ere now.'

George's thoughts were cynical. Charles might be a fool where women were concerned, but he was not such a fool as that. However, it was more than one dared say to Barbara. Roger had his uses. Not only was he a complaisant husband but he supplied a good and valid reason why Barbara was not Queen of England.

'It seems as though fortune does not favour us, cousin,' said George. 'And the lady in the cradle – is she preparing herself to be nice to Papa when he calls?'

'She will be nice to him.'

'You should get him to own her.'

'He shall own her,' said Barbara.

'Roger spoke of the child as though there could be no doubt that she is his.'

'Let him prate of that in public.'

'The acknowledgement by her rightful father should not be too private, Barbara.'

'Nay, you're right.'

'And there is something more I would say to you. Beware of Edward Hyde.'

'Edward Hyde? That old fool!'

'Old, it is true, my dear; but no fool. The King thinks very highly of him.'

Barbara gave her explosive laugh.

'Ah yes, the King is your minion. You lead him by the nose. I know, I know. But that is when he is with you, and you insist he begs for your favours. But the King is a man of many moods. He changes the colour of his skin like a chameleon on

49

a rock, and none is more skilled at such changing than he. Remember Hyde was with him years ago in exile. He respects the man's judgement, and Hyde is telling him that his affair with you is achieving too much notoriety. He is warning him that England is not France, and that the King's mistress will not be accorded the honours in this country which go to His Majesty's cousin's women across the water.'

'I'll have the fellow clapped into the Tower.'

'Nay, Barbara, be subtle. He's too big a man to be clapped into the Tower on the whim of a woman. The King would never consent to it. He would promise you in order to placate you, and then prevaricate; and he would whisper to his Chancellor that he had offended you and he had best make his peace with you. But he will not easily turn against Edward Hyde.'

'You mean I should suffer myself to be insulted by that old ... old ...'

'For the time, snap your fingers. But beware of him, Barbara. He would have the King respectably married and his mistresses cast aside. He will seek to turn the King against you. But do nothing rash. Work stealthily against him. I hate the man. You hate the man. We will destroy him gradually ... but it must be slowly. The King is fickle to some, but I fancy he will not be so with one who has been so long his guide and counsellor. His Majesty is like a bumble bee – a roving drone – flitting from treasure to treasure, sipping here and there and forgetting. But there are some flowers from which he has drunk deep and to these he returns. Know you that he has given a pension to Jane Lane who brought him to safety after Worcester? All that time, and he remembers – our fickle gentleman. So will he remember Edward Hyde. Nay, let the poison drip slowly ... in the smallest drops, so that it is unnoticed until it has begun to corrode and destroy. Together, Barbara, you and I will rid ourselves of one who cannot be anything but an enemy to us both.'

She nodded her agreement; her blue eyes were brilliant. She longed to be up; she hated inactivity.

'I will remember,' she said. 'And how fare you in your married life?'

'Happily, happily,' he said.

'And Mary Fairfax – does she fare happily?'

50

'She is the happiest of women, the most satisfied of wives.'

'Some are easily satisfied. Does she not regret Chesterfield?'

'That rake! Indeed she does not.'

'She finds in you a faithful husband?' said Barbara, cynically and slyly.

'She finds in me the perfect husband – which gives greater satisfaction.'

'Then she must be blind.'

'They say love is, Madam.'

'Indeed it must be. And she loves you still?'

'As she ever did. And so do the entire family. It is a most successful marriage.'

Barbara's woman came in and was about to announce that Chesterfield was on his way, when the Earl himself came into the room.

He and Buckingham exchanged greetings. Chesterfield went to the bed, and, taking the hand Barbara gave him, pressed it to his lips.

'You are well?' he asked. 'You are recovered?'

'I shall be about tomorrow.'

'I rejoice to hear it,' said Chesterfield.

Buckingham said he would take his leave. Matters of state called him.

When he had gone, Chesterfield seized Barbara in his arms and kissed her with passion.

'Nay! she cried, pushing him away. 'It is too soon. Do you not wish to see the child, Philip?'

He turned to the cradle then. 'A girl,' he said. 'Our child.'

'You think that?'

'Yes,' he said. 'It is ours.'

'You are proud to own her, Philip. Well, we must see that your interest in the little girl does not become known to your Lady Elizabeth.'

His face darkened at the memory of the scene he had so recently experienced with his wife.

'I care not,' he said.

She tapped him sharply on the arm.

'*I* care,' she said. 'I'll not have you bruit it abroad that this child is yours.'

'You are reserving her for a higher fate? Barbara, you witch!'

'Philip, soon I shall be well.'

'And then . . .'

'Ah! We shall meet ere long, I doubt not. Why, you are a more eager lover than you once were!'

'You become a habit, Barbara. A habit . . . like the drink or gaming. One sips . . . one throws dice, and then it is an unbearable agony not to be able to sip or throw the dice.'

'It pleases me that you came so quickly to my call.'

He was holding her hands tightly, and she felt his strength. She looked into his face and remembered that occasion four years ago in the nuttery. 'The first time,' she said. 'I remember. It was nothing less than rape.'

'And you a willing victim.'

'A most unwilling one. 'Twas forced upon me. You should have been done to death for what you did to me. Dost know the punishment for rape?'

The woman came in. She was agitated. 'My lady, Madam . . . the King comes this way.'

Barbara laughed and looked up at her lover.

'You had better leave,' she said.

Chesterfield had drawn himself up to his full height.

'Why should I leave? Why should I not stay here and say. "By God, Your Majesty, I am honoured that you should come so far to see my daughter"?'

Barbara's face was white and tense with sudden anger. 'If you do not leave this chamber this minute,' she said, 'I will never see you again as long as I live.'

She meant it, and he knew she meant it.

There were moments when he hated Barbara, but, whether he hated or loved, the knowledge was always with him that he could not live without her.

He turned and followed the woman out of the chamber; he allowed himself to be led ignobly out through a back door that he might run no risk of coming face to face with the King.

*

Charles stepped into the room while his accompanying courtiers stayed in the corridor.

Barbara held out her hand and laughed contentedly.

'This is an honour,' she said. 'An unexpected one.'

Charles took the hand and kissed it.

'It pleases me to see you so soon recovered,' he said. 'You look not like one who has just passed through such an ordeal.'

'It was a joyful ordeal,' she said, 'to bear a royal child.'

Eagerly she watched his face. It was never easy to read his feelings.

He had turned from her to the child in the cradle.

'So the infant has royal blood?'

'Your Majesty can doubt it?'

'There are some who doubtless will,' he said.

She was reproachful. 'Charles, you can talk thus while I lie so weakly here!'

He laughed suddenly, that deep, low musical laugh. 'Od's Fish, Barbara, 'tis the only time I would dare do so.'

'Think you not that she is a beautiful child?'

' 'Tis hard to say as yet. It is not possible to see whether she hath the look of you or Palmer.'

'She'll never have a look of Palmer,' said Barbara fiercely. 'I'd be ready to strangle at birth any child of mine who had!'

'Such violence! It becomes you not ... at such a time.'

Barbara covered her face with her hands. 'I am exhausted,' she murmured brokenly. 'I had thought myself the happiest of women, and now I find myself deserted.'

The King drew her hands from her face. 'What tears are these, Barbara? Do they spring from sorrow or anger?'

'From both. I would I were a humble merchant's wife.'

'Nay, Barbara, do not wish that. It would grieve me to see our merchants plagued. We need them to further the trade of our country, which suffers great poverty after years of Cromwell's rule.'

'I see that Your Majesty is not in serious mood.'

'I could be naught but merry to see that motherhood has changed you not a whit.'

'You have scarce looked at the child.'

'Could I look at another female when Barbara is at hand?'

Her eyes blazed suddenly. 'So you do not accept this child as yours ...?' Her long, slender fingers gripped the sheet. Her eyes were narrowed now and she was like a witch, he thought, a wild and beautiful witch. 'If I had a knife here,' she said, 'I would plunge it into that child's heart. For would it not be better for her, poor innocent mite, that she should never know life at all than know the ignominy of being disowned by her own father!'

The King was alarmed, for he believed her capable of any wild action. He said: 'I beg of you do not say such things, even in a jest.'

'You think I jest then, Charles? Here am I, a woman just emerging from the agony of childbed; in all my sufferings I have been sustained by this one thought: the child I bear is a royal child. Her path shall be made easy in the world. She shall have the honours due to her and it shall be our delight – her father's and mine – to love her tenderly as long as we shall live! And now . . . and now . . .'

'Poor child!' said Charles. 'To be disowned by one because she could be owned by many.'

'I see you no longer love me. I see that you have cast me aside.'

'Barbara, should I be here at this time if that were so?'

'Then you would take your pleasure and let the innocent suffer. Oh, God in Heaven, should such an unfortunate be condemned to live? As soon as I saw her I saw the King in her. I said, "Through my daughter Charles lives again." And to think that in my weakness that father should come here to taunt me. . . . It is more than I can bear.' She turned her face from him. 'You are the King, but I am a woman who has suffered much, and now I beg of you to leave me, for I can bear no more.'

'Barbara,' he said, 'have done with this acting.'

'Acting!' she raised herself; her cheeks were flushed, her hair tumbled, and she looked very beautiful.

'Barbara,' he said, 'I beg of you, control yourself. Get well. Then we will talk on this matter.'

She called to her woman. The woman came nervously, curtseying to the King as her frightened eyes went from him to Barbara.

'Bring me the child!' cried Barbara.

The woman went to the cradle.

'Give the child to me,' said the King. The woman obeyed. And because he loved all small and helpless creatures, and particularly children, the King was deeply touched by the small, pink, wrinkled baby who might possibly be his own flesh and blood.

He looked down at the serving woman and gave her one of those smiles which never failed to captivate all who were favoured with them.

'A healthy child,' he said. 'Methinks she already has a look of me. What say you?'

'Why, yes ... Your Majesty,' said the woman.

'I remember my youngest sister when she was little more than this child's age. They might be the same ... as my memory serves.'

Barbara was smiling contentedly. She was satisfied. The King had come to heel. He had acknowledged her daughter as his, and once more Barbara had her way.

The King continued to hold the child. She was a helpless little thing; he could easily love her. He owned to many children; so what difference did one more make?

*

Spring had come to England, and once more there was expectation in the streets of London. It was exactly a year since the King had returned to rule his country.

The mauve tufts of vetch with golden cowslips and white stitchwort flowers gave a gentle colour to the meadows and lanes which could be seen from almost every part of the city. The trees in St James's Park were in bud and the birdsong there sounded loud and jubilant as though these creatures were giving thanks to the King who had helped to build them such a delightful sanctuary.

The last year had brought more changes to the city. The people were less rough than they had been; there were fewer brawls. French manners had been introduced by the King and courtiers which subdued the natural pugnacity of the English. The streets had become more colourful. Maypoles had been set up; new hawkers had appeared, shouting their wares through the streets; wheels continually rattled over the cobbles. On May Day milkmaids danced in the Strand with flower-decorated pails. New pleasure-houses had sprung up, to compete for public patronage with the Mulberry Garden. Cream and syllabub was served at the World's End tavern in the village of Knightsbridge. There was Jamaica House at

Bermondsey; there were the Hercules Pillars in Fleet Street and Chatelins at Covent Garden – a favourite eating house since it was French and the King had brought home with him a love of all things French. Chatelins was for the rich, but there were cheaper rendezvous for the less fortunate, such as the Sugar Loaf, the Green Lettuce and the Old House at Lambeth Marshes; and there were the beautiful woods of Vauxhall in which to roam and ramble and seek the sort of adventures which were being talked of more openly than ever before, to listen to the fiddlers' playing, and watch the fine people walking.

Yes, there were great changes, and these were brought about through the King.

There was a new freedom in the very air – a gay unconcern for virtue. It might be that the people of the new age were not more licentious than those of the old; but they no longer hid their little peccadilloes; they boasted of them. They would watch the King's mistress riding through the town, haughty and so handsome that none could take his eyes from her. All knew the position she held with the King; he made no secret of it; nor did she. They rode together; they supped together four or five nights a week, and the King never left her till early morning, when he would take his walks and exercise in the gardens of his Palace of Whitehall.

It was a new England in which men lived merrily and were more ashamed of their virtue than their lack of morals. To take a mistress – or two – was but to ape the King, and the King was a merry gentleman who had brought the laughter back to England.

Charles was enjoying his own. The weather was clement; he loved his country; his exile was too close behind him for him to have forgotten it; he revelled in his return to power.

He was a young man, by no means handsome, but he was possessed of greater charm than any man in his Court; moreover he was royal. Almost any woman he desired, be she married or single, was his for the asking. He could saunter and select; he could enter into all the pleasures which were most agreeable to him. He could sail down the river to visit his ships – himself at the tiller; he could revel in their beauty, which attracted him so strongly. He could take his own yacht whither he wished, delighting in its velvet hangings and its damask-covered furniture, all made to his taste and his designs.

He could spend thrilling hours at the races; he could stand beside his workmen in the parks, make suggestions and give commands; he could watch the stars through his telescope with his astronomers and learn all they had to tell him. He could play bowls on his green at Whitehall, he could closet himself with his chemist and concoct cordials and medicines in his laboratory. Life was full of interest for a lively and intelligent man who suddenly found himself possessed of so much, after he had lived so long with so little.

He longed to see plays such as he had seen in France.

He was building two new theatres; he wished to see more witty plays produced. There were to be tall candles and velvet curtains – and women to act!

These were great days of change, but there was one thing which existed in abundance in this colourful and exciting city: dirt. It was ever present and therefore, being so familiar to all, passed unnoticed. In the gutters decaying matter rotted for days; sewage trickled over the cobbles; servants emptied slops out of the upper windows, and if they fell on to passers-by that merely added gaiety and laughter – and sometimes brawls – to the clamouring, noisy city.

Noise was as familiar as dirt. The people revelled in it. It was as though every citizen were determined to make up for the days of Puritan rule by living every moment to the full.

Manners had become more elegant, but conversation more bold. Dress had become more alluring, and calculated to catch the eye and titillate the senses. The black hoods and deep collars were ripped off, and dresses were cut away to reveal feminine charms rather than to hide them. Men's clothes were as elaborate as those of women. In their plumed hats and breeches adorned with frilly lace they frequented the streets like magnificent birds of prey, as though hoping to reduce their victims to a state of supine fascination by their brilliance.

And now the arches, which would be adorned with flowers and brocades, were being set up; the scaffolding was being erected. People stood about in groups to laugh and chatter of the change which had taken place in their city since the King came home. They would turn out in their thousands to cry 'A Health unto His Majesty' when the King rode by on his way to be crowned, and drink to him from the conduits flowing with wine.

*

Charles, driving his chariot with two fine horses through Hyde Park, bowing to the people who called their loyal greetings to him, was, for all his merry smiles, thinking of a subject which never failed to rouse the melancholy in him: Money.

A Coronation was a costly thing, and these people who rejoiced to see the scaffolding erected, and talked of the changed face of London, did not alas realize that they were the ones who would be asked to pay for it.

Charles had a horror of inflicting taxes. It was the surest way to a people's disfavour. And, he thought, I like my country so well, and I have travelled so much in my youth, that I have no wish ever to set foot outside England. It would therefore grieve me greatly if I were asked to go travelling again.

Money! How to come by it?

His ministers had one solution on which they continually harped. Marry a rich wife!

He would soon have to marry; he knew that; but whom should he marry?

Spain was anxious that the woman he married should have some ties with their country. The Spanish ambassador had put forth some suggestions tentatively. If Charles would consider a Princess from Denmark or Holland, Spain would see that she was given a handsome dowry.

Charles grimaced. He remembered the 'foggy' women of those capitals in which he had sojourned as an exile. His ministers wished him to take a rich wife; it was imperative for the state of the country's finances that he did so. And for the sake of my comfort, he had begged, let her be not only rich but comely.

His ministers thought this a frivolous attitude. He had his mistresses to be beautiful; suffice it that his wife should be rich.

Hyde was a strong man. He had deliberately flouted Barbara; and only a strong man would do that, thought Charles grimly. Hyde had forbidden his wife to call on Barbara, and Barabara remembered insults. She was going to be angry when she heard that the King was giving him the Earldom of Clarendon at the Coronation. Why do I give way to Barbara? he asked himself. Why? Because she could amuse him far more than any woman; because there was no physical satisfaction equal to that which Barbara could give. And why was this so? Perhaps because in her great gusto of passion she herself could enjoy so wholeheartedly. One could dislike Barbara's cupidity, her cruelty, her blatant vulgarity, yet Barbara's lusty beauty, Barbara's overwhelming sensuality chained a man to her side; it was not only so with himself. There were others.

But he must not think of Barbara now. He must think of a means of raising money.

When he returned to the Palace Lord Winchelsea was waiting to see him. Winchelsea had recently returned from Portugal, and he had news for the King which he wished to impart to him before he did so to any other.

'Welcome, my lord,' said the King. 'What saw you in Portugal that brings such brightness to your eyes?'

'I think mayhap,' said Winchelsea, 'that I see the solution to Your Majesty's pecuniary difficulties.'

'A Portuguese wife?' said Charles, wrinkling his brows.

'Yes, Sire. I had an interview with the Queen Regent of Portugal, and she offers you her daugher.'

'What manner of woman is she?'

'The Queen is old and earnest, most earnest, Your Majesty.'

'Not the Queen – I have not to marry her. What of the daughter?'

'I saw her not.'

'They dared not show her to you! Is she possessed of a harelip, a limp, a squint? I'll not have her, Winchelsea.'

'I know not how she looks, but I have heard that she is mightily fair, Your Majesty.'

'All princesses are mightily fair when they are in the field for a husband. The fairness is offered as part of their dowry.'

'Ah, Sire, the dowry. Never has there been such a dowry as this Princess would bring to England – should Your Majesty agree to take her. Half a million in gold!'

'Half a million?' cried the King, savouring the words. 'I'll swear she has a squint, to bring me half a million.'

'Nay, she is fair enough. There is also Tangier, a seaport of Morocco, the island of Bombay – and that is not all. Here is an offer which Your Majesty cannot afford to miss. The Queen of Portugal offers free trade to England with the East Indies and Brazil. Sire, you have but to consider awhile what this will mean to our merchants. The treasure of the world will be open to our seamen. . . .'

The King laid his hand on Winchelsea's shoulder. 'Methinks,' he said, 'that you have done good work in Portugal.'

'Then you will lay this proposition before your ministers, Sire?'

'That will I do. Half a million in gold, eh! And our sailors to bring the treasure of the world to England. Why, Winchelsea, in generations to come Englishmen will call me blessed. 'Twould be worth while even if . . .'

'But I have heard naught against the lady, Sire. I have but heard that she is both good and beautiful.'

The King smiled his melancholy smile. 'There have been two miracles in my life already, my friend. One was when I escaped after Worcester; the other was when I was restored to my throne without the shedding of one drop of blood. Dare I hope for a third, think you? Such a dowry, and a wife who is good . . . and beautiful!'

'Your Majesty is beloved of the gods. I see no reason why there should not only be three but many miracles in your life.'

'You speak like a courtier. Still, pray for me, Winchelsea. Pray that I get me a wife who can bring much good to England and pleasure to me.'

Within a few days the King's ministers were discussing the great desirability of the match with Portugal.

*

On the scaffolding the people had congregated to watch a procession such as they had never seen before. They chattered and laughed and congratulated one another on their good sense in calling the King back to his country.

Tapestry and cloth of gold and silver hung from the windows; the triumphal arches shone like gold in the sunshine; the bells pealed forth.

The King left his Palace of Whitehall in the light of dawn and came by barge to the Tower of London.

On St George's Day the great event took place. The procession was dazzling, all the noblemen of England and dignitaries of the Church taking part; and in their midst rode the King – the tallest of them all, dark and swarthy, bareheaded and serene with the sword and wand borne before him on his way to Westminster Abbey.

That was a day for rejoicing, and all through it the city was thronged with sightseers. They were on the river and its banks; they crowded into Cheapside and Paul's Walk; they waited to see the King, after his crowning, enter Westminster Hall, passing through that gate on which were the decomposing heads of the men who had slain his father.

'Long live the King!' they shouted; and Charles went into the building which was the scene of his father's tragedy. And when he sat at the great banqueting table, Dymoke rode into the hall and flung down the gauntlet as a challenge to any who would say that Charles Stuart, the second of that name, was not the rightful King of England.

Music was played while the King supped merrily, surrounded by his favourites of both sexes; and when it was over he took to his gilded barge and so to Whitehall.

But the merriment continued in the streets where the fountains flowed with wine; the bonfires which sprung up about the city cast a fantastic glow on the revellers.

Men and women drunk with wine and excitement lay together in the alleys and told each other that these were King Charles's golden days, while others knelt and drank a health unto His Majesty.

The glow of bonfires was like a halo over the rejoicing city, and from a thousand throats went up the cry: 'Come, drink the health of His Majesty.'

*

A few weeks after his people had crowned him King, Charles called together his new Parliament at the House of Commons and welcomed them in a speech which charmed even those who were not outstandingly Royalist in their sympathies.

'I know most of your faces and names,' said Charles, 'and I can never hope to find better men in your places.'

Charles had come to a decision. He had to find money some-how. The revenue granted him was not enough by some £400,000 to balance the country's accounts. Charles was grieved because the pay of his seamen – a community in which he was particularly interested, for indeed he considered them of the utmost importance to the Nation's security – was in arrears. He had had to raise money in some way, and had bor-rowed from the bankers of the city since it was the only way of carrying on the country's business; and these bankers were demanding high rates of interest.

How wearisome was the subject of money when there was not enough of it!

So he had come to his decision.

'I have often been put in mind by my friends,' he told his Parliament at that first sitting, 'that it is high time to marry, and I have thought so myself ever since I came into England. If I should never marry until I could make such a choice against which there could be no foresight of inconvenience, you would live to see me an old bachelor, which I think you do not desire to do. I can now tell you that I am not only resolved to marry, but whom I resolve to marry if God please. . . . It is with the daughter of Portugal.'

As the ministers had already been informed of what went with the daughter of Portugal the house rose to its feet and showed the King in boisterous manner that it applauded his choice.

*

Barbara heard the news. She was perturbed. The King to marry! And how could she know what manner of wife this Portuguese woman would be? What if she were as fiercely demanding as Barbara herself; what if she resolved to drive the King's mistress from her place?

Barbara decided she was against the marriage.

There were many people to support Barbara. Her power was such that she had but to drop a hint as to her feelings and there would be many eager to set in motion any rumour that would please her.

'Portugal!' said Barbara's friends. 'What is known of Portugal? It is a poor country. There is no glass in the win-dows even of the palaces. The King of Portugal is a poor simple fellow – more like an apprentice than a king. And what of the Spaniards who are the enemies of the Portuguese? Where will this marriage lead – to war with Spain?'

Barbara demanded of the King when they were alone together: 'Have you considered these things?'

'I have considered all points concerning this match.'

'This dowry! Her mother must be anxious to marry the girl. Mayhap she can only marry her to someone who has never seen her.'

'I have reports that she is dark-haired and pretty.'

'So you are already relishing your dark-haired pretty wife!'

' 'Tis well to be prepared,' said the King.

Barbara turned on him fiercely. There was a flippancy about his manner which frightened her. Of all her lovers he was the most important by reason of his rank; the others might seek consolation elsewhere, and she would not care with whom; with the King it was another matter. There must be no woman who could in his estimation compare with Barbara.

'Ah,' sighed Barbara. 'I am an unfortunate woman. I give myself ... my honour ... and I must be prepared to be cast off when it pleases you to cast me aside. It is the fate of those who love too well.'

'It depends on whom they love,' said the King. 'Themselves or others.'

'Do you suggest that I think overmuch of myself?'

'Dearest Barbara, none could help loving you beyond all others – so how could you yourself help it?'

'It amuses you to tease me. Now tell me that you will not let this Portuguese woman come between us.'

She put her arms about his neck; she lifted her eyes to his; they were wet with tears. Barbara was a clever actress and, even though he knew this, her tears could always move him. Barbara tender was almost a stranger.

He said: 'There is only one, Barbara, who could prevent my loving you.'

'And who is that?'

'Yourself.'

'Ah! So I have let my feelings run away with me, have I? How easy it is for some to be calm and serene. .... They do not love. They do not care. But when emotions such as mine are involved ...' She threw back her head and laughed suddenly. 'But what matters it! You have come to see me. We are here together. ... This night we may be together, so let the devil take the rest of my life. ... I still have this night!'

Thus she could change from tearful reproaches to urgent passion; always unaccountable, always Barbara.

Nothing should alter his relationship with her. He assured her of that. 'Not a hundred Portuguese women who brought me ten million pounds, twenty foreign towns and all the riches of the Indies.'

*

That year passed pleasantly for Charles. There was business to be conducted, affairs of state to be attended to, there was sauntering in the Park, bowls and tennis; there was racing, sailing and all the pleasures that a King could enjoy who was full of health and vigour.

He had made inquiries of Portugal. He had written letters to Catherine of Braganza, charming letters which reflected his own personality, the letters of a lover into which he was able to infuse the illusion that the marriage which was to take place was not as one arranged by their two countries but based on pure love.

By the end of the year Barbara was pregnant again. She was exultant.

'I am glad!' she cried. 'I would have the whole world know that I bear your royal child. This time there shall be no doubts. Charles, if you doubt this one to be yours, I'll not have it, I swear. I'll find some means of destroying it ere it is born ... If that fails, I'll strangle it at birth.'

The King soothed her. The child was his. He was as sure of that as she was.

'Then what will you do to prove it? How long shall I remain plain Barbara Palmer?'

It was more than a hint, and the King was not slow to act. It seemed only fair to him that Roger Palmer should be rewarded for his complaisance.

It was during that autumn that Charles wrote to his Secretary of State: 'Prepare a warrant for Mr Roger Palmer to be

Baron of Limerick and Earl of Castlemaine, these titles to go to the heirs of his body gotten on Barbara Palmer, who is now his wife.'

Barbara was delighted when she heard she was to be the Countess of Castlemaine.

*

She could not rest until she had sought out Roger.

She flung the news at him like a gauntlet.

'Now you see what marriage with me has brought you!'

'I know what marriage with you has brought me.'

'Come, Roger, why do you not rejoice in your good fortune? How many women are there in the world who can bring an earldom to their husbands?'

'I had rather you remained plain Barbara Palmer.'

'Are you mad? I, plain Barbara Palmer! You fool! I see I work in vain to bring honour to you.'

'It is so easy ... so natural for you to bring dishonour on all those connected with you.'

'You sicken me.'

'As your conduct does me.'

'Roger Palmer, I despise you. You stand there, so sanctimonious ... such a hypocrite. Do you think I see not the lust in your eyes? Why, I have only to beckon you and you'd be panting for me ... dishonour or not. ... You fool! Why should you not share in the honours and riches I can bring to us? Do not think that this is all I shall have. Nay! This is but the beginning.'

'Barbara,' he said, 'be not too sure. There will be a Queen of England on the throne ere long. Then it may be that the King will be engaged elsewhere and may not come a-supping with you night after night.'

Barbara flew at him, and the marks of her fingers lingered on his cheek long afterwards.

'Don't dare taunt me with that! Do you think I'll allow that miserable little foreigner to come between me and my plans?' Barbara spat over her shoulder; she liked to indulge in the crude manners of the street; it was as though it brought home to herself as well as others that she had no need to act in any way other than the mood of the moment urged upon her. 'She's hump-backed, she squints! The only way her mother can find a husband for her is by giving away half her kingdom.'

'Barbara . . . for the love of God, calm yourself.'

'I'll be calm when I wish to be. And wild when I wish to be. And I'll tell you this, Master Roger Palmer – who cannot bend his stiff neck to say a gracious thank you for the earldom his wife has conferred upon him – I'll tell you this: the coming of this Queen will make no difference to my relationship with the King.' She put her hands on her stomach. 'In here,' she cried, 'is his child. Yes . . . his . . . his . . . his! And by the saints, I swear this child shall be born in the royal apartments of Whitehall. Yes! even if my confinement should take place during the honeymoon of this Portuguese idiot.'

Her eyes flamed. She turned away and paced the floor.

She was eager to tell the King of her plans for lying-in when her time came at his Palace of Whitehall.

*

Christmas came. Charles had laughingly waved aside the question of Barbara's lying-in. It was six months away, and he never let events so far ahead cast a shadow over the pleasure of the moment.

Marriage plans were going forward. It seemed very likely that by the spring the little Portuguese would be in England.

The thought of her excited him, as the thought of any new woman would. That again was an excitement for the future. In the meantime there was Barbara to be placated, and enjoyed.

Barbara was brooding, still determined to be confined in his Palace. He wondered if he had been right to confer a great title on her husband that she might enjoy it. To give a little was to be asked for much. His experience of a lifetime told him that.

Still, there were occasions when he could remind even Barbara that he was the King, and he foresaw that when he had a wife such occasions might occur with greater frequency.

That again was a matter for the future.

So it was a merry Christmas – the merriest since he had come into England, for last Christmas had been overshadowed by the deaths of his brother and sister. It was good fun to revive those merry customs which had been stamped out by the Puritans – the old revelries of Christmas and Twelfth Night.

There was sadness to come in the New Year. His aunt, Elizabeth of Bohemia, who was at his Court, died there, and it was to him that she turned in her last moments.

He was saddened; he was indeed a family man; he could not bear that any member of his family, which had been so tragically torn apart in his youth, should die.

He had been fond of his aunt.

'So few of us are left now,' he pondered. 'There is James and Mam and Minette . . . and Mam is ailing, and Minette has never been strong . . . as James and I are.'

He wrote to his sister then: 'For God's sake, my dearest sister, have a care of yourself and believe me that I am more concerned for your health than I am my own.'

She understood him as, he often thought, no one else in the world had ever understood him.

She wrote to him that she was thinking of sending him a little girl to be a maid-of-honour to his Queen when she arrived in England. 'She is the prettiest girl in the world,' wrote Minette, 'and her name is Frances Stuart.'

The Earl of Sandwich was soon on his way to Portugal. Arrangements were being made to receive the King's bride in England; and there was always Barbara to placate.

He was spending as much time in her company as he ever had.

He was now supping at her house every night, and the whole city was talking of the King's infatuation for its most handsome woman, which did not diminish even though he was negotiating for a wife.

He but takes his fill of Castlemaine until the Queen arrives, said the people. Then we shall see the lady's handsome nose put out of joint.

Charles was treated to the whole range of Barbara's moods during that spring. She would plead with him not to let the Queen's coming make the slightest difference to her position; she would scorn him for a coward; she would cover him with caresses as though to remind him of the physical satisfaction which she alone could give.

She was determined to bind him more closely to her than ever.

She talked continually of the child – his child – which was to be denied its rightful bedchamber when it came into the world. She pitied herself; she flew into rages and threatened to murder the child before it left her womb.

She demanded again and again that she should have her lying-in at Whitehall Palace.

'That is impossible,' said the King. 'Even my cousin Louis would not so insult his wife.'

'You did not think of your wife when you got me with child!'

'A King constantly thinks of his Queen!'

'So I am scorned.'

'For the love of God, Barbara, I swear I cannot much longer endure such tantrums.'

Then she wept bitterly; she wished that her child had not been conceived; she wished that she herself had not been born; and he was at his wits' end to stop her doing herself some damage.

But on one thing he was adamant. It seemed likely that her child would be born just at the time of his Queen's arrival in England and the child must be born in Barbara's husband's house.

'What will become of me?' wailed Barbara. 'I see I am of no account to you.'

'You shall have a good position at Court.'

She was alert. 'What position?'

'A high position.'

'I would be a lady of the Queen's bedchamber.'

'Barbara, that is almost as bad as the other.'

'Everything I ask is bad. It is because you are tired of me. Very well. You no longer care for me. I shall take myself to Chesterfield. He is mad for me. He would leave that silly little wife of his tomorrow if I but lifted my finger.'

'I will do much for you,' said the King. 'You know it well.'

'Then promise me this. I will go quietly to my husband's house and there bear our child. I will not embarrass you while you receive your wife. And for that ... I shall be made a lady of your wife's bedchamber.'

'What you ask is difficult.'

'Are you a King to be governed? Are you not a King to command?'

'It seems that you would command *me*.'

'Nay! It is that hump-backed, squint-eyed woman who would do that. Come, Charles. Show me that I have not thrown away all my love on one who cherishes it not. Give me this small thing. I shall be a woman of your wife's bedchamber and I swear ... I swear that I will then be so discreet ... so gracious ... that she will never know that there has been aught between us two.'

He was weary of her tirades. He longed to rouse the passion in her ... he wanted to find the Barbara who returned his passion so gloriously when she was in that abandoned mood which made her forget to ask for what she considered to be her rights.

She was near that mood. He knew the signs.

He murmured: 'Barbara. . . .'

She leaped into his arms. She was like a lovely animal – a graceful panther. He wanted her to purr; he was tired of snarls.

'Promise,' she whispered.

And weakly he answered, for now it seemed that the moment was all-important to him, and the future a long way off: 'I promise.'

THREE

IN THE apartments at the Lisbon Palace sat Catherine of Braganza, her eyes lowered over a piece of embroidery, and it was clear to those who were with her that her attention was not entirely on her work.

She was small in stature, dark-haired, dark-eyed; her skin was olive and she had difficulty in covering her front teeth with her upper lip. She was twenty-three years of age and not uncomely in spite of the hideous garments she wore. The great farthingale of gaberdine was drab in colour and clumsy, so that it robbed her figure of its natural grace; her beautiful long hair was frizzed unbecomingly to look like a periwig and, as it was so abundant, her barber was forced to spend much time and labour in bringing about this disfigurement.

But, since this hair-style and the farthingale were worn by all Portuguese ladies, none thought their Infanta was disfigured by them.

The two ladies who sat on either side of her – Donna Maria de Portugal, who was Countess de Penalva and sister of the Portuguese Ambassador to England, Don Francisco de Mello, and Donna Elvira de Vilpena, the Countess de Ponteval – were very conscious of the disquiet of their Infanta and, because of certain rumours of which Donna Maria had learned through her brother, she was gravely disturbed. Her outward demeanour gave no hint of this, for Portuguese dignity demanded that a lady should never betray her feelings.

'Sometimes it would seem,' Catherine was saying, 'that I shall never go to England. Shall I, do you think, Donna Maria? And you, Donna Elvira?'

'If it be the will of God,' said Donna Elvira. And Donna Maria bowed her head in assent.

Catherine looked at them and smiled faintly. She would not dare tell them of the thoughts which came to her; she would not dare tell them how she dreamed of a handsome bridegroom, a chivalrous prince, a husband who would be to her as her great father had been to her mother.

Tears filled her eyes when she thought of her father. It had always been so. Yet she must learn to control those tears. An Infanta did not show her feelings, even for a beloved father.

It was five years since he had died. She had been seventeen at that time – and how dearly she had loved him! She was more like him than like her clever, ambitious mother. We were of a kind, dearest father, she often thought; had I been in your position I too should have wanted to shut myself away with my family, to live quietly and hope that the might of Spain would leave us unmolested. Yes, I should have been like that. But Mother would not have it. Mother is the most wonderful person in the world – you knew that, and I know it. Yet mayhap if we had lived quietly, if you had never been called to wrest our country from the yoke of Spain, if we had remained as we were at the time of my birth – a noble family in a captive country, a vassal of Spain – mayhap you would be here with me now and I might talk to you about the prince whose wife I may become. But, of course, had you remained a humble nobleman, I should never have been sought by him in marriage.

'I have a letter from him,' went on Catherine, 'in which he calls me his lady and his wife.'

'It would seem now,' said Donna Elvira, 'that God has willed that the marriage should go forward.'

'How strange it will be,' said Catherine, her needle poised, 'to leave Lisbon; perhaps never again to look from these windows and see the Tagus; to live in a land where, they say, the skies are more often grey than blue; where manners and customs are so different.' Her face showed fear suddenly. 'I have heard that the people are fond of merrymaking; they laugh often; they eat heartily; and they are very energetic.'

'They need to be,' said Donna Maria. 'It keeps them warm since they rarely feel or see the sun.'

'Shall I miss it?' mused Catherine. 'I see it often from my window. I see it on the water and on the buildings; but I seem only to look on the sunshine, not to be in it.'

'It would seem that you have a touch of it to talk thus,' said Donna Elvira sharply. 'What should the Infanta of Portugal be expected to do – wander out into the sun and air like a peasant?'

They had been with her – these two – since her childhood, and they still treated her as a child. They forgot that she was twenty-three, and a woman. So many were married long before they reached her age, but her mother had long preserved her for this marriage – marriage with England, for which she had always hoped, because in her wisdom Queen Luiza had foreseen that Charles Stuart would be recalled to his country, and as long ago as Catherine's sixth birthday she had decided that Charles Stuart was the husband for her daughter.

At that time the fortunes of the Stuarts were low indeed; yet, although Charles I had been in sore need of the money a rich Portuguese wife could bring him, he had decided against the match for his son. Catherine of Braganza was a Catholic and it may have been that he – at that time the harassed King – was beginning to understand that his own ill fortune might in some measure be traced to the fiercely Catholic loyalties of his own wife.

71

Disaster had come to the Stuarts and the first Charles had lost his head, yet, with that foresight and instinct for taking action which would be useful to her country, Luiza had still clung to her hopes for union with England.

'I do not think I shall miss the sun,' Catherine said. 'I think I shall love my new country because its King will be my husband.'

'It is unseemly to speak so freely of a husband you have not seen,' Donna Maria reminded her.

'Yet I feel I know him. I have heard so much of him.' Catherine cast down her eyes. 'I have heard that he is the most fascinating King in the world and that the French King, for all his splendours, is dull compared with him.'

Donna Maria lifted her eyes momentarily to Donna Elvira's; both looked down again quickly at their work. But not before Donna Elvira had betrayed by the slightest twitch of her lips that she was aware of what was in Donna Maria's mind.

'I think,' went on Catherine, 'that there will be a bond between us. You know how deeply I loved my father; so must he have loved his. Do you know that when his father was condemned to death by the Parliament, Charles – I must learn to call him Charles, although in his letter to me he signs himself Carlos – Charles sent to them a blank paper asking them to write what conditions they would and he would fulfil them in exchange for his father's life. He offered his own life. You see, Donna Elvira, Donna Maria, that is the man I am to marry. And you think I shall miss the sun!'

'You talk with great indiscretion,' said Donna Maria. 'You, an unmarried Princess, to speak thus of a man you have never seen. You will have to be more discreet than that when you go to England.'

'It is surprising to me,' said Donna Elvira, 'that you can so little love your mother ... your brothers and your country as to rejoice in leaving them.'

'Oh, but I am desolate at the thought of the parting. I am afraid ... so very afraid. Please understand me. I sometimes awake with terror because I have dreamed I am in a strange land where the people are rough and dance in the streets and shout at me. Then I long to shut myself into a convent where I could be at peace. So I think of Charles, and I say to myself: No matter what this strange new land is like, he will be there. Charles, my husband, Charles, who stopped the people torturing those men who had killed his father; Charles, who said: "Have done with hanging, let it sleep"; Charles, who offered his life and fortune for that of his father. Then I am less afraid, for whatever awaits me, he will be there; and he loves me already.'

'How know you this?' asked Donna Maria.

'His goodness, you mean? I have heard it from the English at our Court. And that he loves me? I have his letter here. He writes in Spanish, for he knows no Portuguese. I shall have to teach him, as he must teach me English; for the nonce we shall speak in Spanish together. I will read it, then you will stop frowning over that altar cloth and you will understand why the thought of him makes me happy.

' "My Lady and wife," ' she read. ' "Already at my request the good Count da Ponte has set off for Lisbon; for me the signing of the marriage has been great happiness; and there is about to be despatched at this time after him one of my servants charged with what would appear necessary; whereby may be declared on my part the inexpressible joy of this felicitous conclusion, which, when received, will hasten the coming of Your Majesty.

' "I am going to make a short progress into some of my provinces; in the meantime, whilst I go from my most sovereign good, yet I do not complain as to whither I go; seeking in vain tranquillity in my restlessness; hoping to see the beloved person of Your Majesty in these kingdoms, already your own; and that, with the same anxiety with which, after my long banishment, I desired to see myself within them ... The presence of your serenity is only wanting to unite us, under the protection of God, in the health and content I desire. ..." '

Catherine looked from one woman to the other and said, 'He signs this: "The very faithful husband of Your Majesty whose hand he kisses. Carlos Rex."

'Now, Donna Elvira, Donna Maria, what say you?'

'That he hath a happy way with a pen,' said Donna Elvira.

'And if,' added Donna Maria, rising and curtseying before Catherine with the utmost solemnity, 'I may have the Infanta's permission, I will retire, as there is something I wish to say to your royal mother.'

Catherine gave the required permission.

She returned to her needlework.

Poor Donna Maria! And poor Donna Elvira! It was true that they would go to England with her, but not to them would come the joy of sharing a throne with the most fascinating prince in the world.

*

As a result of her interview with Donna Maria, the Queen Regent sent for her daughter and, when she arrived, dismissed all attendants that they might talk in the utmost privacy.

Catherine was delighted to dispense with the strict etiquette which prevailed at the Court of Portugal; it was great happiness to sit on a stool at her mother's feet and lean against her.

At such times a foretaste of great loneliness would come to Catherine, for she would suddenly imagine what life would be like in a strange country without her mother.

Queen Luiza was an unusual woman; strong and fiercely ambitious for her family as she was, she was the tenderest of mothers and loved her daughter more than her sons. Catherine reminded Luiza poignantly of her husband – tender, gentle, the best husband and father in the world, yet a man who must be prodded to fight for his rights, a man who could be persuaded more by his conscience than his ambition. But for Luiza, Portugal would have remained under the yoke of Spain, for the Duke of Braganza had, in the early days of his marriage, seemed content to retire with his wife and two sons to the palace of Villa Viçosa in the province of Alemtejo surrounded by some of the loveliest country in Portugal, and there live with his family the life of a nobleman. For a time Luiza herself had been content; she had savoured with delight the charms of a life far removed from intrigue; there in that paradise her daughter had been conceived and, on the evening of November 25th, St Catherine's Day, in the year 1638, little Catherine had been born.

In spite of her practical outlook, Queen Luiza was something of a mystic. From the time the child was two she had

74

believed that Catherine was destined to lead her country to security and be as important a factor in its history as she knew herself to have been. For it was on the child's second birthday that greatness was thrust upon the Duke of Braganza and, had it not been for his two-year-old daughter, it might have happened that the great opportunity to rescue Portugal from Spanish tyranny would have been lost.

Never would Luiza forget that November day when the peace of the Villa Viçosa had suddenly given place to ambition. Portugal had been a vassal state to Spain since the mighty Philip II had made it so, and during the course of sixty years of bondage there had crept into the minds of the new generation a lassitude, a dull acceptance of their fate. It needed such as Luiza to rouse them.

Into the Villa Viçosa had come Don Gaspar Cortigno; he talked long and eloquently of the need to break away from the Spanish tyrants; he brought assurances that if the Duke of Braganza, the last of the old royal line, would agree to lead the revolt, many of the Portuguese nobility would follow him.

The Duke had shaken his head; but Luiza had been filled with ambition for her husband, her sons and her daughter. They were happy, she agreed, but how could they be content, knowing themselves royal, to ignore their royalty? How could they ever be content again if they did not keep faith with their ancestors?

'We are happy here,' said the Duke. 'Why should we not go on being happy all the days of our lives?' His eyes pleaded with her, and she loved him; she loved her family; yet she knew that never would her husband be completely happy again; always there would be regrets, reproaches and doubts in his mind. She knew that it might well be their children who, on reaching maturity, would accuse their parents of robbing them of their birthright. Then beside her was her little daughter catching at her hand, begging to be noticed; and inspired with the certainty that this appeal must not be turned aside, Luiza caught the child to her and cried: 'But, my lord, here is an omen. It is two years since this child was born. Our friends are with us to celebrate her birthday. This is a sign that it is the will of Heaven that your sons should regain the crown of which we have long been deprived. I regard it as a happy presage that Don Gaspar comes this day. Oh, my lord and husband, can you find it in your heart to refuse to confer on this child the rank of King's daughter?'

The Duke was struck by the glowing countenance of his wife, by the strange coincidence of the messenger's coming on the birthday of his daughter; and he thereupon agreed to relinquish his peaceful life for one of bloodshed and ambition.

Often he regretted that decision; yet he knew that he would have regretted still more had he had to reproach himself for refusing to take it. As for Luiza, she was certain that Catherine's destiny was entwined with that of Portugal.

It was for this reason that she had kept Catherine so long unmarried; it was for this reason that she had determined to wait for the conclusion of the match with England.

And, during the years which had followed the Duke's decision, success had come to his endeavours and he had regained the throne; but the struggle had so impaired his health that he had died worn out with his efforts; and since Don Alphonso, his elder son, was somewhat simple-minded, his mother Luiza was Queen Regent and ruler of Portugal, for so ably had she advised her husband that on his death, when the government of the country was left entirely in her hands, she continued to preserve Portugal from her enemies and became known as one of the ablest rulers in Europe.

But now, as she confronted her daughter and thought of the life which lay before her in what she knew to be fast gaining a reputation as the most profligate Court in Europe, and a rival to the French, she was wondering whether she had been as wise in conducting her family affairs as she had been in managing those of her country. Catherine was twenty-three, a normal and intelligent young woman, yet so sheltered had her life been that she was completely ignorant of the ways of the world.

She had seen the felicitous relationship of her father and mother and did not realize that men such as the Duke of Braganza – faithful husband and loving father, gentle yet strong, full of courage, yet tender and kind – were rare indeed. Catherine in her innocence would think that all royal marriages resembled that of her father and mother.

'My dearest daughter,' said the Queen, embracing

Catherine, 'I pray you sit here beside me. I would talk to you in private and most earnestly.'

Catherine sat at her mother's feet and rested her head against her farthingale. It was in moments of intimacy such as this that she was allowed to give vent to her tender feelings.

Luiza let her hand rest on her daughter's shoulder.

'Little daughter,' she said tenderly, 'you are happy, are you not? You are happy because there is now every likelihood that this marriage will come to pass?'

Catherine shivered. 'Happy, dearest mother? I think so. But I am not sure. Sometimes I am a little frightened. I know that Charles is the most charming King in the world, and the kindest, but all my life I have been near you, able to come to you when I was in any difficulty. I am happy, yes. I am excited. But sometimes I am so terrified that I almost hope the arrangements will not be completed after all.'

'It is natural that you should feel so, Catalina, my dearest child. Everything you feel is natural. And however kind your husband is to you and however happy you are, you will sometimes long for your home in Lisbon.'

Catherine buried her face in the serge farthingale. 'Dearest Mother, how can I ever be completely happy away from you?'

'You will learn in time to give all your devotion to your husband and the children you will have. We shall regularly exchange letters, you and I. Perhaps there may be visits between us. But they would be infrequent; that is the fate of royal mothers and daughters.'

'I know. But, Mother, do you think in the whole world there was ever such a happy family as ours has been?'

'It is given to few to know such happiness, it is true. Your father was deeply conscious of that. He would have lived peacefully in the Villa Viçosa and shut his eyes to his duty for the sake of the happiness he could have had with us. But he was a king, and kings, queens and princesses have their duties. They must not be forgotten for the sake of quiet family happiness.'

'No, Mother.'

'Your father agreed on that before he died. He lived nobly, and that is the way in which *we* must live. My dearest Catherine, it is not only that you will be marrying a very attractive King who will be a good husband to you, you will be making the best possible marriage for the sake of your country. England is one of the most important countries in Europe. You know our position. You know that our enemies, the Spaniards, are ever ready to snatch from us that which we have won. They will be less inclined to attack us if they know that our family is united in marriage with the royal family of England, that we are no longer alone, that we have a powerful ally at our side.'

'Yes, Mother.'

'So it is for the sake of Portugal that you will go to England; it is for your country's sake that you will do there all that is expected of a queen.'

'I will do my best, dear Mother.'

'That brings me to one little matter with which I must acquaint you. The King is a young man who will soon be thirty-two years of age. Most men marry before they reach that age. The King is strong, healthy and fond of gay company. It is unnatural for such a man to live alone until he reaches that age.'

'To live alone, Mother?' said Catherine, puzzled.

'To live unmarried. He, like you, could only marry one who was royal, and therefore suitable to his state. It would have been unwise for him to marry while in exile. So ... he consoled himself with one who cannot be his wife. He had a mistress.'

'Yes, Mother,' said Catherine. 'I think I understand.'

'It is the way of most men,' said Luiza. 'There is nothing unusual in this.'

'You mean there is a woman whom he loves as a wife?'

'Exactly.'

'And that when he has a wife in truth he will no longer need her? She will not be very pleased to see me in England, will she?'

'No. But her feelings are of no account. It is the King's which are all-important. He might dismiss his mistress when he takes a wife, but it has come to my ears that there is one lady to whom he is deeply attached.'

'Oh ...' breathed Catherine.

'You will not see her, for naturally he will not let her enter your presence, and you must avoid all mention of her. And eventually the King will cease to require her, and she will

78

quietly disappear. Her name is Lady Castlemaine, and all you have to do is avoid mentioning her name to anyone – anyone whatsoever – and foremost of all to the King. It would be a grave breach of etiquette. If you hear rumours of her, ignore them. It is a very simple matter really. Many queens have found themselves similarly placed.'

'Lady Castlemaine,' repeated Catherine; then she suddenly stood up and threw herself into her mother's arms. She was shivering violently, and Luiza could not soothe her for some time.

'There is nothing to fear, dearest,' she murmured again and again. 'Little daughter, it happens to so many. All will be well. In time he will love you . . . only you, for you will be his wife.'

*

Every day the arrival of the Earl of Sandwich was expected. He was to come to Lisbon with ships so that he might conduct Catherine and her entourage to England.

Still he did not come.

Catherine, bewildered by the sudden change the last months had brought, wondered whether he ever would. She had not left the Palace more than ten times in the whole of her life, so determined had her mother been to keep her away from the world. Exercise had been taken in the Palace gardens and never had she been allowed to leave her duenna; now that she was Queen of England – for she had been proclaimed as such since the marriage treaty had been ratified in Lisbon – she had left the Palace on several occasions. It had been strange to ride out into the steep streets, to hear the loyal shouts of the people and to bow and smile as she had been taught. 'Long life to the Queen of England!' they shouted. She was now allowed to visit churches, where she prayed to the saints that her marriage might be fruitful, and that long prosperity might come to the sister countries of Portugal and England.

When she was alone she took out the miniature which had been brought to her by Sir Richard Fanshawe who was in Portugal to help further the match, and she would feel that she already knew the man pictured there. He was as dark and swarthy as her own brothers, so that she felt he was no foreign prince; his features were heavy, but his eyes were so kindly. She thought of him as the man who had offered his life for the sake of his father and, although she was frightened of leaving her home and her mother, although she was fearfully perplexed at the thought of a woman named Lady Castlemaine, she longed to meet her husband face to face.

But still the Earl of Sandwich did not come.

*

Luiza, anxiously awaiting the arrival of the Earl, began to be afraid. This marriage with England meant so much to her. If it should fall through she could see that the honour and comparative security, which she and her husband had won for Portugal during the long years of endurance, might be lost.

The Spaniards were doing all in their power to prevent the marriage; that in itself showed how important it was. Already they were massing on the frontiers, ready for an attack, and she, being obliged to raise forces without delay, had been hard put to it to find the money to do this, so that it had been necessary to use some of that which she had set aside for her daughter's dowry – that very dowry which had made Catherine so attractive to the English King. The thought of what she would do when the time came for Catherine's embarkation and the handing over of the dowry gave her many a sleepless night; but she was a woman of strong character who had faced so many seemingly insurmountable difficulties in her life that she had learned to deal only with those which needed immediate attention, and trust in good fortune to help her overcome the others when it was absolutely necessary to do so.

There was another matter which gave her grave concern. She was sending her daughter into a strange country to a man she had never seen, without even the security of marriage by proxy.

'I send you my daughter the Infanta, unmarried,' she had written, 'that you may see what confidence I have in your honour.'

But she doubted whether that would deceive the King of England and his ministers. They would know that the Papal See, which was still the vassal of Spain, had never acknowledged Catherine as the daughter of a king; the Pope, when he gave the dispensation for the Infanta to marry a prince of the Reformed Faith – and the marriage could not be performed in Portugal without such a dispensation – would give her title not as Infanta of the Royal House of Portugal, but merely as the daughter of the Duke of Braganza. And that, Luiza felt, was a greater shame than any which could befall her.

So she, a determined woman grappling with many problems, had decided to act boldly. But if the Earl of Sandwich did not come soon, the Spaniards would be marching on Lisbon.

So each day she waited, but in vain.

Had the English learned that she could not find the money for the dowry? How could she know what spies there were in her Court? The Spaniards were cunning; they had been conquerors for a long time; and she was a poor Queen fighting a lonely battle for the independence of her country and the glory of her royal house.

Soon news came to her. The Spaniards were on the march. They were forging ahead towards the unfortified towns on the Portuguese seaboard.

Luiza was in despair. This attack was to be stronger than any the Spaniards had ever launched against their neighbours. Their aim was to see that, by the time the King of England's ambassadors came to claim the daughter of the royal house of Portugal, there would be no royal house. They were throwing great forces into the struggle; for ever since the defeat of their 'invincible' Armada in the reign of the great Elizabeth, the Spaniards had held the English in dread, and it was their endeavour to prevent at all costs the alliance between little Portugal and that country whose seamen they feared beyond any mortal beings.

So all her schemes had been in vain, thought Luiza. Her people would fight; but they had never had to face such a mighty army as now came against them. She saw ahead years of weary warfare, of frustration and struggle, the English marriage repudiated, and Catherine growing too old for matrimony.

She could no longer bear to look ahead. She shut herself into her apartments. She wanted to be alone to consider her next move.

She would not give up. She would somehow send Catherine to England. The King had promised to marry her. He must marry her.

*

She had said she was not to be disturbed, but Catherine came running into the apartment. Her face was flushed, and she ran as best she could, greatly impeded by her cumbrous farthingale.

'Catherine,' said her mother sternly; for in that moment Catherine bore no resemblance to an Infanta of the royal house.

'Mother! Dearest Mother ... quickly! Come and look.'

'What has happened, my child? What has happened to make you so far forget...'

'Come, Mother. It is what we have been waiting for so long. The English are here. They have been sighted in the bay.'

Luiza turned to her daughter and embraced her. There were tears on her cheek, for she too had forgotten the formal etiquette of the Court.

'They have come in time!' she said.

And she looked in wonder at this daughter who, she had always known, had been born to save her country.

*

There was rejoicing throughout Lisbon as the English came ashore. The Infanta Catherine, the Queen of England, had been born to save them; and here was another sign from heaven to assure her people that this was so. The commanders of the Spanish army, having heard the news and remembering the terrible havoc wrought on their country's ships by the Satanic *El Draque* in another century, would not stay to face the English. They turned back to the border and retreated as quickly as they could to safety. Some had seen the ships in the bay – the *Royal Charles*, the *Royal James*, and the *Gloucester* with their accompanying fleet of vessels. To those Spanish soldiers, brought up on the story of that ill-fated Armada which had broken the hopes of great Philip II when it came into conflict with a fleet of inferior vessels yet led by a man of supernatural powers, one glimpse was enough. The great ships seemed to have about them a quality which was not of this world, for it seemed that with them they had brought the spirit of Drake. So the army turned tail, and the Portuguese were saved from their enemies; and how would they dare attack again, knowing that the English were united with their little neighbour through marriage!

Luiza fell on to her knees and uttered prayers of thankfulness to God and His saints. The greatest danger was over; but there still remained the matter of the dowry. However, that could be shelved for the moment; since God had willed that her daughter should be born to save her country, Luiza doubted not that He would show her some way out of the difficulty.

In the meantime there must be a great welcome for the saviours of her country. The people did not need to be ordered to hang out their banners. They were wild with the happiness which comes from relief; they were ready to rejoice. The best bulls had already been brought to Lisbon in readiness for the welcome; it was only a matter of hours before the streets were hung with banners of cloth of gold and tapestry; crowds were on the banks of the river as Don Pedro de Almeida, Controller of Alphonso's household, rowed out in the royal barge to welcome the ambassadors of the King of England. The guns roared as the Earl of Sandwich and his friends were brought ashore. The people cheered as the King's coach carried him to the Palace of the Marquez Castello Rodrigo, where Alphonso was waiting to receive him.

Now the city of Lisbon showed the English what a royal welcome it could give to its friends. Banners, depicting the King of England and the Portuguese Infanta, hands joined, were carried through the streets; the bells of all the churches rang out, bull-fight followed bull-fight, and every Englishman was a guest of honour.

'Long live the King and Queen of England!' cried the people throughout the city of Lisbon, and that cry was echoed in those towns and villages which had so recently been spared the tyranny of Spain.

*

Queen Luiza chose a moment when the Earl of Sandwich had returned from a lavish entertainment, given in his honour, to ask him to her council chamber. On the previous day he had suggested to her that his master was impatient for his bride, and that he wished not to incur His Majesty's displeasure by further delay. The Queen knew he had been late in arriving at Lisbon, because he had found it necessary to subdue the pirates of the Mediterranean, who must be taught to respect the English flag; moreover, taking possession of Tangier, the task with which he had been commissioned before coming to convey the Infanta to England, had not been accomplished as quickly as he had hoped. The Moors had offered some opposition, and it had been necessary to overcome that. He anticipated no further trouble there, but had been obliged to leave a garrison in the town. As he considered these matters he thought he should lose no time in making his preparations to return; and so was eager to begin immediately to get the dowry aboard.

Luiza had known then that there was nothing for her to do but to explain her difficulties. She therefore arranged this Council meeting to take place after the Earl had been assured once more of the love the Portuguese had for his master and his master's country.

The miracle for which she had hoped had not come to pass. There was no means of providing the money she had promised. There was therefore nothing to be done but admit the truth.

She faced him boldly. 'My lord, in these last months we have faced troublous times. Our old enemy had determined to do all in his power to prevent the match which is so desired by both our countries. When the marriage was ratified the dowry was ready and waiting to be shipped to England, but our enemies stole upon us, and it was necessary to raise men and arms against them. For that reason we were forced to use part of the money, which was intended for our daughter's dowry, in the defence of our country.'

The Earl was dumbfounded. He had been ordered to bring back with him that money which he knew to be the very reason why his impecunious master had found the Portuguese match so desirable.

Luiza, watching the expressions of dismay flit across his face, knew he was wondering whether he should abandon Catherine and return to England without her. Panic filled her. She visualized not only the retreat of the English, but ignominious defeat at the hands of the Spaniards. Then she remem-

84

bered that Catherine was destined to save her country, and her confidence returned.

The Earl of Sandwich was meanwhile taking into consideration the fact that he had at some cost gained possession of Tangier, and had left an English garrison there. He was also calculating the cost of conveying that garrison back to England.

Meanwhile Luiza went on: 'Half the portion shall be delivered on board the King of England's ships without delay, and I pledge myself to send the other half before another year has passed.'

The Earl made a quick decision. Half the money was better than nothing; and the whole affair had gone too far for withdrawal; so, bowing before the Queen, he declared that, since it was his Queen in whom His Majesty of England was primarily interested, he would accept half the marriage portion now, and the other half within a year as the Queen had suggested; and, as soon as the moiety was on his ship he would be ready to convey the King's bride to England.

Luiza smiled. The rest would be simple. She would merely have bags of sugar and spices and such commodities shipped aboard the English fleet in place of the money which it was quite impossible to supply.

*

Luiza held her daughter in a last embrace. Both knew that they, who had been so close, might never see each other's face again. Neither shed a tear; they knew they dare not, for if they once allowed any sign of weakness to be visible they would break down completely before all the grandees and *fidalgos* of the Portuguese Court and the seamen of England.

'Always remember your duty to the King your husband, and to your country.'

'I will, Mother.'

Luiza still clung to her daughter. She was wondering: Should I warn her once more against that evil woman Castlemaine, for whom they say the King of England has an unholy passion? No! It is better not. Catherine in her very innocence may discover a way to deal with the woman. Better for her not to know too much.

'Remember all I have taught you.'

'Goodbye, dearest Mother.'

'Goodbye, my child. Remember always that you are the saviour of your country. Remember always to obey your husband. Goodbye, my love, my little one.'

I should not grieve, thought Luiza. All I wished for has happened. The Spaniards no longer molest us; we have the English as our allies, bound to us by the ties of affection and marriage.

That little matter of the dowry had been satisfactorily settled, although she had been afraid that the Earl of Sandwich was on the point of refusing to accept the sugar and spices in place of the gold. However, he had agreed to take it, after it had been arranged that Diego Silvas, a clever Jew, should accompany the sugar and spice to England and there make arrangements to dispose of it for gold which would be paid into the English Exchequer.

God and the saints be praised! thought Luiza. All difficulties have been surmounted, and I have nothing to fear now. There is just that grief which a mother must feel when parting with a beloved daughter.

How young Catherine looked! Younger than her years. Has she been too sheltered? Luiza anxiously demanded of herself. Does she know too little of the world? How will she fare in that gay Court? But God will look after her. God has decided on her destiny.

The last embrace, the last pressure of the hand had taken place, and Catherine was walking between her elder brother, the King, and her younger brother, the Infante. She turned before entering the waiting coach to curtsey to her mother.

Luiza watched them, and a hundred pictures from the past flashed through her mind as she did so. She remembered their birth, the happy days at Villa Viçosa and that important occasion of Catherine's second birthday.

'Goodbye,' she murmured. 'Goodbye, little Catherine.'

Through the streets went the royal coach, under the triumphal arches past the cheering people to the Cathedral, where Mass was celebrated. Catherine, who had rarely left the seclusion of the Palace, felt as though she were living through a fantastic dream. The shouting, cheering people, the magnificence of the streets, and their decorations of damask and cloth of gold, the images of herself and Charles were like pictures conjured from the imagination. After the ceremony the coach took her, her brothers, and their magnificent retinue to the Terreiro do Paço where she was to embark on the barge which would carry her to the *Royal Charles*.

Among those who were to go with her were Maria de Portugal and Elvira de Vilpena. 'You will not feel lonely,' her mother had said, 'for you will have, as well as your suite of six ladies and duenna, those two old friends of your childhood who together will try to be what I have always been to you.'

The ceremony of going aboard was a very solemn one. A salute was fired from the *Royal Charles*, which carried 600 men and 80 brass cannon, and all the noblest in the retinue which had accompanied her to the Paço knelt before her to kiss her hand. Catherine stepped into the royal barge, and to the sound of music and cheering was rowed out to the *Royal Charles*.

As she became conscious of the swell beneath her feet a feeling of terrible desolation swept over her. She had been living in dreams; she had thought continually of her husband – the perfect King, the gentle Prince who had offered his life in exchange for his father's, the lover who had written such tender notes. And now she became acutely aware of all that she was losing – her home, the love of her brothers and, most of all, her mother.

And Catherine was afraid.

Elvira was beside her. 'Your Majesty should go at once to your cabin. And you should stay there until we set sail.'

Catherine did not answer, but she allowed herself to be led to the cabin.

Maria said to her: 'The King himself designed your cabin in this his best beloved ship. I have heard it is the most magnificent cabin that ever was in a ship.'

Catherine was thinking: So it may be, but how can I think of my cabin now, even though he planned it for me? Oh, Mother. ... I am twenty-three, I know, and a woman, but I am only a little girl really. I have never left my home before; I have rarely left the Palace ... and now I have to go so far away, and I cannot bear it ... I cannot ... for I may never return.

Now they were inspecting the cabin. In it, they were saying, was all that a Queen could wish for. A royal cabin and a state room! Had she ever seen the like? Both apartments were decorated with gold, and lined with velvet. Would she take a look at the bed? It was red and white and richly embroidered. Could she believe that she was on board a ship! Look at the taffeta and damask at the windows, and the carpets on the floor!

Now she must rest, and stay in her cabin until the ship reached England, for it would not be meet for a Queen and lady of the royal house of Portugal to show herself to the sailors.

But Catherine had turned away. The closeness of the cabin with its rich decorations seemed to suffocate her. She could not remain there. She could not now consider Portuguese etiquette.

She turned and went on to the deck, determined to look at her native land as long as it was in view.

All that day and the night that followed, the *Royal Charles* with Catherine on board lay becalmed in the bay of Lisbon; but in the morning a wind sprang up and, accompanied by the *Royal James, Gloucester*, and fourteen men-of-war, the ship crossed the bar and sailed out to sea. It was a magnificent sight.

On the deck, waving aside all those who would come near her, was Catherine, Queen of England, Infanta of Portugal, straining to see, through the tears she could no longer restrain, the last of her native land.

*

After seventeen days at sea, to the great relief of all aboard, the English coast came into view. Elvira had suffered from a fever during the voyage. Catherine herself felt exhausted and weak and as the days passed she was beset by many doubts. It was one thing to dream of the perfect marriage with the perfect man, but when to accomplish it meant leaving behind her home and beloved family, she could not experience complete joy.

She had even had doubts about her husband's virtues as the voyage progressed. It might have been that, in imminent peril of losing their lives, those about her had not succeeded in hiding their feelings as they had in calmer moments. Catherine knew that those who loved her were afraid for her; she knew that they were thinking of the woman Castlemaine, of whom she must never speak. She herself was afraid. As she lay in her cabin, tossed by the erratic movement of the ship, she had felt so ill that she had almost wished for death. But then it had seemed that her mother was near her, urging her to remember her duty, not only to her husband, but to Portugal.

She had wept a little; she had cried for her mother, cried for her home and the quiet of the Lisbon Palace.

It was well that her weakness could be kept secret from those about her.

But she had felt happier when they had come in sight of land and, as they approached the Isle of Wight, the Duke of York's squadron hove in sight. Immediately word was sent to her that the Duke, brother to the King, had sent a message craving her permission to come aboard the *Royal Charles* that he might kiss her hand.

Soon he had come, with the gentlemen of his suite; the Duke of Ormond, the Earl of Chesterfield, the Earl of Suffolk and other fine gentlemen.

They were all dazzlingly dressed, and as her brother-in-law approached to kiss her hand, Catherine was glad that she had disregarded Maria's and Elvira's injunctions to receive the visitors in her native dress. She realized that it would seem strange to these gentlemen and that they would expect her to be dressed as the ladies of their Court. So she wore a dress which had been provided for her by the indefatigable and so tactful Richard Fanshawe; it was made of white and silver lace, and Elvira and Maria held up their hands in horror at the sight of her. It was, they declared, indecent compared with her Portuguese costume.

But she refused to listen to them and, in the cabin which had been hastily turned into a small presence chamber, she received these gentlemen.

The Duke set out to charm her, and this he succeeded in doing, for, although his manners with ladies were considered somewhat clumsy by the members of his brother's Court, Catherine sensed his great desire to please, and she was only too ready to be pleased.

They talked in Spanish and, as the Duke was eager to dispense with ceremony, Catherine was delighted to do so. She asked for news of the King, and James told her many things concerning her husband: how he loved ships, and what care he had spent in decking this one out that it might be worthy to receive his bride; how he loved on occasion to take a hand at the tiller himself; he told of the improvements he had made in his parks and houses; how he loved a gamble at the races; how he made experiments in his laboratories, and grew strange herbs in his physic garden; he told her a great deal about his brother and mentioned the names of many ladies and gentlemen of the Court, but never once did the name of Castlemaine pass his lips.

Catherine received him daily when he would be rowed out to the *Royal Charles* in his launch; and they talked together, becoming the best of friends, so that Catherine felt her fears diminishing. And when the *Royal Charles* sailed to Portsmouth, James followed and was at hand again, when she left the great ship, to accompany her to port in the royal barge.

Once on land she was taken to one of the King's houses in Portsmouth, where the Countess of Suffolk, who had been appointed a lady of her bedchamber, was waiting to receive her.

The Duke advised her to despatch a letter to the King, telling him of her arrival, when he would with all haste come to greet her.

Eagerly she awaited his coming.

She shut herself into her apartment and told all her attendants that she wished to be alone. Elvira was still suffering from her fever, and Maria was exhausted; as to her six ladies-in-waiting, and their duenna, they too were feeling the effects of the journey and, like their mistress, were not averse to being left alone to recover.

Catherine lay in the solitude of her chamber and once more took out the miniature she had carried with her.

Soon he would be here. Soon she would see him in the flesh – this man of whom she had dreamed so persistently since she had known he was to be her husband. She knew what his face was like. He was tall, rather sombrely dressed, for he was not a man who greatly cared for finery. This much she had heard. No! He would not care for finery; vanity in dress was for smaller men! He was witty. That alarmed her. He will think me so very stupid, she thought. I must try to think of clever things to say. No, I must be myself. I must apologize because I am simple and have seen so little of the world. He will have seen so much. He has wandered over Europe, an exile for years before he came into his kingdom. What will he think of his poor simple bride?

She prayed as she lay there: 'Make me witty, make me beautiful in his eyes. Make him love me, so that he will not regret giving up that woman whose name I will not mention even to myself.'

I shall walk in his parks with him and I shall love the plants and bushes and trees because he has planted them. I shall love his little dogs. I shall be their mistress as he is their master. I shall learn how to take clocks to pieces and put them back. All his interests shall be mine, and we shall love each other.

'He is the most easy-going man in the world,' they said of him. 'He hates unpleasantness. He avoids scenes and looks the other way when there is trouble. Smile always, be gay . . . if you will have him love you. He has had too much of melancholy in his life. He looks for gaiety.'

I will love him. I will make him love me, she told herself. I am going to be the happiest Queen in the world.

There was commotion below. He had arrived. He had had news of her coming, and he had ridden with great speed from London.

She should have had time to prepare herself. She rose from her bed, called frantically to her women.

'Quickly! Quickly! Dress me in my English dress. Loosen my hair. I will wear it as the English wear it . . . just at first. Where are my jewels? Oh, come . . . come . . . we must not delay. He must see me at my best. . . . I should have been prepared.'

The Countess of Suffolk hurried into the chamber as her women bustled about her.

'Your Majesty, a visitor has come to see you.'

'Yes . . . yes . . . bring him in. I am ready.'

She half closed her eyes. She would not be able to bear to look at him. This was the most important moment in her life. Her heart was fluttering like a frightened bird.

She heard the Countess say: 'This is Sir Richard Fanshawe. He has letters for you . . . messages from the King.'

Sir Richard Fanshawe!

She opened her eyes as Sir Richard came into the apartment.

He knelt. 'Your Majesty, I bring letters from the King's Majesty. He sends loving greetings to you. He commands me to tell you that he will be with you as soon as he can conveniently travel. At this time imperative business detains him in London.'

Imperative business! What business could it be, she wondered, to keep a man from the wife whom he had not yet seen, a King from his Queen who had undertaken a perilous journey to come to him? She wished that she could banish the name of Lady Castlemaine from her mind.

*

The bells were ringing in London. The people stood about in groups, as they did when great events were afoot. The Queen had arrived at Portsmouth; and now it would not be long before the ceremony of marriage took place in England; there would be more pageantry; more revelry; and it would be amusing to see what would happen when the new Queen and Lady Castlemaine came face to face.

The King himself had received the news of the Queen's arrival. He had heard also of the bags of sugar and spices that she had brought with her.

He let the communication drop from his hands. So he had a wife at last; but the very reason for her coming – that half a million of money which he so badly needed – was to be denied him.

The Queen Mother of Portugal had promised the rest would follow. In what form, he wondered; fruit? More spices? He had been deceived by that wily woman, for she had known that the reason he had agreed to marry her daughter was that the dowry would help to save his country from bankruptcy.

He must see Clarendon, his Chancellor. But no. Clarendon had been against the match; Clarendon had wished him to marry a Protestant wife, and had only agreed to support the Portuguese marriage when he was overruled by the majority of the King's ministers. And why had they agreed to this marriage? Simply because of that half a million in gold.

So, said Charles to himself, I have a wife and much sugar and spice; I have a port on the coast of Morocco which is going to cost me dearly to maintain – did the sly woman wish me to have it because she could no longer afford to keep it? – and I have the island of Bombay, which I may discover to be equally unprofitable. Oh, my marriage is a very merry one, I begin to believe!

The Queen was here. She was waiting for him at Portsmouth, and he was expected to go and greet her ... her and her sugar and spice.

Barbara was plaguing him; she had never given up the idea of having her lying-in at Whitehall. Barbara might even by now have heard the story of the sugar and spices; if so, she would be laughing herself hoarse with merriment.

He strode up and down the apartment. Mayhap this Jew they had brought with them would soon set about converting the cargo into money. Mayhap the Queen of Portugal would fulfil her promises in due time!

'Tis no fault of that poor girl! he mused. 'Tis her mother who has tricked me. But a fine laughing-stock I shall be when the story of the sugar and spice is bruited about.

He lifted his shoulders characteristically; and went to sup at Barbara's house.

Barbara was delighted to receive him.

She was now very large, for her confinement would take place within the next few weeks. She embraced the King warmly, having signed to all to leave them, for it was Barbara who on such occasions gave orders like a Queen.

She had had prepared his favourite dishes. 'For,' she told him, 'I heard of the manner in which these foreigners had cheated you, and I was assured that you would come to me this night for comfort.'

'It would seem,' said the King with a frown, 'that news of my affairs reaches you ere it comes to me.'

'Ah, all know how solicitous I am for your welfare. Your troubles are mine, my dearest.'

'And what else have you heard, apart from the description of the cargo?'

'Oh, that Her Majesty is small of stature and very brown.'

'Your informants were determined to please you.'

'Nay, I had it from those that hate me. They say that her teeth do wrong her mouth, and that her hair is dressed in a manner most comic to behold. She has a barber with her who spends many hours dressing it. I hear too that she wears a fantastic costume. It is a stiff skirt designed to preserve Portuguese ladies from the sleight of hand of English gentlemen.'

Barbara burst into loud laughter, but there was an uneasiness in it which the King did not fail to detect.

'Doubtless,' he said, 'I shall soon see those wonders for myself.'

'I marvel that you are not riding with all speed to Portsmouth.'

'Had I not promised to sup with you?'

'You had. And had you not kept your word I should not have let you forget it.'

'Methinks, Barbara, you forget to whom you speak.'

'Nay, I forget not.' Her jealousy of the Queen was too strong to be subdued. 'No,' she added on a louder note, 'I forget not. I speak to the father of this child I carry, this poor mite who will be born in a humble dwelling unworthy of his rank. He will be born in this miserable dwelling instead of the Palace in which he belongs. But then – he is not the first!'

The King laughed. 'You speak of the child as though he were holy. Od's Fish, Barbara, you bear no resemblance to the Blessed Virgin!'

'Now you are profane. But mayhap I shall not survive this confinement, for I have suffered so much during my pregnancy. Those who should cherish me care not for me.'

'And the sufferings you have endured have been inflicted by yourself. But I do not come here to quarrel. Mayhap, as you say, I should be on my way to Portsmouth.'

'Charles . . . pray sit down. I implore you. I beg of you. Do you not understand why I am nervous this night? I am afraid. Yes, it is my fear that makes me so. I am afraid of this woman with her cruel teeth, and her odd hair, and her farthingale. I am afraid that she will hate me.'

'I doubt not that she would – should your paths cross.'

Barbara had turned pale. She said quietly: 'I beg you eat of this pheasant. I had it specially prepared for you.'

She held out the dish to him; her blue eyes were downcast.

For the rest of the meal she did not mention the Queen; but she became gay and amusing, as she well knew how to be. She was soothing; she was the Barbara he had always hoped she would be, and her pregnancy had softened the rather hard beauty of her face; and lying on a couch, a brilliantly coloured rug hid her awkwardness, and her lovely auburn hair fell loose about her bare shoulders.

After a while others came to join them, and Barbara was merry. And when they had gone, and left the King alone with her – as it was their custom to do – he stayed talking to her; and she was tenderly tearful, telling him that she was sorry for her vicious ways towards him, and that she hoped in the future – should she live – to improve her manners.

He begged her not to talk of dying, but Barbara declared she had a feeling that she might not be long for this world. The ordeal of childbirth was no light matter, and when one had suffered during the weeks of pregnancy as she had suffered, death was often the result.

'You suffered?' asked the King.

'From jealousy, I fear. Oh, I am to blame, but that did not lessen my suffering. I think of all the sins I have committed, as one does when one approaches death, and I longed for a chance to lead a better life. Yet, Charles, there is one thing I could never do. I could never give you up. Always I shall be there if you should want me. I would rather face damnation than lose you.'

The King was disturbed. Not that he entirely believed her, but he thought she must be feeling very weak to be in such a chastened mood. He comforted her; she made him swear that he would not let this marriage interfere with their relationship; she must have a post which would result in her seeing him frequently; but she knew that, if she lived, she would have it, for had he not promised her the post in his wife's bedchamber? She would be content with that, but she could never give him up.

'No matter,' she said, 'if a hundred queens came to marry you bringing millions of bags of sugar and spices, still there would be one to love you till she died – your poor Barbara.'

And to be with Barbara, meek and submissive, was an

adventure too strange and exciting to be missed.

It was early morning before he left Barbara's house; and all London took notice that the King passed the night at his mistress's house while his Queen lay lonely at Portsmouth. Outside the big houses of the city, bonfires had been lighted in honour of the Queen's coming; but it was seen that there was none outside the door of that house in which the King spent the night with Lady Castlemaine.

*

What was detaining him? Catherine wondered. Why did he not come? Imperative business? What was that? After the second day she ceased to care, for she was smitten with that fever from which Elvira had suffered during and just after the voyage. Her throat was so sore and she was so feverish that she spent the hours lying in her bed while her maids of honour brought her dishes of tea, that beverage of which she was particularly fond and which was rarely drunk in England.

She would lie in her bed thinking of him, wondering when he would come. She longed to see him, yet she did not want him to come and see her as she was now, with dark shadows under her eyes, and her hair lustreless. She was terrified that he might turn from her in disgust.

Lady Castlemaine, she supposed, would be very beautiful. The mistresses of kings were beautiful because they were chosen by the kings, whereas their wives were thrust upon them.

She knew that her maids whispered together and wondered, as she did, what detained him. Perhaps they knew. Perhaps among themselves they murmured that name which, her mother had impressed on her, must never pass her lips.

Could it be that he, in her imagination the hero of a hundred romances, could so far discard his chivalry as to neglect his wife? Was he so angry about the dowry? Each day there came for her those charming letters from his pen. He wrote like a lover; he wrote of his urgent business as though he hated it, so it surely could not be Lady Castlemaine. He longed to be with her, he declared; he was making plans for the solemnization of their nuptials; ere long he would be with her to assure her in person of his devotion. She treasured the let-

96

ters. She would keep them for ever. Through them lived again the romantic hero of her imagination. Yet the days passed – three ... four ... five – and still there was no news of the King's coming.

The fever left her, but, said the physicians, she was to remain in bed. And on the fifth day news came to her that the King had left his capital.

It was two days later, and she was still confined to her bed, but there had been a miraculous change in her. She wondered how long the journey from London to Portsmouth would take, and she pictured him, having done with his 'imperative business', riding with all speed to her, and thinking of her as she thought of him.

It was afternoon and Catherine was sitting up in bed, her luxuriant hair falling about her shoulders, when Elvira and Maria came hurrying into her room to say that the King was below.

Catherine was flustered. 'I must be dressed ... at once. How can I receive him thus? I pray thee, Donna Maria ... call my women. I must wear my English dress. ... Or should it be my own ... ?'

'You are trembling,' said Elvira.

'It is because I shall not be at my best when the King arrives.'

Elvira said: 'The doctors' orders are that you shall not leave your bed. Why, if you were to take a chill now ... who knows what would happen? Nay! The King shall wait. We will let His Majesty wait to see you, as you have waited to see him.'

But at that moment there was a knock on the door and the Earl of Sandwich was craving permission to enter.

Elvira stood back and he came into the room, bowing to the Queen.

He said: 'The King has ridden from London that he may be with his Queen. Your Majesty, he is ready to wait upon you now....'

Elvira said: 'Her Majesty is indisposed. She has been ill these several days. ... Mayhap tomorrow she will be well enough to receive His Majesty.'

But at that moment there was the sound of footsteps outside. A low musical voice cried: 'Wait until tomorrow? Indeed

I'll not. I have ridden far to see the Queen, and I'll see her now.'

And there he was, just as she had imagined him – tall, very dark, and smiling the most charming smile she had ever seen. He was as he had been in her dreams, only so much more kingly, she told herself afterwards, so much more charming.

Her first thought as he approached the bed was: Why was I afraid? I shall be happy. I know I shall be happy, because he is all and more than I hoped he would be.

Sweeping off the big plumed hat, he had taken her hand; his eyes had twinkled as he smiled at her.

Now the room was filling with his attendants. The ambassadors were there, the Marquis de Sande and his gentlemen who had accompanied him to England; there were the King's cousin, Prince Rupert, my lord Sandwich, my lord Chesterfield, and others. Elvira had grown pale with horror on seeing so many gentlemen in the bedchamber of a lady.

The King said: 'I am most happy at last to greet you. Alas, I do not speak your tongue. Nor you mine, I understand. 'Tis a merry beginning. We must speak in Spanish, which means that I must needs pause to think before I utter a word. And that may not·be a bad thing, do you agree?' He was still holding her hand, pressing it firmly, and his eyes said: You are afraid. Of what? Not of me! Look at me. Do you think you should ever be afraid of me? Of these men! They are of no account, for you and I are their King and Queen, to rule over them.

She smiled tremulously, and her dark eyes never left his.

'It grieves me much to see you indisposed,' he continued. And then he did a strange thing which no Portuguese gentleman would have dreamed of doing: he sat on the bed as though it had been a couch; and he still kept his grip on her hand. He threw his hat from him. One of the gentlemen caught it.

He went on: 'Catherine, my happiness on this occasion would have been greatly diminished had your doctors not assured me that there is no cause for anxiety concerning your indisposition.'

'Your Majesty is graciously kind to be so concerned,' she said.

He smiled and waved to the people who had come into the

room to retire a little, that he and the Queen might converse together in more privacy.

The courtiers moved back and stood in little groups while the King turned to his Queen.

'We shall have time in the future,' he said, 'for more private conversation. Then we shall be quite alone. Just now it would seem that your duennas are eager that you and I should not be left quite alone together.'

'That is so,' she said.

'And are you as solemn as they are?'

'I do not know. I have never had any opportunity to be other than solemn.'

'You poor little Queen! Then we must contrive many opportunities for making you the reverse of solemn. You shall see what I have planned for you. I thank God you have come to me in summertime, for our winters are long, and doubtless you will find them very cold. But we shall have sylvan entertainments; we shall have river pageants. I mean to show you that your new country can look tolerably well in summertime. I trust you will not be displeased with it.'

'I know I shall be very pleased.'

'It shall be our earnest endeavour to make you so. Ah! you smile. I am glad you smile so readily. I am an ugly fellow who likes those about him to look pleasant – and what is more pleasant than smiling faces?'

'But indeed you are not ugly,' she said.

'No? Doubtless the light of your bedchamber is favourable to me.'

'No. Never, never ugly. . . .'

'Ah, it would seem I have not made such an ill impression after all. . . . I rejoice in that. Now you must get well quickly, for your mother will expect our nuptials to take place as early as can be arranged. As soon as you are fit to leave your bed the ceremony must be performed.'

'I shall soon be well,' she promised him.

Her face was flushed, but not with fever, and her eyes were bright.

He rose from the bed. 'Now I shall leave you, for this was a most unceremonious call. But you will soon learn that I am not over-fond of ceremony. I wished to see my bride. I could contain myself no longer, so great was my eagerness. And now

99

I have seen her, and I am content. I trust you too are not entirely disappointed?'

How kind he looked – eager, anxious, determined to tell her she must not be afraid!

It was as though that romanticized figure of her dreams had materialized; and in the flesh he was more charming than her dreams had fashioned him, for the simple reason that, before meeting him, she would not have believed so much that was charming and fascinating could be concentrated in one person.

'I am content,' she said; and she spoke from the bottom of her heart.

Then he kissed her hand again.

She heard her women, whispering together after he had gone, and they were talking of him. They were shocked because he had come thus unceremoniously, but she did not care. She would not care what they said in future. She was only anxious that she should please him.

She whispered to herself: 'I am content.' He had said that; and she had answered: 'I am content.'

*

The King was pensive as he left the apartment. He was pleasantly surprised. From some reports, and in view of the way the Queen Mother had cheated him over the dowry, he had half expected a bride who looked more like a bat than a woman. It was true that she was no beauty, and he was such an admirer of beauty; but he realized that he could hardly have expected a woman who was suitable as a wife to be also a suitable mistress.

He liked very much her manner; quiet, innocent, eager to please. That was such a change after the imperious conduct of Barbara. Had his Queen the temper of his mistress he would have visualized a very stormy life ahead.

No. He believed he had good reason to congratulate himself.

He could grow fond of his little Catherine; he could find it easy to forgive her for not bringing him the promised dowry – and indeed how could a man of his nature do aught else, since it was in truth no fault of hers?

He would be kind to her; he would help her overcome her fears; he would be a gentle lover and husband, for he knew that was what she would want. He would make her happy; and they would have a fine family – several sons as handsome as young James Crofts, Lucy Water's boy – and he would no longer have any need to sigh with regret every time his eyes fell on that young man.

He smiled, thinking of her shyness. What a life she must have led in her solemn Portuguese Court; and if her mother was anything like those drags who had come to guard her daughter, it was no wonder that the poor child was eager for affection.

Have no fear, little Catherine, he mused. You and I can bring much good to one another.

He was looking forward to the nuptials, for a new woman was always a new adventure. Her eyes are good, mused the connoisseur, and there is certainly nothing in her face which could in the least way disgust one. In fact there is as much agreeableness in her lips as I ever saw in any woman's face, and if I have any skill in physiognomy, which I think I have, she must be a good woman. Her voice is agreeable and I am sure our two humours will agree. If I do not do all in my power to make her happy – in spite of the spice and sugar – I think I shall be the worst man on Earth, and I do not believe I am that, although I am far from saintly.

It was not in his nature to grieve unnecessarily. He doubted not that this Jew, whom Queen Luiza had sent with the cargo, would be able to dispose of it satisfactorily; and it should be his pleasure to care for his new wife, to make her feel welcome in her new country, and perhaps in some measure compensate her for having led such a dull life before she came to England.

*

The meeting with the King had had its effect on Catherine. The remains of her illness had disappeared by the morning; she felt radiantly happy.

During that day and night she thought continually of her husband. That was real affection she had seen in his eyes; he had spoken so sincerely when he had said he was glad to see her and they would be happy together. And how he had smiled! And the manner in which he had sat on her bed had been most amusing – and quite charming. He had thrown his hat from him for one of the gentlemen to catch, a somewhat boyish and unkingly act! she thought indulgently; yet in what a kingly manner he had done it! He was so perfect that every gesture, every word, had a ring of nobility and became exactly right just because they were his.

He came to her that morning early, to the room which he called her presence chamber. He chatted easily and familiarly, and his warm dark eyes watched her closely. She blushed a little under the scrutiny, for she did not quite understand the meaning behind those eyes and she was very eager for his approval.

If he did not love me, she thought, I should want to die. And she found that every minute in his company increased her wish to please him.

He told her that their marriage should take place that day. 'For,' he added, 'your mother has shown great trust in me to send you to me thus.' He did not add, though he felt a temptation to do so: 'And in particular considering she has sent me spice and sugar instead of the money she promised.' He could not say anything that might hurt her; he could see that she was vulnerable; and he had determined to make her happy, to keep from her anything that might prove hurtful, for he could well imagine how easily she could be wounded. She was a gentle creature and she should be treated gently.

'Catherine,' he said, 'the ceremony shall take place here in this house and be registered in the church of St Thomas A'Becket here in Portsmouth. Unfortunately you and I are not of the same religion; and my people, I think, should not be reminded that my Queen is a Catholic. It would be an unfortunate beginning to your life here if the Catholic ceremonial should be performed. So, my plan is that we shall dispense with it, and that there shall only be our Church of England ceremony.'

He was unprepared for the look of horror which came into her face.

'But . . .' she stammered '. . . to dispense with the ceremony of my church! It would be as though we are not married.'

'None could say that, Catherine. In this country all would consider the church ceremony completely binding.'

She looked about her in distress. She longed for her mother. Her mother would tell her what she ought to do. She feared to displease Charles, and yet she was sure her mother would never have agreed to her dispensing with the Catholic rites.

Charles regarded her with the mildest exasperation. Then he said: 'Oh, I see you have set your heart on it. Well, we must find some means of pleasing you. It would not do for us to disappoint you on your first few days in our country, would it?'

She was immediately radiant. It amused him to see the fear fade from her face and joy take its place.

He took her hand and kissed it; then, with an expert gesture, he drew her towards him and kissed her on the lips. Catherine gasped with pleasure.

'There!' he said. 'You cannot say I do not do my utmost to win your love! I will even submit to this ceremony – and I confess to you here and now that you will find me a wicked man who has no love for such ceremonies – and all to please you!'

'Oh, Charles . . .' she cried, and she felt as though she might weep or swoon with the delight which swept over her; but instead she laughed, for she guessed intuitively that that would please him more than any other expression of her pleasure. 'I begin to feel that I am the most fortunate woman in the world.'

He laughed with her. 'But wait!' he warned in mock seriousness. 'You do not know me yet!'

Then he embraced her – an action which both terrified and thrilled her.

He was gay and lighthearted; she felt so moved by her emotions that she told herself: 'If I should die now I know that I have discovered more happiness than I ever hoped to possess.'

*

The Catholic rites were performed in her bedroom with the utmost secrecy. How he loves me! she thought. For this is not easy for him. It must be done in secret because his people do not love Catholics. He himself is not a Catholic, yet he submits to this because he knows it gives me solace. He is not only the most charming man in the world, he is the most kind.

He whispered to her when the ceremony was over: 'Now see what you have done! You will have to marry me twice instead of once! Do you think you can bear that?'

She could only smile and nod her head. She was afraid to speak, lest before witnesses she should find the words escape her which she knew it would not be wise to utter. She wanted to cry: 'I love you. Even the man of whom I dreamed, I realize now, was a poor thing compared with the reality. You are good, and never did one seek to cover his goodness as you do. Never did such a kindly, courtly gentleman cover his virtues with a laugh and such disparaging remarks concerning himself. I love you, Charles. And I am happy . . . happier than I ever thought to be.'

The Church of England ceremony took place in the afternoon of the same day.

Her six maids of honour helped her to dress in the pale pink gown cut in the English manner. This dress was covered in knots of blue ribbon, and secretly Catherine thought it most becoming, although all the Portuguese ladies were not so sure. They declared it almost gave her the appearance of the type of person modesty forbade them to mention. Perhaps, thought Catherine, it was the excitement of marrying the finest man in the world which made her look like that.

As soon as she was dressed, the King came to her and, taking her hand, led her into the great hall where there was a throne containing two seats set under an elaborately embroidered canopy. One end of the chamber was crowded with those of the King's ministers and courtiers who had come with him to Portsmouth.

Catherine was trembling as the King drew her down with him on to the throne; she scarcely heard Sir John Nicholas read the marriage contract. She was only aware of Charles's twinkling eyes which belied the solemnity of his tones as he plighted his troth before them all. She tried to speak when it was indicated that she should join in the responses, but she found she had forgotten the unfamiliar English words which she had learned.

She was afraid, but Charles was beside her to indicate with his smiles that it did not matter; she was doing well all that was expected of her.

She was thinking: All through my life he will be there to support me; I need never be afraid again. He is the kindest, most affectionate of men.

When the ceremony was over, all the people in the hall cried: 'Long may they live!' And the King took her hand once more and whispered to her in Spanish that it was over; she was truly his wife, and she could not run home to Portugal now if she wished to.

If she wished to! She wondered whether her eyes betrayeed to him the depth of her feeling. I would die rather than leave you, she thought; and was astonished afresh that she could love so deeply, so completely, a man whom she had only known a few hours. Ah, she reminded herself, but I knew him long ago. I have known for long that he offered his life for his father; I knew then that he was the only man in the world whom I could love.

'Now we must go to my apartments,' he told her, 'and they will all come to kiss your hand. I pray you do not grow too weary of kissing this day, for I would you should save a few to bestow on me this night.'

Those words made her heart beat so fast that she thought she would faint. This night the nuptials would be consummated, and she was afraid. Afraid of him? Perhaps afraid that she would not please him, that she was ignorant and would be stupid and mayhap not beautiful enough.

In his apartment the ladies and gentlemen took her hand and kissed it as they knelt to her. She stood beside Charles and every second she was conscious of him.

He was making jocular remarks as though this were not a most solemn occasion. I am not witty enough, she thought; I must learn to laugh. I must learn to be witty and beautiful, for if I do not please him I shall wish to die.

The Countess of Suffolk took one of the bows of blue ribbons from Catherine's dress and said she would keep it as a wedding favour; and then everyone was demanding wedding favours, and Lady Suffolk pulled off knot after knot and threw the pieces of blue ribbon to those who could catch them.

And amid much laughter Catherine's dress was almost torn to pieces; and this the English – and the King in particular – seemed to find a great joke, but the Portuguese looked on in silent disapproval as though they wondered into what mad company their Infanta had brought them.

When the merriment was ended, the King was the first to

notice how pale Catherine had become. He put his arm tenderly about her and asked if she were feeling well; and she, overcome by the excitement of the ceremony and her own emotions, would have slipped to the floor in a faint but for his arms which held her.

He said: 'This has been too much for the Queen. We forget she is but recently up from a sick bed. Let us take her back to it that she may rest until she is fully recovered.'

So the Queen was taken to her bedchamber, and her ladies disrobed her; and as she lay back on her pillows a feeling of despair came to her.

This was her wedding day and she had been unable to endure it. He would be disappointed in her. What of the banquet that was to be given in her honour? She would not be there. A wedding banquet without a bride! Why had she been so foolish? She should have explained: I am not ill. It was the suddenness of my emotions ... this sudden knowledge of my love, which makes me uncertain whether to laugh or cry, to exult or to despair.

She could not bear that he should be disappointed in her, and she was on the point of calling to her women to help her dress that she might join the company in the banqueting hall, when the door was opened and trays of food were brought in.

'Your Majesty's supper,' she was told.

'I could eat nothing,' she answered.

'But you must,' said a voice which brought back the colour to her cheeks and the sparkle to her eyes. 'I declare I'll not eat alone.'

And there he was, the King himself, leaving his guests in the great banqueting hall, to sup with her alone in her bedroom.

'You must not!' she cried.

'I am the King,' he told her. 'I do as I will.'

Once more he sat on the bed; once more he kissed her hands, and those dark eyes, which were full of something she did not understand, were smiling into hers.

So he took supper sitting on her bed, and he laughed and joked with those who served them as though they were his closest friends. He was intimate with all, it seemed, however lowly; he was perfect, but he was less like a great King than she would have believed anyone would be. Now all the ladies and gentlemen had left the banqueting hall and came to sup in her room.

And all the time he joked so gaily Catherine understood, from the very tender note which crept into his voice when he addressed her, that he was telling her he understood her fears and she was to dismiss them.

'You must not be afraid of me,' he whispered to her. 'That would be foolish. You see that these serving people are not afraid of me. So how could you be, you my Queen, whom I have sworn to love and cherish?'

'To love and to cherish,' she whispered to herself. To share this merry life all the rest of her days!

What a simpleton she had been! She had not realized there could be joy such as this. Now the glorious knowledge was with her. There was no room for fear, there was no room for anything but joy – this complete contentment which came of giving and receiving love.

*

The royal honeymoon had begun, and with it the happiest period of Catherine's life.

Charles knew well how to adapt himself to her company; to Catherine he was the perfect lover, all that she desired; he was tender, gentle, and loving, during those wonderful days when he devised a series of entertainments for her pleasure. There were river pageants and sunny hours spent sauntering in the fields about Hampton Court whither they had gone after leaving Portsmouth; each evening there was an amusing play to watch, and a ball at which to lead the dancers in company with the King. There was none who danced so gracefully as Charles; none who was so indefatigable in the pursuit of pleasure.

She believed that he gave himself to these pleasures so wholeheartedly because he wished to please her; she could not tell him that the happiest times were when they were alone together, when she taught him Portuguese words and he taught her English ones, when they burst into laughter at the other's quaint pronunciations; or when she was in bed and he, with a few of his intimates, such as his brother the Duke of York and the Duchess, sat with her and shared with her the delights of drinking tea, of which they declared they were growing as fond as she was.

But they were rarely alone. Once she shyly mentioned this to Charles because she wished to convey to him the tenderness of her feelings towards him, and how she never felt so happy, so secure, as at those times when there was no one else present.

'It is a burden we must carry with us, all our lives,' said Charles. 'We are born in public, and so we die. We dine in public; we dance in public; we are dressed and undressed in public.' He smiled gaily. 'That is part of the price we pay for the loyalty of our subjects.'

'It is wrong to regret anything,' she said quietly, 'when one is as happy as I am.'

He looked at her quizzically. He wondered if she were with child. There was hardly time yet. He could not expect her to be as fertile as Barbara was. He had had news that Barbara had been delivered of a fine son. It was a pity the boy was not Catherine's. But Catherine would have sons. Why should she not? Lucy Water had given him James Crofts, and there were others. There was no reason to suppose that his wife could not give him sons as strong and healthy as those of his mistresses.

Then he began to think longingly of Barbara. She would have heard of the life of domestic bliss he was leading here at Hampton Court; and that would madden her. He trusted she would do nothing to disturb the Queen. No, she would not dare. And if she did, he had only to banish her from Court. Banish Barbara! The thought made him smile. Odd as it was, he was longing for an encounter with her. Perhaps he was finding the gentle adoration of Catherine a little cloying.

That was folly. He was forgetting those frequent scenes with Barbara. How restful, in comparison, how charmingly idyllic was this honeymoon of his!

He would plan more picnics, more pageants on the river. There was no reason why the honeymoon should end yet.

As he was leaving Catherine's apartment a messenger came to him and the message was from Barbara. She was in Richmond which was, he would agree, not so far from Hampton that he could not ride over to see her. Or would he prefer her to ride to Hampton? She had his son with her, and she doubted not he would wish to see the boy – the bonniest little boy in England, whose very features proclaimed him a Stuart. She had much to tell him after this long separation.

The King looked at the messenger.

'There is no answer,' he said.

'Sire,' said the young man, fear leaping into his eyes, 'my mistress told me . . .'

How did Barbara manage to inspire such fear in those who served her? There was one thing she had to learn; she could not inspire fear in the King.

'Ride back to her and tell her that there is no answer,' he said.

He went to the Queen's apartment. The Duchess of York was with her. Anne Hyde had grown fat since her marriage and she was far from beautiful, but the King was fond of her company because of her shrewd intelligence.

The Queen said: 'Your Majesty has come in time for a dish of tea?'

Charles smiled at her but, although he looked at her so thoughtfully and so affectionately, he was not seeing Catherine but another woman, stormy, unaccountable, her wild auburn hair falling about her magnificent bare shoulders.

At length he said: 'It grieves me that I cannot stay. I have urgent business to which I must attend without delay.'

Catherine's face reflected her disappointment, but Charles would not let that affect him. He kissed her hand tenderly, saluted his sister-in-law, and left them.

Soon he was galloping with all speed towards Richmond.

*

Barbara, confined to her bed after the birth of her son, fumed with rage when she heard the stories of the King's felicitous honeymoon. There were plenty of malicious people to tell her how delighted the King was with his new wife. They remembered past slights and humiliations which Barbara had inflicted on them, and they came in all haste to pass on any little scrap of gossip which came their way.

'Is it not a charming state of affairs?' the Duchess of Richmond asked her. 'The King has at last settled down. And what could be happier for the Queen, for the country and the King's state of mind than that the person who should bring him so much contentment should be his own wife!'

'That crow-faced hag!' cried Barbara.

'Ah, but she is pretty enough when properly dressed. The King has prevailed upon her not to employ her Portuguese barber, and now she wears her hair as you and I do. And hers is so black and luxuriant! In an English dress one realizes that beneath that hideous farthingale she is as shapely as any man could wish. And such sweet temper. The King is enchanted.'

'Sweet temper!' cried Barbara. 'She would need to have when the King remembers how he has been swindled.'

'He is, as you would know better than any, the most forgiving of monarchs.'

Barbara's eyes glinted. If only I were up and about! she told herself. If I had not the ill luck to be confined to my bed at such a time, I would show this black bat of a Portuguese Infanta what hold she has on the King.

'I long to be on my feet again,' said Barbara. 'I long to see all this domestic bliss for myself.'

'Poor Barbara!' said Lady Richmond. 'You have loved him long, I know. But alas, there is a fate which often overtakes many of those who love Kings too well. Remember Jane Shore!'

'If you mention that name again to me,' cried Barbara, suddenly unable to control her rage, 'I shall have you banished from Court.'

The Duchess rose and haughtily swept out of the room; but the supercilious smile on her face told Barbara that she for one was convinced that Lady Castlemaine would no longer have the power to decide on such banishment.

After she had gone Barbara lay brooding.

There was the child in the cradle beside her – a bonny child, a child any man or woman would be proud of. And she had named him Charles.

The King should be at her side at such a time. What right had he to neglect his son for his bride, merely because they had chosen to arrive at the same time?

She thumped her pillows in exasperation. She knew that her servants were all skulking behind doors, afraid to come near her. What could she do? Only shout at them, only threaten them – and exhaust herself.

She closed her eyes and dozed.

When she awoke the child was no longer in his cradle. She shouted to her servants. Mrs Sarah came forward. Mrs Sarah, who had been with her since before her marriage, was less afraid of her than anyone in the household; she stood now, arms akimbo, looking at her mistress.

'You're doing yourself no good, you know, Madam,' she said.

'Hold your tongue. Where's the child?'

'My lord has taken him.'

'My lord! How dare he! Whither has he taken him? What right has he . . . ?'

'He has a right, he would say, to have his own son christened.'

'Christened! You mean he's taken the boy to a priest to be christened? I'll kill him for this. Does he think to bring the King's son up in the Catholic religion, just because he himself is a half-witted oaf who follows it?'

'Now listen to Mrs Sarah, Madam. Mrs Sarah will bring you a nice soothing cordial.'

'Mrs Sarah will get her ears boxed if she comes near me, and her nice soothing cordial flung in her face.'

'In your condition, Madam . . .'

'Who is aggravating my condition? Tell me that. You are – and that fool I married.'

'Madam, Madam . . . there are scandals enough concerning you. Tales are carried to the people in the street about your rages. . . .'

'Then find out who carries them,' she screamed, 'and I'll have them tied to the whipping-post. When I'm up, I'll do the whipping myself. When did he take my son?'

'It was while you slept.'

'Of course it was while I slept! Do you think he would have dared when I was awake? So he came sneaking in . . . while I could not stop him. . . . At what o'clock?'

'It was two hours ago.'

'So I slept as long as that!'

'Worn out by your tempers.'

'Worn out by the ordeal through which I have gone, bearing the King's child while he sports with that black savage.'

'Madam, have a care. You speak of the Queen.'

'She shall live to regret she ever left her native savages.'

'Madam ... Madam ... I'll bring you something nice to drink.'

Barbara lay back on her pillows. She was quiet suddenly. So Roger had dared to have the child baptized according to the Catholic rites! She was tired of Roger; he had served his purpose. Perhaps this was not a matter to be deplored after all, for she could see all sorts of possibilities arising from it.

Mrs Sarah brought her a dish of tea, the merits of which beverage Barbara was beginning to appreciate.

'There! This will refresh you,' said Mrs Sarah, and Barbara took it almost meekly. She was thinking of what she would say to Roger when she next saw him.

Mrs Sarah watched her as she drank. 'They say the King is drinking tea each day,' she commented, 'and that the whole Court is getting a taste for it.'

'The King was never partial to tea,' said Barbara, absently.

Mrs Sarah was not a very tactful woman. It seemed to her that Barbara had to become accustomed to the fact that, now the King had married, her position would no longer be of the same importance.

'They say the Queen drinks it so much that she is giving the King a taste for it.'

Barbara had a sudden vision of tea-time intimacy between the foolish simpering Queen and the gallant and attentive King. She lifted the dish and flung it against the wall.

As Mrs Sarah was staring at her in dismay, Roger and some of his friends came into the room. A nurse was carrying the child.

Barbara turned her blazing eyes upon them.

'How dared you take my child from his cradle?'

Roger said: 'It was necessary that he should be baptized.'

'What right have you to make such decisions?'

'As his father, the right is solely mine.'

'His father!' cried Barbara. 'You are no more his father than any of these ninnies you have there with you now. His father! Do you think I'd let you father my child?'

'You have lost your senses,' said Roger quietly.

'Nay! It is you who have lost yours.'

Roger turned to the company. 'I beg of you, leave us. I fear my wife is indisposed.'

When they were alone Barbara deliberately assumed the manner of an extremely angry woman but inwardly she was quite calm.

'So, Roger Palmer, my lord Castlemaine, you have dared to baptize the King's son according to the rites of the Catholic Church. Do you realize what you have done, fool?'

'You are legally married to me, and this child is mine.'

'This child is the King's, and all know it.'

'I demand the right to have my child baptized in my own faith.'

'You are a coward. You would not have dared to do this had I been up and able to prevent you.'

'Barbara,' said Roger, 'could you be calm for a few minutes?'

She waited, and he went on: 'You must face the truth. When you get up from that bed, your position at Court will no longer be the same as it has been hitherto. The King is now married, and his Queen is young and comely. He is well pleased with her. You must understand, Barbara, that your role is no longer of any importance.'

She was seething with rage but with a great effort she kept a strong control over herself. As soon as she was up she would show them whether a miserable little foreigner with prominent fangs, a little go-by-the-ground, who could not speak a word of English, should oust her from her position. But in the meantime she must keep calm.

Roger, thinking she was at last seeing reason and becoming reconciled to her fate, went on: 'You must accept this new state of affairs. Perhaps we could retire to the country for a while. That might make things a little more comfortable for you.'

She was silent; and Roger went on to talk of the new life they might build together. It would be foolish to pretend he could forget her behaviour ever since their marriage, but might they not live in a manner which would stop malicious tongues clacking? They would not be the only married pair in the country who shelved their differences and hid them from public view.

'I have no doubt there is something in what you say,' she

said as calmly as she could. 'Now leave me. I would rest.'

So she lay making plans. And when she was up and about again she sought a favourable opportunity when Roger was absent for a few days, to gather together all her valuables and jewels; and, with the best of the household's servants, she left Roger's house for that of her brother in Richmond, declaring she could no longer live with a husband who had dared to baptize her son according to the rites of the church of Rome.

*

The King was more attentive to his Queen than ever he had been. Our love is strengthened day by day, thought Catherine, and Hampton Court will always be to me the most beautiful place in the world because therein I first knew my greatest happiness.

Often she would wander through the gallery of horns and look up at those heads of stags and antelopes which adorned it; it seemed to her that the patient glass eyes looked sadly at her because they would never know – as few could – the happiness which was hers. She would finger the beautiful hangings designed by Raphael, but it was not their golden embroidery depicting the stories of Abraham and Tobit, nor the Caesarean Triumphs of Andrea Montegna, which delighted her; it was the fact that within these elaborately adorned walls she had become more than the Queen of a great country; she had found love which she had not believed existed outside the legends of chivalry. She would look at her reflection in the mirror of beaten gold and wonder that the woman who looked back at her could really be herself grown beautiful with happiness. Her bedroom in the Palace was so rich that even the English ladies marvelled at it, and the people who crowded in to see her, as was the custom, would gasp at the magnificence of the colourful hangings and the pictures on the walls as well as the cabinets of exquisite workmanship which she had brought with her from Portugal. But most admired of all was her bed of silver embroidery and crimson velvet, which had cost £8,000 and had been a present to Charles from the States of Holland. To Catherine this bed was the most valuable of all her possessions because the King had given it to her.

Now, as the summer days passed, there seemed to be nothing he would not give her.

Tiresome state business often detained him, but on his return to her he would be more gallant, more charming than he had seemed before, if that were possible. Never, thought Catherine, did humble shepherd and shepherdess – who chose each other for love, without any political motive – lead a more idyllic existence.

She could have been perfectly happy but for her fears for her country. She had had news from her mother. The Spaniards had been frightened off by the sight of English ships in Portuguese waters, the danger to the country was less acute than it had been, now that Portugal and England were united by the marriage, but England was far away, and Spain was on the borders of Portugal.

When the King asked tenderly what was causing her apprehension, she told him.

Then greatly daring, for she knew that the request she was about to make was one which the monarch of a Protestant country would be loth to grant, she told him what was in her mind.

'It is because you are so good to me, because you are always so kind and understanding, that I dare ask.'

'Come!' said the King. 'What is this you would ask of me? What do you wish? I doubt if I shall find it in my heart to deny it.'

He smiled at her tenderly. Poor little Catherine! So different from Barbara. Catherine had never yet asked for anything for herself; Barbara's demands were never-ending. He was foolish to see her so often, foolish to ride so frequently to Richmond, foolish to have acknowledged the new child as his own. But what a charming creature that small Charles was! What flashing eyes, and there was such a witty look about the little mouth already! He was undoubtedly a Stuart, for how like a Stuart to get himself – the King's bastard – born at the time of his father's marriage! He was more foolish still to have acted as Sponsor to the boy, with the Earl of Oxford and the Countess of Suffolk, at the time of his christening in accordance with the rites of the Church of England. And now that Barbara had declared she would never again live with Roger Palmer, and Palmer himself had left the country in his fury, there was certain to be more trouble; but if he could prevent its touching poor little Catherine, he would do so.

His one concern was to keep from the Queen knowledge of the state of his relationship with Lady Castlemaine; and as all those about him knew this was his wish, and as he was a most optimistic man, he did not doubt his ability to do so.

In the meantime he wished to indulge Catherine in every possible way; it pleased him to see her happy, and it seemed the easiest thing in the world to make her so. Now he listened to her request almost with eagerness, so ready was he to grant it.

'It is my country,' she said. 'The news is not good. Charles, you do not hate the Catholics?'

'How could I, when that would mean hating you?'

'You are being charming as usual, and not saying all you mean. You do not hate them for other reasons?'

He said: 'I owe much to Catholics. The French helped me during my exile, and they are Catholics. My little sister is a Catholic, and how could I hate her! Moreover, a Mr Giffard, who did much to make possible my escape after Worcester, was also a Catholic. Indeed no, I do not hate Catholics. In truth, I hold it great folly to hate men because their opinions differ from my own. Women of course I should never hate in any circumstances.'

'Charles, be serious to please me.'

'I am all seriousness.'

'If the Pope would promise his protection to my country, it would have less to fear from Spain.'

'The Pope will support Spain, my dear. Spain is strong, and Portugal is weak, and it is so much more convenient to support that which is in little danger of falling down.'

'I have thought of a way in which I might appeal to the Pope, and with your permission I would do it.'

'What is this way?'

'I am a Catholic, here in a Protestant country. I am a Queen, and it may be that all the world knows now how good you are to me.'

Charles looked away. 'Nay,' he said quickly. 'Nay ... I am not so good as I ought to be. Mayhap the whole world but you knows that.'

She took his hand and kissed it.

'You are the best of husbands, and I am therefore the happiest of wives. Charles, would you grant me this permission? If you did, it would make my happiness complete. You see, the Pope and others will know how you love me, and they will think I am not without influence with you ... and thus this country. If I might write to the Pope and tell him that now that I am in England I will do everything within my power to serve the Catholic Faith, and that my reason for coming here was not for the sake of the crown which would be mine but for the sole purpose of serving my faith, I think the Pope will be very pleased with me.'

'He would indeed,' said Charles.

'Oh, Charles, I would not attempt to persuade you to act against your conscience.'

'Pray you, have less respect for my conscience. He is a weak, idle, and somnolent fellow who, I fear, often fails in his duty.'

'You joke. You joke continually. But that is how I would have it. It is that which makes the hours spent in your company the happiest I have ever known. Charles, if I could make the Pope believe that I would work for the Catholic Faith in England, I could at the same time ask for his protection of Portugal.'

'Yes, that is so; and I doubt not that you would get it for such a consideration.'

'And Charles, you ... you ... would agree?'

He took her face in his hands. 'I am the King of a Protestant country,' he said. 'What think you my ministers would say if they knew I had allowed you to send such a letter?'

'I know not.'

'The English are determined never to have a Catholic Monarch on their throne. They decided that, more than a hundred years ago on the death of Bloody Mary, whom they will never forget.'

'Yes, Charles. I see you are right. It was wrong of me to ask this of you. Please forget it.'

As he continued to hold her face in his hands, he asked: 'How would you convey such a letter to Rome?'

'I had thought to send Richard Bellings, a gentleman of my household, whom I can trust.'

'You suffer because of your country's plight,' he said gently.

'So much! If I could feel that all was well there, I should be happy indeed.'

He was thinking how sweet she was, how gentle, how loving. He wanted to give her something; he wanted to give all that she most desired. A letter to the Pope? What harm in that? It would be a secret matter. What difference could such a letter make to him? And how it would please her! It might be the means of securing Papal protection for the poor harassed Queen Regent of Portugal, who had trials enough with her half-imbecile son as King and the Spaniards continually threatening to depose the pair of them. What harm to him? What harm in promises? And he felt a guilty need to make Catherine happy.

'My dearest wife,' he said gently, 'I ought not to allow this. I know it well. But, when you ask me so sweetly, I find it mighty hard to refuse.'

'Then Charles, let us forget I asked you. It was wrong of me. I never should have asked.'

'Nay, Catherine. You do not ask for jewels or money, as so many would. You are content to give of your love, and that has given me great pleasure. Let me give something in return.'

'You ... give me something! You have given me such happiness as I never knew existed. It is not for you to give me more.'

'Nevertheless I shall insist on granting this. To please me, you shall write this letter and despatch it. But do this yourself – let none know that I have any part in it, or the thing would be useless. Tell the Pope what you intend, ask his protection. Yes, Catherine, do it. I wish it. I wish to please you ... greatly.'

'Charles, you make me weep ... weep with shame for asking more of you who have given so much ... weep for the joy of all the happiness which has come to me, so that I wonder why Heaven should have chosen me to be so singularly blessed.'

He put his arms about her and kissed her gently.

While she clung to him he remembered a paper he carried in his pocket, which he had meant to present to her at a convenient moment.

He patted her arm gently and disengaged himself.

'Now, my dearest, here is a little matter for you to attend to.'

He took the scroll from his pocket.

'But what is this?' she asked, and as she was about to look over his shoulder, he handed it to her.

'Study it at your leisure. It is merely a list of ladies whom I recommend for appointments in your household.'

'I will look at it later.'

'When you can no longer feast your eyes upon your husband!' he said lightly. 'You will find all these ladies worthy and most suitable for the posts indicated. I know my Court far better than you can in such a short time, so I am sure you will be happy to accept these suggestions of mine.'

'Of a certainty I shall.'

She put the scroll away in a drawer and they went out into the gardens to saunter with a few ladies and gentlemen of the Court.

It was some time later when Catherine took out the scroll and studied the list of names.

As she did so her heart seemed to stop and plunge on; she felt the blood rush to her head and drain away.

This could not be real. This was a bad dream.

At the head of the list which the King had given her was the name Barbara, Countess of Castlemaine.

It was some time before, trembling with fear and horror, she took a pen and boldly crossed out that name.

*

The King came to the Queen and dismissed all attendants so that they were entirely alone.

He began almost suavely: 'I see that you have crossed out the name of one of the ladies whom I suggested you should take into your household.'

'It was Lady Castlemaine,' said Catherine.

'Ah, yes. A lady to whom I have promised a post in your bedchamber.'

Catherine said quietly: 'I will not have her.'

'But I have told you that I myself promised this post.'

'I will not have her,' repeated Catherine.

'Why so?' asked the King. His voice sounded cold, and Catherine had never known coldness from him before.

'Because,' she said, 'I know what relationship this woman once had to you, and it is not meet that she should be given this post.'

'I consider it meet, and I have promised her this post.'

'Should a lady have a post in the Queen's bedchamber against the wishes of the Queen?'

'Catherine, you will grant this appointment because I ask it of you.'

'No.'

He looked at her appraisingly. Her face was blotched with weeping. He thought of all he had done for her. He had played the loving husband for two months to a woman who aroused no great desire within him, and all because her naïvety stirred his pity. Being considerate of her feelings he had never once reminded her of the fact that her mother had cheated him over the dowry. He had only yesterday given her permission to write a letter to the Pope, which he should not have done, and yet because he had wished to give her pleasure he had agreed that she should write it. And now when he asked this thing of her because he, in a weak moment, had promised the appointment to a woman of whose rages he was afraid, Catherine would not help him to ease the situation.

So she knew of his liaison with Barbara, yet she had never uttered a word about it. Then she was not so simple as he had thought. She was not the gentle, loving creature he had believed her to be. She was far more subtle.

If he allowed her to have her way now, Barbara's rage would be terrible and Barbara would take her revenge. Barbara would doubtless lay bare to this foolish Queen of his the intimacies which had taken place between them; she would show the Queen the letters which he had carelessly written; and Catherine would suffer far more through excluding Barbara from her bedchamber than by accepting her.

How could he explain to the foolish creature? How could he say, 'If you were wise you would meekly accept this woman. You have your dignity and through it could subdue her. If you would behave now with calm, dignified decorum in this matter, if you would help me out of a difficult position in which I, with admittedly the utmost folly, have placed myself, then I would truly love you; you would have my devotion for ever more. But if you insist on behaving like a silly jealous girl, if you will not make this concession when I ask you – and I know it to be no small thing, but I have given you in these last two months far more than you will ever know – then I shall love you truly, not with a fleeting passion but with the respect I should give to a woman who knows how to make a sacrifice when she truly loves.'

'Why are you so stubborn?' he asked wearily.

'I know what she was to you ... this woman.'

He turned away impatiently. 'I have promised the appointment.'

'I will not have her.'

'Catherine,' he said, 'you must.'

'I will not. I will not.'

'You have said you would do anything to please me. I ask this of you.'

'But not this. I will not have her – your mistress – in my service ... in my own bedchamber.'

'I tell you I have promised her this appointment. I must insist on your giving it to her.'

'I never will!' cried Catherine.

He could see that she was suffering, and his heart was immediately touched. She was, after all, young and inexperienced. She had had a shock. He should have prepared her for this. But how could he when she, in her deceit, had given him no indication that she had ever heard of Lady Castlemaine?

Still he realized the shock she had sustained; he understood her jealousy. He must insist on her obeying him, but he wished to make the surrender as easy as possible for her.

'Catherine,' he said, 'do this thing for me and I shall be for ever grateful. Take Lady Castlemaine into your service, and I swear that if she should ever be insolent to you in the smallest degree I will never see her again.'

He waited, expecting the floods of tears, the compliance. It would be so easy for her, he was sure. Queens had been asked to overcome these awkward situations before. He thought of Catherine de' Medici, wife of Henri Deux, who had long and graciously stood aside for Diane de Poitiers; he thought of the many mistresses of his respected ancestor Henri Quatre. He was not asking his wife anything to compare with what those monarchs had asked of theirs.

But he had been mistaken in Catherine. She was not the soft and tender girl. She was a determined and jealous woman.

'I will not receive her into my household,' she said firmly.

Astonished and now really angry, the King turned abruptly and left her.

*

Charles was in a quandary. It grieved him to hurt Catherine, yet less than it would have done a week before, for it seemed to him that her stubborn refusal to understand his great difficulty clearly showed that her vanity and self-love was greater than her love for him; he was able to tell himself that he had been deceived in her; and this helped him to act as he knew he would have to act. Charles wanted to be kind to all; to hurt anyone, even those whom he disliked, grieved him; revenge had always seemed to him a waste of time, as was shown by his behaviour when those men who had been instrumental in bringing about his father's death and his own exile had been brought to trial; he wished to live a pleasant life; if some painful act had to be performed it was his main desire to get it over as quickly as possible or look the other way while someone else carried it out.

Now he knew that he was going to hurt Catherine, for he was sure that to allow Barbara to disclose to the Queen the intimate details of their relationship – which Barbara had hinted she might do, and he knew her well enough to realize that she was capable of carrying out her threat – would result in hurting Catherine more than would quietly receiving Barbara into her household.

Catherine had right on her side to a certain extent, but if she would only be reasonable, if she would only contemplate his difficulties instead of brooding on her own, she would save them all much trouble.

But she was obstinate, narrow-minded and surrounded by a group of hideous prudes; for it was a fact that those ladies-in-waiting and duennas of hers would not sleep in any beds unless all the linen and covers had been changed – lest a man might have slept there before them and so would, they believed, defile their virginity.

Catherine had to grow up. She had to learn the manners of

a Court less backward than that ruled over by her stern old mother.

He would not plead with her any more; that only resulted in floods of tears; but he was convinced that to allow her to flout him would be folly. It was bad enough to have Barbara flouting him. He had to be firm with one of them; and Barbara had the whip-hand – not only because of the revelations she could make, but because of her own irresistible appeal.

So he made up his mind that if Barbara could be presented to Catherine – and Barbara had promised that she would behave with the utmost decorum, and so she would, provided she had her way – the Queen would not make a scene in front of a number of people; and then, having once received his mistress, she would find there was nothing very extraordinary in doing so.

Catherine was holding a reception in her presence room, and many of the ladies and gentlemen of the Court were with her there.

Charles was not present and Catherine, heart-broken as she was, could not prevent her gaze straying every now and then to the door. She longed for a sight of him; she longed to return to that lost tender relationship. She let herself dream that he came to her full of sorrow for the way in which he had treated her; that he implored her to forgive him and declared that neither of them should ever see or speak of Lady Castlemaine again.

Then she saw him. He was making his way to her, and he was smiling, and he looked so like the Charles he had been in the early days of their marriage. He laughed aloud and the sound of that deep attractive voice made her whole body thrill with pleasure. He had caught her eye now; he was coming towards her and his smiles were for her.

She noticed his companion then. He was holding her hand, as he always held the hands of those ladies whom he would present to her. But Catherine scarcely looked at the woman; she could see none but him, and absorb the wonderful fact that he was smiling at her.

He presented the lady, who curtsied as she took Catherine's hand and kissed it.

The King was looking at the Queen with delight, and it seemed in that moment of incomparable joy that their differences had been wiped out. He had stepped back, and the lady he had presented remained at his side; but he continued to look at Catherine, and she felt that only he and she existed in that large assembly.

Then quite suddenly she became aware of tension in the atmosphere; she realized that the ladies and gentlemen had stopped murmuring; it was almost as though they held their breath and were waiting for something dramatic to happen.

Elvira, who was standing behind her chair, leaned forward.

'Your Majesty,' whispered Elvira, 'do you know who that woman is?'

'I? No,' said the Queen.

'You did not catch the name. The King deliberately mispronounced it. It is Lady Castlemaine.'

Catherine felt waves of dizziness sweeping over her. She looked round at that watching assembly. She noted the smiles on their faces; they were regarding her as though she were a character in some obscene play.

So he had done this to her! He had brought Lady Castlemaine to her reception that she might unwittingly acknowledge his mistress before all these people.

It was too much to be borne. She turned her eyes to him, but he was not looking her way now; his head was bent; he seemed absorbed in what that woman was saying.

And there stood the creature – the most lovely woman Catherine had ever seen – yet her loveliness seemed to hold an evil kind of beauty, bold, brazen, yet magnificent; her auburn curls fell over bare shoulders, her green and gold gown was cut lower than all others, her emeralds and sparkling diamonds about her person. She was arrogant and insolent – the King's triumphant mistress.

No! She could not endure it. Her heart felt as though it were really breaking; she suffered a violent physical pain as it leaped and pranced like a mad and frightened horse.

The blood was rushing to her head. It had started to gush from her nose. She saw it, splashing on to her gown; she heard the quick intake of breath as the company, watching her, gasped audibly.

Then she fell swooning to the floor.

*

The King was horrified to see Catherine in such a condition; he ordered that she be carried to her apartments, but when he realized that only the feelings of the moment – which he preferred to ascribe to anger – had reduced her to such a state, he allowed himself to be shocked by such lack of control.

He, so ready to seek an easy way out of a difficulty, so ready to accept what could not be avoided, felt his anger increasing against his wife. It seemed to him that it would have been so simple a matter to have received Barbara and feigned ignorance of her relationship with himself. That was what he himself would have done; that was what other Queens had done before her.

He knew that he must placate Barbara; he had promised to, and she would see that this was one of the promises he kept. He hated discord, so he decided that he would shift to Clarendon the responsibility of making Catherine see reason.

He sent for his Chancellor.

He was not so pleased with Edward Hyde, Earl of Clarendon, as he had once been. In the days when he had been a wandering exile he had felt unsafe unless Clarendon was beside him to give the benefit of his wisdom and advice. It was a little different now that he was a King. He and Clarendon had disagreed on several matters since their return to England; and Charles knew that Clarendon had more enemies in England than he ever had in exile.

Clarendon wished to go back to the pre-revolutionary doctrine. He believed that the King should have sole power over the militia; and he wished to inaugurate in place of Parliament a powerful privy council who would decide all matters of state.

The King agreed with him on this, but on very little else. Clarendon continually deplored the King's wish to shape his own monarchy in the pattern of that of France. The King was too French in his outlook; he looked to his grandfather, Henri Quatre, as a model, not only in his numerous love affairs but in his schemes of government. Again and again Clarendon had pointed out that England was not France, and that the temperament of the two countries was totally different.

They also disagreed on religious matters. Clarendon thought Charles's policy of toleration a mistaken one. There were many in the Court who sensed the mild but growing estrangement between the King and his most trusted minister, and they were ready enough to foster that growth. Buckingham was one, and with him in this was his kinswoman, Lady Castlemaine.

Clarendon, as a wise old man, knew that his enemies were watching, quietly as yet but hopefully.

Still he persisted in his frankness with the King; and although he had been against the Portuguese marriage he now attempted to take the side of the Queen.

'Your Majesty is guilty of cruelty towards the Queen,' he said; 'you seek to force her to that with which flesh and blood cannot comply.'

Charles studied the man. He no longer completely trusted him. A few years ago he would have listened respectfully and he might have accepted Clarendon's view; but he now believed that his Chancellor was not wholly sincere, and he looked for the reasons which had impelled him to take such views as he now expressed.

Charles knew that Clarendon hated Barbara. Was this the reason why he now urged the King not to give way to his mistress's cruel desires, but to support his wife? How could he be sure?

'I have heard you say,' went on the Chancellor, 'when you saw how King Louis forced his wife to receive his mistresses, that it was a piece of ill nature that you would not be guilty of, for if ever you had a mistress after you had a wife – which Your Majesty hoped you never would have – she should never come where your wife was.'

'It is good for a man who has a wife not to have a mistress,' said Charles testily, 'but if he has, he has, and there's an end of it. We would all like to be virtuous, but our natures drive us another way. I hold that when such a matter as this arises the best road from it is for good sense to be shown all round. If the Queen had quietly received my Lady Castlemaine there would not then be this trouble.'

'Your Majesty, I would beg you to please your wife in this, for she is the Queen and the other but your mistress. I can assure Your Majesty that Ormond and others agree with me in this. You should repudiate my Lady Castlemaine and never allow her to enter into your wife's household.'

The King was rarely angry, but he was deeply so on this

occasion. He remembered the hypocrisy of Clarendon when the Duke of York had married his daughter. Then he had said he would have rather seen Anne James's mistress than his wife. It seemed at that time he had a little more respect for mistresses, since he was eager to see his daughter one.

No! He could trust none. Clarendon, Ormond, and the rest urged him to repudiate Barbara, not because she was his mistress, but because she was their enemy. They would have been howling for the destruction of the Queen if they did not think her an ineffectual puppet who could harm them not.

Then Charles fell into one of his rare moods of obstinacy.

He said: 'I would beg of you all not to meddle in my affairs unless you are commanded to do so. If I find any of you guilty in this manner I will make you repent of it to the last moments of your lives. Pray hear what I have to say now. I am entered upon this matter, and I think it necessary to counsel you lest you should think by making stir enough you might divert me from my resolution. I am resolved to make my Lady Castlemaine of my wife's bedchamber; and whosoever I find using any endeavours to hinder this resolution, I will be his enemy to the last moment of his life.'

Clarendon had never seen the King so stern, and he was shaken. He remembered all his enemies at Court, and how again and again when he was in danger from them it was the King who had come to his aid.

He hated Lady Castlemaine; he hated her not only because she was his enemy but because of the influence she had over the King. But he knew that in this instance, the King's will being so firm, he must remember he was naught else but the King's servant.

'Your Majesty has spoken,' he said. 'I regret that I have expressed my opinions too freely. I am Your Majesty's servant, to be used as you will. I beg you forgive the freedom of my manners, which freedom has grown out of my long affection for Your Majesty.'

The King, regretting his harshness almost immediately, laid his hand on Clarendon's shoulder.

He gave a half-smile. 'I am pledged to this. It's a mighty unpleasant business. Come, my friend, extricate me; stand between me and these wrangling women. Be my good lieutenant as you have been so many times before, and let there never more be harsh words between us.'

There were tears in the older man's eyes.

The charm of the King was as potent as it had ever been.

Oddly enough, thought Clarendon, though one believes him to be in the wrong, one desires above all things to serve him.

*

Clarendon made his way to the Queen's apartment and asked for audience.

She received him in bed. She looked pale and quite exhausted after her upset, but she greeted him with a faint smile.

Clarendon intimated that his business with her was secret, and her women retired.

'Oh, my lord,' she cried, 'you are one of the few friends I have in this country. You have come to help me, I know.'

'I hope so, Madam,' said Clarendon.

'I have been foolish. I have betrayed my feelings, and that is a bad thing to do; but my feelings were so hard to bear. My heart was broken.'

'I have come to give you my advice,' said the Chancellor, 'and it is advice which may not please Your Majesty.'

'You must tell me exactly what you mean,' she said. 'I can glean no help from you if you do not talk freely of my faults.'

'Your Majesty makes much of little. Has your education and knowledge of the world given you so little insight into the conduct of mankind that you should be so upset to witness it? I believe that your own country could give you as many – nay more – instances of these follies, than we can show you here in our cold climate.'

'I did not know that the King loves this woman.'

'Did you imagine then that a man such as His Majesty, thirty-two years of age, virile and healthy, would keep his affections reserved for the lady he would marry?'

'I did not think he loved her still.'

'He has the warmest feelings for you.'

'Yet his for her are warmer.'

'They would be most warm for you if you were to help him in this,' said the Chancellor slyly. 'I come to you with a message from him. He says that if you will but do what he asks on this one occasion he will make you the happiest Queen in the world. He says that whatever he entertained for other ladies before your coming concerns you not, and that you must not inquire into them. He says that if you will help him now he will dedicate himself to you. If you will meet his affection with the same good humour, you will have a life of perfect felicity.'

'I am ready to serve the King in all ways.'

The Chancellor smiled. 'Then all is well. There is no longer discord between you.'

'Save,' went on Catherine, 'in this one thing. I will not have that woman in my household.'

'But only by helping the King in this – for he has given a promise that it should be so – can you show that devotion.'

'But if he loved me he could not ... could not suggest it! By insisting on such a condition he exposes me to the contempt of the Court. If I submitted to it I should believe I was worthy to receive such an affront. No. No. I will not have that woman in my household. I would prefer to go back to Lisbon.'

'That,' said Clarendon quickly, 'it is not in your power to do. Madam, I beg of you, for your own sake, listen to my counsel. Meet the King's wishes in this. It is rarely that he is so insistent. Pray try to understand that he has given his word that Lady Castlemaine should have a post in your bedchamber. Demean yourself in this – if you consider you should demean yourself by so obeying your husband – but for our future happiness do not remain stubborn.'

Catherine covered her face with her hands.

'I will not,' she moaned. 'I will not.'

Clarendon left her and her women came round her, soothing her in their native tongue. They cursed all those who had dared insult their Infanta; they implored her to remember her state; they swore to her that she would forfeit all respect, not only of the Court but of the King, if she gave way.

'I cannot have her here,' Catherine murmured. 'I cannot. Every time I saw her my heart would break afresh.'

So she lay back and her women smoothed her hair away from her brow and spread cooling unguents on her heated face; they wiped away the tears which she could not restrain.

*

That night the King came to her chamber.

Clarendon had failed, and Charles no longer felt impelled to pretend he cared for her. She had disappointed him. Her charm had been in her soft tenderness, her overwhelming desire to please. Now she was proving to be such another termagant as Barbara, and not nearly so handsome a one.

They are alike, thought the King; only the method of getting what they want is different.

'Charles,' she cried tearfully, 'I pray you let us have done with this matter. Let us be as we were before.'

'Certainly let us have done with it,' he said. 'You can decide that quicker than any of us.'

'I could not bear to see her every day in my chamber. . . . I could not, Charles.'

'You who have talked of dying for me . . . could not do this when I ask it?' He spoke lightly, maliciously.

She said: 'When you speak thus I feel as though a hundred daggers pierce my heart.'

'That heart of yours is too easily reached. A protection of sound good sense might preserve it from much pain.'

'You are so different now, Charles. I scarcely know you.'

'You too are different. I feel I knew you not at all. I had thought you gentle and affectionate, and I find you stubborn, proud and wanting in your sense of duty.'

'I find you wanting in affection and full of tyranny,' she cried.

'You are inexperienced of the world. You have romantic ideals which are far from reality.'

'You have cynical ideas which shock and alarm me.'

'Catherine, let us have done with these wrangles. Let us compromise on this. Do this one thing for me and I promise you that Lady Castlemaine shall never, in the smallest way, show the slightest disrespect for you; she shall never, for one moment, forget that you are the Queen.'

'I will never have her in my household!' cried Catherine hysterically. 'Never . . . never. I would rather go back to Portugal.'

'You would do well to discover first whether your mother would receive you.'

Catherine could not bear to look at him. He was so aloof and angry, and anger sat so unfamiliarly on that dark face.

That he could talk so coldly of her going home frightened her.

He went on: 'Your Portuguese servants will soon be going back, so doubtless they could lay this matter of your return before your mother; then we should see whether she would be willing to receive you.'

'So you would send my servants away from me – even that?'

Charles looked at her in exasperation. She was so innocent of the world, so ignorant of procedure. She thought that in sending her servants from her he would be guilty of another act of cruelty; she did not understand that in all royal marriages a bride's servants stayed with her only until she was settled into the ways of her new country, and that it was considered unwise for them to stay longer since they created jealousy and were inclined to make great matters of small differences – such as this one – which arose between a king and his queen.

He did not explain to her; he was exasperated beyond endurance. Moreover it seemed to him she was ready to misconstrue all his actions and doubtless would not believe anything he told her.

'I did not know,' she said, 'that you could find it in your heart to treat me so ill. My mother promised me that you would be a good husband to me.'

'Your mother, alas, made many promises which were not fulfilled. She promised a handsome dowry which has not yet been delivered.'

He immediately hated himself for those words, for he had told himself again and again that the defalcation of her mother was no fault of Catherine's.

He longed to be done with the matter. It was absurd. A quarrel between two women, and he was allowing it to give him as much anxiety as the threat of a major war. He was wrangling with her through the night in such loud tones that many in the Palace would hear him.

It was undignified; it was folly; and he would do it no more.

He hurried from the apartment, leaving Catherine to weep through the rest of the night.

*

The days passed most wretchedly for Catherine. She seldom spoke to the King. She would see him from the windows of her apartment sauntering with his friends; she would hear their laughter; it seemed that wherever he was there was merriment.

She was lonely, for although she was the Queen, there was no one in the Palace who did not know of the estrangement between herself and the King, and many who had been eager to please her in the hope of receiving her favour, no longer considered her capable of bestowing benefits.

She knew something of what was said of her. The King's devotion of the last two months had been given out of the kindness of his heart: there had been no real love, no passion. How could there be? There were many ladies of the Court more beautiful than the Queen, and the King was deeply affected by beauty.

For months he had given his affections exclusively to her, and she, being simple and ignorant, had not realized what a great sacrifice that was for the King to make.

She was humiliated and heart-broken. She did not know how foolish she was; she did not realize that, since there could be no happiness for her while the King was displeased with her, she could quite easily win back his grateful devotion. Charles hated to be on bad terms with anyone, particularly a woman; his tenderness for her sex was apparent in all he did; even to those women who attracted him not at all he was invariably courteous. He was sorry for Catherine; he understood her difficulties; he knew she was an idealist while he was very much a realist; and if at the time she had given way in this matter, if she had understood his peculiar problem, if she had been able to see him as the man he was – charming, affable, easy-going, generous, good-natured but very weak, particularly in his relationship with women – Catherine could have won his affectionate regard for all time; and although she could never have roused his passion she could have been his very dear friend. But her rigid upbringing, her lack of worldly knowledge, her pride and the influence of her prudish Portuguese attendants robbed her of not only her temporary peace of mind but of her future happiness.

So she sat aloof, sometimes sullenly, sometimes weeping bitterly; and the King ignored her, his courtiers following his example. Thus Hampton Court, the scene of those first weeks of triumphant happiness, became the home of despair.

*

Henrietta Maria, the King's mother, arrived in England; she wished to meet her son's wife and let the whole world know how she welcomed the marriage.

Then it was necessary for Charles to behave towards Catherine as though all was well between them.

They rode out from Hampton Court side by side while a brilliant cavalcade accompanied them. The people lined the roads to cheer them, and Catherine felt new pride stir within her when she realized how the English loved their King.

That was a happy day, for Charles was chatting with her as though there had been nothing to disturb their relationship; and when they arrived at Greenwich, Henrietta Maria, determined to dispense with ceremony, took her daughter-in-law in her arms and assured her in her volatile way that this was one of the happiest moments in her life of one whose many sorrows had made her call herself *la reine malheureuse*.

She accepted a fauteuil and sat on the right hand of Catherine. Charles sat next to his wife, and on his left hand sat Anne Hyde the Duchess of York, while the Duke stood behind his mother.

It was Henrietta Maria who talked continually, studying the face of her daughter-in-law, trying not to let her eyes betray the fact that she was wondering if she were yet pregnant. Those lively dark eyes missed little, and she could see no signs of a child.

'This is indeed a pleasure, my dearest daughter. And how like you your country, eh? I thank the saints that you have come to it in summer weather. Ah, I remember my first visit to this country. That was in the days of my youth . . . the happiest time of my life! But even then I had my little worries. I was so small – smaller than you, my dear daughter – and it grieved me lest my husband should wish me taller. How we suffer we princesses sent to strange lands! But I found my husband to be the best man in the world . . . the kindest and most faithful husband . . . the best of fathers. . . .'

Charles interrupted: 'I beg of you, Mam, say no more. My wife will expect too high a standard of me.'

'And why should she not expect you to be like your father! I trust that you may bring her as much happiness as he brought me ... though ... through my love of him I suffered much. But is not that the way with love? To love is to suffer ...'

Catherine said fervently: 'It is true, Your Majesty. To love is to suffer.'

'Well, let us not talk of suffering on such a happy occasion,' said the King. 'Tell me, Mam, how is my sister?'

Henrietta Maria frowned. 'She has her trials. Her husband is not kind to her.'

'I am sorry for her,' said Catherine.

'Ah ... indeed, yes. When I think of the regard the King of France has for her ... when I think of what might have been. ...'

'It is useless to dwell on what might have been,' said the King. 'It grieves me that my sister is not happy.'

'You must not be jealous of his love for his sister,' said Henrietta Maria to Catherine. 'I declare that my daughter's husband is jealous of hers for him. They have been devoted all their lives.'

The Duke of York joined in the conversation and Henrietta Maria chattered on in her garrulous way; her manner faintly cool to the Duchess of York whom Charles had forced her to accept, but James had always been a favourite of hers. She made little attempt to veil her likes and dislikes. She asked how fared that man Hyde – she refused to give him his title of Earl of Clarendon – and she asked if her son was still as strongly under his influence as he always had been.

The King turned aside her awkward remarks with his easy manner, and Catherine felt more deeply in love with him than ever before.

She could not be unhappy while they were together thus, for although it might only have been for the sake of etiquette, the King would turn to her again and again, and it was delightful to enjoy the warmth of his smiles and his tender words once more.

She felt desolate when it was time to return to Hampton Court, but she found that the King's manner towards her did not change as they rode away from London. He remained friendly and charming; though of course she knew that he would not be her lover.

Even then she did not see how much happier her life might have been had she given way on this one matter; and although she had been able to set aside her misery during the visit to Greenwich, still she determined to nurse it, and the matter of Lady Castlemaine's admittance to the household was still between them.

Henrietta Maria visited the King and Queen at Hampton Court, and during the month of August Catherine made her first public entry into the capital of her new country.

She rode down the river in the royal barge; and by her side was Charles, delighted to be on water, and returning to his capital. Full of charm and gaiety he was tender and affectionate. The Duke and the Duchess of York were with them in the brilliantly decorated barge, as well as those Princes, cousins of the King, Rupert and Edward, with the Countess of Suffolk; other members of the royal household followed. All along the river banks cheering people watched them; and when they were within a short distance of London they left the barge for a large boat with glass windows. The awnings were covered in gold-embroidered crimson velvet.

Now they were ready for the triumphal entry.

'And this,' Charles told his wife, 'is all in honour of you.'

The river was crowded with craft of all description, for the Lord Mayor and companies had turned out in force to play their Queen, to the tune of sweet music, into her capital. On the deck of their boat, beneath the canopy which had been made in the form of a cupola with Corinthian pillars decorated with flowers, sat Catherine and Charles.

To Catherine it was inspiring and thrilling. The music enchanted her as did the shouts of the people acclaiming their loyalty to the royal pair; but what delighted Catherine more than anything else was the fact that Charles was beside her, her hand was in his, and his affable smiling face turned again and again from his cheering people to herself.

It was possible to believe that their differences were forgotten, that all was well between them, and that they were lovers again.

And so to Whitehall, of which the King had often talked

to her, where the public crowded into the banqueting hall to watch the royal party dine.

Catherine realized now how much a part of this merry boisterous existence Charles himself was, how his ready smiles to the humblest, how his quick retorts, his dispensing with royal dignity, appealed to the people. They were delighted – those who crowded about Whitehall and came into the private apartment to see their royal family – with the easy manner of their King and his friendliness to all; they were enchanted with the extravagance of his Palace and glittering splendour of the gentlemen of his Court and the beauty of the ladies.

They loved their King not only because of his good nature – and when he had returned to England he had brought with him a colourful way of life – but also for his weaknesses, for providing them with many a titbit of scandal; they loved him for his love affairs, which could always be relied upon to raise a laugh in any quarter, and were such a contrast to the dull, drab and respectable existence of men such as Cromwell and Fairfax.

Now he joked with the Queen and his mother at the royal table, and the crowd looked on and enjoyed his wit.

Catherine was shocked when, before them all, he discussed the possibility of her bringing an heir to England.

'I believe he will soon put in an appearance,' said Charles.

'This is wonderful news!' cried Henrietta Maria.

Catherine looked from one to the other, trying to follow the conversation which was taking place in English.

The King turned to her and explained what had been said.

Catherine blushed hotly, and the people laughed.

She stammered in English: 'You lie.'

At which the whole assembly burst into loud laughter on hearing the King so addressed; and none laughed more heartily than the King.

He said: 'And what will my people think of the way in which I am treated by my wife? These are the first words in English she has uttered in public.' His face wore a look of mock seriousness. 'And she says I lie!'

He then turned to her and said that she must talk more in English, for that was what his people would like to hear; and he made her say after him such phrases as set the people rocking with hilarious laughter in which all the noble company joined.

*

But Catherine's joy was short-lived, for it was not long before Barbara appeared at Whitehall. No more was said as to her becoming a lady of the bedchamber; she was just there, always present, brilliantly beautiful; so that whenever Catherine compared herself with Charles's notorious mistress she felt plain – even ugly – quite dull and completely lacking in charm.

She grew sullen; she sat alone; she would not join any group if Barbara was there, and, as the King always seemed to be where Barbara was, all the brilliant and amusing courtiers were there also.

Almost everyone deserted the Queen; the Earl of Sandwich, who had been so charming when he had come to Portugal, no longer seemed to have any time to spare for her; young Mr James Crofts, a very handsome boy of about fifteen, scarcely noticed her at all, and moreover she felt that the fact that he was received at Court was an affront to herself, for she knew who he was – the son of a woman as infamous as Lady Castlemaine. And the boy's features, together with a somewhat arrogant manner would have proclaimed him to be Charles's son – even if the King did not make it openly obvious that this was so.

James Crofts was often with the King; they could be seen sauntering in the Park, arm in arm.

Catherine heard what was said of the King and this boy. 'Greatly His Majesty regrets that he was not married to the mother of such a boy, for it is clear that handsome Mr James Crofts is beloved by his father.'

James gave himself airs. He was at every state occasion magnificently dressed, and already ogling the ladies. He was a fervent admirer of Lady Castlemaine and sought every opportunity of being in her company; and there was nothing this lady liked better than to be seen with the King and his son, when they laughed and chatted together.

There were some who said that young James's feeling for his father's mistress was becoming too pronounced, and that the lady was not displeased by this, but that when the King realized that this boy of his was fast becoming a man he would be less fond of Master James. The King however was human and, like all parents, took far longer than others to become aware that his son was growing up.

Although the King was outwardly affectionate to his wife, all knew of his neglect of her. It was said that he was pondering whether he might not proclaim Mr Crofts legitimate, give him a grand title, and make him his heir. If he did this it would mean that he had decided no longer to hope for an heir from the Queen; and all understood what that implied.

So Catherine grew more and more wretched during those summer months. It seemed to her that she had only two friends at Court. Most of her attendants were returning to Portugal and all her most intimate friends were to leave her, with the exception of Maria the Countess de Penalva for, it was said, the King thought Maria too old and infirm to influence Catherine and support her in her stubbornness.

That other friend was a younger brother of the Earl of Sandwich – Lord Edward Montague – who held the post of Master of Horse in her household.

Edward Montague had by his demeanour shown his sympathy with her and had told her that he considered she was shamefully treated.

She found some pleasure therefore in listening to his words of sympathy, for it was comforting to think that in the royal household there was at least one who understood her.

When she said goodbye to her servants she continued to believe that Charles had deprived her of their company in order to spite her. She would not accept the fact that custom and the wishes of English members of the household demanded their departure.

She withdrew herself more than ever; she began to see that in refusing to accept Lady Castlemaine she had brought nothing but sorrow to herself. She had lost the King's affection, which had been given to a meek and gentle woman; and at the same time Lady Castlemaine had become a member of her household in spite of her dissent. Now James Crofts was made Duke of Monmouth, and was taking precedence over every other Duke in the kingdom with one exception – that of the King's brother James.

She herself was of no account; she had brought no good

to her husband; her dowry was unpaid; her country was begging for England's military help; valuable English ships were kept in the Mediterranean to assist Portugal should Spain attack.

She was the most wretched of Queens for, in spite of all she had suffered, she continued to love her husband.

*

She paced up and down her apartment.

Her country was in danger, she knew. If Charles withdrew his fleet Portugal would be once more the vassal of Spain. All the political advantages which this marriage had been intended to secure would be lost.

And it was due to her obstinacy. Was it obstinacy? She did not know. Was it her pride? Was it her vanity? She had dreamed of his chivalry; she had set him up in her mind and heart as the perfect man; and when she had met him in the flesh she had discovered him to be – so she had thought – more lovable than her ideal. That ideal had been noble, a little stern; she had never thought of his making merry. The reality had seemed noble but never stern; he was fond of laughter; he was affectionate – the kindest man in the world.

And suddenly one night as she lay alone, the knowledge came to her. She loved him; she would always love him; she loved him not only for his virtues but for his faults. She no longer wanted that ideal; she wanted Charles the living man. Suddenly she realized that she was married to the most fascinating Prince in the world and that, although she was not sufficiently beautiful or charming, so kindly was his nature that she could still expect much affection from him.

He had asked one thing of her, and she failed to give it because it had seemed impossible to give. He had asked her to accept him as he was – frail, a lover of women other than herself – and she had failed him in the one important thing he had asked of her.

She remembered now the kindness with which he had first received her; she remembered how, when he had come into her bedchamber, he had made her feel that she was beautiful and desirable, not because he found her so, but because he knew that that was what she wished to be. He would deceive in order to please; she had failed to appreciate that. She had

139

set him stern rules, conventional rules; she had tried to make a saint of the most charming sinner in the world, little realizing that saints are often uncomfortable people and that their saintliness is often attained at the cost of that kindly good nature which was an essential part of Charles's character.

She saw clearly his side of their disagreement, as she had never thought to see it, and she cursed herself for a fool because she had failed him when he asked her help.

She loved him; any humiliation was not too much to suffer for the sake of his affection.

She determined to regain that affection. She would not tell him of her decision; she would startle him by her friendly manner towards Lady Castlemaine. Mayhap it was not too late.

*

In the early hours of the morning as he left his mistress's apartment in the Cockpit and strolled back to his own in the main Palace, Charles was thinking of Catherine. He wondered how many people in the Court knew of these nightly wanderings of his to and from Barbara's apartment. Did Catherine know? Poor Catherine! He had been wrong to show coldness to her. He had asked too much of her. Could he have expected an innocent and ignorant girl, brought up as she had been, to understand his *blasé* point of view?

No! Catherine had acted in accordance with what she had considered to be right. She had clung to her duty. He, who would have sought an easy way out of the difficulty, must admire her for her strength of purpose. She had endured his neglect without much complaint, and he had behaved very badly.

She was the Queen, and he must put an end to this state of affairs. Barbara was often unbearable. He would tell her she must leave the Court. That should be his first concession to Catherine. Gradually he would let her see that he wished them to return to a happier relationship.

Poor homely little Catherine! She was a good woman, though a stubborn one, but well within her rights he doubted not.

'I will see what may be done about remedying this difference between us,' he mused.

And so, salving his conscience, he returned to his apartment.

*

Catherine's change of manner towards Lady Castlemaine caused great astonishment.

It was so sudden, for not only did she speak with her as hitherto she had not done, but she seemed actually to enjoy that lady's company more than that of any other. She referred to Barbara as 'my friend Lady Castlemaine'.

Poor Catherine! So eager was she for the King's regard that, having once made up her mind to turn about, she could not do so quickly enough.

Those few who had sought to curry favour with the Queen for what it might be worth, were now alarmed and tried to remember what derogatory remarks they had made about Barbara. Those who had ignored Catherine were equally astonished.

Clarendon thought her inconsequent and unreliable. 'This,' he said to Ormond, 'is the total abandonment of her greatness. She has lost all dignity; for, although I continued to warn her against her stubborn conduct, yet I was forced to admire it. In future none will feel safe with her. The Castlemaine herself is more reliable.'

The King, too, was astonished. He had not asked for such affability. He would have preferred her to have been cool with Barbara. It seemed folly to have expressed such abhorrence and now to have assumed a completely opposite attitude.

I was a fool, he told himself. I worried unduly. She is not the woman I thought her. She gives way to sudden passions. Her persistent refusal to receive Barbara did not grow out of her sense of rightness; it was pure perversity.

He shrugged his shoulders and decided to let matters take their course.

*

It was the end of the year – Catherine's first in England – and the King gave a grand ball in his Palace of Whitehall to mark the passing of the old year and the coming of the new.

Into the great ballroom the public crowded to watch the dancing. There was the King, the most graceful dancer of all, more merry than any, clad in black with flashing diamonds adorning his person, surrounded by his fine courtiers and beautiful ladies. A little apart sat the Queen with Edward Montague and a few of her friends; and although she smiled often, chatted in her quaint English and seemed to be enjoying the ball, it was noticed how her eyes wistfully went back and back again to the tall figure of her husband.

She watched him leading the Duchess of York out for the brantle. And how ungainly was the Duchess beside such an elegant partner! The Duke led the Duchess of Buckingham, poor Mary Fairfax, for whom Catherine had a feeling of deep sympathy, for Mary was plain, ungainly and so eager to please the brilliant handsome man she had married; Catherine noticed how all eyes were on that other pair which joined the brantle with the King's group. Tall, dark James Crofts, the Duke of Monmouth, looking amazingly like his father, had chosen for his partner the most strikingly handsome woman in the ballroom. There were gasps from the people who had come in from the streets to watch the royal party at their pleasure; there was a titter of grudging admiration for the auburn-haired beauty with the flashing blue eyes.

Her jewels were more brilliant than those of any woman in the room, and she held herself imperiously as though conscious of her power; and now she was amused because she knew that the King was aware of the warm looks of this very young boy who was her partner in the dance.

A murmur went through the crowd. ' 'Tis my Lady Castlemaine! Was there ever such a woman, such beauty, such jewels?'

The courtiers followed her with their eyes. None could refrain from looking at Barbara. Some of the jewels she was now wearing had been Christmas presents to the King, but already Barbara had grasped them with greedy hands. And as she danced in the brantle the King watched her, Monmouth watched her, and Lord Chesterfield watched her, but none watched her quite so closely nor so sadly as the Queen of England.

The brantle over, the King led the dancers in a coranto; and when that was ended and more stately dances followed, the King, with more energy than that possessed by most of his courtiers, signed to the fiddlers to play the dances of old

England, with which country dances, he declared, none could compare.

'Let the first be "Cuckolds all awry"! The old dance of old England.'

The Court grew very merry in the light of tall wax candles, and the crowds cheered and stamped with pleasure to see the old English dance; and they laughed and shouted to one another that Charles was indeed a King, with his merry life and his bland good humour, and the smiles he lavished freely on his subjects; they wanted no saint on the throne, who knew not how to laugh and found a virtue in forbidding pleasure to others.

They looked at the sad-faced Queen who did not seem to share in the fun; and from her they turned their gaze on dazzling Barbara.

The King was a man whom the English would never cease to love. And at the great Court ball in Whitehall Palace on the last night of the year 1662, all those present rejoiced once more that their King was a merry monarch and that he had come home to rule his kingdom.

FOUR

IN THE great ballroom at Windsor Castle the most brilliant ball of the year was taking place. This was to celebrate not only St George's Day but the marriage of the young man whom the King delighted to honour, his son, the Duke of Monmouth.

Catherine watched the dancers, and beside her sat the little bride, Lady Anne Scott, the heiress of Buccleugh and one of the richest in the kingdom; but the bridegroom seemed more interested in Lady Castlemaine than in his bride, and the young girl gazed at the pair with apprehension.

How sad it was, thought the Queen, that so many seemed to love those who were not their lawful partners! No wonder the King with sly humour liked to summon them all to dance 'Cuckolds all awry'. Was he the only man who knew that he could rely on the good faith of his wife? Yet he seemed not to love her the more for her fidelity, and to love Barbara none the less for the lack of it in her. It was said that Sir Charles Berkeley and George Hamilton were Barbara's lovers now and it seemed as though, before many weeks were out, young Monmouth might be; for the youth of the latter would be no deterrent to Barbara. She would look upon that as piquant. Catherine heard that she took lovers on the spur of the moment merely because some novelty in them appealed to her. She did not care whether they were noble or not; a lusty groom, she had been heard to say, was a better bedfellow than an impotent noble lord. The King also would hear these rumours, yet they seemed to affect him little; he still visited her on several nights each week and was often seen coming back early in the morning and all alone through the privy gardens. How could one hope to please such a husband as Catherine's by one's chastity?

Chastity! Who at Court cared about that? Their King clearly did not, and the courtiers were only too ready to follow his lead.

The Court was growing extremely elegant; Charles was introducing more and more French customs; he wrote continually to his sister, the wife of the French King's brother, asking her to send him any novelties which had appeared in the Court of her brother-in-law. Making love was the main pursuit, it seemed, of all; rarely did any drink to excess at the Court; there again the custom of the King was followed. There was less gambling now, although this was a sport much loved by Lady Castlemaine. The King would anxiously watch her at play; he had good reason, for she was a reckless gambler, and who would pay her debts but himself? He did not forbid her or any of the ladies whom he so admired, to gamble; he could not bring himself to spoil their pleasure, he admitted; but he tried to lure them from the gaming tables with brilliant balls and masquerades. How indulgent he was to the women he loved!

Why could they not be content with the partners whom they had married? Catherine wondered. She looked at little Anne beside her and felt a wave of tenderness for her. Poor child! She was young yet, but Catherine felt that if she ever grew to love her handsome young husband she was going to suffer deeply.

Lady Chesterfield was standing beside the Queen's chair and Catherine turned to her and smiled. A very charming lady – Elizabeth Butler now Lady Chesterfield – and married to that man who had seemed as much a slave of Barbara's as the King himself.

Catherine had been sorry for Elizabeth Chesterfield; she had felt she understood her sadness for she had heard how innocent she had been when she married the profligate Earl, and how she had tried to win his love only to be repulsed.

Catherine said in her faltering English: 'I rejoice to see you look so well, Lady Chesterfield.'

Lady Chesterfield bowed her head and thanked Her Majesty.

Yes, she had changed, thought Catherine; she had lost her meek looks. Her dress of green and cloth of silver fell from beautifully rounded shoulders, and her thick hair was in ringlets falling about them; her eyes sparkled and she watched the dancers almost speculatively.

So she had come to terms with life, thought Catherine. She had decided not to grieve because her husband preferred the evil beauty of Lady Castlemaine.

The Earl of Chesterfield had come to his wife's side, and would have taken her hand to lead her into the dance, but Elizabeth had withdrawn it and seemed not to see him standing there.

Catherine heard the whispered words.

'Come, Elizabeth. I would lead you to the dance.'

Elizabeth's voice was lightly mocking. 'Nay, my lord, your place is by the side of another. I would not deprive you of your pleasure in her company.'

'Elizabeth, this is folly.'

'Nay, 'tis sound good sense. And I advise you to watch what is afoot, for your dear friend seems mightily taken with the young Duke. You endanger your chances with her by dallying with me. Ah, here comes my cousin George Hamilton to claim me in the dance. George, I am ready.'

And the graceful creature had laid her hand in that of George Hamilton, her cousin, who, it was said, had lately been the lover of my Lady Castlemaine. Chesterfield stood watching them with a frown between his eyes. It was like a mad dance, thought Catherine, in which, after a clasping of hands and a merry jig, they changed partners. Was Chesterfield more interested in the wife who flouted him than in one who had been ready to love him? Or was it merely his pride which was wounded?

She noticed, however, that as the evening progressed his eyes were more frequently on his wife than on Lady Castlemaine.

Nor was he the only one who had seemed to change the course of his affections.

Catherine, whose eyes never strayed far from the King, saw that he was giving much of his attention to one of her maids of honour.

Frances Theresa Stuart was a distant relative of the King's; she was the daughter of Walter Stuart, the third son of Lord Blantyre, and Henrietta Maria had brought her to England when she came over, and had left the girl with Catherine to act as maid of honour.

Henrietta Maria had told Catherine that Louis Quatorze had been interested in her, and had suggested that she remain in his Court. 'But,' said Henrietta Maria, 'I thought it well not to leave her there; for her family lost much during the Civil War and I have a duty to them. I would not wish to see her become one of Louis's mistresses. She has been brought up to live virtuously, so I pray you take her into your household and let her serve you.'

Catherine had not wondered then whether removing Mrs Stuart from the lecherous orbit of Louis to that of Charles was not after all somewhat pointless, because at that time she had regarded the King's attachment to Lady Castlemaine as largely the result of an evil spell which that woman had put upon him. Now she was beginning to understand her husband and to realize that if there had been no Lady Castlemaine there would have been others.

Previously Frances had been looked upon as little more than a child, but it seemed that in her dazzling gown and the few jewels she possessed, this night she had become a young woman; and Catherine realized that if Barbara's beauty had a rival it was in this lovely girl.

Frances's hair was thick, fair and hung in curls over her shoulders; her pink and white complexion was dazzling; her eyes were blue; and she was tall and very slender; Barbara had a rare beauty with which any woman would find it difficult to compete, but Frances, in addition to beauty, was possessed of an elegance which she had acquired during her education at the French Court; her manners were gentle and quite modest – a complete contrast to the vulgarity of Lady Castlemaine. Barbara was, of course, full of wiles, full of cunning, and compared with her Frances Stuart seemed simple as a child. It was perhaps these qualities, as much as her youth, which had made Catherine regard her as a little girl.

But on this night she seemed to have grown up, and the King was noticing the change in her.

Others were noticing it too. Barbara's enemies, ever on the watch for her decline, were triumphantly asking each other and themselves: Could this be the end of her long domination of the King? Never had they seen Charles so completely absorbed in another woman, while Barbara was present, as he was in Frances.

Catherine was sad at heart. She had believed that one day the King would come to notice what a vulgar woman Barbara was and, full of shame and repentance, he would turn to his wife and they would resume that idyllic relationship they had enjoyed at Hampton Court.

Now she must wonder whether he ever would turn to her again, whether she had lost him for ever when she had failed to do that one thing which he had asked of her.

She continued to watch Lady Chesterfield who, flushed and triumphant, had many admirers now, including her husband perhaps. There was the Duke of York, watching her with dark, slumberous eyes. James was so clumsy in his devotion to women that he always aroused the amusement of the Court, and particularly of Charles. Catherine doubted not that ere long there would be whispers concerning the attraction Lady Chesterfield was exerting over the susceptible Duke.

It was a strange world, this Court of her husband. She was once more reminded that it was a Court in which beauty and the power to charm were of greater importance than virtue. Lady Chesterfield provided an example. Could Catherine herself follow it?

There was young Edward Montague who was often at her side. But were his feelings for her inspired by pity for her plight rather than admiration for her person?

Now she must dance, and here was the Duke of Monmouth, in whose honour the ball was held, ceremoniously asking for the hand of the first lady of the Court.

Catherine rose and put her hand in his. He was a very graceful dancer, and Catherine, who loved to dance, found herself enjoying this one.

How like Charles he was! A young, more handsome Charles, but lacking that kingliness, that great elegance, that wit, that charm. In comparison Monmouth was merely a pretty boy.

And as he danced with her – holding his plumed hat in his hand, since he danced with the Queen – Charles came to them and, there before the whole assembly, in an access of tenderness for this boy whom it was his delight to honour, stopped the dance, took the boy in his arms, kissed him on both cheeks and bade him put on his hat and continue the dance.

Everyone was astonished at this action of the King's. It could mean only one thing, it was whispered. The King so doted on his handsome son that he determined to make him legitimate. Then the Duke of Monmouth would be heir to the throne.

Rumour began to grow. Had the King truly married Lucy Water? Had the creature prevailed upon him to go through a ceremony of marriage? Charles had been an exile then, and all knew how easy-going he was with his women.

Catherine sadly continued to dance; she feared that the King's regard for her was so slight that he was telling her – and the Court – that whatever children she might bear him, they could not mean more to him than did young Monmouth.

*

In the little octagonal building which was part of Whitehall Palace and was called the Cockpit, Barbara had her apartments and here she held court. Hither flocked those ambitious men who believed that through Barbara lay the way to glory.

The chief of these was George Villiers, the Duke of Buckingham and Barbara's second cousin once removed; he was recognized, not only as one of the most handsome men of the day, but one of its most brilliant statesmen.

He saw in close association with Barbara a means of getting that power for which he had always longed, and there was one man whom he felt stood between him and his goal; that man was Clarendon, and in their hatred of the Chancellor, he and Barbara were united.

There in her rooms at the Cockpit they would meet frequently, and about them would gather all those who hoped to follow them to power. In the light of candles they would make merry, for, in addition to being a wily statesman, Buckingham was a man of many social graces: he was one of the most entertaining men at Court, and his imitations of well-known figures could set guests laughing so much that they became almost hysterical, so clever was he at caricaturing those little vanities and dignities of his enemies to make them appear utterly ridiculous. He used this gift in order to bring ridicule to those he disliked, and his caricature of Clarendon was in constant demand.

Another great enemy of Clarendon's who came to Barbara's parties was the Earl of Bristol. He was bold and vivacious but somewhat unreliable. He had written a book about the Reformation and, during the course of writing this, had become a Catholic; he was looked upon as the leader of the Catholic party in England and because of this was watched eagerly by those who hoped to see the Catholics more firmly established in the land. There was not a man at Court who hated the Chancellor more than did the Earl of Bristol.

Henry Bennet, who had been with the King in exile, was another; he was a clever, ambitious but rather pompous man who bore a scar on his nose of which he was so proud that he called attention to it by wearing a patch over it which was far greater than the scar warranted; this was meant to be a constant reminder to the King that he had been wounded in the Royalist Cause. Henry Bennet had shared Lucy Water with Charles when they were in Holland, and it was a matter of opinion whether Lucy's daughter Mary was Bennet's child or the King's. Barbara had included Bennet in her own little circle of men she could use, and it was largely through her that he had replaced Nicholas as Secretary of State.

It was these three men – Buckingham, Bristol and Bennet – with whom Barbara sought to intrigue after that New Year's ball during which the King had clearly shown his interest in Frances Stuart.

They all wished to bring about the downfall of Clarendon,

and at the same time it was Barbara's desire to damage Frances Stuart in the eyes of the King.

Barbara was seriously alarmed about Frances Stuart. The girl had in the first place seemed to be a simpleton. She was young and artless and seemed unaware of the fact that there was not a woman at Court whose beauty could compare with hers; and in a Court where the King was instantly moved by beauty in any form – and in particular the beauty of women – that meant a passport to power.

Barbara watched Frances closely. Each day she seemed to grow in beauty. The girl was perfect; her figure was enchanting; her face, with that expression of supreme innocence, delightful. Had she not been the most beautiful girl at Court, her very grace of movement would have made her stand out among them all, and allied with this was a charming air of innocence. She laughed easily; she prattled of nothing in a lighthearted way; she seemed almost simple-minded in her childishness. But Barbara had her own ideas. She did not believe in Mrs Stuart's innocence. She remembered the case of Anne Boleyn, who had remained haughty, pure and aloof, and had murmured to an enamoured King: 'Your wife I cannot be; your mistress I will not be.'

Barbara was furious with the girl, but the situation was too delicate to allow her to give full vent to that fury. Barbara was in her twenties; Frances in her teens; Barbara lived riotously, never denying her senses what they craved; Frances slept the sleep of the innocent each night and arose in the mornings fresh as a spring flower.

Barbara had realized that where this sly little prude was concerned she would have to play a wary game.

So she took Frances under her wing. She believed that, if she had not, the King might have been found supping where Frances was and Barbara was not. She made Frances her little friend; she even had her sleep in her bed.

She knew, of course, that the King had made the usual advances to the girl – the languishing looks, the pressing of hands, the stolen kisses, the gifts. All these she had received with wide-eyed pleasure as though the insinuation which acccompanied them was quite beyond her understanding.

So Barbara played those games which Frances loved, childish games which made the simple little creature shriek with pleasure. They played 'marriage' – with Barbara the husband and Frances the wife, and they were put to bed with a sack posset and the stocking was flung. Unfortunately the King had come in while that game was in progress and had declared that it was a shame poor Frances had been married to one of her own sex. He was sure she would have preferred a man for her husband; he therefore would relieve Barbara of conjugal responsibilities and take them on himself. What shrieks of laughter from sly Mrs Stuart! What nudging and whispering of those participating in the game! Had the bride been anyone else, Barbara knew full well that the frolic of that night would not have ended as it did. But sly, virtuous Mrs Stuart knew when to draw back; and Barbara, with murder in her heart, believed the sly creature was contemplating very high stakes indeed.

So the dearest wish of Barbara's heart was to see Mrs Stuart exposed in the eyes of the King as a wanton. She knew that he was growing more and more tender towards the girl, that he believed in all that innocence, and that it was having a devastating effect which might prove disastrous to Barbara. Dearly as she wished to see the fall of Clarendon she wished even more to see the fall of Mrs Stuart.

It was in the Cockpit that she conferred with her friends.

'It should not be difficult now,' she said, 'for you gentlemen to assure the King of how this man works against him.'

'The King is too easy-going,' growled Bennet.

'Yet,' said Buckingham, 'his opposition to the Declaration of Liberty for Tender Consciences has, I am certain, incensed the King.'

'I have assured him,' said Barbara, 'that Clarendon opposed the Declaration, not because he believed it to be wrong, but because of his hatred towards those who promoted it.'

'And what said he to that?'

Barbara shrugged her shoulders. 'He said that Clarendon was a man of deep conscience. He had reason to know it, for he knew the man well.'

'Still he was displeased with Clarendon.'

'Indeed he was,' said Bristol, 'and it was solely because of his need for money that he agreed to those laws which deal harshly with all who differ from the Act of Uniformity.'

'And now,' said Buckingham, 'he has been forced to

proclaim that Papists and Jesuits will be banished from the kingdom, although I have good reason to believe that he will do everything in his power to oppose the banishing. You know his great wish for tolerance, and it is solely because he needs money so badly that he is forced to fall in with the Parliament's wishes.'

'But he loves them all a little less for forcing him to agree,' said Barbara. 'And he knows that it is Clarendon who has led those against him.'

'So,' cried Bristol, 'now is the time to impeach the fellow. If the King fails to support him as he failed to support the King, all those who feign friendship towards him will drop away like leaves in an autumn gale.'

'Yes,' said Barbara, 'now is the time.'

'There is another matter,' said Bristol. 'I am a Catholic and I know how friendly the King has been to Catholics. There are rumours – and always have been – that one who can be so lenient towards Papists must surely be of their Faith.'

'It is nonsense,' said Barbara. 'He is often more lenient when he does not agree. It is due to some notion he has of respecting all points of view.'

'Clarendon deplores his tolerance,' said Buckingham. 'I have it! Someone has been spreading reports of the King's devotion to the Catholic cause. It might well be Clarendon.'

'It shall be Clarendon!' said Barbara.

'Moreover,' said Bristol, 'I have heard that a correspondence has taken place between the Queen and the Pope. His Majesty is weary of the Queen; that much is certain. There is no sign of a child. Doubtless the woman is unfruitful; princesses often are. And the King has proved his ability – nay his great good fortune – in getting children elsewhere. It may be that he would wish to rid himself of the Queen.'

Barbara's eyes were narrowed. Could it be that these friends of hers were concocting some plot of which she was not acquainted? Had Bristol betrayed it; and could it by any chance concern Frances Stuart?

'Nay,' she said quickly, 'I warn you. If you should try to turn the King against the Queen you would be greatly mistaken.'

Better, thought Barbara, a plain little Portuguese Catherine as Queen than beautiful Frances Stuart.

'Barbara is right in that,' said Buckingham. 'Let us not

152

take the plot too far as yet. Let us settle this one matter first, and we will deal with others afterwards. Let us rid ourselves of the Chancellor; let us set up a new Chancellor in his place. . . .' Buckingham looked at Bristol, and Bristol looked at the ceiling. Why not Buckingham? thought Buckingham. Why not Bristol? thought Bristol. Bennet was smugly content as Secretary of State.

They parted soon afterwards. Barbara was hoping the King would call upon her.

*

A few days later she had an opportunity of speaking to Buckingham alone.

She immediately began to discuss Frances.

'Do you believe she is as virtuous as she feigns to be?'

'There is no proof that she is otherwise.'

'Mayhap no one has tried hard enough.'

'The King is a skilful player. Would you not say he is trying very hard indeed?'

'George, you may not be the King, but you are the handsomest man at Court.'

Buckingham laughed.

'Dear cousin,' he said, 'I know full well how mightily it would please you should I take the Stuart for my mistress. It is galling for one of your high temper to see His Majesty growing more deeply enamoured every day. It would be pleasant for me to bask in your approbation, Barbara, but think what goes with it: the fury of the King.'

'Nay, he'd not be furious. It is her seeming virtue that plagues him. He only half believes in it. Prove it to be a myth and he'll love you better than he loves the silly Stuart.'

'And you too, Barbara?'

But Buckingham went away thinking of this matter. He *was* a handsome man; he was irresistible to many. Might it not be that for all his royalty, Charles as a man had failed to appeal to Frances? Might it not be that she realized that Charles in pursuit might be more amusing – and profitable – than Charles satisfied?

He decided to cultivate the fair Stuart.

*

Barbara whispered to Sir Henry Bennet: 'She is beautiful, is she not – Frances Stuart?'

'She is indeed. Apart from yourself, I would say there is not a more handsome woman at the Court.'

'I know that you admire her.'

' 'Tis a pity she is determined not to take a lover.'

'So far!' said Barbara.

'What mean you by that?'

'Mayhap the man she would wish for has not yet claimed her!'

'The King, it is said, has had ill fortune in his pursuit of her.'

'The King may not always be victorious. I have heard it said that Lucy Water, who knew you both well, had a more tender heart for Henry than for Charles.'

Bennet was a vain man. He postured and laughed aloud at the memory of Lucy Water.

And when he left Barbara, he was thoughtful.

*

The plot to discredit Clarendon failed completely, largely through Charles's interference. Charles fully realized that the charge had been brought against him, not because those who brought it believed that Clarendon was working against him and the country, but because the plotters were working against Clarendon.

The Chancellor's judges decided that a charge of high treason could not be brought by one peer against another in the House of Lords; and that even if those charges against Clarendon were true, there was no treason in them. The House of Lords therefore dismissed the charges.

Bristol, who had been the prime mover against Clarendon in this case, seeking to justify himself with the King and believing that Charles wished to rid himself of Catherine, added a further charge against Clarendon, declaring that he had brought the King and Queen together without any settled agreement about marriage rites, and that either the succession would be uncertain, in case of Catherine's being with child, for want of the due rites of matrimony, or His Majesty would be exposed to suspicion of being married in his own country by a Romanish priest.

When the King heard of this he was indignant.

'How dare you suggest that there would be an inquiry into the secret nuptials between myself and the Queen?' he demanded.

'Your Majesty, I thought that in raising this point I should be acting as you wished.'

'You carry your zeal too far.'

'Then I crave Your Majesty's pardon.'

'It would be easier to grant it if I did not have to see you for a little time. I would have you know – and all those who are with you – that I will not have slights cast on the Queen.'

'There was no desire to slight the Queen, Your Majesty.'

'Then let us hear no more of the matter. It is astonishing to me that you, a Catholic yourself, should have added this article to the impeachment of Clarendon. What caused your conversion to Catholicism?'

'May it pleasure Your Majesty, it happened whilst I was writing a book for the Reformation.'

The King turning away, said with a half smile: 'Pray, my lord, write a book for Popery.'

It was necessary after that for the Earl of Bristol to absent himself from Court for a while.

The people in the streets and about the Court had said that Bristol and his friend had cast the Chancellor on his back past ever getting up, but Clarendon retained his post, although the rift between the King and his Chancellor had widened.

*

The Queen had become very happy. She was certain now that she was to have a child.

This made the King very tender towards her; he longed for a legitimate heir. He had not proclaimed Monmouth legitimate and he had denied the rumours that he had married Lucy Water. He was seen often in company with the Queen; but he was deeply in love with Frances Stuart.

He still continued to visit Barbara, who retained her hold over him, and she kept her title as his first mistress.

She made no attempt to control her temper, and she was pregnant again.

'It would seem,' she said, 'that I have no sooner borne a

child than the next is conceived. Charles, I hope our next will be a boy.'

'*Our* next?' said Charles.

'Indeed it is our next!' shouted Barbara.

The King looked about him. Barbara was not the only one who had her apartments in the Cockpit, for the building was large and had been built by Henry the Eighth to lodge those whom he wished to keep near him. Clarendon had a suite of rooms there; so had Buckingham.

Charles knew that these people were quite aware of the stormy nature of his relationship with Barbara, but he did like to keep their quarrels private.

'I doubt it,' said Charles. 'I very much doubt this one to be mine.'

'Whose else could it be?'

'There you set a problem which you might answer more readily than I, though I confess you yourself might be hard put to it to solve it.'

Barbara looked about for something that she might throw at him; there was nothing to hand but a cushion; she would not throw that; it would seem almost coy.

'Oh, Barbara,' said the King, 'let another man father this one.'

'So you would shift your responsibilities!'

'I tell you I do not accept this responsibility.'

'You had better change your mind before the child is born ... unless you would like me to strangle it at birth and set it up in the streets with a crown upon its head proclaiming it the King's son.'

'You're fantastic,' said the King, beginning to laugh.

She laughed with him and leaping towards him threw her arms about his neck. In the old days such a gesture would have been a prelude to passion, but today the King was pensive and did not respond.

*

In Frances Stuart's apartment the light of wax candles shone on all the most favoured of the gallant gentlemen and beautiful ladies of the Court.

The King sat beside Frances who looked more beautiful than even she had ever looked; she was dressed in black and white, which suited her fair skin, and there were diamonds in her hair and about her throat.

From her seat at another table Barbara watched the King and Frances.

Frances seemed unaware of everything except the house of cards she was building. She was like a baby! thought Barbara. Her greatest delight was in building card-houses; and everyone who sought to please her must compete with her in the ridiculous game. There was only one who could build as she did; that was Buckingham.

They built their card-houses side by side. The King was handing Frances her cards; Lady Chesterfield was handing Buckingham his; all the other builders of card-houses had given up the game to watch these two rivals. Frances was breathless with excitement; Buckingham was coolly cynical; but his hand was so steady that it seemed that his calmness would score over Frances's excitement.

Imbecile! thought Barbara. Is she really so infantile that a card-house can give her that much joy? Or is she acting the very young girl in the hope that the King is weary of such as I? We shall see who wins in the end, Mrs Frances.

Lady Chesterfield caught Barbara's attention momentarily; she had changed much since those days when she had first married Chesterfield and had been another simpleton such as Frances would have them believe she was. Simplicity had not brought Lady Chesterfield all she desired. Now George Hamilton sought to be her lover – and he had been Barbara's lover too – and the Duke of York was paying her that attention with which he was wont to honour ladies; it consisted of standing near them and gazing longingly at them in a manner which made all secretly laugh, or writing notes to them which he pushed into their pockets or muffs; and as the ladies concerned were not always willing to accede to his advances, there had been much amusement when the notes had been allowed to fall, as though unnoticed, from muff or pocket and left lying about for any to read.

Barbara thought of Chesterfield, her first lover, her first experience in those adventures which were more important to her comfort than anything else. Chesterfield had been a good lover.

She realized with some dismay that it was a long time since

he had been to see her. She verily believed that he was more interested in another woman than he was in herself; and it was rather comic that that woman should be his wife.

Ah, but he had turned too late to Lady Chesterfield, who would not forget the humiliation she had suffered at his hands. It delighted her now to be cold to him, to accept the admiration of George Hamilton and to return the yearning gazes of the Duke of York, to set new fashions in the Court such as this one of green stockings which had begun with her appearing in them.

The King's attention was all for the fair Stuart; Chesterfield's for his wife; and Buckingham – for naturally Barbara and Buckingham had slipped into amorous relationship now and then – was also paying attention to the Stuart, although, Barbara reminded herself, it was at her suggestion he did this.

Three of her lovers looking at other women! It was disconcerting.

George Hamilton too, she remembered, was paying attention to Lady Chesterfield and hoping to persuade her to break her marriage vows.

Could it be that Barbara, Countess of Castlemaine, was finding herself deserted?

Not deserted, never deserted. There would always be lovers, even if she chose one of her grooms – although she would not do that unless he was a very appealing fellow. Yet it was disconcerting to find so many of those who had once sought her favours eagerly looking elsewhere. It was certainly time Frances Stuart was exposed to the King as a hypocrite and humbug. He would find it harder to forgive her infidelity than he ever had Barbara's, for Barbara's he took for granted. He knew Barbara; she was like himself. They could not curb their desires; he understood that of her as she did of him. They were not the sort to wrangle if the other took an odd lover or two.

The building of card-houses was over; Buckingham had allowed Frances to win, and now was singing one of his songs set to his own music. He was a good performer and he sang in French and Italian as well as English. His poor, plain Duchess looked on with wistful tenderness as he performed. They were rarely together, but Frances liked husbands and wives to come to her gatherings; she was so very respectable, thought Barbara cynically.

Now there was dancing; and it was left to Monmouth to partner Barbara.

A spritely young fellow, thought Barbara, but she had not allowed him to become her lover; she was not sure how the King would feel about that. Monmouth, as his son, would be in a different category from other men; and she was not going to offend Charles more than she could help at this point.

When they were tired of dancing, Frances called on Buckingham to do some of his imitations, and that night the Duke excelled himself. He did his favourite – Clarendon, carrying a shovel in place of the mace, so full of self-importance, slow and ponderous; and this made the company roll and bend double with merriment; then he did the King, the King sauntering, the King being very gallant to a lady – who, of course, it was implied, was Frances herself. Charles led the laughter at this. And finally the versatile Duke approached Frances and began to make what he called a dishonourable proposal. It was Bennet to the life. The phrases were Bennet's, slow, flowery and wordy, spiced with those quotations with which Bennet liked to adorn his parliamentary addresses.

Frances shrieked with laughter and clutched the King in a very paroxysm of merriment – all of which delighted the King mightily; and made of that evening a very merry one.

The French ambassador who was present was, after the merriment subsided a little, so delighted with the company that he whispered to the King that he had heard Mrs Stuart was possessed of the most exquisite legs in the world, and he wondered whether he dared ask the lady to show him these – up to the knee; he would dare ask for no more.

The King whispered the request to Frances; who opened her blue eyes very wide and said but of course she would be delighted to show the ambassador her legs. Whereupon, still in the manner of a very young girl, she stood on a stool and lifted her skirt as high as her knees that all might gaze on the legs which had been proclaimed the most beautiful in the world.

The King was quite clearly enchanted with Frances's manners, with her ingenuity and with the grace she displayed.

The French ambassador knelt and said that he knew of no

way in which to pay homage to the most beautiful legs in the world except to kneel to them.

Then was the whole assembly made aware of how deep was the passion of the Duke of York for Lady Chesterfield, for he said in his somewhat ungracious way that he did not consider Mrs Stuart's legs the most beautiful in the world.

'They are,' he declared, 'too slender. I would admire legs that are plump, and not so long as Mrs Stuart's. Most important of all, the legs I most admire should be clothed in a green stocking.'

The King burst into merry laughter, for, like everyone else, he knew that the Duke was referring to Lady Chesterfield who had introduced the green stocking to Court; Charles clapped his brother on the back and pushed him in the direction of the lady.

Barbara continued to watch this horse-play. She saw Lord Chesterfield's angry glance at the royal brothers.

To think, thought Barbara, in rising fury, that I should ever live to see Chesterfield in love with his own wife!

She looked about her for the man whom she would invite to her bed that night. It would not be the King, nor Buckingham, nor Chesterfield, nor Hamilton.

She wished to have a new lover, someone young and lusty, who would take the memory of this evening with its warning shadows from her mind.

*

The Chesterfield scandal burst suddenly on the Court. It was astonishing to all, for Chesterfield was known as a rake and a libertine, and none would have suspected him of having any deep feelings for a woman, least of all for his own wife.

Music was the delight of the Court, and Tom Killigrew, one of the leading lights in the theatrical world, had brought with him from Italy a company of singers and musicians who had a great success at Court. One of these, Francisco Corbetta, was a magnificent performer on the guitar, and it was due to this that many ladies and gentlemen determined to learn the instrument. Lady Chesterfield had acquired one of the finest guitars in the country, and her brother, Lord Arran, learned to play the instrument better than any man at Court.

Francisco had composed a Sarabande, and this piece of

music so delighted the King that he would hear it again and again. All at Court followed the King's example, and through courtyards and apartments would be heard the Sarabande, in deep bass and high sopranos, played on all kinds of musical instruments, but the favourite way of delivering the Sarabande was to strum on the guitar and to sing at the same time.

When the Duke of York expressed his desire to hear Arran play the Sarabande on his sister's guitar, Arran immediately invited the Duke to his sister's apartments.

Chesterfield, hearing what was about to happen, stormed into his wife's chamber and accused her of indulging in a love affair with the Duke of York.

Elizabeth, laughing inwardly, and remembering that occasion when she had first discovered that the husband she loved was in love with the King's mistress, merely turned away and would neither deny nor admit that the Duke was her lover.

'Do you think,' cried Chesterfield, 'that I shall allow you to deceive me . . . blatantly like this?'

'My thoughts are never concerned with you at all,' Elizabeth told him.

She sat down and took up the guitar, crossing those plump legs encased in green stockings for which the Duke had displayed public admiration.

Chesterfield cried: 'Is he your lover? Is he? Is he?'

Elizabeth's answer was to play the first notes of the Sarabande.

She looked at him coolly, and she remembered how she had loved him in the first weeks of their marriage, how she had sought to please him in every way, how she had dreamed of a marriage as happy as that enjoyed by her parents.

And then, when she had known that Barbara Castlemaine was his mistress – that woman of all women, that blatant, vulgar woman of whom there were so many stories current, that woman who had lost count of her lovers – when she had allowed herself to imagine them together, when she had seen how foolish she had been to hope for that happy marriage, quite suddenly she had ceased to grieve, she had come to believe that she would never care about anything any more. It had seemed to her that in loving there could only be folly. The Court was corrupt; chastity and fidelity were laughed at even by the kindly King. Her feeling for her husband died suddenly. She had stood humiliated as a simple fool; and she would be so no longer.

Then she had discovered that there was much to enjoy in the Court; she had found that she was deemed beautiful. Gradually this understanding had come to her, and it was amusing to dance, to flirt, to astonish all by some extraordinary costume which, on her beautiful form, was charming. Like any other beautiful woman at Court she could have her lover. The King's brother now sought her; mayhap soon the King himself would.

As for her husband, she could never look at him without remembering the acute humiliation he had inflicted on a tender young spirit which had been too childlike to bear such brutality.

One of her greatest joys henceforth would be to try to inflict on him a little of the torture he had carelessly made her suffer. She had never thought to accomplish it; but now the perverse man was, in his stupidity, ready to love a wife who would be cold to him for ever more, although he had turned slightingly away from her youthful love.

That was life. Cynical, cruel. The Sarabande seemed to explain it far better than she could.

'I ask a question!' cried Chesterfield. 'I demand an answer.'

'If I do not wish to answer you, I shall not,' she said.

'So he comes to hear the Sarabande! What an excuse! He comes to see you.'

'Doubtless both,' she said lightly.

'And that brother of yours has arranged this! He is in this plot against me! Do you think I'll stand aside and allow you to deceive me thus?'

'I told you I do not think of you at all. And I do not care whether you stand aside or remain here. Your actions are of the utmost indifference to me.'

She was very beautiful, he thought, insolent and cold, sitting there with her pretty feet and a green stocking just visible below her gown. He often wondered how he could have been such a fool as not to have recognized her incomparable qualities; he had been mad to prefer the tantrums of Barbara to the innocence of the young girl whom he had married. He remembered with anguish her jealousy of his first wife. If he could only arouse that jealousy again he would be happy. Yet he knew that he would never arouse anything within her but cold contempt.

There was no time to say more, for at that moment the arrival of the Duke of York with Arran was announced. The Duke was flatteringly attentive to Lady Chesterfield and it was clear that he was far more interested in her than in her guitar.

Chesterfield refused to leave the little party to themselves, and stood glowering while Arran instructed the Duke in the playing of the famous Sarabande.

But, before the lesson had progressed very far, a messenger arrived to say that Chesterfield's services as Lord Chamberlain to the Queen were required in the royal apartments, as the Muscovite ambassadors were ready to be conducted to her.

Furious at being called away at such a time, Chesterfield had no choice but to comply with instructions and leave Arran as chaperon for Lady Chesterfield and the Duke. When he arrived in the Queen's presence chamber, to his complete horror, he found that Arran was there. The Duke and Lady Chesterfield must be alone together, in her apartments!

A mad fury possessed Chesterfield. He could scarcely wait for the audience to end. He was convinced that a trick had been played on him and that he had been cunningly removed that the Duke might be alone with his wife.

So great was his jealous rage that he went straight to his apartments. Neither the Duke nor Lady Chesterfield were there; and the first thing his eyes alighted on was the guitar; he threw it to the floor and jumped on it again and again till it was broken into many pieces. Then he set about searching for his wife, and the first person he found was George Hamilton, his wife's cousin and admirer; and to him Chesterfield poured out the story of his miserable jealousy.

Hamilton, believing with Chesterfield that the Duke must certainly have succeeded with Lady Chesterfield where he had failed, nursed his own secret jealousy. He could not bear the thought of anyone's enjoying those favours for which he had long sought; he would prefer to lose sight of the lady rather than allow her to enjoy another lover.

'You are her husband,' he said. 'Why not take her to the

country? Keep her where you will know that she is safe and entirely yours.'

This seemed good sense to Chesterfield. He made immediate arrangements and, by the time he saw his wife again, he was ready to leave with her for the country; and she had no alternative but to fall in with his wishes.

So they disappeared from the Court and, in accordance with the lighthearted custom of the time, witty verses were written about the incident, and what more natural than that they should be set to the tune of the Sarabande and sung throughout the Court?

The Duke of York began pushing notes into another lady's muff. But Barbara could not forget that yet another lover had deserted her.

*

Catherine was happier during those months than she had been since the days of her honeymoon. At last she was to bear a child; she saw in this child a new and wonderful happiness, a being who would compensate her for all she had suffered through her love for the King. She pictured him; for, of course, he would be a boy; he would have the manners of his father; yes, and the looks of his father; the kindliness, the affability and the good nature; but he would be more serious – in that alone should he resemble his mother.

She saw him clearly – the enchanting little boy – the heir to the throne of England. She built him as firmly in her imagination as, in the days when she was awaiting her marriage, she had pictured Charles. She found great happiness in daydreams.

And indeed the King was charming to her. He seemed to have forgotten all their differences. He declared she must take the utmost care of herself; he was solicitous that she should not catch a chill; he insisted on her resting from arduous state duties. It was pleasant to believe that he cared, for her sake as well as for that of the child.

They rode hand in hand in the Park, and the people stood in groups to watch and cheer them. She was quite pretty in her happiness, and she heard the people confirm this to one another – for they were not a people to mince their words – as she rode forth in her white-laced waistcoat and her crimson short petticoat which was so becoming, with her hair flowing about her shoulders. Behind her and the King, rode the ladies, and of course Lady Castlemaine was there, haughty and handsome as ever, but just a little out of humour because she had not been invited to ride by the side of the King; and surely a little subdued, for previously she would have pushed her horse forward and made sure that she was seen riding near the King and Queen.

Her face under her great hat with its yellow plume was sullen; and, when she was ready to alight, she was very angry because no gentleman hurried forward to her aid but left her own servants to look after her.

Barbara's day is done, thought Catherine. Had this something to do with her own condition? Or was it because of the meek little beauty who rode with them and was even more lovely than haughty Castlemaine, determined that the people should not see *her* riding side by side with the King when his wife was present, and looking so charming, in her little cocked hat with the red feather, that everyone gasped at such beauty.

Good news came from Portugal of the defeat of the Spaniards at Amexial. The battle had been fierce, for the Spaniards were led by Don John of Austria, but the English and the Portuguese Allies had won this decisive battle on which hung the fate of Portugal. The English had fought with such bravery and resource that the Portuguese had cried out that their allies were better to them than all the saints for whose aid they had prayed.

Catherine, hearing the news, wept with joy. She owed the security of her country to the English; it was true that she had been born to be of great significance to Portugal. She looked upon Charles as the saviour of her country; and when she thought of that, and all he had been to her since their marriage, she wondered afresh how she could have been so blind in the first days as to have refused him the one thing he asked of her. He had given her the greatest happiness she had ever known; he had saved her country from an ignoble fate, and when he had asked her to help him out of a delicate situation, she had not considered his feelings; she had thought only of her own pride, her own wounded love. She could weep for her folly now; but it was too late for tears; all she could do was wait for opportunities to prove her love, to pray that one day she might be able to win back his affection which her stupidity had made her throw away.

Her simple-minded brother had given the English soldiers a pinch of snuff apiece as a token of his gratitude, and she blushed for her brother. Pinches of snuff for a kingdom! The English soldiers had been outraged and had thrown the snuff on the ground; but Charles had saved the situation by ordering that 40,000 crowns should be distributed among them as a reward for their services to his Queen.

She knew how hard pressed he was for money, how often he paid the country's expenses out of his own personal income; she knew the constant demands made on him by women like Barbara Castlemaine, and how his generosity made it impossible for him to refuse what they asked.

She prayed earnestly that her child might be big and strong, a boy of whom he would be proud.

She looked into the future and saw a period of happiness ahead, for she was mellowed; she was no longer a hysterical girl who could not adjust herself to the exigencies of a cynical world.

*

Barbara was thinking seriously.

It might, she supposed, be necessary to have a husband again. If she was to lose the King's favour, she would need the protection of Roger.

As the Queen grew larger, so did she; and was the King going to admit paternity of her child? It was true he came to her nurseries now and then, but that was to see the children who would clamber over him and search his pockets for gifts.

'I see,' he had said on one occasion, 'that you have your mother's fingers.'

He would always look after the children – she need have no fear of that – but he was certainly growing cooler to their mother.

She could, of course, threaten him; she could print his letters. But what of that? All knew of their relationship; there was little fresh to expose.

Moreover, there was a possibility that he might banish her from Court. She knew him well. Like most easy-going people, there came to him now and then a desire to be firm, and then nothing could shake him. Barbara knew that although his great good humour could be relied upon, when he decided to stand firm none could be firmer.

She began to plan ahead and called a priest to her that she might make good study, she said, of the Catholic Faith, for there was something within her which told her that she ought to do this in preparation for a reconciliation with Roger.

The whole Court laughed at the thought of Barbara closeted with her priest; she declared he was teaching her the tenets of the Catholic Faith, but they ribaldly asked each other what *she* was teaching *him*.

Buckingham approached the King concerning his cousin. 'Your Majesty, could you not forbid the Lady Castlemaine from this new religion?'

Charles laughed lightly. 'You forget, my lord,' he said, 'I have never interfered with the *souls* of ladies.'

Barbara heard this and was more alarmed than ever. She was becoming more and more aware that she was losing some of her power over the King.

*

Buckingham had been sent from the presence of Frances Stuart. He was no longer her very good friend. He had dared make improper suggestions to her. She, who had professed to be so innocent, had been by no means at a loss as to how to deal with the profligate Duke.

He returned to the Cockpit and consulted with Barbara. 'It would seem the lady is determined to be virtuous,' he said.

Bennet tried his luck but, when he stood before Frances and made that declaration in the pompous tones which Buckingham had imitated so well, Frances was unable to contain her mirth, for, as she said afterwards, it was well nigh impossible to know whether she was listening to Bennet in person or Buckingham impersonating Bennet.

The King also made his proposals to the beautiful young girl. She was sad and remote. She did not think His Majesty was in a position to say such things to her, she declared; and even though she might incur his displeasure, she could only beg him not to do so.

The King, in exasperation, went to sup at Barbara's house. She was delighted to see him and received him with warmth; she was determined to remind him of all that they had enjoyed together.

She succeeded in doing this so certainly that he was back the next night and the next.

Barbara's hopes began to rise; she forgot her priest and the need to accept the Catholic religion. She ordered a great chine of beef to be roasted for the King; but the tide rose unusually high and her kitchens were flooded, so that Mrs Sarah declared she could not roast the beef. Barbara cried aloud: 'Zounds! Set the house afire but roast that beef.'

And Mrs Sarah, far bolder with Lady Castlemaine than any other servant dared be, told her mistress to talk good sense, and she would carry the beef to be roasted at her husband's house; and as her husband was cook to my Lord Sandwich she doubted not that she could get the beef roasted to a turn.

This was done; and the King and Lady Castlemaine supped merrily, but all London knew of the chine of beef which had to be roasted in the kitchens of Lord Sandwich. It was known too that the King stayed with my Lady Castlemaine until the early hours of the morning.

*

Catherine, resting in the Palace of Whitehall and shut away from rumour, was waiting for her baby to be born. She had allowed herself to believe that when the child came she and Charles would be content with one another. It was true that he was enamoured of the beautiful Mrs Stuart, but Frances was a good girl, who conducted herself with decorum and had made it quite clear that the King must give up all hope of seducing her.

When the child came he would forget his schemes concerning Frances Stuart, Catherine persuaded herself; he would give himself up to the joys of family life. He was meant to be a father; he was tolerant, full of gaiety and a lover of children. There would be many children; and they would be as happy a family as that in which she had been brought up – nay, happier, for they would not have to suffer the terrible anxiety which had beset the Duke of Braganza's.

All this must come to pass as she knew it could, once he was free of that evil woman. The name Castlemaine would always make her shiver, she feared. When she saw it she would always remember that terrible occasion when she had seen it written at the top of the list; and that other when she had given her hand to the woman to kiss, without realizing her identity; and the shame of the scene that followed.

But in the years to come the name of Castlemaine would be nothing but a memory, a memory to provoke a shiver it was true, yet nothing more.

So now she thought exclusively of the child, hoping it would be a boy; but if that should not be, well then, they were young, she and Charles, and they had proved themselves capable of getting children.

I knew I should be happy, she told herself. It was only necessary for him to escape from that evil woman.

The women below her window were giggling together. She wondered what this was about. She gathered it concerned a certain chine of beef. The stupid things women giggled about!

She turned away from the window, wondering when she would see Charles again.

Perhaps she would tell him of her hopes for their future – such confidences were often on her lips, but she never uttered them. Although he was tender and solicitous for her health, he was always so merry; and she fancied that he was a little cynical regarding sentimental dreams.

No! She would not tell him. She would make her dreams become realities.

Donna Maria came to her, and Donna Maria had been weeping. Old and infirm, hating the English climate, not understanding the English manners, Donna Maria constantly longed for her own country, although nothing would have induced her to leave her Infanta.

Poor Donna Maria! thought Catherine. She always had a habit of looking on the dark side of life as though she preferred it to the brighter.

'So you have heard this story of the chine of beef?' she asked.

'Well, I heard some women laughing over it below my window.'

'It was for the King's supper, and the kitchens were flooded, so it must needs be carried to my Lord Sandwich's kitchens to be cooked.'

'Is that the story of the chine of beef?'

'A noisy story because Madam Castlemaine cried out to burn the place down – but roast the beef.'

'Madam . . . Castlemaine!'

'Why, yes, have you not heard? The King is back with her. He is supping with her every night and is as devoted to her as he ever was.'

Catherine stood up. Her emotions were beyond control as they had been on that occasion when the King had presented Lady Castlemaine to her without her knowledge and consent.

All her dreams were false. He had not left the woman. In that moment she believed that as long as she lived Lady Castlemaine would be her evil genius as she was the King's.

'Why . . . what ails you?' cried Donna Maria.

She saw the blood gushing from Catherine's nose as it had on that other occasion; she was just in time to catch the Queen as she fell forward.

*

The King stood by his wife's bed. She looked small, frail and quite helpless.

She was delirious; and she did not know yet that she had lost her child.

Donna Maria had explained to him; she had repeated the last words she had exchanged with Catherine.

I have brought her to this, thought the King. I have caused her so much pain that the extreme stress of her emotional state has brought on this miscarriage and lost us our child.

He knelt down by the bed and covered his face with his hands.

'Charles,' said Catherine. 'Is that you, Charles?'

'I am here,' he told her. 'I am here beside you.'

'You are weeping, Charles! Those are tears. I never thought to see you weep.'

'I want you to be well, Catherine. I want you to be well.'

He could see by the expression on her face that she had no knowledge of the nature of her illness; she must have forgotten there was to have been a child. He was glad of this. At least she was spared that agony.

'Charles,' she said. 'Hold my hand, Charles.'

Eagerly he took her hand; he put his lips to it.

'I am happy that you are near me,' she told him.

'I shall not leave you. I shall be here with you . . . while you want me.'

'I dreamed I heard you say those words.' A frown touched her brow lightly. 'You say them because I am ill,' she went on. 'I am very ill. Charles, I am dying, am I not?'

'Nay,' he cried passionately. 'Nay, 'tis not so.'

'I shall not grieve to leave the world,' she said. 'Willingly would I leave all . . . save one. There is no one I regret leaving, Charles, but you.'

'You shall not leave me,' he declared.

'I pray you do not grieve for me when I am dead. Rejoice rather that you may marry a Princess more worthy of you than I have been.'

'I beg of you, do not say such things.'

'But I am unworthy . . . a plain little Princess . . . and not a Princess of a great country either. . . . A Princess whose country made great demands on you . . . a Princess whose country you succoured and to whom you brought the greatest happiness she ever knew.'

'You shame me.' And suddenly he could no longer control his tears. He thought of all the humiliations he had forced her to suffer, and he swore that he would never forgive himself.

'Charles . . . Charles,' she murmured. 'I know not whether to weep or rejoice. That you should care so much for me . . . what more could I ask than this? But to see you weep . . . to see you so stricken with sorrow . . . that grieves me . . . it grieves me sorely.'

Charles was so overcome with remorse and emotion that he could not speak. He knelt by her bed, his face hidden, bent over the hand that he held. As she drifted into unconsciousness, she felt his tears on her hand.

Donna Maria came to stand beside the King.

'Your Majesty can do no good to the Queen . . . now,' she said.

He turned wearily away.

*

He was at her bedside night and day. Those about the Queen marvelled at his devotion. Was this the man who had supped nightly with my Lady Castlemaine, the man who was

171

deeply in love with the beautiful Mrs Stuart? He wished that his should be the hand to smooth her pillows, his the face she would first see should she awake, his the voice she should hear.

She was far gone in fever, and so lightheaded that she thought she was the mother of a son.

Perhaps she was thinking of the tales she had heard of Charles's babyhood, for she murmured: 'He is fine and strong, but I fear he is an ugly boy.'

'Nay,' said the King, his voice shaken with emotion, 'he is a very pretty boy.'

'Charles,' she said, 'are you there, Charles?'

'Yes, I am here, my love.'

'Your love,' she repeated. 'Is it true? But I like to hear you say it as you did at Hampton Court before ... Charles, he shall be called Charles, shall he not?'

'Yes,' said the King, 'he shall be called Charles.'

'It matters not if he is a little ugly,' she said. 'If he be like you he will be the finest boy in the world, and I shall be well pleased with him.'

'Let us hope,' said the King, 'that he will be better than I.'

'How could that be?' she asked.

And the King was too moved to continue the conversation. He bade her close her eyes and rest.

But she could not rest; she was haunted by the longing for maternity.

'How many children is it we have, Charles? Three, is it? Three children ... our children. The little girl is so pretty, is she not?'

'She is very pretty,' said Charles.

'I am glad of that, for I should not like you to have a daughter who was not lovely in face and figure. You care so much for beauty. If I had been blessed with great beauty ...'

'Catherine,' said the King, 'do not torment yourself. Rest. I am here beside you. And remember this: I love you as you are. I would not want to change you. There is only one thing I wish; it is that you may get well.'

*

Newly slaughtered pigeons were laid at her feet; she was bled continuously; a night-cap, made of a precious relic, was put upon her head; but the King's presence at her bedside seemed to give her more comfort than any of these things.

In the streets the people talked of the Queen's serious illness which might end in death; and it was generally believed that, if she were to die, the King would marry the beautiful Frances Stuart whose virtue had refused to allow her to become the King's mistress.

This thought excited many. Buckingham, in spite of his being banished from Mrs Stuart's company on account of his suggestion that she should become his mistress, had been restored to her favour. No one could build card-houses as he could; no one could sing so enchantingly, nor do such amusing impersonations; so Frances had been ready to forgive him on the understanding that he realized there were to be no more attempts at love-making. Buckingham, who thrived on bold plans, was already arranging in his mind for the King, on the death of the Queen, to marry Frances; and Frances's greatest friend and adviser would be himself.

Barbara, knowing these plans were afoot, was watching her relative cautiously. Buckingham had been her friend, but he could easily become her enemy. So Barbara was one of those who offered up prayers for the recovery of the Queen.

As for the King, he was so assiduous in his care for Catherine, so full of remorse for the unhappiness which he had caused her, that his mind was occupied solely with his hopes for her recovery.

The Duke and Duchess of York also prayed for Catherine's recovery, for it was said that she would be unable to bear children; and if this were true and she lived, it would mean that the King would be unable to remarry, thus leaving the way clear for their children to inherit the throne.

Speculation ran high through the Court and the country, but this ended when Catherine recovered.

One morning she came out of her delirium, and her anguish on discovering she was not a mother was considerably lessened by the sight of her husband at her bedside, and the belief that she might be a beloved wife.

He continued full of care for her, and the days of her convalescence were happy indeed. The King's hair had turned so white during her illness that he laughingly declared he looked such an old man that he must follow the fashion of the day and adopt a periwig.

'Could those grey hairs have grown out of your anxiety as to what would become of me?' she asked.

'Assuredly they did.'

'Then I think mayhap I shall enjoy seeing you without your periwig.'

He smiled, but the next time she saw him he was wearing it. He looked a young man with the luxuriant curls falling over his shoulders, although his face was lined and on his dark features there were signs of the merry life he lived. But he was tall and slender still and so agile. Then she remembered with horror that she had had all her beautiful hair cut off when the fever was on her, and that she must be plainer than she had ever been before.

Yet he seemed determined to assure her of his devotion; and when she was told that she must impute her recovery to the precious relics which had been brought to her in her time of sickness, she answered: 'No. I owe my recovery to the prayers of my husband, and the knowledge that he was beside me during my trial.'

FIVE

ALAS, as Catherine's health improved the King's devotion waned. It was not that he was less affectionate when they were together; it was merely that they were less frequently together. Irresistible attractions drew him away from Catherine's side.

Barbara had been delivered of a fine son whom she called Henry. The King had refused to own him as his child, yet Catherine knew that he often visited Barbara's nurseries to see those children whom he did accept, and it had been reported to her that he was mightily wistful when he regarded the new baby, and that Barbara was hopeful.

What a cruel fate this was! Barbara had child after child; in fact it seemed that no sooner was one born than another was on the way; and yet Catherine, who so longed for a child, who so *needed* a child, had lost hers and she was so weak after her

174

long illness that it was doubtful whether she would be fit to have another for some time.

It was a source of grief and humiliation to her to know that Barbara championed her, so little did the woman regard her as a rival. She had heard that Barbara had prayed fervently for her recovery – not out of love for her, of course, but because as a Queen she was so ineffectual that there was not the slightest need to be jealous of her.

The woman whom all were watching now, some with envy, some with speculation, was Frances Stuart. The King was becoming more and more enamoured every day, and Frances's determination not to become his mistress, while it might have seemed laudable to some, was ominous to others.

The affair of the calash seemed significant.

This beautiful glass coach, the first of its kind ever seen in England, was a French innovation which Louis's ambassador, hoping to ingratiate himself and his country with the King, had presented to Charles. The entire Court was enchanted by the dazzling vehicle and, as Charles gave most of his presents to one of his mistresses – usually Barbara – it was Lady Castlemaine who immediately declared her intention of being the first to be seen in it.

Barbara visualized the scene – herself ostentatiously cutting a fine figure in Hyde Park with the crowd looking on. They would have heard of the presentation of the calash, and they would realize when they saw her within it that her favour was as high as ever with the King.

There had been a reconciliation between Charles and her, for, although the King was in love with Frances Stuart, he could not remain faithful to a woman who denied him her favours, and he was still supping now and then at Barbara's house, although often it was necessary for her to have Frances as a guest in order to ensure the King's attendance.

Barbara was pregnant again, and although the King had not yet accepted Henry, she was certain that he would do so ere long, and she assured him that the child she now carried was undoubtedly his.

It was evening of the day when Gramont had presented the glass coach, and the King and Barbara were at last alone. Barbara, remembering how soulful Charles had looked while he watched the simpering little Stuart building her card-houses after she had insisted on the company's joining her in a madcap and very childish game of blind man's buff, had determined to show the Court and the world that her hold on the King was still firm.

'Tomorrow,' she announced, 'the calash should be shown to the people.'

'Ah, yes,' said the King absently. He was wondering whether Frances had seemed a little more yielding this evening. When he had kissed her during the game of blind man's buff she had not turned away; she had just laughed on a note of shrill reproof which might not have been reproof after all.

'You know how they hate things to be hidden from them, and they will have heard of the calash. They will expect to see it in Hyde Park as soon as the weather permits.'

' 'Tis true,' said the King.

'I would wish to be the first to ride in it.'

'I hardly think that would be meet,' said the King.

'Not meet! In what way?'

'The Queen has said that she would wish to ride in it with my brother's wife. She says that is what the people will expect.'

'The people will expect no such thing.'

'You are right,' said the King ruefully. 'And that points to our bad conduct in the past.'

'Bad conduct!' snorted Barbara. 'The people want to see the calash, not the Queen.'

'Then since it is the calash they wish to see, and the purpose of the ride is to please them, it matters not who rides in it. Therefore the Queen and the Duchess of York should do so.'

Barbara stood up, her eyes flashing. 'Everything I ask is denied me. I wonder that you can treat me thus!'

'I have always thought the truth much more interesting than falsehood,' said the King. 'You know you have been denied very little, and it is tiring to hear you assert the contrary.'

Barbara's common sense warned her. Her position with the King was not what it had been. Her great sensuality could stand her in good stead only for the immediate future. She knew that Frances Stuart had first place in the King's heart. But it maddened her now to think that it might have been Frances herself who had suggested that the Queen should be the first to ride in the calash. The sly creature was for ever declaring her devotion to the Queen; it was part of her campaign, like as not.

But Barbara was determined to ride in the calash.

She cried: 'So you are tired of me! You have taken my youth . . . all the best years of my life . . . and now that I have borne so many children . . .'

'Of whose parentage we must ever remain in doubt.'

'They are your children. Yours . . . yours! It is no use denying your share in the making of them. I have devoted my life to you. You are the King, and I have sought to serve you . . .'

'Barbara, I beg of you, make no scenes now. I have had enough of them.'

'Do not think to silence me thus. I am to have our child . . . our child, sir. And if you do not let me ride first in the calash I shall miscarry this child. Aye, and all the world shall know it was through the ill-treatment I received from its father.'

'They would not be very impressed,' said Charles lightly.

'Do not dare to laugh at me, or I shall kill myself . . . as well as the child.'

'Nay, Barbara. You love yourself too well.'

'Oh, will I not!' She looked about her and called wildly: 'A knife! A knife! Bring me a knife. Mrs Sarah! Do you hear me?'

The King went to her swiftly and placed his hand over her mouth. 'You will make it impossible for me to visit you,' he said.

'If you did not, I should make you repent it!'

'I shall repent nothing. It is only the righteous who repent.'

'You will. I swear you will. All the world shall know of what has been between us.'

'Calm yourself, Barbara. The world already knows half and the other half it will guess.'

'Don't dare talk to me thus.'

'I am weary of quarrels.'

'Yes, you are weary of everything but that smug-faced idiot. Do you imagine that she would interest you beyond a week? Even her simple mind realizes that. It is why she is so simperingly virtuous. She knows full well that once she gave way you'd be sick to death of her simple-mindedness. Simple-minded! She is half-witted. "Play a game of blind man's buff, sire?"' squealed Barbara and curtsied, viciously demure. ' "I do like a nice game of blind man's buff, because I can squeal so prettily, and say Nay, nay, nay when Your Majesty chases me!" Bah!'

In spite of his annoyance, Charles could not help laughing, for her mimicry, though cruelly exaggerated, had a certain element of truth in it.

'Charles,' she wheedled, 'what is it to you? Pray you let me ride in the calash ... just once; and after that let the Queen and the Duchess take the air in Hyde Park. You know the people would rather see me than the Queen or the Duchess. Look at me. ...' She tossed back her hair and drew herself to her full magnificent height. 'Would the calash not become me, think you? 'Twould be a pity to let it take its first airing in the Park without the most becoming cargo.'

'Barbara, you would wheedle the crown off my head.'

And I would, she thought, but for my cursed husband! And while I am fettered to him, Mrs Stuart stays coy and hopeful; and doubtless, in spite of all her piety and friendship for the Queen, she prays for Catherine's death.

Still, the calash, not the crown, was the immediate problem, and she believed that Charles was about to give way. She knew the signs so well.

Abruptly she stopped speaking of it and gave herself up to passion with such abandonment that she could not fail to win his response.

But when he left her in the early morning his promises about the calash were vague, and she was faintly worried.

*

Many heard the loud quarrels between Charles and Barbara. Now the Court was saying that Barbara had declared her intention of miscarrying the child – which she insisted was the King's – providing she was not the first to ride in the calash.

The Queen heard this and remembered with humiliation her request to the King that she and the Duchess should be the first to use it.

What mattered it, thought Catherine, who rode in the coach? It was not the actual riding which was significant.

The King put off the decision. He wanted to please the Queen, yet he was afraid of Barbara. He could not be sure what she would do. She made wild threats; she was always declaring that she would strangle this child, murder that servant, if her whims were not satisfied. So far as he knew, she had not carried out these threats to kill, but her temper was violent and he could not be sure to what madness it would lead her.

The Court sniggered about the wrangle concerning the calash. The country heard and murmured about it. It was a great joke – the sort of joke with which the King so often amused his people. But the calash was not seen in the Park, simply because the King did not wish to offend the Queen and dared not offend Barbara.

A few evenings later the King was supping in the apartments of Frances Stuart, and as she was sitting at the table – with him beside her – Frances's beautiful blue eyes were fixed on the flimsy structure of cards before her, while the King's passionate dark ones were on Frances. She turned to him suddenly and said: 'Your Majesty has often declared that you would wish to give me something which I clearly desired.'

'You have but to ask, as you know,' said the King, 'and it is yours.'

Everyone was listening. All were deciding: This is the end of her resistance. Frances has decided to become the King's mistress.

'I desire to be the first to ride in the calash,' said Frances.

The King hesitated. This was unexpected. He was beginning to wish he had never been presented with the thing.

He was aware of Barbara's burning blue eyes on him; he saw the danger signals there.

Frances continued to smile artlessly and continued: 'Your Majesty, the coach should be seen. The people long to see it. It would greatly please me to be the first to ride in it.'

Barbara stepped up to the table. With an impatient gesture she knocked down the house of cards. Frances gave a little cry of dismay, but the eyes which looked straight into Barbara's were pert and defiant.

Barbara said in a low voice: 'I have told the King that if I am not the first to ride in the coach I shall miscarry his child.'

Frances smiled. 'It is a pity,' she said. 'And if *I* am not the first to ride in the coach I shall never be with child.'

It was a challenge. There were three contestants now. The Court laughed more merrily than before.

They were sure it would be a battle between Barbara and Frances.

The King, faintly exasperated by this public display of rivalry, said: 'This calash seems to have turned all heads. Where is my lord Buckingham? Ah, my lord Duke, sing to us ... sing, I pray you. Sing of love and hate, but sing not of coaches!'

So Buckingham sang; and Barbara's blazing eyes were fixed on the slender, youthful figure of Frances Stuart while he did so.

*

The battle was over.

The Queen sat sadly in her apartments. She almost wished that she had not recovered from her illness. She mused: While I was ill he loved me. If I had died then I should have died happy. He wept for me; his hair turned grey for me; it was he who smoothed my pillows. I remember his remorse for all the jealousy I had been made to suffer on his account. He was truly sorry. Yet, now that I am well, I suffer as I ever did.

Barbara's jealousy took another form.

She strode up and down her apartment, kicking everything in her path out of the way. No servants would come near her except Mrs Sarah, and even she took good care to keep well out of reach.

All thought Barbara might do herself some injury; many hoped she would.

In her rage she tore her bodice into shreds; she pulled her hair; she called on God to witness her humiliation.

Meanwhile Frances Stuart was riding serenely in Hyde Park, and the calash made a very pleasant setting for such a beautiful jewel.

The people watched her go by and declared that never – even in those days when Lady Castlemaine had been at the height of her beauty – had there been such a lovely lady at the Court.

*

Catherine, watching the game Charles played with the women of his Court, often wondered whether he were capable of any deep feeling. Barbara took lovers shamelessly yet remained the King's mistress; in fact, he seemed quite indifferent to her amatory adventures which were the scandal of the Court. He seemed only to care that she received him whenever he was ready to visit her.

Frances, after the affair of the calash, had continued to hold back. She had promised nothing, she declared; and her conscience would not allow her to become the King's mistress.

Catherine was unsure of Frances. The girl might be a skilful coquette – as Barbara insisted that she was, for Barbara made no secret of her enmity now – or she might indeed be a virtuous woman.

Catherine believed her to be virtuous. It certainly seemed to her that Frances was sincere when she confided to the Queen that she wished to marry and settle down in peace away from the Court.

'Your Majesty must understand,' she had said, 'that the position in which I find myself is none of my making.'

Catherine determined to believe her, and sought to help her on every occasion.

She pondered often on the King's devotion to women other than herself. She remembered too the case of Lady Chesterfield. The Chesterfields remained in the country, but news came that the Earl was as much in love with his wife as he had been at Court, and that she continued to scorn him.

Catherine talked of this with Frances Stuart, and Frances answered: 'It was only when he saw how others admired her that he began to do so. That is the way of men.'

And I, thought Catherine, admired Charles wholeheartedly. I showed my admiration. I was without guile. He knew that no other man had ever loved me.

Edward Montague was often in attendance. He would look at her sadly when such affairs as that of the calash took place; it was clear that he pitied her. He was invariably at her side at all gatherings; his position as master of her horse necessitated that, but she was sure his feelings for her were stronger than those of a servant.

She often studied Edward Montague; he was a handsome young man and there was surely something of which to be proud in the devotion of such as he; so she smiled on him with affection, and it began to be noticed that the friendship between them was growing.

Catherine knew this, but did nothing to prevent it; it was, after all, a situation she had striven to create.

Montague's enemies were quick to call the King's attention to this friendship with the Queen; but Charles laughed lightly. He was glad that the Queen had an admirer. It showed the man's sound good sense, he said, because the Queen was worthy to be admired.

He was certainly not going to put a stop to the friendship; he would consider it extremely unfair to do so since he enjoyed so many friendships with the opposite sex.

Catherine, seeing his indifference to her relationship with her handsome master of horse, made another of those mistakes which turned the King's admiration for her to indifference.

Catherine's great tragedy was that she never understood Charles.

It so happened that, when she alighted from her horse and he took her hand, Montague held it longer than was necessary and pressed it firmly. It was a gesture of assurance of his affection and sympathy for her, and Catherine knew this; but when, longing for Charles's attention and desperately seeking to claim it, she artlessly asked what a gentleman meant when he held a lady's hand and pressed it, she was feigning an innocence and ignorance of English customs which were not hers.

'Who has done this?' asked the King.

She answered: 'It is my good master of horse, Montague.'

The King looked at her with pity. Poor Catherine! Was she trying to be coy? How ill it became her!

He said lightly: 'It is an expression of devotion, but such expressions given to kings and queens may not indicate devotion but a desire for advancement. Yet it is an act of insolence for Your Majesty's master of horse to behave thus to you, and I will take steps to see that it does not happen again.'

She believed she had aroused his jealousy. She believed he was thinking: So other men find her attractive; and she waited to see what would happen next.

Alas, Charles's attention was still on his mistresses and Catherine merely lost her one admirer.

Edward Montague was dismissed his office; not on account of the King's jealousy, but because Charles feared that Catherine's innocence might betray her into indiscretion if the man remained.

*

The King's love for Frances did not diminish.

He was subdued and often melancholy; a listlessness – so unusual with him – crept into his behaviour. He had accepted her reluctance at first as the opening phase in the game of love; but still she was unconquered; and he began to believe that she would never surrender.

His feelings were more deeply stirred than they had ever been before. For the first time in his life the King was truly in love.

Sometimes he marvelled at himself. It was true that Frances was very beautiful, but she completely lacked that quick wit which he himself possessed and which he admired in others. Frances was just a little stupid, some might say; but that seemed to make her seem more youthful than ever. Perhaps she provided such a contrast to Barbara. She never flew into tantrums; she was invariably calm and serene; she rarely spoke in an ill-natured fashion of anyone; she asked for little – the affair of the calash was an exception, and he believed she may have been persuaded to that, possibly by Buckingham whose head was, as usual, full of the most harebrained schemes; all she wished was to be allowed to play those games which delighted her. Frances was like a very young and guileless girl and as such she deeply touched the heart of the King.

It was Frances who now adorned the coinage – a shapely Britannia with her helmet on her charming head and the trident in her slender hands.

He brooded on her constantly and wrote a song to explain his feelings.

> 'I pass all my hours in a shady old grove,
> But I live not the day when I see not my love;
> I survey every walk now my Phyllis is gone,
> And sigh when I think we were there all alone;
> O then, 'tis O then, that I think there's no hell
> Like loving like loving too well.
> While alone, to myself I repeat all her charms,

She I love may be locked in another man's arms,
She may laugh at my cares, and so false may she be
To say all the kind things she before said to me;
O then, 'tis O then, that I think there's no hell
Like loving too well.
But when I consider the truth of her heart,
Such an innocent passion, so kind without art;
I fear I have wronged her, and hope she may be
So full of true love to be jealous of me;
And then 'tis, I think, that no joy be above
The Pleasures of love.'

And while the King brooded on his unfulfilled passion for
Frances, state matters were not progressing satisfactorily. He
would be called to hasty council meetings and there were long
consultations with Clarendon, whose dictatorial manner was
often irritating. But, like Clarendon, Charles was alarmed
by the growing hostilities on the high seas between the Dutch
and the English.

The Duke of York, who had won fame as an Admiral of
the Fleet, was growing more and more daring. He had the
trading classes of the country behind him; and it was becoming clear that these people were hoping for a war with Holland. The Duke had captured Cape Corso and other Dutch
colonies on the African coast, a matter which had caused
some concern to the Chancellor which he had imparted to
Charles. The conquests, insisted Clarendon, were unjust and
were causing bad blood between the two countries. The Duke's
retort to Clarendon's warnings was to capture New Amsterdam on the coast of North America and immediately rename
it New York. He declared that English property in North
America had been filched by the Dutch, and it was only
seemly that it should be filched back again. Meanwhile there
were frequent hostile incidents when the ships of both nations
met.

Charles could see that if events continued to follow this
course there would indeed be war, for it seemed that he and
the Chancellor were the only men in the country who did not
wish for it. He himself was very much bound by his Parliament, and Clarendon was fast becoming the most unpopular
man in the country. The Buckingham faction had set in

progress rumours damaging to Clarendon, so that every difficulty and disaster which arose was laid at his door. It was
now being whispered that the selling of Dunkirk to the French
had been Clarendon's work, and that he had been heavily
bribed for his part in this, which was untrue. Dunkirk
had been sold because it was a drain on the expenses of
the Exchequer which was in urgent need of the purchase
money. Clarendon had only helped set the negotiations in
motion once it had been decided that the deal should go
forward.

So these were melancholy days for Charles. State affairs
moving towards a climax which might be dangerous; Charles
for the first time in love and denied the satisfaction he asked.

*

Mary Fairfax, the Duchess of Buckingham, was giving a ball.

While her maids were dressing her she looked at her reflection in the Venetian mirror with a fearful pride. Her jewels
were of many colours, for she liked to adorn herself thus and
she knew she wore too many and of too varied colours, but she
could never decide which she ought to discard. She was too
thin, completely lacking the slender grace of Frances Stuart;
she was awkward, and never knew what to do with her large
hands, now ablaze with rings. She feared though that the
jewels she wore did not beautify; they merely called attention to the awkwardness of those hands. Her nose was too
large as was her mouth; her eyes large and dark, but too
closely set together. She had always known she was no beauty;
and she could never rid herself of the idea that brightly
coloured gowns and many jewels would help her to hide her
deficiencies; it was only when she was in the company of some
of the beauties of the Court – ladies such as Lady Chesterfield,
Miss Jennings, Lady Southesk, Barbara Castlemaine and, of
course, the most beautiful Mrs Stuart – that she realized that
all of them, including Barbara, had achieved their effects by
less flamboyant means than she had employed.

She was neglected by her husband, the great Duke, but she
never resented this; she was constantly aware that she, Mary
Fairfax, was the wife of the handsomest man she had ever
seen; not only was he handsome, but he was witty, amusing,
sought after by the ambitious; and she continually told herself

that she was the most fortunate of women merely to be his wife.

She was remembering, as her maids dressed her, that happy time immediately following her marriage, before the King's return to England, when the Duke had played the faithful husband, and her father had told her so often that he rejoiced in her marriage.

Mary's husband was a strange man. He was brilliant, but it seemed that always there must be some plot forming itself within his mind. What joy when that plot had been to marry Mary Fairfax; and afterwards, when he had planned to make Mary a good husband! They had lived quietly in the country – she, her dearest George, and her father. How often had she seen them, her father and her husband, walking arm in arm while George talked of the book he was planning to write on her father's career. Those had been the happiest days of her life and, she ventured to think, of his. But the quiet life was not for him; and with the Restoration it was only reasonable that he should become a courtier and statesman. At Court it was natural that he should become the King's companion and the friend of those profligate gentlemen who lived wildly and consorted with women whose reputations were as bad as their own.

'Marriage,' he had said, 'is the greatest solitude, for it makes two but one, and prohibits us from all others.' A different cry that from the words he had so often spoken immediately before and after their marriage. Nor did he accept this 'solitude'; nor did he 'prohibit himself from all others'.

Life had changed, and she must accept the change; she was grateful for those occasions when she did see him, when, as on this one, he needed her help. It was rarely that he did so and it was not often that they were together.

Her father worried a great deal about the change in their relationship; he complained bitterly of the way in which George treated her. She was fortunate to be so loved by a great man like her father, but now he blamed himself because he had brought about this marriage; and again and again she soothed him and assured him that he had not wished for the marriage more than she had. All knew that Buckingham neglected her, that he had married her when his fortunes were at a low ebb and it had seemed as though the Monarchy would never be restored, but that marriage with the daughter of an old Parliamentarian was the best a man could make. She was glad that she had turned from Lord Chesterfield to Buckingham; she would never regret it, never, even though those who wished her well were sorry for her. Only recently one of the Duke's servants had made an attempt on his life when they had spent the night at the Sun Inn at Aldgate after returning from the Newmarket races. George had quickly disarmed the man. But the affair became widely known; and it was disconcerting that the point of the story should not be that the Duke was almost done to death by a mad servant, but that he should have been about to spend the night with his own wife.

Such slights, such humiliations, she accepted. They were part of the price which a plain and homely woman paid for union with one of the greatest Dukes in the country.

Now she asked her maids: 'How like you my gown?'

And they answered: 'Madam, it is beautiful.'

They were sincere. They really thought so.

'Ah,' said Mary quickly, 'if I could but get me a new face as easily as I get me a new gown, then I might be a beauty.'

The maids were excited because they knew that this was to be a very grand ball, and the King himself was to be present.

They did not know the purpose of the ball.

George had explained it to his wife. It was one of his plots and in this his conspirators were Lord Sandwich and Henry Bennet – who was now Lord Arlington.

'We cannot,' George had said, 'allow the King to become morose. He neglects his state business and he is not so amusing as he once was. The King wants one thing to make him his merry self again; and we are going to give it to him: Frances Stuart.'

'How will you do this?' she had asked. 'Is it not for Frances Stuart to make the necessary decision?'

'We shall be very, very merry,' said the Duke. 'There will be dancing and games such as Frances delights in. There shall be drink . . . potent drink, and we must see that Frances partakes of it freely.'

Mary turned a little pale.

'You mean that she is to be made incapable of knowing what she does!'

'Now you are shocked,' said the Duke lightly. 'That is your puritan stock showing itself. My dear Mary, stop being a hopeless prude, I beg of you. Move with the times, my dear. Move with the times.'

'But this girl is so young and . . .'

'And wily. She has played her games long enough.'

'George, I . . .'

'You will do nothing but be hostess to the guests; and make sure that we have a rich apartment ready for the lovers when they need it.'

She had wanted to protest; but she could not bear his displeasure. If she *must* play such a part for the sake of her Duke, she had not alternative but to do so.

She took one last look at herself and went downstairs to be ready to greet her guests.

And when she was in that glittering assembly she knew at once that her jewels were too numerous, the bright scarlet of her gown unbecoming to one of her colouring; she realized afresh that she was the ugly Duchess of the most handsome of Dukes.

*

Mrs Sarah wanted a word with her mistress, and she wanted it in private.

Barbara left her friends to hear what her servant had to say. She knew that Mrs Sarah, while often denouncing her to her face, was loyal.

Mrs Sarah began: 'Now, if I tell you something your ladyship won't like to hear, will you promise to hear me out without throwing a stool at me?'

'What is it?' said Barbara.

'Your promise first! It's something you ought to know.'

'Then unless you tell me this instant I'll have the clothes torn from your back and I'll lay about you with a stick myself.'

'Now listen to me, Madam.'

'I am listening. Come closer, you fool. What is it?'

'There is a ball this night at my lord Buckingham's.'

'And what of that? The fool can give a ball if he wishes to, without asking me. Let him sing his silly songs; let him do his imitations. . . . I'll warrant he has a good one of me.'

'The King is to be present.'

Barbara was alert. 'How know you this?'

'My husband, who is cook to my lord Sandwich . . .'

'I see . . . I see. The King is there; and is that sly slug there with him?'

'She is, Madam.'

'Playing card-houses, I'll swear. Let them. That's all the game he'll play with that lily-livered virgin.'

'Mayhap not this night.'

'What do you mean, woman?'

'There is a plot to bring them together this night. My lord Arlington . . .'

'The pompous pig!'

'And my lord Sandwich . . .'

'That prancing ape!'

'And my lord Buckingham . . .'

'That foul hog!'

'I beg of you remember, Madam, stay calm.'

'Stay calm! While that merry trio work against me? For that is what they would do, Sarah. They strike at me. They use that simpering little ninny to do so, but they strike at me. By God and all the saints, I'll go there and I'll let them know I understand their games. I'll throw their silly cards in their faces and I'll . . .'

'Madam, remember; so much is at stake. I beg of you do nothing rash. *She* remains calm. That is why she keeps his regard.'

'Are you telling me what to do, you . . . *you* . . .'

'Yes, I am,' said Sarah. 'I don't want you to hurt yourself.'

'Hurt myself! It is not I who shall get hurt. Do you think I do not know how to look after myself?'

'Yes, Madam, I do think that. I think that, had you been calmer and more loving and not so ready to fly into tantrums, His Majesty would have continued to love you even though, such being the royal nature, he hankered after Frances Stuart. Let me finish what I began to say. This night they plan to bring this affair to a conclusion. They will so bemuse Mrs Stuart this night that it will be easy to overcome her resistance. And when that is done, there will be the apartment waiting and the royal lover to conduct her to it.'

'It shall not be. I'll go there and drag the little fool away, if I have to pull her by her golden hair.'

'Madam, think first. Be calm. Do not demean yourself. There is one other who would not wish for the surrender of Mrs Stuart. Why not let her do your work this night? It would be better so if you would hold His Majesty's regard, for I verily believe that she who takes from him the pleasure he anticipates this night will not long hold his love.'

Barbara did not answer immediately; she continued to look at Mrs Sarah.

*

The two women faced each other.

This is the woman, thought Catherine, who has destroyed my happiness. She it was who, as a mere name long ago in Lisbon, filled me with misgivings.

Barbara thought: I would not barter my beauty for her plain mien even though the crown went with it. Poor Charles, he is indeed gallant to feign tenderness for such a one. She could never have appealed to him during all those weeks when he played the loving husband.

Barbara said: 'Your Majesty, this is not a time when two women should weigh their words. A plot is afoot this night to make an innocent girl a harlot. That is putting it plainly, but it is none the less the truth. The young girl is Frances Stuart, and I beg of Your Majesty to do something to prevent this.'

Catherine felt her heart beat very fast; she said: 'I do not understand your meaning, Lady Castlemaine.'

'Buckingham is giving a ball. The King is there. And so is Mrs Stuart. It is the Duke's plan to make her so bemused that she will be an easy victim.'

'No,' cried Catherine. 'No!'

' 'Tis so, Your Majesty. You know the girl. She is not very intelligent but she is virtuous. Can you stand aside and allow this to happen?'

'But no,' said Catherine.

'Then may I humbly beg of Your Majesty to prevent it?'

'How could I prevent that on which the King has set his heart?'

'You are the Queen. The girl is of your household. Your Majesty, if you attended this ball ... if you brought her back with you to your apartments, because you had need of her services, none could say you nay. The King would not. You know that he would never humiliate you . . . on a matter of etiquette such as this would be.'

Catherine felt her cheeks burning. She gazed at the insolent woman, and she knew her motive for wishing to rescue Frances had nothing to do with the preservation of Frances's virtue. Yet she could not allow Charles to do this. She could not allow Frances to become his unwilling mistress.

She was not sure what it was that prompted her to act as she did. It might have been jealousy. It might have been for the sake of Frances's virtue, for the sake of Charles's honour. She was sure that in all his numerous love affairs there could never yet have been an unwilling partner.

She turned to Barbara and said: 'You are right. I will go to the ball.'

*

It was three o'clock when the Queen arrived.

By this time the fun was fast and the games very wild and merry. Frances, the centre of attraction, had been induced to drink far more than usual; she was flushed and her eyes bright with the excitement which romping games could always rouse in her.

The King had scarcely left her side all the evening. Three pairs of eyes watched Frances – Buckingham's, Arlington's and those of Sandwich – and their owners were sure that very soon Frances would be ready to fall into the arms of the King.

And then the Queen arrived.

Buckingham and his Duchess must declare their delight in this unexpected honour. They hoped Her Majesty would stay and join the dance.

She danced for a while, and then she declared that she would return to Whitehall and take Frances Stuart with her.

If Frances left there was nothing to detain the King at the ball; so the evening ended very differently from the way in which it had been planned, and Frances and the King left for Whitehall in the company of the Queen.

*

Affairs of state were occupying the King continuously, so that he had little time for following pleasure. The Parliament were declaring that the damage inflicted on English ships was doing a great deal of harm to English trade. The merchants were demanding that the Dutch be taught a lesson. Dutch fishermen met English fishermen in the North Sea and fought to the death. On the Africa coasts Dutch and English sailors were already at war. In Amsterdam scurrilous pamphlets were published concerning the life of the King of England; and pictures were distributed showing a harassed King pursued by women who tried to drive him in all directions.

Charles was anxious. He loathed the thought of war, which he believed could bring little profit even to the victors. He had seen much of the sufferings due to war; his thoughts went back to that period of his life which would ever live vividly in his memory. He remembered Edgehill where he and James had come near to capture; but more clearly than anything that had ever happened to him would be the memory of disaster at Worcester and those weeks when he had skulked, disguised as a yokel, afraid to show his face in the country of which he called himself King.

But he knew that his wishes would carry little weight, for the whole country was calling out for war with the Dutch.

Every day, instead of sauntering in the Park he was on the Thames, inspecting that Fleet of which he was more proud than anything else he possessed.

He had told of his pride in it to the Parliament when he had asked them for money to maintain that Fleet.

'I have been able to let our neighbours see that I can defend myself and my subjects against their insolence. By borrowing liberally from myself out of my own stores, and with the kind and cheerful assistance which the City of London hath given me, I have a Fleet now worthy of the English nation and not inferior to any that hath set out in any age.'

After that speech he had been voted the great sum of two and a half million pounds for the equipment and maintenance of the Fleet; and although his pride in it was high, he was fervently hoping to avoid making open war on the Dutch.

That winter was the coldest that men remembered; but the great news was not of the phenomenal weather; it concerned the exploits of Dutchmen, for if Charles had a great Fleet, so had they, and they were as much at home on the high seas as were the English.

Barbara had given birth to another child – this time a daughter whom she named Charlotte. She declared she was the King's child, and this time the King was too immersed in matters of state to deny this.

By March it was necessary to declare war on Holland, and the whole country was wild with excitement. The City of London built a man-of-war which they called *Loyal London*, and the Duke of York took command of the Fleet.

The spring came, warm and welcome after the long, hard winter, and all at home waited news of the encounter between the Dutch and English navies. In London the gunfire out at sea could be heard, and the nation was tense yet very confident. They did not know that the money voted by Parliament for the conduct of war – a sum which seemed vast to them – was inadequate. There was one man who knew this and suffered acute anxiety. This was the King; he knew the state of the country's finances; he knew that he could not go on indefinitely subscribing to the maintenance of the Fleet in war out of his inadequate allowance; he knew that the Dutch were wealthier than the English, and that they were as worthy seamen.

When the news came of the victory over the Dutch, when the bells of the city pealed out and the citizens ran into the streets to snatch up anything that would make a bonfire, the King was less inclined to gaiety than any; he had heard news that Berkeley – recently become the Earl of Falmouth – had perished in the battle. He had known Berkeley well, and he guessed that he would be but one of many to suffer if the war continued.

Then in the streets of London there appeared a more cruel enemy than the Dutch.

In that warm April a man, coming from St Paul's into Cheapside, was overcome by his sickness, and lay down on the cobbles since he could go no farther. Shivering and delirious, he lay there, and in the morning he was dead; and those who approached him saw on his breast the dreaded macula, and, shuddering, ran from him. But by that time others were falling to the pestilence. From the Strand to Aldgate men and women on their ordinary business would stagger and hurry blindly to their homes. Some of those stricken in the streets could go no farther; they lay down and died.

The plague had come to London.

*

Who could rejoice wholeheartedly? It was true that the

English had taken eighteen capital ships from the Dutch off Harwich, and had destroyed another fourteen. It was known that Admiral Obdam had been blown up with his crew and would no longer worry the English. And all this had been achieved for the loss of one ship. It was true that many good sailors had been lost – Falmouth among them – with Marlborough and Portland and the Admirals Hawson and Sampson.

But the plague was on the increase, and its effect was already being severely felt in London. The weather was hotter than usual after the bleak winter. Stench rose from the gutters; refuse was emptied from windows by people who could not leave their houses since they kept a plague victim there. Men and women were dying in the streets. It was dangerous to give succour to any who fell fainting by the roadside. All indisposition was suspect. Many were frightened into infection in that plague- and fear-ridden atmosphere. Death was in the air and terror stalked the streets.

The river was congested with barges carrying away from the city those who were fortunate enough to be able to leave the plague spots.

The Court had retired, first to Hampton, and then, when the plague stretched its greedy maw beyond the metropolis, farther afield to Salisbury.

Albemarle took command of London and, with the resourcefulness of a great general, made plans for taking care of the infected and avoiding the spread of the plague. He arranged that outlying parishes should be ready to take in all those who could arrive uninfected from the city.

London continued to suffer in the heat.

Grass was now growing among the cobbles, for the business of every day had ceased. Those merchants who could do so, left their businesses; those who could not, stayed to nurse their families and to die with them. Trade had come to a standstill and the city was like a dead town. Those who ventured into its streets did so muffled in close garments covering their mouths that they might not breathe the polluted air.

Almost every door bore a red cross with the inscription 'Lord Have Mercy Upon Us' to warn all to keep away because the plague was in the house; by night the pest-carts roamed the streets to the tolling of a dismal bell and the dreadful cry of 'Bring out your dead'.

By the time that terrible year was over about 130,000 people had died of the plague in England. The citizens returned to London to take possession of their property, but the losses of life and trade were so great that the country, still engaged in war, was in a more pitiable plight than it had ever been in during the whole of its history.

It was at this time that Catherine discovered she was pregnant, and her hopes of giving birth to an heir were high.

*

The year 1666 dawned on a sorrowing people.

The plague had crippled the country more cruelly than many suspected. Since trade had been brought to a standstill during the hot summer months there was no money with which to equip the ships of the Navy. The French chose this moment to take sides with the Dutch, and England, now almost bankrupt and emerging from the disaster of the plague, was called upon to face two enemies instead of one.

The English were truculent. They were ready for all the 'Mounseers', they declared; but the King was sad; he was alarmed that that nation, to which his own mother belonged and to which he felt himself bound so closely, should take up arms against his; moreover two of the greatest Powers in the world were allied against one crippled by the scourge of death which had lately afflicted it and by lack of the means to carry on a successful war.

In March of that year bad news was brought from Portugal, but on the King's advice it was not immediately imparted to the Queen.

'It will distress her,' said Charles, 'and in view of her delicate health at this time I would have the utmost care taken.'

But it was impossible to keep the news long from Catherine. She knew by the tears of Donna Maria that something had happened, and she guessed that it concerned their country, for only then would Donna Maria be so deeply affected.

And at length she discovered the secret.

Her mother dead! It seemed impossible to believe it. It was but four years since they had said their last goodbyes.

Much had happened in those four years, and perhaps in her love for her husband Catherine had at times forgotten her mother; but now that she was dead, now that she knew she would never see her again, she was heart-broken.

She lay in her bed and wept silently, going over every well-remembered incident of her childhood.

'Oh, Mother,' she murmured, 'if you had been here to advise me, mayhap I should have acted differently; mayhap Charles would not now regard me with that vague tolerance which seems so typical of his feelings for me.'

Then she remembered all her mother had bidden her do; she remembered how Queen Luiza had determined on this match; how she had again and again impressed on her daughter that she, Catherine, was destined to save their country.

'Mother, dearest Mother, I will do my best,' she murmured. 'Even though he has nothing more than a mild affection for me, even though I am but the wife who was chosen for him and there are about him beautiful women who he has chosen for himself, still will I remember all that you have told me and never cease to work for my country.'

Tempers ran high during those anxious months.

When Catherine decreed that, in mourning for her mother, the Court ladies should appear with their hair worn plain, and that they should not wear patches on their faces, Lady Castlemaine was openly annoyed. She was affecting the most elaborate styles for her hair and set great store by her patches. Several noticed that, with her hair plain and her face patchless, she was less strikingly beautiful than before.

This made her ill-humoured indeed; and in view of the King's continued devotion to Frances Stuart, her temper was not improved.

As Catherine sat with her ladies one day in the spring, and Barbara happened to be among them, they talked of Charles.

Catherine said she feared his health had suffered through the terrible afflictions of last year. He had unwisely taken off his wig and pourpoint when he was on the river and the sun proved too hot; he had caught a chill and had not seemed to be well since then.

She turned to Barbara and said: 'I fear it is not good for him to be out so late. He stays late at your house, and it would be better for his health if he did not do so.'

Barbara let out a snort of laughter. 'He does not stay late at my house, Madam,' she said. 'If he stays out late, then you must make inquiries in other directions. His Majesty spends his time with someone else.'

The King had come into the apartment. He looked strained and ill; he was wondering where the money was coming from to equip his ships; he was wondering how he was going to pay his seamen, and whether it would be necessary to lay up the Fleet for lack of funds; and if that dire calamity should befall, how could he continue the war?

It seemed too much to be borne that Catherine and Barbara should be quarrelling about how he spent his nights – those rare occasions when he sought a little relaxation in the only pastime which could bring him that forgetfulness which he eagerly sought.

He looked from Catherine to Barbara and his dark features were stern.

Catherine lowered her eyes but Barbara met his gaze defiantly.

'Your Majesty will bear me out that I speak the truth,' she said.

Charles said: 'You are an impertinent woman.'

Barbara flushed scarlet, but before she could give voice to the angry retorts which rose to her lips, Charles had continued quietly: 'Leave the Court, and pray do not come again until you have word from me that I expect to see you.'

Then, without waiting for the storm which his knowledge of Barbara made him certain must follow, he turned abruptly and left the apartment.

Barbara stamped her foot and glared at the company.

'Is anybody here smiling?' she demanded.

No one answered.

'If any see that which is amusing in this, let her speak up. I will see to it that she shall very soon find little to laugh at. As for the King, he may have a different tale to tell when I print the letters he has written to me!'

Then, curbing her rage, she curtsied to the Queen who sat stiff and awkward, not knowing how to deal with such an outrageous breach of good manners.

Barbara stamped out of the apartment.

But on calmer and saner reflection, considering the King's

cares of state and his melancholy passion for Mrs Stuart, she felt she would be wise, on this one occasion, to obey his command.

Barbara left the Court.

*

Barbara was raging at Richmond. All those about her tried in vain to soothe her. She was warned of all the King had had to bear in the last few years; she was discreetly reminded of Frances Stuart.

'I'll get even with him!' she cried. 'A nice thing if I should print his letters! Why, these Hollanders would have something to make pamphlets of then, would they not!'

Mrs Sarah warned her. She must not forget that although Charles had been lenient with her, he was yet the King. It might be that he would forbid her not only the Court but the country; such things had happened.

'It is monstrous!' cried Barbara. 'I have loved him long. It is six years since he came home, and I have loved him all that time.'

'Others have been his rivals in your affections, and fellow-guests in your bedchamber,' Mrs Sarah reminded her.

'And what of *his* affection and *his* bedchamber, eh?'

'He is the King. I wonder at his tenderness towards you.'

'Be silent, you hag! I shall send for my furniture. Do not imagine I shall allow my treasures to remain at Whitehall.'

'Send a messenger to the King,' suggested Madam Sarah, 'and first ask his permission to remove your possessions.'

'Ask his permission! He is a fool. Any man is a fool who chases that simpering ninny, who stands and hold cards for her card-houses, who allows himself so far to forget his rank as to play blind man's buff with an idiot.'

'He might not grant that permission,' suggested Mrs Sarah.

'If he should refuse to let me have what is mine . . .'

'He might because he does not wish you to leave.'

'You dolt! He has banished me.'

'For your insolence before the Queen and her ladies. He may be regretting that now. You know how he comes back again and again to you. You know that no one will ever be quite the same as you are to him. Send that messenger, Madam.'

Barbara gazed steadily at Mrs Sarah. 'Sarah, there are times when I think those who serve me are not all as doltish as I once thought them to be.'

So she took Sarah's advice and asked the King's permission to withdraw her goods; the answer she had hoped for came to her: If she wished to take her goods away she must come and fetch them herself.

So, with her hair exquisitely curled, and adorned by a most becoming hat with a sweeping green feather, and looking her most handsome, she took barge to Whitehall. And when she was there she saw the King; and, taking one look at her, and feeling, as Mrs Sarah had said he did, that no one was quite like Barbara, he admitted that her insolence at an awkward moment had made him a little hasty.

Barbara consented to remain at Whitehall. And that night the King supped in her apartments, and it was only just before the Palace was stirring to the activities of a new day that he left her and walked through the privy gardens to his own apartments.

*

All that summer the fear of plague was in the hearts of the citizens of London; the heat of the previous summer was remembered, and the dreadful toll which had been taken of the population. Through the narrow streets of wooden houses, the gables of which almost met over the dark streets, the people walked wearily and there was the haunting fear on their faces. From the foul gutters rose the stink of putrefying rubbish; and it was remembered that two or three times in every hundred years over the centuries the grim visitor would appear like a legendary dragon, demanding its sacrifice and then, having taken its fill of victims, retreat before the cold weather only to strike again, none knew when.

Catherine found this time a particularly anxious one. She was worried about her brother Alphonso who she knew was unfit to wear the crown; she knew that Pedro, her younger brother, coveted it; and now that the restraining hand of her mother would not be there to guide them, she wondered continually about the fate of her native country.

The condition of her adopted country was none too happy at this time. She knew of Charles's anxieties. She knew too that he was beginning to despair of her ever giving him an heir. Again her hopes had been disappointed. Why was it that so many Queens found it hard to give their husbands sons, while those same Kings' mistresses bore them as a matter of course? Barbara had borne yet another child – this time a handsome boy, whom she called George Fitzroy. Barbara had, as well as her voluptuous person, a nursery full of children who might be the King's.

In June of the year which followed that of the great plague the Dutch and English fleets met. De Ruyter and Van Tromp were in charge of the Dutchmen, and the English Fleet was under Albemarle. There were ninety Dutch ships opposed to fifty English, and when the battle had been in progress for more than a day, the Dutch were joined by sixteen sail. Fortunately Prince Rupert joined the Duke of York and a mighty battle was the result; both sides fought so doggedly and so valiantly that neither was victorious; but, although the English sank fifteen Dutch ships and the Dutch but ten English, the Dutch had invented chain-shot with which they ruined the rigging of many more of the English ships; and all the latter had to retire into harbour for refitting.

Yet a few weeks later they were in action once more, and this resulted in victory for the English, with few English losses and the destruction of twenty Dutch men-of-war.

When the news reached England, the bells rang out in every town and hamlet and there was general rejoicing in London which, but a year ago, had been like a dead and desolate city.

These celebrations took place on August 14th. Hopes were high that ere long these proud and insolent Dutchmen would realize who would rule the sea.

It was less than two weeks later when, in the house of Mr Farryner, the King's baker, who lived in Pudding Lane, fire broke out in the early morning; and as there was a strong east wind blowing and the baker's house was made of wood, as were those of his neighbours, in a few hours all Pudding Lane and Fish Street were ablaze and the streets were filled with shouting people who, certain that their efforts to quench the raging furnace were in vain while the high wind persisted, merely dragged out their goods from those houses which were in danger of being caught by the flames, wringing their hands, and declaring that the vengeance of God was turned upon the City.

Through the night, made light as day by the fires, people shouted to each other to come forth and flee. The streets were filled with those whose one object was to salvage as many of their household goods as was possible; and the wind grew fiercer as house after house fell victim to the flames. People with blackened faces called to each other that this was the end of the world. God had called vengeance on London, cried some, for the profligate ways of its people. Last year the plague and the Dutch wars, and now they were all to be destroyed by fire!

Showers of sparks shot into the air and fell like burning rain when a warehouse containing barrels of pitch and tar sent the blaze roaring to the sky. The river had suddenly become jammed with small craft, as frantic householders gathered as many as possible of their goods together and sought the green fields beyond the City for safety. Many poor people stood regarding their houses with the utmost despair, their arms grasping homely bundles, loth to leave their homes until the very last minute. Pigeons, which habitually sheltered in the lofts of these houses, hovered piteously near their old refuge and many were lying dead and dying on the cobbles below, their wings burned, their bodies scorched.

And all through the night the wind raged, and the fire raged with it.

*

Early next morning Mr Samuel Pepys, Secretary of the Navy, reached Whitehall and asked for an audience with the King; he told him all that was happening in the City, and begged him to give instant orders that houses be demolished, for only thus could such a mighty conflagration be brought to a halt. The King agreed that the houses which stood in the way of the fire must be pulled down, as only by making such gaps could the conflagration be halted, and gave orders that this should be done.

Pepys hurried back to the City and found the Lord Mayor in Cannon Street from where he was watching the fire and shouting in vain to the crowds, imploring them to listen to him, and try to fight the fire.

'What can I do?' he cried. 'People will not obey me. I have been up all night. I shall surely faint if I stay here. What can I do? What can any do in such a raging wind?'

The Secretary, thinking the man was more like a fainting woman than a Lord Mayor, repeated the King's order.

'I have tried pulling down houses,' wailed the Lord Mayor. 'But the fire overtakes us faster than we can work.'

They stood together, watching the flames which, in some places, seemed to creep stealthily at first, as tongues of fire licked the buildings and then suddenly, with a mighty roar, would appear to capture yet another; the sound of falling roofs and walls was everywhere; the flames ran swiftly and lightly along the thatches; now many streets were avenues of flame. People screamed as the fire-drops caught them; flames spread like an arch from one side of London Bridge to the other; the air was filled with the crackling sound of burning and the crash of collapsing houses. It was almost impossible to breathe the dense smoke-filled air.

*

On Tuesday morning the fire was still raging, and the King decided that he dared no longer leave the defence of his capital to the Lord Mayor and the City Fathers.

Fleet Street, the Old Bailey, Ludgate Hill, Warwick Lane, Newgate, Paul's Chain and Watling Street were all ablaze. The heat was so fierce that none could approach near the fire, and when a roof fell in great showers of sparks would fly out from the burning mass to alight on other dwellings and so start many minor fires.

The King with his brother, the Duke of York, were in the centre of activity. It was they who directed the blowing-up of houses in Tower Street. The citizens of London saw their King then, not as the careless philanderer, but the man of action. It was he, his face blackened by smoke, who directed the operations which were to save the City. There he stood passing the buckets with his own hands, shouting to all that their help was needed and they would be rewarded for the work they did this day. There he stood, with the dirty water over his ankles, encouraging and, being the man he was, not forgetting to joke. It was while he stood in their midst that the people ceased to believe those stories which the Puritans had murmured about God's vengeance. This fire was nothing but the result of an accident which had taken place in a baker's kitchen and, on account of the high wind, the dry wood and thatch of the houses all huddled so closely together, had turned the fire in Pudding Lane into the Fire of London.

By Thursday the fire showed signs of being conquered. The heat from smouldering buildings was still intense; fires raged in some parts of the City, but that great ravaging monster had been checked.

It was said that day that all that was left of London owed its existence to the King and his brother James.

*

Now it was possible to look back and see the extent of the disaster.

The fire, following so soon on the plague, had robbed the country of the greater part of its wealth. London was the centre of the kingdom's riches, for more than a tenth of the population had lived in the Capital. Now the greater part of the City lay in ruins, and for months afterwards ashes, charred beams, and broken pieces of furniture were found in the fields of the villages of Knightsbridge and Kensington; and the people marvelled that the effects of the great fire could still be seen at such great distance.

But there were more terrible effects to be felt. In the fields the homeless huddled together, having nowhere to go. The King rode out to them, bags of money at his belt; he distributed alms and ordered that food and shelter should be found for these sufferers.

His heart was heavy. He knew that never before in her history had England been in such a wretched plight. There was murmuring all over the country and in particular throughout the stricken City. England was no longer merry, and people were beginning to think of the period of Puritan rule as the 'good old days'. The wildest rumours were in the air. New terrors stalked the smouldering streets. The fire was the work of Papists, said some. Those who were suspected of following the Catholic religion were seized and ill-treated and some were done to death by the mob. Feeling ran high against the Queen. She was a Papist, and trouble had started during the last King's reign, declared the people, on account of his

Papist wife. Others said the profligate life led by the King and his associates was responsible for the fire.

'This is but the beginning,' cried some. 'The destruction of England is at hand. First the plague; then the war; and now the great fire. This is Sodom and Gomorrah again. What next? What next?'

The King realized that there was nothing to be done but lay up the Fleet, for where in his suffering country could he get means to maintain it? And to lay up the Fleet meant suing for peace.

Sailors were rioting in the stricken City's streets because they had not been paid. There was revolution in the air. Charles himself rode out to do what he could to disperse the groups of angry seamen. In vain did his Chancellor and those about him seek to restrain him. His subjects were in an ugly mood; insults had been hurled at the King on account of his way of life. But Charles insisted on going among them. He was bankrupt in all save that one thing which had stood him in good stead all his life; his charm was inviolate as was his courage.

So he rode out into the midst of the brawling crowds of angry sailors who stood about in the heart of the City amid the blackened buildings and heaps of ashes and rubble. He knew their mood; yet he was smiling, with that charming rueful smile. His manner was dignified, yet all those men were aware of the easy affability which had always been shown to any who came near him whatever their rank, and which had done much to make all submit to his charm.

They fell back before him; they would have expected him to come with soldiers behind him; but he came alone, and he came unarmed. So they fell back before him and they were silent as he spoke to them.

It was true they had not been paid. The King would remedy that as soon as it were possible to do so. They had fought gallantly. Would they tell themselves that they had fought for their country, and would that suffice for a temporary reward? He promised them that they should be paid – in time. They would be wise men to wait for that payment rather than to persist in acts which would lead themselves and others into misfortune likely to end in the traitor's fate on the gallows.

They had all suffered terribly. The plague last year; the fire this. Never in the country's history had such calamities befallen it. Yet had they not given good account of insolent Dutchmen? Let them all stand together; and if they would do this, their King doubted not that ere long they would have little cause for complaint.

Then suddenly someone in the crowd cried: 'Long live the King!' and then others joined in and helped to disperse the mob.

On that occasion trouble had been avoided, but revolt continued to hang in the air.

The people looked about them for a scapegoat and, as usual at such times, their thoughts turned to the Chancellor. Crowds gathered outside the fine house he had built for himself in Piccadilly; they murmured to one another that he had built the palace with the bribes he had been paid by the French King to advise the selling of Dunkirk. It was remembered that he, the commoner, was linked with the royal family through the marriage of his daugher Anne Hyde with the King's brother. It was said that he had procured Catherine of Braganza for the King because he knew she would never bear children and thus leave the succession clear for the offspring of his own daughter. Everything that was wrong in the country was blamed on Clarendon; and this attitude towards the poor Chancellor was aggravated by such men as Buckingham – urged on by Lady Castlemaine – Arlington, and almost all the King's ministers.

A gibbet was set up on a tree outside the Chancellor's house, and on it was an inscription:

'Three sights to be seen—
Dunkirk, Tangier, and a barren Queen.'

For the sale of Dunkirk, the possession of an unprofitable seaport and the Queen's inability to bear children successfully were all laid at Clarendon's door.

The King sought to throw off his melancholy and was already instructing his architect, Christopher Wren, to make plans for the rebuilding of the City; he was urging the Parliament to find money somehow for the refitting of his ships that they might, with the coming of spring, be ready to face their Dutch enemies. He sought to find consolation among the many ladies who charmed him, but he found that his desire for the still unconquered Frances Stuart made contentment impossible.

*

There were men about the King now who, perceiving his infatuation for Frances Stuart, reminded him of how his predecessor, Henry VIII, had acted in similar circumstances. Chief among these was the Duke of Buckingham who, much to Barbara's annoyance, had made himself chief adviser and supporter of Frances Stuart.

What if there were a divorce? The Queen's religion displeased the people. After the disaster of the fire it could easily be suggested that this had been started by Papists. No English man or woman would desire then to see the King remain married to a member of that wicked sect. Moreover, the Queen was barren and surely that was a good enough reason for divorcing her. It was necessary for the King to have an heir and Charles had proved again and again that he was not to blame for this unfruitful marriage.

'It should not be difficult to obtain a divorce,' said Buckingham. 'Then Your Majesty would be free to marry a lady of your own choice. I doubt that Mrs Stuart would say no to a crown.'

The King was tempted. Frances had become an obsession. Through her he was losing his merry good humour. He was angry far more often than he used to be. He was melancholy; he wanted to be alone, whereas previously he had enjoyed company; he was spending more and more time in his laboratory with his chemists, but what compensation could that offer? It was Frances whom he wanted; he was in love. If Frances would become his mistress he was sure that he could forget, for long spells at a time, the sorry condition of his realm and all the troubles that were facing him.

Then he remembered Catherine – the Catherine of the honeymoon – so naïvely eager to please him, so simple, so loving. He had wronged her when he had made her accept Barbara. No! In spite of his love for Frances he would not agree to ill-treat Catherine.

He continued melancholy; but his temper blazed out when Clarendon again took up his tutorial attitude towards him.

'It is more important to Your Majesty to give attention to state matters that to saunter and toy with Lady Castlemaine.' How often had the man said those or similar words, and how often had they been received with a tolerant smile!

Now the Chancellor was told to look to his own house and not try to set that of his master in order.

Clarendon was unrepentant; he prided himself on his forthright manners. He knew he was unpopular but he did not care; he said that all that mattered to him was that he should do his duty.

The Chancellor began to look upon Frances Stuart as an unhealthy influence, and thought that the best thing she could do was to marry. Her cousin, the Duke of Richmond – another Charles Stuart – was one of the many young men who were in love with her and having recently become a widower was eager to marry her. He was rich, of high rank, being distantly related to the King as Frances was. The Chancellor therefore called the young Duke to him and urged him to continue with his wooing. And when he had seen him and discovered that was just what the young man was most eager to do, he sought an audience with the Queen.

They looked at each other – Queen and Chancellor.

Catherine's appearance had not been improved by all she had suffered. She knew of the people's animosity towards herself; she knew that they hated her because she was a Catholic, and concocted rhymes about her which they sang in the streets; and that these rhymes were witty and ribald after the manner of the day.

She guessed too that certain of the King's ministers had spoken against her, because Charles had been particularly kind to her of late, which meant, she realized now that she had come to know him, that he felt sorry for her and was doubtless urging himself not to listen to his ministers' advice.

There was a numb desolation in Catherine's heart. She knew that they were advising him to rid himself of her. What would become of her? she wondered. Whither should she go? Home to Portugal where her brothers wrangled for the crown, a disgraced Queen, turned away by her husband because she could not bear him children and had failed to win his love and that of his subjects? No! She could not go back to Portugal. What was there for her, but a nunnery! She thought of the years stretching out ahead of her – she was a young woman still – of matins and complines, of bells and prayers; and all the time within her there would be longings which she must stifle, for whatever happened she would never forget Charles; she would love him until the day she died.

Last night he had stayed with her; he had resisted all temptation to go to one of his mistresses. She had been sick and overtaken with trembling, so fearful was she of what the future held for her.

How she despised herself! When she had the opportunity of being with him she was unable to make use of it. How could she hope to arouse anything but pity within him? His kindness she enjoyed was due, not to her attractiveness nor her cleverness, but merely to his goodness of heart. When she had been sick it was he who had brought the basin, and held her head and spoken soothing words; it was he who had called her women, to make her clean and comfortable, while uncomplaining he left the royal bed and moved to another room.

She could enjoy his kindness, but never his love.

Those were her thoughts when Clarendon was shown into her presence.

The Chancellor spoke in his usual blunt but somewhat pompous and authoritative manner.

'Your Majesty will have heard rumours concerning Mrs Stuart?'

'Yes, my lord, that is true,' agreed Catherine.

'I am sure Your Majesty will agree with me that the Court would be a happier place if Mrs Stuart were married, and mayhap left it for a while. Her cousin, the Duke of Richmond, would be an excellent match. It would be well for those of us who wish Mrs Stuart good to do all in our power to bring such a match about.'

'You are right, my lord.'

'Perhaps a word to the Duke from Your Majesty would be of use; and, as Mrs Stuart's mistress, Your Majesty might see that the young people have every opportunity to meet.'

Catherine clenched her hands tightly together and said: 'I will do all in my power to bring this matter to a happy conclusion.'

Clarendon was pleased. He, the Queen, and the Duke of

Richmond were determined to bring about this marriage. There was one other who would be equally delighted to see it take place. That was Lady Castlemaine. And if Frances herself could be made to realize the advantages of the match, it must surely come about.

*

Barbara, whose spies were numerous, discovered that the Duke of Richmond was often in the company of Frances Stuart and that the conversations which took place between them were of a tender nature. Infuriated by the rumours she had heard of the King's contemplating a divorce that he might marry Frances, Barbara had one object in mind – and that was to ruin Frances in the King's eyes.

She did not believe that Frances was seriously contemplating marriage with her cousin, the Duke of Richmond. What woman, thought Barbara scornfully, would become a Duchess when the prospect of becoming a Queen was dangling before her?

She suspected Frances of being very sly and, in spite of her apparent ingenuousness, very clever. Barbara could be angry with herself when she came to believe that she, no less than others, had been duped by Frances's apparent simplicity.

No! said Barbara. What the sly creature is doing is holding on to her virtue where the King is concerned, following the example of other ladies in history such as Elizabeth Woodville and Anne Boleyn. It may even be that she is not averse to entertaining a lover in private!

One day she discovered through her spies that the Duke of Richmond was in Frances's apartment, and she lost no time in seeking out the King.

She waved away his attendants in a manner which annoyed him, but he did not reprove her for this until they had left.

Then she shouted at him: 'Would you have them remain to hear what I have to say? Would you have them know – though doubtless they do already – what a fool Frances Stuart makes of you?'

The King's calmness could always be shaken by the mention of Frances, and he demanded to know to what she referred.

'We are so virtuous, are we not?' mimicked Barbara. 'We cannot be your mistress because we are so pure.' Her blue eyes flashed, and her anger blazed forth. 'Oh, no, no, no! We cannot be your mistress because we think you may be fool enough to make us your Queen.'

'Be silent!' cried the King. 'You shall leave the Court. I'll never look on your face again.'

'No? Then go and look on hers now ... Go and catch her and her lover together, and then thank me for showing you what a fool that sly slut has made of you.'

'What is this?' demanded the King.

'Nothing ... Nothing at all. Merely that your pure little *virgin* is at this moment languishing in the arms of another Charles Stuart. It would seem that she hath a fancy for the name. Only one is a King and to be dangled on a string, and the other ... is merely a Duke, so there is no sense in being *quite* so pure with him.'

'You lie,' growled the King.

'You are afraid of what you'll discover. Go to her apartment now. Go ... Go! And then thank me for opening your besotted eyes.'

The King turned and hurried from the room. He went immediately to Frances's apartments; he pushed aside her attendants and went straight into that chamber where Frances was lying on a couch and the Duke of Richmond was sitting beside her holding her hand.

The King stood, legs apart, looking at them.

The Duke sprang to his feet. Frances did likewise.

'Sire ...' began the Duke.

'Get out of here,' said the King ominously; and the Duke backed to the door and hurried away.

'So,' said the King, turning to Frances, 'you entertain your lovers alone at times. Did you find his proposals to your liking?'

Frances said: 'They were honourable proposals.'

'Honourable! And he here alone in your apartment?'

'Your Majesty must see that ...'

'I know nothing of your behaviour to this man,' said the King. 'I can only draw conclusions, and I see this: that you, who have been so careful not to be alone with me, employ not the same care in his case.'

Frances had never seen Charles angry with her before, and she was alarmed; but she did not tremble before him; she knew he would not harm her.

She said: 'Your Majesty, the Duke came hither to talk to me in an honourable fashion. He has no wife.'

'How far has this gone?'

'No farther than you saw. How could it? I would never submit to any man except my husband.'

'And you plan that he shall be that?'

'I plan nothing . . . yet.'

'Then he should not be here in your apartments.'

'Are the customs of the Court changing then?'

'We have always heard that you were set apart, that you did not accept the standards of the rest of us frail folk.'

He took her by the shoulders suddenly; his face was dark with passion.

'Frances,' he pleaded. 'Have done with folly. Why do you so long hold out against me?'

She was frightened; she wrenched herself free and, running to the wall, clutched at the hangings as though childishly wishing to hide herself among them.

'I beg of Your Majesty to leave me,' she said.

She realized that his anger was still with him. He said: 'One day mayhap you will be ugly and willing! I await that day with pleasure.'

Then he left her, and she knew that her relationship with the King had taken a new turn.

*

Frances, her fear still upon her, sought audience with the Queen.

She threw herself at Catherine's feet and burst into tears.

'Your Majesty,' she cried, 'I beg of you to help me. I am afraid. I have aroused the wrath of the King, and I have never seen him angry before. I fear that when his wrath is aroused it is more terrible than in those to whom anger comes more often.'

'You had better tell me what has happened,' said Catherine.

'He disturbed me with the Duke. He was furious with us both. The Duke has fled from Court. I know not what to do.

He has never looked at me as he did then. He suspected . . . I know not what.'

'I think,' said Catherine sadly, 'that he will not long be displeased with you.'

'It is not that I fear his displeasure, Your Majesty. He believes the Duke to be my lover; and I fear he will not have the same respect for me as hitherto.'

'That may be true,' agreed Catherine.

She felt then that she hated the beautiful face which was turned up to hers, hated it as much as she hated that other bold and arrogant one. These women with their beauty! It was cruel that they should have the power to take so easily that for which she longed, and longed in vain.

At that moment she would have given her rank and all she possessed to be in Frances Stuart's place, loved and desired by the King.

He was angry with this girl, she was thinking; yet with me he never cared enough to be anything but kind.

She was aware of a rising passion within herself. She longed to rid the Court of all these women who claimed his attention. She believed he was tiring of Barbara, whose continual tantrums were at last wearing him down; but this young girl with her matchless beauty and her girlish ways was different. He loved this girl; he had even contemplated making her his wife. Catherine was sure of this.

She said suddenly: 'If you married the Duke you would have a husband to protect you. You would show the King that he was mistaken in thinking you had taken a lover. Would you marry the Duke? He is the best match you could make.'

'Yes,' said Frances, 'if it were possible. I would marry the Duke.'

'Can you keep a secret?'

'But of course, Madam.'

'Then say nothing of this, but be ready to leave the Palace should the summons come.'

'Whither should I go?'

'To marriage with the Duke.'

'He has gone away. I do not know where he is.'

'Others will have means of knowing,' said the Queen. 'Now go to your room and rest. Be ready to leave the Palace if need be.'

When Frances had gone, Catherine marvelled at herself. I

have come alive, she mused. I am fighting for what I desire more than anything on Earth. I have ceased to sit placidly waiting for what I want. Like others, I go out to get it.

Then she summoned one of her women and bade her bring the Chancellor to her.

Clarendon came, and they talked long and secretly together.

*

The King's fury and sorrow, when he learned that Frances had eloped, was boundless.

He could not bear to think of Frances and her Duke together. He knew the young husband to be a worthless person, a devotee of the bottle, and he did not believe that Frances was in love with him. That she should have chosen such a man increased his rage. He declared he would never see Frances again. He blamed himself for having caused that scene in her apartments; he suspected several people of being concerned in helping the lovers to elope, and he vowed that he would never forgive them. The only person he did not suspect was the Queen.

He believed Clarendon to be the prime mover in the affair, and both Buckingham and Barbara confirmed this belief.

Barbara was delighted. Not only was she rid of her most dangerous rival, but Clarendon was in disgrace because of it.

The King's natural easy temper deserted him on this occasion. He accused Clarendon and his son, Lord Cornbury, of conspiring to bring about the elopement, and for once would not let them speak in their defence. He was unable to hide his grief. All the Court now understood the depth of his feeling for Frances and that it was very different from the light emotions he felt for his mistresses.

This was the most unhappy time of his life. He dreaded the coming of the spring when his ships, still laid up and in need of repairs, would be required to set out to face their enemies; he did not know how he was going to make good the country's losses which were a direct result of the plague and the fire.

His position was wretched, and there was only one person at that time who could have made him feel that life was worth while. Now he had to think of her – for he could not stop thinking of her – in the arms of another man.

His rage and grief stayed with him; and at length he turned to one whose very outspoken vulgarity seemed to soothe him.

Barbara was in the ascendant again, and it seemed that the King was spending as much time with her as he had in the first days of his infatuation.

Barbara was determined that Buckingham should not go unpunished for his support of Frances Stuart, which was blatantly inimical to her interests.

Buckingham had become involved with a woman, notorious for her love affairs. This was Lady Shrewsbury, a plump, languorous beauty whose lovers were said to be as numerous as those of Barbara herself. She was a woman who seemed to incite men to violence, and several duels had been fought on her account. When he fell under her spell, Buckingham appeared to become more reckless than even he had been before, and was continually engaged in quarrelling with almost everyone with whom he came into contact. His passion for Lady Shrewsbury increased as the months passed. He followed her wherever she went; and she was by no means loth to add the brilliant and witty, as well as rich and handsome, Duke to her list of lovers. On their first meeting, the Earl of Shrewsbury had quarrelled with Buckingham, but neither Lady Shrewsbury nor Buckingham took the slightest notice of their marriage vows; and both the Earl and Lady Buckingham should, from their long experience, not have expected them to take such notice. Buckingham could not tear himself away from his new love; he was drinking heavily; he quarrelled with Lord Falconbridge, and the quarrel threatened to end in a duel. He tried to quarrel with Clarendon; he attacked the Duke of Ormond; at a committee meeting he pulled the nose of the Marquess of Worcester; he insulted Prince Rupert in the street, whereupon the Prince pulled him off his horse and challenged him on the spot. Only the King could pacify his infuriated cousin. There was a quarrel at the theatre whither he had gone with Lady Shrewsbury. Harry Killigrew, who was in the next box and was one of Lady Shrewsbury's discarded lovers, began attacking them both and shouting to all in the theatre that Lady Shrewsbury had been his mistress – and declaring indeed there was not a man in the theatre who might not aspire to the lady's favours, for she was insatiable in her demand for lovers – and that if the Duke believed he was her sole lover they could wager the very shirts on their backs that he was wrong.

The audience watched with great interest while the Duke ordered Killigrew to be quiet, and Lady Shrewsbury leaned forward in her box, sleepy-eyed, half smiling; for, next to getting men to make love to her, she liked setting them to fight each other; nor did she in the least mind being stared at.

Killigrew drew his sword and struck the Duke with the flat side of it. Buckingham thereupon sprang out of his own box and into Killigrew's, but Killigrew had already leaped out of his and was scuttling across the theatre. The Duke flew after him, to the delight of the audience who found this far more entertaining than the play which was being performed on the stage. The Duke caught Killigrew, snatched off his periwig and threw it high in the air; then he set upon the man until he begged for mercy.

Killigrew was given a short term of imprisonment for the offence, and banished; and Barbara persuaded the King that her relative should also be banished until he learned to be less quarrelsome.

So Buckingham departed for the country, taking with him his wife and Lady Shrewsbury. There, he declared, he was content to stay. He had his music and his mistress, his chemists and his uncomplaining wife.

He knew though that Barbara was responsible for his banishment, and he promised himself that he would not let her escape punishment altogether, although he agreed that in trying to promote a marriage between Frances and the King he had not acted in the interest of his fiery cousin.

In his pastoral retreat he would have stayed, had not one of those men, who had professed to be his friends, made an accusation of high treason against him; the charge was of forecasting the King's death by horoscope.

He was ordered to return to London and sent to the Tower.

Barbara was now furious that a member of her family should be so imprisoned. She had merely wished that he should receive a light rap over the knuckles for having supported Frances's interest against hers.

She had forgotten that the King was no longer in love with

her, and that it was only his acute sorrow in the loss of Frances which had made him turn to her. She believed her power to be as great as it had ever been, and she strode into his apartments, as soon as she heard the news, and cried aloud: 'What means this? You would imprison your best servant on the false testimony of rogues!'

The King cried in exasperation: 'You are a meddling jade who dabbles in things of which she knows nothing.'

Barbara was furious. 'You are a fool!' she shouted, not caring who heard her.

'Be careful!' he warned.

'Fool! Fool! Fool!' was Barbara's retort. 'If you were not one, you would not suffer your business to be carried on by fools that do not understand it, and cause your best subjects and those best able to serve you to be imprisoned.'

'Have done, you evil woman,' cried the King.

He strode away and left her; she fumed up and down the apartment, declaring that ere long she would have her cousin free. It should be learned that any who dared imprison a noble Villiers was the enemy of the entire family.

By that she meant Clarendon.

And it was not long before Barbara had her way. No case could be proved against Buckingham. The paper on which he was supposed to have drawn up the horoscope was given to the King, who confronted Buckingham with it; but the Duke declared he had never before seen it, and asked the King if he did not recognize his (Buckingham's) sister's writing upon it.

'Why, 'tis the result of some frolic of hers about another person whose birthday happens to be the same as Your Majesty's. Your Majesty's name does not appear on the paper.'

The King studied the paper afresh; he considered the whole matter to be too trivial for his attention, and he said so.

'Have done with this business,' he cried. 'There is no need to press the matter further.'

Buckingham was released, though he was wise enough to know that he must not yet appear at Court.

Clarendon had imprisoned him. He decided, and Barbara agreed, that Clarendon's day must soon be over.

*

The Fleet was crippled; the navy in debt to the extent of over a million pounds. There were two alternatives: not to repair the ships but to keep them laid up, and sue for peace; or bankruptcy.

Charles, with his brother, their cousin Rupert, and Albemarle passionately declared that the ships should be refitted at whatever cost to the nation; but the will of the Council prevailed.

The Dutch, however, were not prepared to make an easy peace. Why should they? They had had peaceful months in which to refit their ships; they had spent three times as much on the war as the English had. They believed that action was better than words at a conference table; and they were not going to lay up their ships merely because their enemy had been forced to do so.

It seemed to all Englishmen in the years to come that in June of the year 1667 there fell upon their land the greatest calamity which had ever touched its pride and honour.

On that warm summer's day some nine months after the Fire of London, the Dutch fleet sailed up the Medway as far as Chatham. They burnt the *Royal Oak,* the *Royal James* and the *Loyal London,* together with other men-of-war; they blew up the fortifications, and, towing the *Royal Charles,* they returned the way they had come, while their trumpeters impudently played the old English song 'Joan's Placket is Torn'; and on either side of the river Englishmen looked on, powerless to prevent them.

Crippled by the great plague and the great Fire of London, England suffered the most shameful defeat of her history.

*

The people were numb with shame and anger.

They could not understand how such an insult could be aimed at them. They had believed they were winning the war against Holland. They had shown themselves to be seamen equal to – nay, better than – the Dutchmen. They had not been defeated in action. It was plague and fire which had defeated them, together with the threat of bankruptcy.

Revolution was again in the air. Much money had been raised for the conduct of the war; why had it come to such a shameful end?

Someone was wrong. Someone must be blamed. And it was the custom to look to the most unpopular man in the kingdom on whom to fix blame.

Mobs pulled up the trees in front of Clarendon's Piccadilly house. It was true, shouted the people, that he had betrayed them. Was he not the friend of the French, and were the French not siding with the Dutch enemies of England? Who had sold Dunkirk? Who had married the King to a barren Queen that his own grandchildren might inherit the throne of England?

The people needed a scapegoat and, as Charles studied their mood, he knew that they must have him before Parliament reassembled.

Clarendon had been universally disliked since the early days of the Restoration; never had a man possessed more enemies. But for Charles's protection over the last years he would have long ago been set down from his high post.

Now Charles himself no longer desired his services. He had grown tired of the man's continual reproaches. No Chancellor should speak to a King as Clarendon talked to his. Charles had always been ready to listen to reproaches from men of virtue, because he knew that he himself was far from virtuous. He had always maintained that every man had a right to his opinion and to the expression of that opinion. It was a view with which Clarendon had not approved. But, thought Charles, while those virtuous people, who spoke their minds freely concerning the faults of others, might in many cases have right on their side, they became increasingly unattractive; moreover it was other people's faults which they surveyed with such contempt, while they were apt to turn a blind eye to their own. Such as Clarendon believed that if a man lived a pious life and was faithful to one woman – and she his wife – intolerance, cruelty and carelessness of the feelings of others were no sins. That is where I differ, thought Charles; for I hold malice to be the greatest of sins; and I cannot believe that God would wish to make a man miserable for the sake of taking a little pleasure out of his way.

But Clarendon must go. The country was demanding it; and if he stayed, the people might be incited to revolution. Moreover, Charles did not feel inclined to protect a man who, he was sure, had done everything in his power to rob him of Frances Stuart.

But he did not wish Clarendon to suffer more than need be. He remembered the good advice the old man had given him when he was a wandering prince.

So he called the Duke of York to him – for, after all, James was Clarendon's son-in-law – and they talked together concerning the Chancellor.

'He has to go,' said Charles.

James did not think so. James was a fool, alas. Charles wondered what would happen to him if he lived to wear the crown, which might easily come to pass, as he, Charles, was possessed, it would seem, of a barren wife.

'He is blamed for the conduct of the war,' said Charles. 'Did you not know that on the day the Dutch sailed up the Medway the mob broke his windows and pulled down the trees before his house?'

'He is not to blame. He took little part in the conduct of the war and only agreed to the suggestions of the experts.'

'People rage against him. They say he has excluded the right men from ministerial posts and given those posts to those whom he considered to be of the nobility. Since you made his daughter a possible queen, he has, you will admit, been inclined to be haughty to the more lowly.'

James's mouth was stubborn. Charles knew that in supporting his father-in-law he was obeying his wife, for James was known to be under Anne Hyde's control. Only a short while ago, Charles remembered, he had likened his brother to the henpecked husband in *Epicene*, or *The Silent Woman*, a play which had afforded him much amusement. Charles remembered ruefully that when he had mentioned this, one of the wits who surrounded him – and whom he had ordered to forget 'His Majesty' in the cause of wit – had wanted to know whether it was better to be henpecked by a mistress than a wife.

That made him think momentarily of Barbara. He was wishing that he could rid himself of her. Her rages were becoming more and more unbearable; they ceased to amuse as they had once done. If only Frances were at Court, and amenable!

The memory of Frances turned his thoughts back to

Clarendon who, he was sure, had done his best to arrange Frances's marriage.

He said: 'The people accuse him of advising me to rule without a Parliament.'

'That,' said James, 'was what our father tried to do.'

'I have no intention of doing it. James, face the truth. The peace we have concluded with the French and Dutch at Breda is a shameful one. The people must have a scapegoat. They demand a scapegoat, and none will do but Clarendon. Do you know that I have been threatened with the same fate which befell our father if I do not part with him? As for myself, his behaviour and humours are insupportable to me and all the world else. I can no longer live with it. I must do those things which must be done with the Parliament, or the Government will be lost. James, do you want to set out on your wanderings once more? Have you forgotten The Hague and Paris? Have you forgotten what it means to be an exile? But mayhap we were lucky to be exiles. Our father was less fortunate. Be practical, brother. Be reasonable. He is your father-in-law. He was my old friend. I forget not his services to me. Do not let his enemies seize him and make a prisoner of him. God knows what would be his fate if he were taken to the Tower. Go to him now. Urge him to retire of his own free will. I doubt not that then he will be saved much trouble.'

The Duke at length saw the wisdom of his brother's plan and agreed to do this.

*

After his interview with the Duke of York, Clarendon came to see the King. He still spoke in the manner of a schoolmaster. 'And have you forgotten the days of your exile so soon then?' he asked. 'Can you be so ungrateful as to cast off an old and faithful servant?'

Charles was moved to pity. He said: 'I warn you. I am sure that you will be impeached when the next Parliament sits. Too many are your enemies. If you value your own safety, resign now. Avoid the indignity of being forced to do so.'

'Resign! I have been your chief minister ever since you were a King in fact – and indeed before that. Resign because my enemies blame me for the Dutch disaster! Your Majesty knows that my policy was not responsible for that defeat.'

Charles said: 'The plague, the fire, our lack of money – they are responsible for our disasters. I know that, my friend. I know it. But you have many enemies, many who have determined on your ruin. You are growing old. Why should you not spend your remaining days in comfortable retirement? That is what I should wish for you. I implore you, give up the Seal on your own account, before they take it from you and inflict God knows what. They are in an ugly mood.'

'I shall never give up the Seal unless forced to do so,' said Clarendon.

Charles lifted his shoulders and left the apartment.

*

Barbara knew that Clarendon was with the King; she knew that the old man was receiving his dismissal. She was hilarious in her delight. For years she had worked for this – ever since the day he had refused to allow his wife to visit her.

Now she waited in her bedchamber and joked with those who had gathered round her to witness what they knew to be the humiliating dismissal of the Chancellor.

'Who was he to forbid his wife to see me!' demanded Barbara. 'I was the King's mistress; his daughter was the Duke's before she duped him into making her his wife. And do you remember how he disowned her ... how he declared he would rather see her James's mistress than his wife! Yet he thought his family too fine ... too virtuous to consort with me. Old fool! Mayhap he wishes he had not been so fine and virtuous now.'

'He has left the King,' cried one of her friends. 'He comes across the gardens now.'

Barbara ran out into her aviary that she might not miss the sight of the old man's humiliation.

'There he goes!' she called. 'There goes the man who was the Chancellor. Look you! He holds not his head so high as he once did.'

Then she broke into peals of mocking laughter, in which her companions joined.

Clarendon walked quickly on as though he did not hear them.

*

Clarendon's enemies, led by Buckingham, were not content with Clarendon's dismissal. They were determined to arraign him on a charge of high treason. Charges were drawn up, among which was one accusing him of betraying the King's confidences to foreign Powers, and as this was nothing less than high treason it was clear that his enemies were after the ex-Chancellor's blood.

Charles was perturbed. He agreed that Clarendon was too old for his task, that his manner caused nothing but trouble to all those – including the King himself – who came into contact with him; he knew that his enemies had determined to destroy him.

He wished to be rid of Clarendon; yet he would not stand by and see an old friend forced to the executioner's block if he could help it.

He sent word in secret to Clarendon, telling him that unless he left the country at once he would find himself facing a trial for high treason.

Clarendon at last saw reason.

On the night after he had received Charles's message he was on his way to Calais.

*

Barbara was delighted with the dismissal of Clarendon. She felt that her ascendancy over Charles was regained. She was congratulating herself on the disgrace of Frances Stuart who, she was sure, had wounded the King's *amour propre* to such an extent that she would never be taken back into favour again.

Barbara laughed over the affairs of Mrs Stuart and Clarendon with her newest lover – little Henry Jermyn, one of the worst rakes at Court, and one of the smallest men to be met there; it was amusing to have for lovers the little Jermyn and the six-foot-tall King. Barbara was momentarily contented.

As for Catherine, she was hopeful. She did not believe that Charles was really in love with Barbara, and she knew that he was deeply wounded by the elopement of Frances; she often rode out with the King, and the people who, blaming Clarendon for the Dutch disaster, had taken Charles back completely into their affection, would cheer them.

Everywhere the King went was sung the latest song from the

play *Catch that Catch Can* or *The Musical Companion*; and it was sung wholeheartedly.

> 'Here's a health unto His Majesty,
> With a fa, la, la;
> Conversion to his enemies,
> With a fa, la, la.
> And he that will not pledge his health,
> I wish him neither wit nor wealth,
> Nor yet a rope to hang himself,
> With a fa, la, la.'

Catherine would discuss with Charles his plans for rebuilding the City and, as he seemed to cease mourning over past failures and had his eyes firmly fixed on the future, she found that she could follow his lead.

If only she could have a child! Then she believed that, with his own legitimate son and a wife who was ready to love him so tenderly, she and Charles could build a very happy relationship. God knew that she was willing and she could not believe that he, who was the kindest man in the world, could feel otherwise.

Charles believed that the new cabinet council would succeed where Clarendon had failed. This was already beginning to be called the 'Cabal' because of the first letters of the names of the five men who were its members: Clifford, Arlington, Buckingham, Ashley, and Lauderdale. He was seeing Christopher Wren every day, and it seemed that before long a new City would spring up to replace the old one of wooden houses and narrow streets.

Catherine was delighted to hear good news from her own country, and to learn that her brother, Don Pedro, had now succeeded in deposing his brother Alphonso; for Alphonso had become duller-witted as time passed and now, being almost an imbecile, it had seemed that unless there could be a peaceful abdication and the security of Portugal assured by Pedro, the Spaniards might march and subdue the disunited land.

Everything is working towards some good end, decided Catherine.

But one day Donna Maria asked her if she had noticed that the King was visiting the theatre more regularly than usual.

Donna Maria had heard that there was a reason for this, other than the play itself.

*

Barbara was fuming.

'I can scarcely believe it!' she cried. 'So His Majesty will demean himself as far as that! He will go to a theatre and, because some minx on the stage leers boldly enough, the King is delighted. The King is in love with a low playing-wench.'

'Madam,' said Mrs Sarah, 'I beg of you make no scenes in public.'

Barbara slapped the woman's face, but not too hard. She valued Mrs Sarah too much.

'Madam,' said Mrs Sarah, standing back a little and placing her hands on her hips, 'the King is enamoured of a wench at the play. She dances a merry jig, and that pleases him.'

'A pretty state of affairs! No wonder the young men of this City are such that modest maidens dare not go abroad. No wonder no woman is safe!'

Mrs Sarah had turned aside to hide a titter.

'Don't dare laugh at me, woman, or you'll wish you'd never been born.'

'Come, my lady, *you're* not afraid to go abroad!'

'By God, no!' cried Barbara. 'Nor to go to the theatre and to order the crowd to pelt the lewd creature with oranges and to hoot her off the stage.'

'The King would not be pleased.'

'The King will not be pleased! And should I be pleased to see him so demean himself?'

Mrs Sarah turned away. Even she dared not say that there were some who would consider he demeaned himself far more by his subservience to Lady Castlemaine than by any light fancy he might have for a play-actress.

Barbara demanded that her hat with the yellow plume be brought for her, her carriage called.

'You're not going to the play, my lady?' cried Mrs Sarah.

'Of a certainty I am going to the play,' retorted Barbara.

With the patch under her right eye to set off the brilliance of those features, and the small spot by her mouth to call attention to the fullness of her lips, and ablaze with jewels to the value of some £40,000, she set out to see Dryden's new play *The Maiden Queen,* for the part of Florimel was played by an Eleanor Gwyn, and it was said that the King was somewhat taken with the actress, although he was more deeply involved with another play-girl named Moll Davies.

'Play-girls!' muttered Barbara. 'This is too much to be borne.' She would sit in her box – next to the King's – and she would look haughtily at the stage, and then perhaps he would compare her with the low creature who, it was said, had caught his fancy with her merry jig and playing of a part.

She was aware of the interest of the pit as she took her place in the box. She looked over their heads and appeared to be concentrating on the stage. She liked the common people to stare at her, and she was glad she was glittering with jewels, and that the yellow plume in her hat so became her. The orange girls stared at her in candid admiration; all eyes in the house were on her. The King and his brother, however, were watching the stage, and that maddened her.

And there was the girl – a small, bright, slender thing with tumbled curls and a cockney wit which the part would not suppress. A low-born player! thought Barbara; yet the King and the Duke were intent. And the player knew it; that was evident from the way in which she darted quick glances at the royal box.

The King knew Barbara was there; but he was growing very indifferent to Barbara – even to the scenes she would create. He kept his eyes on the stage.

But now one of the players had caught Barbara's attention. He was one of the handsomest men she had ever set eyes on, and what physique! Her eyes glittered and narrowed; mayhap there was an attraction about these players.

She turned to the woman who had accompanied her, and pointed to the man.

'Charles Hart, my lady. Eleanor Gwyn, they say, is his mistress.'

Barbara felt an inclination to laugh. She said to her woman: 'You will go to Mr Charles Hart and tell him that he may call on me.'

'Call on your ladyship!'

'Are you deaf, fool? That was what I said. And tell him there should be no delay. I will see him at eight of the clock this night.'

The woman was alarmed, but, like all those in Barbara's service, realizing the need for immediate obedience, left Barbara's box.

Barbara sat back, vaguely aware of the King in his box, of the girl on the stage, and the play which was about to end.

'I am resolved to grow fat and look young till forty,' said the impudent little player, 'and then slip out of the world with the first wrinkle and the reputation of five and twenty.'

The pit roared its approval and called: 'Dance your jig, Nelly. Dance your jig!'

The girl had come forward and was talking to them, and the King was laughing and applauding with all those in the pit.

Charles Hart! thought Barbara. 'What a handsome man!' Why had she not come to the theatre to look for a lover before now? And how piquant to take the lover of that brazen creature who was daring to throw languorous glances at the King!

*

The King was visiting Barbara less frequently; his relationship with the Queen had settled into a friendly one, but Catherine knew that she was as far as ever from reaching that relationship which she had enjoyed during the honeymoon. And it seemed to her that morals at the Court were growing more and more lax with the passing of the years.

The affair of Buckingham was characteristic of the conduct of the times. The Earl of Shrewsbury had challenged the Duke to a duel on account of his misconduct with Anna Shrewsbury, and on a cold January day they met. Their seconds engaged each other and one was killed, another badly wounded, so Buckingham and Shrewsbury were left to fight alone. Buckingham fatally wounded Shrewsbury, and a week or so later Shrewsbury was dead. There was an uproar in the Commons against the duellists even before Shrewsbury died, and the King promised that he would impose the extreme penalty in future on any who engaged in duelling; sober people were disgusted that one of their chief ministers should have engaged himself in a duel over his mistress; and when Shrewsbury died, Buckingham came very near to being expelled from the Cabal. Wild rumours were circulated. It was said that Lady Shrewsbury, disguised as a page, had held her lover's horse and witnessed her husband's murder, and that the two lovers, unable to suppress their lust, satisfied it there and then, while Buckingham was still bespattered with the husband's blood.

Buckingham was reckless and quite indifferent to public abuse. When Lady Shrewsbury was a widow he took her to Wallingford House, where the Duchess of Buckingham was living, and when she protested that she and her husband's mistress could not live under the same roof, he answered her coolly: 'I did think that also, Madam. Therefore I ordered your coach to carry you back to your father's house.'

Some of those who followed the course of events were shocked; more were merely amused. The King had his own seraglio; it was understandable that those about him should follow his example. Lady Castlemaine had never contented herself with one lover; as she grew older she seemed to find the need for more and more.

After her association with Charles Hart she discovered a fancy for other players.

One day, masked and wrapped in a cloak, she went to St Bartholomew's Fair and saw there a rope-dancer – who immediately fascinated her. His name was Jacob Hill, she was told, and after his performance she sent for him.

He proved so satisfactory that she gave him a salary which was far greater than anything he had dreamed of earning; and thus, she said, he could give up his irksome profession for a more interesting one.

Like the King, she was learning that there was a great deal of fun to be had outside Court circles.

Catherine tried to resign herself, to content herself because the news from Portugal was good. Her young brother Pedro had contrived to establish himself firmly on the throne; he had arranged that his sister-in-law, Alphonso's wife, should obtain a divorce and marry him; Alphonso was put quietly away and all seemed well in Portugal. Catherine had hopes that one day the dowry promised by her mother would be paid to Charles; and she marvelled at the goodness of her husband who never but once – and that when he was deeply incensed with her for denying him the one thing he had asked of her – had mentioned the fact that the dowry (the very reason for his marrying her) had not been paid in full.

So, saddened yet resigned, she continued to love her husband dearly and to hope that one day, when he tired of gaiety and his mistresses, he would remember the wife who, for the brief period of a honeymoon at Hampton Court, had been the happiest woman in the world because she had believed her husband loved her.

Then Frances Stuart came back to Court.

*

The King received the news calmly. All were watching him to see what his reaction would be. Barbara was alert. She had her troupe of lovers, but she was as eager as ever to keep the favour of the King; she still behaved as *maîtresse en titre*, but she was aware that the King knew of her many lovers, and the fact that he raised no objection was disconcerting. What would happen, she asked herself, now that Frances had returned? Frances, the wife of the Duke of Richmond and Lennox, might, as a married woman, find herself more free to indulge in a love affair with the King than she had been as an unmarried one. If she did, Barbara believed she would have a formidable rival indeed.

Catherine was uneasy. She knew that a faction about the King had never ceased to agitate for a divorce, and that the powerful Buckingham was at the head of this contingent. Catherine had proved, they said, that she could not bear children; the King had proved that he was still potent. It was unsound policy, declared these men, to continue in a marriage which was fruitless. England needed an heir. These men were influenced by another consideration: If the King died childless, his brother, the Duke of York, would follow him, and the Duke of York had not only adopted the Catholic religion but he was the enemy of many of these men.

Catherine knew that they were her bitter enemies. She was unmoved by the arrival of Frances. Frances could not now become the wife of the King since she had a husband of her own; and if she became the King's mistress, she would now be one of many.

But when the King and Frances met, the King received her

coolly. It was clear, said everyone, that when she had run away with the Duke of Richmond and Lennox she had spoiled her chances with the King.

*

It was not long after Frances's return to Court that all had an opportunity of understanding the depth of Charles's affection for his distant cousin.

Frances was now even more beautiful than when she had left. Marriage with the Duke had sobered her; she was less giddy; if she still played card-houses it was with an abstracted air. The Duke, her husband, was not only besotted, he was indifferent; he had wished to marry her only because the King had so ardently desired her; in fact, Frances had quickly realized that her marriage had been one of the biggest mistakes of her life. She had her apartments in Somerset House, the home of the King's mother, Henrietta Maria, for she was not invited to take up residence in her old apartments in Whitehall. It was very different being merely the wife of the Duke of Richmond and Lennox and a woman who had offended the King so deeply that she would never be taken back into his favour again. There were fewer people to visit her and applaud all she did. Buckingham and Arlington, those devoted admirers, seemed now to have forgotten her existence. Lady Castlemaine laughed at her insolently whenever they met. Barbara was determined to flaunt her continued friendship with the King, which had lasted nearly ten years; Frances's spell of favour had been so very brief.

'The King must amuse himself,' Barbara said in her hearing. 'He takes up with women one week and by the next he finds it difficult to recall their names.'

So Frances, the petted darling of the Court, the King's most honoured friend, found herself neglected because she no longer held the King's favour. There was no point in seeking to please her; for what good could her friendship bring them? It was astonishing how many of those who had sworn she was the most beautiful creature on Earth now scarcely seemed to notice her.

She was beautiful – none more beautiful at the Court; she was far less foolish than she had been, but her circle of friends had dwindled astonishingly and she was often lonely in her rooms at Somerset House. Now and then she thought of returning to the country.

Sitting solitarily, building card-houses, she thought often of the old days; she thought of the charm of the King and compared it with the ungracious manners of her husband; she thought of the Duke's indifference to her and of the King's continual care.

She covered her face with her hands and wept. If ever she had been in love with anyone it had been with Charles.

She left her card-house to collapse on to the table, and went to a mirror; her face looked back at her, perfect in contour and colouring; lacking the simplicity it had possessed when Charles had so eagerly sought her, but surely losing nothing of beauty for that.

She must go to Court; she must seek him out. She would humbly beg his pardon, not for refusing to become his mistress – he would not expect that – but because she had run away and married against his wishes, because she had flouted him, because she had been such a fool as to prefer the drunken Duke to her passionate, but so kind and affectionate King.

She called to her women.

'Come,' she cried. 'Dress me in my most becoming gown. Dress my hair in ringlets. I am going to pay a call ... a very important call.'

They dressed her, and she thought of the reunion as they did so. She would throw herself on to her knees first and beg his forgiveness. She would say that she had tried to go against the tide; she had believed in virtue, but now she could see no virtue in marriage with a man such as she had married. She would ask Charles to forget the past; and perhaps they would start again.

'My lady, your hands are burning,' said one of her women. 'You are too flushed. You have a fever.'

'It is the excitement because I am to pay a most important call ... I will wear that blue sash with the gold embroidery.'

Her women looked at each other in astonishment. 'There is no blue sash, my lady. The sash is purple, and the embroidery on it is silver.'

Frances put her hand to her head. 'Dark webs seem to dance before my eyes,' she muttered.

'You should rest, my lady, before you pay that call.

Even as they spoke she would have fallen if two of them had not managed to catch her.

'Take me to my bed,' she murmured.

They carried her thither, and in alarm they called the physician to her bedside. One of the women had recognized the alarming symptoms of the dreaded smallpox.

*

The Court buzzed with the news.

So Frances Stuart was suffering from the smallpox! Fate seemed determined to put an end to her sway, for only if she came unscathed from the dread disease, her beauty unimpaired, could she hope to return to the King's favour.

Barbara was exultant. It was hardly likely that Frances would come through unmarked; so few people did, and Barbara's spies informed her that Frances had taken the disease very badly. 'Praise be to God!' cried Barbara. 'Madam Frances will no longer be able to call herself the beauty of the Court. Dolt! She threw away what she might have had when she was young and fair and the King sought her; she married her drunken sot, and much good has that done her. I'll swear she was planning to come back and regain Charles's favour. She'll see that the pock-marked hag she'll become will best retire to the country and hide herself.'

The King heard the sly laughter. He heard the whispers. 'They say the most beautiful of Duchesses has become the most hideous.' 'Silly Frances, there'll be no one to hand her her cards now.' 'Poor Frances! Silly Frances! What had she but her beauty?'

Catherine watched the King wistfully. She saw that he was melancholy, and she asked him to tell her the reason.

He turned to her frankly and replied: 'I think of poor Frances Stuart.'

'It has been the lot of other women to lose their beauty through the pox,' said Catherine. 'Her case is but one of many.'

'Nay,' said the King. 'Hers is unique, for the pox could never have robbed a woman of so much beauty as it could rob poor Frances!'

'Some women have to learn to do without what they cannot have.'

He smiled at Catherine. 'No one visits her,' he said.

'And indeed they should not. The infection will still be upon her.'

'I think of poor Frances robbed of beauty and friends, and I find myself no longer angry with her.'

'If she recovers it will bring great comfort to her to know that she no longer must suffer your displeasure.'

'She needs comfort now,' declared the King. 'If she does not have it, poor soul, she will die of melancholy.'

He was thinking of her in her little cocked hat, in her black and white gown with the diamonds sparkling in her hair – Frances, the most beautiful woman of his Court, and now, if she recovered, one of its most hideous. For the pox was a cruel destroyer of beauty, and Frances was suffering a severe attack.

Catherine, watching him, felt such twinges of jealousy that she could have buried her face in her hands and wept in her misery. She thought: If he could speak of me as he speaks of her, if he could care so much for me if I suffered the like affliction, I believe I would be willing to suffer as Frances has suffered. He loves her still. None of the others can mean as much to him as that simple girl, of whom it was once said: 'Never had a woman so much beauty, and so little wit.'

He smiled at Catherine, but she knew he did not see her. His eyes were shining and his mouth tender; he was looking beyond her into the past when Frances Stuart had ridden beside him and he had been at his wits' end to think of means to overcome her resistance.

He turned and hurried away, and a little later she saw him walking briskly to the river's edge where his barge was waiting.

Catherine stood watching him, and slowly the tears began to run down her cheeks.

She knew where he was going. He was going to risk infection; he was going to do something which would set all the Court talking; for he was going to show them all that, although he had been cool towards the lovely Frances Stuart because she had flouted him in her marriage, all was forgiven the poor, stricken girl who was in danger of losing that very beauty which had so attracted him.

For love like that, thought Catherine, I would welcome the pox. For love like that I would die.

*

Frances lay in her bed. She had asked for a mirror, and had stared a long time at the face she saw reflected there. How cruel was fate! Why, she asked herself, should it have made her the most beautiful of women, only to turn her into one of the most hideous! If only the contrast had been less marked! It was as though she had been shown the value of beauty in those days of the Restoration, only that she might mourn its loss. Gone was the dazzling pink and white complexion; in its place was yellow skin covered by small pits which, not content with ravaging the skin itself, had distorted the perfect contours of her face. The lid of one eye, heavily pitted, was dragged down over the pupil so that she could see nothing through it, and the effect was to make her look grotesque.

Nothing of beauty was left to her; even her lovely slender figure was wasted and so thin that she feared the bones would pierce her skin.

Alone she lay, for none came to visit her. How was that possible, who would dare risk taking the dread disease?

And when I am recovered, she thought, still none will visit me. And any who should be so misguided as to do so will be disgusted with what they see.

She wanted to weep; in the old days she had wept so easily. Now there were no tears. She was aware only of a dumb misery. There was none to love her, none to care what became of her.

Perhaps, she pondered, I will go into a convent. How can I live all the years ahead of me, shut away from the world? I am not studious; I am not clever. How can I live my life shut away from the Court life to which I have grown accustomed?

How would it be to have old friends, who once had been eager to admire, turning away from her in disgust? There would be no one to love her; she had nothing to hope for from her husband. He had married the fair Stuart whom the King so desired because he had believed that, the King finding her so fair, she must be desirable indeed. Now . . . there would be none.

She could see from her bed the buhl cabinet inlaid with tortoiseshell and ivory. It was a beautiful thing and a present from the King in those days when he had eagerly besought her to become his mistress. She remembered his pleasure when he had shown her the thirty secret drawers and the silver-gilt fittings. The cabinet was decorated with tortoiseshell hearts, and she remembered that he had said: 'These are reminders that you possess one which is not made of tortoiseshell and beats for you alone.'

Beside her bed was the marquetry table, ebony inlaid, and decorated with pewter – another of Charles's elaborate presents.

She would have these to remind her always that once she had been so beautiful that a King had sought her favours. Few would believe that in the days to come, for they would look at a hideous woman and laugh secretly at the very suggestion that her beauty could ever have attracted a King who worshipped beauty as did Charles.

All was over. Her life had been built on her beauty; and her beauty was in ruins.

Someone had entered the room, someone tall and dark.

She did not believe it was he. She could not. She had been thinking of him so vividly that she must have conjured him up out of her imagination.

He approached the bed.

'Oh, God!' she cried. 'It is the King . . . the King himself.'

She brought up her hands to cover her face, but found she could not touch the loathsome thing she believed that face to be. She turned to the wall and sobbed: 'Go away! Go away! Do not look at me. Do not come here to mock me!'

But he was there, kneeling by the bed; he had taken her hands.

'Frances,' he said, in a voice husky with emotion, 'you must not grieve. You must not.'

'I beg of you go away and leave me in my misery,' she said. 'You think of what I was. You see what I have become. You . . . you of all people must be laughing at me . . . you must be triumphant . . . If you have any kindness in you . . . go away.'

'Nay,' he said. 'I would not go just yet. I would speak with you, Frances. We have been too long bad friends.'

She did not answer. She believed the hot, scalding smart on the face she loathed meant tears.

She felt his lips on her hands. He must be mad. Did he not know that there might still be danger of contagion?

'I came because I could not endure that we should be bad

friends, Frances,' he said. 'You were ill and alone, so I came to see you.'

She shook her head. 'Now go, I beg of you. I implore you. I know you cannot bear to look at anything so ugly as I have become. You cannot have anything but loathing for me now.'

'One does not loathe friends – if the friendship be a true one – whatever befalls them.'

'You desired me for my beauty.' Her voice broke on a cracked note. 'My beauty. . . . I am not only no longer beautiful, I am hideous. I know how you hate everything ugly. I can appeal only to your pity.'

'I loved you, Frances,' he said. 'Od's Fish! I did not know how much until you ran away and left me. And now I find you sick and alone, deserted by your friends. I came hither to say this to you, Frances: Here is one friend who will not desert you.'

'Nay . . . nay . . .' she said. 'You will never bear to look upon me after this.'

'I shall visit you every day until you are able to leave your bed. Then you must return to Court.'

'To be jeered at!'

'None would dare jeer at my friend. Moreover, you despair too soon. There are remedies for the effects of the pox. Many have tried them. I will ask my sister to tell me what the latest French remedies are for improving the skin. Your eye will recover its sight. Frances, do not despair.'

'If I had been less beautiful,' she murmured, 'it would have been easier.'

He said: 'Let us talk of other matters. I will tell you of the fashions of which I hear from my sister. The French are far in advance of us and I will ask her to send French dresses for you. How would you like to come to Court in a dress from Paris?'

'With a mask over my face, mayhap I might,' said Frances bitterly.

'Frances, this is not like you. You used to laugh so gaily when the card-houses of others collapsed. Do you remember?'

She nodded. Then she said sadly: 'Now my house has collapsed, and I see that cards were such flimsy things . . . so worthless with which to build a house.'

He pressed her hands; and she turned to look into his face,

hoping for what she could not possibly expect to find; the tenderness of his voice deceived her.

How could he love her – hideous as she had become? She thought of the flaming beauty of Barbara Castlemaine; she thought of the dainty *gamin* charm of the player with whom she had heard he was spending much time. And how could he love Frances Stuart who had had nothing but her unsurpassed beauty, of which the hideous pox had now completely robbed her?

She had caught him off his guard.

She had allowed him to see her once beautiful face hideously distorted, and he knew and she knew that, whatever remedies there were, nothing could restore its beauty; and she also knew that what had prompted him to visit her was nothing but the kindness of heart he would have for any sick animal. Thus would he have behaved for any of his little dogs or the creatures he kept in his parks.

Of all those who had courted and flattered her in the days when she had enjoyed the power her beauty had brought, there was only one who came now to visit her – the King himself; and, because of this, when she was well and no longer a danger to them, others would come, not because they cared what became of her, but because it was the custom to follow the King.

He had come in her affliction; she would always remember that. He had risked grave sickness and possibly death by coming to her when she had felt prepared to take a quick way out of this world.

Now he sat there on the bed and was trying to act a part; he was trying to be gay, trying to pretend that soon she would be back at Court, and the old game – she evasive, he persuasive – would begin again.

But although he was a tolerably good actor, there had been one moment of revelation when she had seen clearly that he had no feeling for her but one, and that was pity.

SIX

IT WAS springtime, and Catherine was filled with new hope. If all went well this time she might indeed present an heir to the nation.

It was seven years since she had come to England, and she was more deeply in love with Charles than she had been during that ecstatic honeymoon. She no longer hoped to have his love exclusively; it would be enough for her if she might share it with all those who made demands upon it. He had so many mistresses that none was quite sure how many; he had taken a fancy to several actresses whom he saw at the theatre; and, although his passion for these women was usually fleeting, he had remained constant to Eleanor Gwyn, who was affectionately known throughout the Court and country as Nelly. Barbara kept her place at the head of them, but that was largely due to Barbara herself; the King was too lazy to eject her from the position she had taken as a right; and until there came a mistress who would insist on his doing so, it seemed that there Barbara would remain.

As to Catherine, she allowed the King's seraglio to affect her as little as possible. She had her own court of ladies – among them poor, plain Mary Fairfax, who had suffered through her husband as Catherine had through hers. Catherine had her private chapel in the Queen Mother's residence of Somerset House; she had her own priests and loyal servants; the King was ever kind to her and she was not unduly unhappy.

Mary Fairfax, gentle, intelligent, and very patient, would sometimes talk of her childhood and the early days of her marriage which had been so happy, and how at that time she had believed she would continue to live in harmony with her husband all the days of her life.

They had much comfort to bring each other.

They talked of pleasant things; they never mentioned Lady Castlemaine, whom Mary Fairfax regarded as her husband's evil genius almost as much as Catherine regarded her as Charles's.

They talked of the coming of the child and the joy which would be felt throughout the country when it was born.

Lying back in her white *pinner*, the loose folds of which were wrapped about her thickening body, Catherine looked almost pretty. She was imagining Charles's delight in the child; she saw him as a boy – a not very pretty boy because he would be so like his father; he would have bright, merry eyes, a gentle nature, and a sharp wit.

They talked together and an hour passed merrily, but when Mary Fairfax rose to call her ladies to help the Queen disrobe, Catherine suddenly felt ill.

Her women came hurrying in, and she saw the anxiety on their faces; she knew they were wondering: Is the Queen going to miscarry again?

Catherine said quickly: 'Send for Mrs Nun. She is at dinner in Chaffinch's apartments. I may need her.'

There was consternation throughout Whitehall. Mrs Nun had been brought away from a dinner party in great haste at the Queen's command, and this could mean only one thing; the Queen's time had again come too soon.

Within a few days the news was out.

Catherine came out of her sleep of exhaustion, and the tears fell slowly down her cheeks as she realized that, once more, she had failed.

*

The Duke of Buckingham called on Barbara.

When they were alone, he said: 'So Her Majesty has failed again!'

'The King should have married a woman who could bear him children,' declared Barbara.

'Well, cousin,' said the Duke, 'you have proved that you could do that. The only thing that would need to be proved in your case would be that the King had begotten them.'

'It is only necessary for Queens to *bear* them,' said Barbara.

'And does your rope-dancer still give you satisfaction?' asked the Duke.

'I'll be thankful if you will address me civilly,' snapped Barbara.

'A friendly question, nothing more,' said Buckingham airily. 'But let us not quarrel. I have come to talk business. The

King is gravely disappointed. He had hoped for a son.'

'Well, he'll get over the disappointment, as he has been obliged to do before.'

'It is a sad thing when a King, knowing himself to be capable of begetting strong healthy children, cannot get an heir.'

Barbara shrugged her magnificent shoulders, but the Duke went on: 'You indicate it is a matter of indifference. Know you not that if the King gets no legitimate son, one day we shall have his brother on the throne?'

'That would seem so.'

'And what of us when James is King?'

'Charles's death would be calamity to us in any case.'

'Well, he is full of health and vigour. Now listen to me, Barbara; we must rid him of the Queen.'

'What do you suggest? To tie her in a sack and throw her into the river one dark night?'

'Put aside your levity. This is a serious matter. I mean divorce.'

'Divorce!' cried Barbara shrilly. 'That he might marry again! Another barren woman!'

'How do we know she would be barren?'

'Royal persons often are.'

'Don't look alarmed, Barbara. It cannot be Frances Stuart now.'

'That pock-marked hag!' Barbara went into peals of laughter, which the very mention of Frances Stuart's name never failed to provoke. She was serious suddenly: 'Nay! Let the Queen stay where she is. She is quiet and does no harm.'

'She does no good while she does not give the country an heir.'

'The country has an heir in James.'

'I'll not stand by and see the King disappointed of a son.'

'There is nothing else you can do about it, cousin.'

'Indeed there is! Ashley and others are with me in this. We will arrange a divorce for the King, and he shall marry a princess who will bring him sons.'

Barbara's eyes narrowed. She was ready to support the Queen, because the Queen was docile. How did she know what a new Queen would do? Was her position with the King so strong that she could afford to have it shaken? And, horror

239

of horrors, what if he looked about his Court and selected one of the beauties to be his Queen? It might so easily have been Frances Stuart. What if he should choose some fiery creature who would insist on making trouble for Lady Castlemaine?

She would have nothing to do with this plot. She was all for letting things stay as they were.

'The poor Queen!' said Barbara. 'This is shameful. So you plot against her ... you and your mischief-making Cabal. Keep your noses out of the King's marriage; meddle with matters more fitting. I tell you I'll do nothing to help you in this vile plot. I shall disclose it to the King. I shall ...'

The Duke took her by the wrist, but she twisted her arm free and dealt him a stinging blow across the face.

'There, Master George Villiers, that will teach you to lay hands on me!'

It was nothing. There had been quarrels between them before; there had been physical violence and physical tenderness; they were of a kind, and they recognized that in each other.

Now they surveyed each other angrily, for their interests were divided.

Buckingham laughed in her face. 'I see, Madam, that your standing with the King is in such bad case that you fear a new Queen who might decide to banish you for ever.'

'You see too much, sir!' cried Barbara. 'I have given you great support during the last years, but doubtless you forget this, as it suits you to. Do not forget that I, who have done you much good, could do you much harm.'

'Your wings are clipped, Barbara. The King but allows you to stay at Court out of laziness, rather than his desire to keep you there.'

'You lie.'

'Do I? Try leaving and see then how eager he will be to have you back.'

Fear was in Barbara's heart. There was some truth in Buckingham's words.

'Go and do your worst!' she cried. 'See if, without my help – which you consider so worthless – you can rid the country of the Queen.'

'So you have a fellow-feeling with the Queen now,' sneered

Buckingham. 'Two poor deserted women! Mrs Nelly, they say, is an enchanting creature. She is young; she is very pretty, and she makes the King laugh.'

'I pray you, leave my apartment,' said Barbara with dignity; but almost immediately that dignity deserted her. 'Get out, you plotting hog! Get out, you murderer! I wonder poor Shrewsbury does not haunt you, that I do. Get out and plot with Shrewsbury's widow.'

'So you refuse to help me?'

'Not only that; I'll do all in my power to work against you.'

'Think awhile, Barbara. You'll be sorry if you do anything rashly.'

'You dare to tell me I shall be sorry? You'll be sorrier than I could ever be.'

'We Villiers should stand together, Barbara. You said that.'

'Not when it means bringing dishonour to an innocent woman,' said Barbara in a virtuous tone which sent Buckingham into hysterical laughter. Whereupon he gave, for Barbara's benefit, an imitation of Barbara – the real Barbara, and Barbara, virtuous defender of the Queen.

Barbara was furious; she would have flown at him and dug her nails into his face, but he was quick, and before she could reach him he was through the door, and away.

*

Buckingham sought out the King and intimated that he came from the Council with a matter of grave importance to discuss.

'Your Majesty,' he said, 'your Council and your country view with alarm the Queen's sterility.'

Charles nodded. 'It is a source of great disappointment to me. There was no reason for it. No accident. Nothing wrong. It is the same as that which happened previously. Again and again she loses the child she might have.'

'It is the way with some women, Sire. You have but to look back and consider Henry VIII and what difficulties he had in getting an heir. It brought much inconvenience to him.'

'And greater inconvenience to his wives, I fear,' added Charles.

'There was much unrest regarding the succession, because of the sterility of those women.'

'In my case I have a successor in my brother James.'

'Your brother, Sire, has turned to the Catholic Faith. Your Majesty knows what dissatisfaction that causes in the country.'

'James is a fool,' said Charles.

'All the more reason why Your Majesty should make sure that he is not your successor.'

'I have tried to make sure of that, George. God knows' – he smiled wryly – 'I have tried very hard indeed.'

'All know Your Majesty's labours have been tireless. But ... there is no child, and it would seem that the Queen will never have one.'

'Alas, it is a sad fate.'

'Your Majesty would seem to accept it with resignation.'

'I learned in my early youth to accept with resignation that which could not be avoided.'

'There are means of avoiding most things, Sire.'

'Are you back to the divorce?' asked the King.

'It is the only way in which we may reach a satisfactory conclusion to this affair of the succession.'

'On what grounds could one divorce as virtuous a lady as the Queen has proved herself to be?'

'On her inability to bear an heir to the crown.'

'Nonsense! Moreover she is a Catholic and would not agree to be divorced.'

'She might be urged to go into a nunnery.'

The King was silent, and Buckingham was delighted. He did not press the point. He would wait awhile. He believed the King greatly wished to be rid of his wife; it was not that he hated her; he was, in his way, fond of her; but because of her mildness, because of her resignation, she bothered him. She made him continually conscious of the way in which he treated her. He could no more deny himself the pleasure of falling in and out of light love affairs than he could stop breathing; but such was his nature that, knowing this hurt the Queen, he was uneasy in her presence; and it was of the very essence of his nature that he should avoid that which was unpleasant.

A divorce from the Queen! Catherine to spend the rest of her days peacefully in a nunnery!

It was a good idea. And for him the pleasure of choosing a new wife. This time he would choose with the utmost care.

When Buckingham left the King the Duke's hopes were high indeed.

At all costs he must prevent his enemy, the Duke of York, mounting the throne – even if it meant making the bastard Monmouth heir of England.

Wild schemes formed in Buckingham's mind. What if Charles had really been married to Lucy Water! Then Monmouth would in truth be heir to the throne. What if a box were found ... a box containing papers which proved the marriage to have taken place? An excellent scheme but a wild one.

It would be far, far better for the King to divorce Catherine, remarry, and let a new Queen produce the heir.

Well, he decided, he was moving forward. He had discovered something. The King would not be averse to a divorce. He sought out Lauderdale and Ashley to tell them the good news.

*

Barbara's spies quickly brought the information to her.

She sat biting her lips and contemplating the possible danger to herself from a new and beautiful Queen.

I am satisfied with the Queen, she mused. I like the Queen – a mild and sensible lady who understands the King and his ways.

What if the King married? She pictured another such as Frances Stuart ruling the Court. The first thing such a woman would do would be to clear out the seraglio; and who would be the first to go? Those whom she most feared and whom the King was not determined to keep.

Barbara would certainly not allow these plans to proceed, for the deeper they were laid the more difficult they would be to frustrate, and it might well be that her persistent relative would set about making things so very uncomfortable for the Queen that she would sigh for the quiet walls of a convent.

Barbara sought audience with the Queen and, when she was with her, told her that what she had to say was for her ears alone.

She fell on her knees before Catherine and kissed her hand;

then she lifted those bright flashing eyes to Catherine's face and said: 'I have come to warn Your Majesty.'

'Of what?' inquired Catherine. She spoke harshly. She was tormented by hundreds of mental pictures when this woman stood before her. She saw her in the arms of the King; she thought of his passionate love-making; she thought of all she had heard of this infamous woman, of the numerous lovers she took, and how she kept some as servants in her household so that she might call them instantly when she needed them. She thought of those days during her honeymoon, when Lady Castlemaine had been merely a name to be shuddered over and never mentioned.

Barbara boldly answered: 'Of your enemies, who seek to destroy you. They would part you from the King.'

Catherine turned pale in spite of her determination to remain controlled before this woman.

'How ... how could they do that, Lady Castlemaine?'

'Madam, you have failed to give the King children.'

Catherine winced and thought again of the many times this woman had been brought to bed, as she said, of the King's child.

'And,' went on Barbara, 'there are certain of his ministers who seek to have him set you aside. They talk of divorce.'

'I would not agree.'

'Your Majesty should never ... never agree to that!'

'Lady Castlemaine, you have no need to urge me to my duty.'

'Madam, you misunderstand me. Nor do you understand how wicked, how determined are these men who scheme to displace you. They will try persuasion at first, and if that fails they will seek to compel you.'

'They dare not compel me. If they harmed me, they would have to answer to my brother.'

Barbara raised her well-arched brows, indicating that Pedro of Portugal already had too many commitments to leave his country and sail across the seas in what would be a feeble attempt to defend his sister.

'But Madam, I came to tell you of plans I have discovered, plans which are indeed being set on foot to force Your Majesty from the throne.'

'It is fantastic.'

'Nevertheless, Madam, it is true.'

'The King would not consent.'

'The King must have an heir, Madam.'

'He would never treat me thus.'

'He can be persuaded.'

'No ... no. He is too noble ... too good to agree to such a thing.'

'Madam, I warn you. I beg of you, take my advice. The King has a tender heart; we both know that. You must win him to your side against your enemies. You must implore him to protect you against those who would destroy you. The King is tender-hearted. If you can move him with your tears ... if you can but bring him to pity you, your enemies will have no power to harm you.'

The two women looked at each other as though measuring each other's strength and sincerity.

Barbara was ageing and the signs of debauchery were beginning to show on her handsome face, but however old she was, she would still be handsome. Catherine was pale from her miscarriage and in despair because she could not produce the heir so necessary to the country. They had been rivals for so long; they had hated each other; and now it was clear to them both that at last they must become allies.

'I must thank you, Lady Castlemaine,' said the Queen, 'for coming to me thus.'

Barbara knelt and kissed the Queen's hand. For the first time Catherine saw Barbara humble in her presence; and she realized that Barbara feared the future even as she did.

*

It was rarely, Catherine reflected bitterly, that she had an opportunity of being alone with the King. She had become resigned to the relationship between them; she had schooled herself not to show how hurt she was every time she saw him becoming enamoured of a new woman. She had learned to hesitate before entering her own apartments, lest he should be there, kissing one of her maids, and she surprise them.

She had learned to subdue her jealousy; and now she realized that she would endure any humiliations which life with Charles brought her rather than suffer the lonely despair of life without him.

She waited for one of the nights when they were alone together. At such times she felt that he was more her husband than her King. He would then modify that brilliant wit of his and attune his conversation to suit her; he was unfailingly courteous. If she were ill he would tend her carefully; he never failed to be considerate of her health. She fancied that that expression of melancholy regret, which she saw so often on his face when he was in her company, meant that he was sorry because he could not be a better husband to her.

She now said to him: 'Charles, it seems that there are many in your counsels who believe I am incapable of bearing children.'

That light and easy smile flashed across his face as he prevaricated. 'Nay, you must not despair. We have been unfortunate. There have been a few disappointments. . . .'

She looked about the chamber of this apartment in Hampton Court and thought of other queens who had, within these very walls, despaired of their ability to produce an heir to the throne. Was there a curse on queens? she wondered.

'Too many disappointments,' she said. 'It does not happen with . . . others.'

'They are stronger than you. You must take better care of your health.'

'Let us be frank one with the other, Charles. There are men who plan to destroy me.'

'To destroy you! What words are these?'

'They wish to rid you of me, that you may marry again. Buckingham, Ashley, Lauderdale . . . all the Cabal . . . and others. They offer you a new and beautiful wife who can give you sons. Oh, Charles, do not think I cannot understand the temptation. I am not beautiful . . . and you so admire beauty.'

He was beside her; his arms were about her. 'Now, Catherine, what tales are these you have heard? You are my wife. For you I have the utmost affection. I know I am not a good husband, but you took me, Catherine, and, Od's Fish, you'll have to stick to me.'

'They seek to destroy me,' she repeated blankly. 'They seek to send me away from you. Do not deny it. You cannot deny it, can you, Charles?'

He was silent for a while; then he said gently: 'They have thought that there is much of which you disapprove in our sinful Court. They have seen you so devout, and have thought that mayhap you would be happier in a nunnery.'

She looked at him quickly, and she was overcome with anguish. Was that an expression of hopeful anticipation she saw on his face? Was he asking her to leave him for a nunnery?

Sudden determination came to her. She would not leave him. She would fight for what she wanted. She would never give up hope that one day he would turn to her for the love which she was but waiting to bestow upon him. Surely, when they were both old, when he had ceased to desire so many women, surely then he would understand the value of true love, the quiet affection which was so much more lasting than physical desire. She would wait for that. She would never despair of getting it; and she was going to fight all her enemies in this country until that day when Charles turned to her for what he needed most.

He was the kindest man she had ever known; he was the most attractive, the most tolerant; he would have been a saint, she supposed, had he not been entirely sensual. It was that sensuality which caused her such misery, because she herself was not endowed with the necessary weapons to appeal to it in competition with such women as Barbara, Frances Stuart, Moll Davies, Mrs Knight, and Nelly.

But she would never give him up.

She turned to him: 'Charles,' she cried, 'I will never willingly leave you.'

'Of a certainty you shall not.'

She threw herself at his feet. She was suddenly terrified. He was so careless, so easy-going, so ready with light promises; and those about him were ruthless men who stopped at nothing. She thought of Buckingham, determined to destroy her, his hands red with the blood of his mistress's husband. She thought of Ashley, that terrifying little man, with his elegant clothes, his head – adorned with a fair periwig – which seemed too big for his frail body, his sharp wit and that soft and gentle voice which belied the ruthless determination behind it; she thought of other members of the Cabal who had determined to provide a new wife for the King.

'Charles,' she implored, 'save me from those men. Do not let them send me away from you.' She could no longer hide emotion. The tears streamed down her cheeks, and she knew that he could not bear to see a woman's tears. They never failed to move him deeply; he was even ready at all costs to stop the tears of women such as Barbara, who turned them on and off according to whether they would be effective.

'Catherine,' he said in dismay, 'you distress yourself unnecessarily.'

'It is not unnecessary, I know. Charles ... they will do anything to separate us. I know full well it is not merely their hatred of me which makes them determined to ruin me. What do they care for me! Who am I? A poor woman of no importance ... unloved ... unwanted. ...'

'I'll not have you say that. Have I not cared for you?'

She shook her head sadly. 'You have been kind to me. Are you not kind to all? Your dogs enjoy your kindness. ... The animals in your parks benefit from it. And ... so do I. Nay! They do not hate me. I am unworthy of hate ... unworthy of love. They hate your brother. They are his sworn enemies. They are determined he shall not rule. They are determined on a Protestant heir. Oh, this is nothing so simple as their hatred for one poor woman. ... It is a policy ... a policy of state. But, for the sake of that policy, I shall be condemned to a life of misery. Charles, they will trample on my life as Buckingham trampled on Shrewsbury's. Charles, save me ... save me from my enemies.'

He lifted her in his arms and, sitting down, held her on his knee, while he wiped the tears from her face.

'Come, Catherine,' he murmured, as though she were a child. 'Have done with weeping. You have no cause to weep. Od's Fish! You have no cause whatsoever.'

'You are gentle with me. But you listen to them.'

'Listen to their roguery? I will not!'

'Then Charles, you will not let them turn me away?'

'I'll not allow it.'

'My lord Buckingham makes many plots, and this is no less likely to be carried out than others.'

'Nay! You listen to gossip. You and I will not allow them to separate us. If they come to me with their tales,' I shall dismiss them from the Court. And, moreover, we'll foil them! They say we cannot have children. We'll show them otherwise.'

He kissed her and she clung to him passionately.

He soothed her; he was adept at soothing hysterical women.

*

Buckingham, Ashley, and Lauderdale laid their plans before the King.

'Your Majesty, the Queen cannot bear children, and we fear that the country is growing restive because of this.'

'The Queen is a young woman yet,' murmured Charles.

'There has been more than one miscarriage.'

' 'Tis true.'

'If Her Majesty would be happy in a nunnery . . .'

'She has told me that she would never be happy in a nunnery.'

Buckingham murmured in a low and wheedling voice: 'If Your Majesty gave me permission, I would steal the Queen away and send her to a plantation, where she would be well and carefully looked after but never heard of more. The people could be told that she had left Your Majesty of her own free will, and you could divorce her for desertion.'

Charles looked into the cunning, handsome face before him, and said quietly and with that determination which he rarely used: 'Have done and hold your tongue! If you imagine that I shall allow an innocent woman to suffer through no fault of her own, you are mistaken.'

Lauderdale began: 'But Your Majesty would wish to take a new wife. Your Majesty could choose any beautiful princess.'

'I am well satisfied with the ladies of my Court.'

'But the heir . . .'

'My wife is young yet; and hear me this: If she should fail to get children, that is no fault of hers. She is a good and virtuous Princess, and if you wish to keep my good graces you will no more mention this matter to me.'

The three statesmen were aghast.

They were determined that Catholic James should never have the throne. If he ever came to it, their ambitions would be at an end; moreover they foresaw a return to the tyranny of Bloody Mary.

Lauderdale then ventured: 'The Duke of Monmouth is a

brave and handsome gentleman. Your Majesty is justly proud of such a son.'

'You speak truth there,' said Charles.

'Your Majesty must wish,' said Ashley, 'that he were your legitimate son. What joy for England – if you had married his mother!'

'If you had known his mother you might not have thought so. I doubt whether the people of England would have accepted her as their Queen.'

'She is dead,' said Buckingham. 'God rest her soul. And she gave Your Majesty a handsome boy.'

'I am grateful to Lucy for that.'

'If he were but your legitimate son, what a happy thing for England!'

Charles laughed lightly. He turned to Buckingham; he knew him to be a dangerous adventurer but, because he was the most amusing man at his Court, he could not resist his company.

'Have done with making trouble with my brother,' said Charles. 'Try cultivating his friendship instead of arousing his enmity.'

'Your Majesty, I live in terror of the Duke, your brother,' said Buckingham. 'He threatens my very life!'

'I beg of you, no play-acting,' said the King, and he began to laugh. 'I confess that to see you riding in your coach protected by your seven musquetoons for fear my brother will take your life ... is the funniest thing I have witnessed for a long time.'

'I am grateful to have brought a little sunshine into Your Majesty's life.'

'George! Have done with your plotting and scheming. Let matters lie as they are. The Queen and I may yet get an heir. If not ...'

'The Duke of Monmouth is a worthy heir, Your Majesty.'

'A bastard heir for England?'

'We could discover that Your Majesty married his mother. Leave it to me, Sire. I will find a box in which are the marriage lines ... She begged you, she implored you ... for the sake of her virtue ... and Your Majesty, being the man you always are with the ladies, could not find it in your heart to refuse her!'

The King laughed aloud but his eyes were shrewd. He knew they were speaking only half in jest.

He said abruptly: 'Have done! Have done! The Queen stays married to me. I'll not have the poor lady, who is the most virtuous in the land, plagued by you. As for Monmouth, I love the boy. I am proud of the boy. But he is a bastard and I'd see him hanged at Tyburn before I'd make him heir to my throne.'

The members of the Cabal retired, temporarily defeated. And the matter of the divorce was dropped, for another more serious one arose. This concerned the secret treaty of Dover in which the King, unknown to his people and the majority of his ministers, agreed to become a Catholic and lead the country to do the same; for such services to Catholic France he would become the pensioner of that country. The matter had given Charles much grave thought. He was in dire need of money; he was verging on bankruptcy. There were two ways of raising money; one was by taxing his subjects, as Cromwell had done to such extent that they could bear little more; and the other was by making promises to the King of France – which might never be kept – and allowing France to wipe out England's deficit.

These matters occupied his mind continually and, when the sister whom he loved so tenderly came to England as the emissary of the King of France, when he realized how deeply she desired his signature to the treaty and all that his signature would mean to her, and how such a signature could make her unhappy life in France supportable through the love of Louis, he agreed – and the very few of his counsellors who were in the secret were of his opinion – that the best way out of England's troubles was the signing of the treaty.

There were fêtes and balls in honour of the King's sister, and Catherine was moved to see how tender was the love between Charles and Henriette of Orléans.

How sad he was when he bade farewell to his sister; and how much sadder he would have been, could he have known that he would never see her face again, for only a few weeks after her return to France Henriette died suddenly. During the King's grief at the loss of this beloved sister it was Catherine who brought him most comfort. She would sit with him, while he talked of Henriette, and of those rare occasions in her childhood when he had been able to enjoy her company.

He wept, and Catherine wept with him; and she believed that in his unhappiness she meant more to him than any woman of his Court.

She thought then: This is a foretaste of the future.

When he is old, when he no longer feels the need to go hunting every pretty thing that flits across the scene – like a boy with a butterfly net – then he and I shall be together in close unity; and those will be the happiest days of my life, and perhaps of his.

*

Buckingham had not forgotten his threat to punish Barbara for not supporting him in the matter of the Queen's divorce. His spies had informed him that Barbara had whispered to the Queen of his plots against her, even telling her that he had suggested kidnapping her and taking her to a plantation – an idea too fantastic to have been meant in true earnest. And, because she had been warned, the Queen had been able to pour out her tears and pleadings to the King who, softened by these, had determined to turn his thoughts from the idea of divorce.

It was infuriating. For Charles was certainly tired of his Queen; he had never been in love with her; she was a plain little woman and by no means a clever one. Buckingham, Ashley, and Lauderdale had several fascinating and beautiful creatures with whom to tempt the King; but they had been defeated by the Queen's tears which were the result of Barbara's perfidy.

Barbara should be shown that she could not work against her kinsman in this way; it should be borne home to her that her position at Court was far from secure.

When Charles's sister had visited him for the last time she had brought in her train a charming little Breton girl, named Louise de Kéroualle, who had taken Charles's fancy immediately; and, after the death of Henriette, Louis had sent the girl to Charles's Court, ostensibly to comfort him, but more likely to act as spy for France.

She was a very beautiful young girl, and it was clear that the King was ready to fall more deeply in love with her than was his custom.

This meant that Barbara would have a new and very serious rival; and the fact that the King had showered great honours on Barbara was an indication that he was expecting her to retire from Court. She had been created Baroness of Nonesuch Park, Countess of Surrey, and Duchess of Cleveland; he had given her £30,000 and a grant of plate from the jewel house and, as she was already receiving an annual income of £4,700 from the post office, she was being amply and very generously paid off; but Barbara, while accepting these gifts and honours, omitted to remove herself from the Court and continued to pretend that she occupied the place of *maîtresse en titre.*

The King was uneasy. He saw trouble ahead between the newcomer – who, some said, had not yet become his mistress – and Barbara, now known by the grand title of Duchess of Cleveland.

Barbara continued to flaunt her jewels and her person at Court functions; she was often seen at the playhouse wearing her jewels, worth more than £40,000, so that all other ladies, including the Queen and the Duchess of York, seemed far less splendid than she.

She gave up none of her lovers and had even taken a new one – one of the handsomest men about the Court. Barbara's lovers were always handsome.

The latest was John, son of a Sir Winston Churchill, gentleman, of Devonshire. John Churchill had been a page to the Duke of York and had later received a commission as ensign in the Foot Guards. The Duke of York had shown him great favour, which might have been due to the fact that the Duke had cast a covetous eye on John's sister, Arabella.

Barbara had seen the young man and had immediately desired him as her lover. Barbara handsomely paid those whose services she used in this way; she lavished rich presents upon her young men, and made the way to advancement easier for them. If they could please the Duchess of Cleveland, it was said, their fortunes might be made; and John Churchill was soon on the way to making his.

Buckingham watched the affair, and considered that, if he could arrange for the King to catch them *flagrante delicto,* he would by such a device supply the King with a good excuse for ridding himself of a woman who was growing irksome to His Majesty; he would, moreover, be doing the King a good turn while letting Barbara see that she was foolish to work against her cousin.

It was not difficult to discover when the two would be together. Barbara had never made any great secret of her love affairs; and one afternoon, when Buckingham knew that Barbara was entertaining the handsome soldier in her apartments, he begged the King to accompany him thither.

The King agreed to go, and together they made their way to Barbara's apartment. When Buckingham saw the consternation of her women, he guessed that he had come at the right moment. Mrs Sarah made excuses to delay them, saying that she would go to warn her mistress of their arrival, but the Duke pushed her aside and, throwing open the door of Barbara's bedchamber, could not repress a triumphant laugh.

Barbara was in bed, pulling the clothes about her; John Churchill, hearing the commotion without, had managed to scramble into a few of his more essential garments.

Taking one look at the Duke, and seeing the King behind him, the young lover could think of only one thing: escape.

He forthwith ran to the window and leaped out of it. The Duke of Buckingham burst into uproarious laughter; Barbara picked up an ebony-handled brush which lay on a table beside the bed and threw it at her cousin, while the King, striding to the window, called out after the departing figure of Churchill: 'Have no fear, Master Churchill. I hold nothing against you. I know you do it for your bread!'

Barbara, furious at the insulting suggestion that she now found it necessary to pay her lovers, and mad with rage against the Duke, found herself for once without words to express her anger and indignation.

Nor did the King give her time to recover her calm. He strode out of the room. Only Buckingham turned to give a brief imitation of John Churchill, surprised and leaping to safety.

Barbara's rage was boundless and for some hours her servants dared not approach her.

She turned and pummelled her pillows, while Mrs Sarah wondered which of those men she would have preferred to attack: the Duke for his perfidy in exposing her thus; John

Churchill for running away; or the King for his cool and care-less indifference to what lovers she might take.

It was clear that the King had ceased to regard her as his mistress; and very shortly afterwards her name failed to appear on the list of Ladies of the Queen's Bedchamber. Furthermore, when her daughter Barbara was born, and the girl was seen to bear a strong resemblance to John Churchill, the King flatly refused to acknowledge her as his.

Barbara's day was over.

SEVEN

IT WAS sixteen years since Catherine had come to England, and in those years, during which she had lived through many fears, a little happiness and much heartbreak, she had never ceased to love her husband and to hope that one day he would turn, from those brilliant women who so enchanted him, to the plain little wife who adored him.

She had little hope now of bearing a child; and she knew that there were many of her husband's most important ministers who sought to ruin her. If they could have brought some charge against her, how readily would they have done so! But it seemed that, in the profligate Court, there was one virtuous woman, and she was the Queen. There was one matter which they held against her, and this was her religion. There was a growing feeling in the country against Papists and, whenever there was any trouble in this connexion, there was always someone to remind the company that the Queen was a Papist.

Since the Duke of York had announced his conversion to the Catholic Faith there had been a strong and growing faction working against him, and these men never ceased to urge the King to rid himself of the Queen.

The chief of these was Ashley, who had now become Lord Shaftesbury. His principal enemy was the Duke of York, and his enmity towards him had increased since the Duke's marriage, on the death of Anne Hyde, to the Catholic Princess of Modena. The one aim of Shaftesbury's party was to prevent the Duke's becoming King and, since the Queen was barren, they could only hope to do this either through divorce or, as the only other alternative, by the acknowledgement of Monmouth as the heir to the throne.

They were certain that, but for the King's soft-heartedness, they could achieve this, and they had never ceased, over the last ten years, to work for it.

Catherine must therefore live in continual dread that one day they would succeed in their plans.

She was no longer plagued by Barbara, for Barbara was out of favour. It was true that the King had never dismissed her from the Court. It was beyond his nature to do that. Some said that he feared Barbara's threat to print his letters, but what harm would such an act do to him? All knew of his infatuation for her; all knew that she had behaved abominably to him and had not even pretended to be faithful. No, Catherine often thought, it is his sheer kindness of heart and his desire to live easily and comfortably without troublesome quarrels which have made him give no direct rebuff to Barbara, just as they compel him to keep me as his wife. To rid himself of either of us would make trouble. Therefore he says: Let Barbara stay at Court; let Catherine remain my wife. What matters it? I have many charming companions with whom to beguile my hours.

So that woman, Louise de Kéroualle, who had taken Barbara's place, was the Queen of England in all but name. It was she – now Duchess of Portsmouth – who lived as the Queen in Whitehall while Catherine retired to the Dower Palace of Somerset House.

She made excuses for him. He was half French; his mistress wholly so; and in France the King's mistress had invariably ruled in place of the King's wife.

It was true that his neglect of her, and the fact that – now that he no longer hoped that she would give him a child – he rarely visited her, meant that the hopes of her enemies were high; and they continued most energetically to plot for a divorce.

Barbara had gone to France, where she had indulged in a love affair with Ralph Montague, the King's ambassador. But now it seemed he had offended her and she was writing frequently to the King complaining of her ex-lover's conduct of English affairs.

Barbara had, after the installation of Louise de Kéroualle as the King's favourite, continued to amuse London with her many love affairs. She had turned again to the theatre and had found one of the handsomest men in London, William Wycherley, the playwright, who dedicated his *Love in a Wood* to her.

But in spite of her numerous lovers she had found it insupportable to see another take her place with the King. The play-actress she accepted, but she could not tolerate the French woman. In vain did she call the woman a spy, and the King a fool. No one stopped her; they merely ignored her. That was why she had gone to France.

So, as Catherine looked out on the river from her apartments in Somerset House and her wistful gaze wandered in the direction of Whitehall, she told herself that she must be resigned to her position as wife of the King, the wife to whom he was so kind because he could not love her.

*

It was a hot August day, and the King was shortly to ride to Windsor. He was pleased at the prospect. Windsor was a favourite resort of his, and he was looking forward to a little holiday from state affairs. He had decided to take Louise and Nelly – those two whom he never greatly cared to be without – and set off as early as this could be arranged. He was eager to assure himself that his instructions were being carried out regarding the alterations he was having made there, and to see how Verrio's work on the fresco paintings was progressing.

He was about to take his quick morning walk through St James's Park, with which he always liked to begin the day. With him were a few of his friends, and his dogs followed at his heels, barking their delight at the prospect of the walk.

But before he had taken more than a dozen steps a young man, whom he recognized as one who worked in his laboratories, came running towards him.

'Your Majesty,' he cried, falling to his knees, 'I beg of you, allow me to speak a few words to you.'

'Do so,' said the King in some astonishment.

'It would be well if, when walking in the Park, Your Majesty did not stray from your companions.'

'Why so?' said Charles. He was faintly amused by the

man's earnest looks. It was rarely that the King walked abroad and was not asked for something. That he should be asked to keep with his companions was a strange request.

'Your Majesty's life is in danger,' whispered the young man.

Charles was not easily alarmed. He stood surveying the young man, who he now remembered was Christopher Kirby, a merchant who had failed in business and had begged the Lord Treasurer, the Earl of Danby, to employ him as a tax collector; as he had some skill as a chemist, he had been given work to do in Charles's laboratory; and it was in that capacity that the King on one or two occasions had come into contact with him.

'What is this talk?' asked Charles.

'Your Majesty may at any moment be shot at.'

'You had better tell me all you know,' said the King.

'Your Majesty, I can give you a full account. . . . I can give you many details, but to do so I must ask for a private interview.'

'Go back to the Palace,' said Charles, 'and wait there in my private closet for my return. If any ask why you do so, tell them it is at my command.'

The man came closer to the King. 'Your Majesty, on no account leave your companions. Remember . . . men may at this moment be lurking among the trees.'

With that, Kirby bowed and retired.

The King turned to his companions.

'Will Your Majesty continue the walk?' asked one.

The King laughed. 'Ever since the gunpowder plot, in my grandfather's reign, there have always been plots which are purported to threaten the life of the King. Come! Let us enjoy the morning air and forget our chemist. I'll warrant this is nothing more than a dream he has had. He had an air of madness, to my mind.'

The King called to his dogs who came running round him joyfully. He threw a stone and watched them race for it, each striving for the honour of bringing it back to him.

Then he continued his walk, and it was an hour later before he again saw Kirby.

*

When the King returned to his closet, the chemist was waiting for him there.

The King listened to his story as patiently as he could, without believing a word of it.

Two men, according to Kirby, were lurking in the Park waiting for an opportunity of shooting the King.

'Why should they do this?' asked Charles.

'It is for the Jesuits, Your Majesty,' replied Kirby. 'Their plan is to murder you and set your brother on the throne.'

Poor James! thought Charles. He has many enemies. Now these people would seek to add me to their number.

'How did you learn of these matters?' he asked, scarcely able to suppress a yawn.

'It was through a Dr Tonge, Your Majesty. He is the rector of St Michael's in Wood Street, and he has discovered much in the interests of Your Majesty. If Your Majesty would but grant him an interview he could tell you more than I can.'

'Then I dare say we should see your Dr Tonge.'

'Have I Your Majesty's permission to bring him to the Palace?'

'You may bring him here between nine and ten this evening,' said the King.

When Kirby had left, the King summoned the Earl of Danby and told him of all that had passed.

They laughed together. 'The fellow is clearly deranged,' said the King. 'Let us hope this fellow Tonge is not equally so. Yet he was so earnest I had not the heart to deny him the interview. In the meantime keep the matter secret. I would not have the idea of murdering me put into the heads of people who previously have not given the matter a thought.'

*

At the appointed time Kirby arrived with Dr Tonge, a clergyman and schoolmaster of Yorkshire; he was, he told the King, rector of the parishes of St Mary Stayning and St Michael's Wood, and because he had long known the wickedness to which the Jesuits would stoop – even to the murder of their King – he had made it his business to study their ways.

He then began to enumerate the many crimes he had uncovered, until the King, growing weary, bade him proceed with the business which had brought him there.

There were, said Dr Tonge, Jesuits living close to the King, who had plotted his murder.

'Who are these men?' demanded the King.

Dr Tonge thereupon produced a wad of papers and told the King that if he would read these he would find therein that which would shock and enrage him.

'How came you by these papers?' asked the King.

'Sire, they were pushed under my door.'

'By whom?'

'By one who doubtless wished Your Majesty well and trusted that I would be the man to save Your Majesty's life and see justice done.'

The King handed the papers to Danby.

'So you do not know the man who thrust these papers beneath your door?'

'I have a suspicion, Your Majesty, that he is one who has spoken to me of such matters.'

'We may need to see him. Can he be found?'

'I have seen him lately, Your Majesty, walking in the streets.'

The King turned to Danby. He was wishing to be done with the tiresome business, and had no intention of postponing the trip to Windsor because of another Papist scare.

'You will look into these matters, my lord,' he said.

And with that he left.

*

The Earl of Danby was a most unhappy man. He had many enemies, and he knew that a fate similar to that which had befallen Clarendon was being prepared for him. He was in danger of being impeached for high treason when Parliament met, and he was terrified that if there were an investigation of his conduct of affairs he might even lose his life.

He was fully aware that powerful men such as Buckingham and Shaftesbury would welcome a Popish plot. Since the Duke of York had openly avowed his conversion to the Catholic Faith there had been an almost fanatical resentment towards Catholics throughout the country. The Duke of York was heir to the throne, and there was a great body of Englishmen who had vowed never to allow a Catholic monarch to sit again on the throne of England.

Already the slogan 'No Popery' had come into being; and it seemed to Danby that, by creating a great scare at this time, he could turn attention from himself to the instigators of the plot. The people were ready to be roused to fury at the thought of Catholic schemes to overthrow the King; some of the most important of the King's ministers would be ready to devote their great energy exclusively to discrediting the Duke of York and arranging a divorce for the King; and mayhap arranging for the legitimization of the Duke of Monmouth, thus providing a Protestant King to follow Charles.

The papers which he studied seemed to contain highly improbable accusations; but Danby was a desperate man.

He sent for Tonge.

'It is very necessary,' he told him, 'for you to produce the man who thrust these papers under your door. Can you do that?'

'I believe I can, my lord.'

'Then do so; and bring him here that he may state his case before the King.'

'I will do my utmost, sir.'

'What is his name?'

'My lord, it is Titus Oates.'

*

Titus Oates was a man of purpose. When he heard that he was to appear before the King he was delighted. He saw immense possibilities before him, and he began to bless the day when Fate threw him in the way of Dr Tonge.

Titus was the son of Samuel Oates, rector of Markham in Norfolk. Titus had been an extremely unprepossessing child, and it had seemed to him from his earliest days that he had been born to misfortune. As a child he had been subject to convulsive fits, and his father had hated the shuffling, delicate child with a face so ugly that it was almost grotesque. His neck was so short that his head seemed to rest on his shoulders; he was ungainly in body, one leg being shorter than the other; but his face, which was purple in colour, was quite repulsive, for his chin was so large that his mouth was in the centre of his face; he suffered from a continuous cold so that he snuffled perpetually; he had an unsightly wart over one eyebrow; and his eyes were small and cunning from the days when he had found it necessary to dodge his father's blows. His mother, though, had lavished great affection on him. He had none for her. Rather he admired his father whose career he soon discovered to have been quite extraordinary. Samuel, feigning to be a very pious man, had, before he settled in Norfolk, wandered the country preaching his own particular brand of the gospels which entailed baptism by immersion of the naked body in lakes and rivers of the districts he visited. Samuel went from village to village; he liked best to dip young women, the more comely the better; and for this purpose he advised them to leave their homes at midnight, without the knowledge of their parents, that they might be baptized and saved. The ceremony of baptism was so complicated that many of the girls found that they gave birth to children as a result of it. But, in view of these results, dipping had eventually become too dangerous a procedure, and Samuel, after some vicissitudes, had settled down as rector of Hastings.

Meanwhile Titus pursued his own not unexciting career.

He went to the Merchant Taylors' School, where he was found to be such a liar and cheat that he was expelled during his first year there; afterwards he was sent as a poor scholar to a school near Hastings where he managed to hide his greater villainies; and eventually, having taken Holy Orders, he became a curate to his father.

The curate of All Saints, Hastings, quickly became the most unpopular man in the district. The rector was heartily disliked, and the people of Hastings would not have believed it was possible to find a man more detestable until they met his son. Titus seemed to delight in circulating scandal concerning those who lived about him. If he could discover some little peccadillo which might be magnified, he was greatly delighted; if he could discover nothing, he used his amazing imagination and an invention which amounted almost to genius.

Samuel hated his son more than ever and wished he had never allowed him to become his curate; therefore, there arose the problem of how to remove Titus. Titus had his living to earn; and it seemed that, if he remained in Hastings, not only the curate but the rector would be asked to leave. A schoolmaster's post would be ideal, decided Samuel; there was one in a local school, but unfortunately it was filled by a certain

262

William Parker, so popular and of such good reputation that it seemed unlikely he could be dismissed to make way for Titus.

Father and son were not the sort to allow any man's virtues to stand in their way.

Titus therefore presented himself to the Mayor and told him that he had seen William Parker in the church porch committing an unnatural offence with a very young boy.

The Mayor was horrified. He declared he could not believe this of William Parker, who had always seemed to him such an honest and honourable man; but Titus, who was a lover of details and had worked on the plan with great thoroughness, managed to convince him that there was truth in the story.

William Parker was sent to jail and Titus, swearing on oath that he was speaking the truth, gave in detail all he alleged he had seen in the church porch.

Titus was eloquent and would have been completely convincing; but he was not yet an adept at the art of perjury, and he had forgotten that truth has an uncomfortable way of tripping up the liar.

Parker was able to prove that he was nowhere near the porch when the offence was alleged to have taken place; the tables were turned; Titus was in danger of imprisonment, and so he ran away to sea.

It was not difficult to get to sea, for His Majesty's Navy was in constant need of men and did not ask many questions. Titus became ship's chaplain, in which role he had opportunities of practising that very offence of which he had accused Parker, and became loathed by all who came into contact with him; and after a while the Navy refused to employ him.

Samuel had been forced to leave Hastings after the Parker affair and was in London, where Titus joined him; but it was soon discovered that Titus was wanted by the law; he was captured and sent to prison, from which he escaped, only to find himself penniless once more. He joined a club in Holborn, where he made the acquaintance of several Catholics, and it was through their influence that he obtained a post of Protestant chaplain in the household of that staunch Catholic, the Duke of Norfolk.

It was at this time that the Catholic scare was beginning to be felt in England, and it had occurred to Titus that there might be some profit in exposing, in the right quarters, the secrets of Catholics. He thereupon set himself out to be as pleasant as he could to Catholics, in the hope of learning their secrets, and obtaining an authentic background for his imagination.

Dismissed from the service of the Duke of Norfolk, he was again in London where he made the acquaintance of Dr Israel Tonge.

Dr Tonge was a fanatic who was prepared to dedicate his life to the persecution of Jesuits. He had written tracts and pamphlets about their wickedness but, as so many had done the like since the conversion of the Duke of York, there was no sale for those of Dr Tonge. This made him bitter; not against those who refused to buy them, but against the Papists. He was more determined than ever to destroy them; and when he renewed his acquaintance with Oates, he saw in him a man who could be made to work for him in the cause so near his heart.

Titus was at the point of starvation and ready enough to do all that was required of him.

The two men met often and began to plot.

Oates was to mingle with the Catholics who congregated in the Pheasant Coffee House in Holborn; Tonge had heard that certain Catholic servants of the Queen frequented the place. There Titus would meet Whitbread and Pickering, and other priests who came from Somerset House, where Catherine worshipped, in accordance with her Faith, in her private chapel.

There was one person whom those two plotters mentioned often; the condemnation of that person could bring them greater satisfaction than that of any other, for to prove the Queen of England a Papist murderer would enrage the country beyond all their hopes. If they could prove that the Queen was plotting to murder the King, then surely there was not a Jesuit in England who would not be brought to torture and death.

'The King is a lecher,' said Oates, licking his lips. 'He will wish to be rid of the Queen.'

Dr Tonge listened to the affected voice of his accomplice and laid a hand on his shoulder. He knew the story of William

Parker and Titus's tendency to be carried away by his imagination.

He warned him: 'This is no plot against a village schoolmaster. This is a charge of High Treason against the Queen. 'Tis true the King is a lecher, but he is soft with women, including his wife. We shall have to build up our case carefully. This is not a matter over which we can hurry. It may take us years to collect the information we need, and we shall accuse and prove guilty many before we reach the climax of our discovery which shall be the villainy of the Queen.'

Tonge's eyes burned with fanaticism. He believed that the Queen must wish to murder the King; he believed in the villainy of all Catholics, and the Queen was devoutly Catholic.

Titus's sunken eyes were almost closed. He was not concerned with the truth of any accusations they would bring. All he cared for was that he should have bread to eat, a roof to shelter him and a chance to indulge that imagination of his which was never content unless it was building up a case against others.

Dr Tonge's plan was long and involved. Titus should mix with Catholics; he should *become* a Catholic, for only thus could he discover all they would need to build the plot which should bring fame and fortune to them both, and win the eternal gratitude of the King and those ministers of his who desired above all things to see the Queen and the Duke of York dismissed from the Court.

Titus 'became' a Catholic and went to study at a college in Valladolid. When he returned, expelled from the college, he brought with him little knowledge, but a fair understanding of the life lived by Jesuit priests; and he and Dr Tonge, impatient to get on with their work, set about fabricating the great Popish plot.

They would begin by warning the King that two Jesuits, Grove and Pickering – men whom Titus had met at the coffee house in Fleet Street – were to be paid £1,500 to shoot the King while he walked in the park. The death of the King was to be followed by that of certain of his ministers; the French would then invade Ireland and a new King would be set up. This was to be the Duke of York, who would then establish a Jesuit Parliament.

That was the first plot. Others would follow; and when

the people were fully aroused, and the King fully alarmed, they would bring forth evidence of the Queen's complicity.

Titus was excited. He saw here a chance to win honours such as had never before come his way.

So when Dr Tonge returned to his lodgings and told Titus that the man who had uncovered the hellish Popish plot and had thrust the papers concerning it under the door of Dr Tonge was ordered to appear before the King, Titus was eager to tell his story.

*

Charles looked at Titus Oates and disliked him on sight.

Oates knew this but was unperturbed; he was accustomed to looks of disgust. He cared for nothing; he had a tale to tell, and he felt himself to be master of his facts.

He was glad now of the affair of William Parker as it had taught him such a lesson.

Beside the King was the Duke of York, for Charles had said he must be present since this matter of plots and counter-plots concerned him as much as Charles himself.

'A preposterous tale,' said Charles when he had read the papers. 'False from beginning to end.'

His eyes were cold. He hated trouble, and these men were determined to make it.

'So you have studied in Valladolid?' he asked Titus.

'It is true, Your Majesty.'

'And you became a Jesuit, that you might mingle with them and discover their secrets?'

'That is so, Your Majesty.'

'What zeal!' commented the King.

' 'Twas all in the service of Your Most Gracious Majesty.'

'And when you were in Madrid you conferred with Don John of Austria, you say in these papers.'

' 'Tis true, Your Majesty.'

'Pray, describe him to me.'

'He is a tall, spare, and swarthy man, if it please Your Majesty.'

'It does not please me,' said Charles with a sardonic smile. 'But doubtless it would please him, for he is a little, fat, fair man, and I believe would desire to appear taller than he is.'

'Your Majesty, it may be that I have made a mistake in

the description of this man. I have met so many.'

'So many of the importance of Don John? Ah, Mr Oates, I see you are a man given to good company.'

Titus stood his ground. He could see that if the King did not believe him, others were ready to do so. The difference was that they wanted to, whereas the King did not.

'You say,' went on the King, 'that the Jesuits will kill not only me but my brother, if he should be unwilling to join them against me, and that they received from Père la Chaise, who is Confessor to Louis Quatorze, a donation of £10,000.'

'That is so, Your Majesty.'

Those about the King seemed impressed. It was true that Père la Chaise was Confessor to the French King.

'And that there was a promise of a similar sum from another gentleman?'

'From De Corduba of Castile, Your Majesty.'

Again Titus was aware of his success. He made sure of facts. The visit to Spain had been well worth while. What if he had made a mistake in his description of a man; those about the King did not consider that to be of any great importance.

'So la Chaise paid down £10,000, did he? Where did he do this, and were you there?'

'Yes, Your Majesty. It was in the house of the Jesuits, close to the Louvre.'

'Man!' cried the King. 'The Jesuits have no house within a mile of the Louvre!'

'I doubt not,' said Titus slyly, 'that Your Majesty during your stay in Paris was too good a Protestant to know all the secret places of the Jesuits.'

'The meeting is over,' said Charles. 'I will hear no more.'

And, putting his arm through that of his brother, the King led James away, murmuring: 'The man is a lying rogue. I am certain of it.'

*

But the news of the great Popish plot was spreading through the streets of London. The citizens stood about in groups discussing it. They talked of the Gunpowder Plot; they recalled the days of Bloody Mary, when the fires of Smithfield had blackened the sky and a page of English history.

'No Popery!' they shouted. Nor were they willing to wait

for trials. They formed themselves into mobs and set about routing out the Catholics.

Coleman, who had been secretary of the Catholic Duchess of York, and one of the suspects at whom Titus had pointed, was found to be in possession of documents sent him by that very Père la Chaise, for Coleman was in truth a spy for France.

All the King's scepticism could do nothing to quieten rumour. The people's blood was up. They believed in the authenticity of the plot. The Jesuits were rogues who must be tracked down to their deaths; Titus Oates was a hero who had saved the King's life and the country from the Papists.

Oates was given lodgings in Whitehall. He was heard in royal palaces talking of Popery in his high nasal and affected voice interspersed with the coarsest of oaths; he was at the summit of delight; he had longed for fame such as this; he was no longer a poor despised outcast; he was admired by all. He was Titus Oates, exposer of Jesuits, the man of the moment.

The King, still declaring the man to be a fake, went off to Newmarket, leaving his ministers to do what they would.

And Titus, determined to hold what he had at last achieved, concocted fresh plots and looked for new victims.

*

Catherine was afraid.

In her apartments at Somerset House she sensed approaching doom. She felt she had few friends and owed much to the Count of Castelmelhor, a Portuguese nobleman, who had been loyal to Alphonso and had found it necessary to leave the country when Pedro was in control. He had come to Catherine for shelter and had brought great comfort to her during those terrible weeks.

Her servants brought her news of what was happening, and from her stronghold she would often hear the sound of shouting in the streets. She would hear screams and protests as some poor man or woman was set upon; she would hear wild rumours of how this person, whom she had known, and that person, for whom she had a great respect, was being taken up for questioning. 'No Popery! No slavery!' was the continual cry. And Titus Oates and Dr Tonge with their supporters were banded together to corroborate each other's stories and fabricate wilder and still wilder plots in order to implicate those they wished to destroy.

The King, disgusted with the whole affair and certain that Titus was a liar, was quick to sense the state of the country. He had to be careful. His brother was a confessed Catholic. It might be that that clause in the secret treaty of Dover was known to too many, and that he himself might be suspect; he was afraid to show too much leniency to Catholics. He was shrewd, and the tragic events of his life had made him cautious. He remembered – although he had been but a boy at the time – the feeling of the country in those days before the Civil War, which had ended in the defeat of his father, had broken out. He sensed a similar atmosphere. He knew that Shaftesbury and Buckingham with other powerful men were seeking to remove the Duke of York; he knew too that they plotted against Catherine and were determined either to see him divorced and married to a Queen who could provide a Protestant heir, or to see Monmouth legitimized.

He must walk very carefully. He must temporize by giving the people their head; he must not make the mistakes his father had made. He must allow those accused by the odious Titus Oates to be arrested, questioned and, if found guilty, to suffer the horrible death accorded to traitors.

He was grieved, and the whole affair made him very melancholy. He would have liked to have put Titus Oates and his friends in an open boat and sent them out to sea, that they might go anywhere so long as they did not stay in England.

But he dared not go against the people's wishes. They wanted Catholic scapegoats, and they were calling Oates the Saviour of England for providing them. They must be humoured, for their King was determined to go no more a-wandering in exile. So he went to Windsor and spent a great deal of time fishing, while he indulged in melancholy thought; and Titus Oates lived in style at Whitehall Palace, ate from the King's plate and was protected by guards when he walked abroad. All tried not to meet his eye, and if they were forced to do so, responded with obsequious and admiring smiles, for Titus had but to point the finger and pretend to remember an occasion when a man or woman had plotted against the King's life, and that man or woman would be thrown into jail.

Titus was content; for all those powerful men who had for ten years been seeking to bring about a divorce between the King and Queen saw Titus as a means of perfecting their plans, and to Titus they gave their support.

Catherine knew this.

She longed for the King to come and see her, but she heard that he was at Windsor. There was no one to whom she could turn for advice except those immediately about her, and they were mostly Catholics who feared for their own lives.

She began to realize that the trap into which many of her servants were in danger of falling was in reality being prepared for herself.

There came news that a certain magistrate of the City, Sir Edmund Berry Godfrey, had been murdered. He it was who had taken Titus's affidavit concerning the Popish Plot. He was known as a Protestant although he had Catholic friends, and the manner of his meeting his death was very mysterious. Titus accused the Papists of murdering him, and the magistrate's funeral was conducted with great ceremony while Titus and his friends did everything they could to incite the citizens to fury against his murderers, declared by Titus to be Catholics.

Charles had offered £500 reward for anyone bringing the murderer of Godfrey to justice, although he half suspected that the man had been murdered by Titus's agents for the purpose of rousing the mob to fresh fury, for it seemed that whenever this showed signs of lagging, some such incident would take place, some new plot would be discovered.

It was then that William Bedloe made himself known and came before the Council with a terrible tale to tell.

Bedloe was a convict, and he had met Titus when they were both in Spain. At that time Bedloe had been living on his wits and posing as an English nobleman, with his brother James acting as his manservant. He was handsome and plausible, and had managed during his free life to live at the expense of others, but he had served many sentences in Newgate and had just been released from that prison.

He was attracted by the King's promised reward of £500 and by the fact that his old friend Titus, whom he had last known as a very poor scholar of dubious reputation in Valla-dolid, was now fêted and honoured with three servants at his beck and call and several gentlemen to help him dress and hold his basin whilst he washed.

Bedloe did not see why he should not share in his friend's good fortune, so he came forward to offer his services.

*

It seemed to Catherine that she was always waiting for some-thing to happen; she was afraid when she heard a movement outside her door. She believed that these men were preparing to strike at her, and she was not sure when and how the blow would fall.

It was dusk, and she had come from her chapel to that small chamber in which her solitary meal would be served. And as she was about to sit at her table, the door was thrown open and two of her priests came in to throw themselves at her feet.

'Madam, Madam!' they cried. 'Protect us. For the love of God and all the Saints, protect us.'

They were kneeling, clutching at her skirts, when she lifted her eyes and saw that guards had entered the chamber.

'What do you want of these men?' she asked.

'We come to take them for questioning, Madam,' was the answer.

'Questioning? On what matter?'

'On the matter of murder, Madam.'

'I do not understand.'

'They are accused of being concerned in the murder of Sir Edmund Berry Godfrey.'

'But this is not true. It is quite ridiculous.'

'Madam, information has been laid with the Council which may prove them guilty.'

'You shall not take them,' cried Catherine. 'They are my servants.'

'Madam,' said the guard who was spokesman, 'we come in the name of the King.'

Her hands fell helplessly to her side.

*

When they had taken the two priests away, she went into her chapel and prayed for them.

271

Oh, these terrible times! she mused. What will happen next? What will happen to those two servants of mine? What have they done – those two good men – what have they done to deserve punishment, except to think differently, to belong to a Faith other than that of Titus Oates?

She was on her knees for a long time, and when she went back to her apartment she was conscious of the tension throughout her household.

She was aware of strained and anxious faces.

Walsh and le Fevre today. Who next? That was what all were asking themselves. And every man and woman in her service knew that if they were taken it would be because, through them, it might be possible to strike at the Queen.

They trembled. They were fond of their mistress; it would be the greatest tragedy in their lives if they should betray her in some way. But who could say what might be divulged if the questioners should become too cruelly determined to prise falsehood from unwilling lips!

'There is nothing to fear,' said Catherine, trying to smile. 'We are all innocent here. I know it. These cruel men, who seek to torture and destroy those of our Faith, cannot do so for long. The King will not allow it. The King will see justice done. They cannot deceive him.'

No! It was true that they could not deceive him; but he was a man who loved peace; he was a man who had wandered across Europe for many years, an exiled Prince; he was a man whose own father had been murdered by his own countrymen.

The King might be shrewd; he might be kind; but he longed for peace, and how could they be sure whether he would bestir himself to see justice done?

And at the back of Catherine's mind was a terrible fear.

She was no longer young; she had never been beautiful. What if the temptation to put her from him was too great; what if the wife they offered him was as beautiful as Frances Stuart had been in the days before her disfigurement?

Who could tell what would happen?

The Queen of England was a frightened woman during those days of conspiracy.

*

The Duchess of Buckingham brought her the news. She and Mary Fairfax had always been great friends, for there was much sympathy between them. They were both plain women and, if one had been married to the most charming man in England, the other had been married to one of the most handsome.

Mary Fairfax knew that her husband was one of the Queen's greatest enemies; she loved her husband but she was too intelligent not to understand his motives, and she could not resist coming to warn the Queen.

'Your Majesty,' she cried, 'this man Bedloe has sworn that Sir Edmund Berry Godfrey was murdered by your servants.'

'It cannot be true. How could they do such a thing? They were nowhere near the place where his body was found.'

'They have trumped up a story,' said Mary. 'They declare that Godfrey was invited to Somerset House at five o'clock in the afternoon, and that he was brought into one of the rooms here and held by a man of my Lord Bellasis' whilst Walsh and le Fevre stifled him with the aid of two pillows.'

'No one can believe such a tale.'

'The people believe what they want to believe at a time like this,' said Mary sadly. 'They say that the body lay on your back staircase for two days. Many have been arrested. The prisons are full. The crowds are congregating outside and shouting for them to be brought out, hung, drawn, and quartered.'

The Queen shuddered. 'And my poor innocent priests . . .?'

'They will prove their innocence.'

'These lies are monstrous. Will no one listen to the truth?'

'Your Majesty, the people are treating this man Oates as though he is a god. They are arresting all sorts of people. Do you remember Mr Pepys of the Navy Office, who did such good service at the time of the great fire? He was taken up, and God alone knows what would have become of him had not one of his accusers – his own butler – come suddenly to his deathbed and, fearing to die with the lies on his lips, confessed that he had borne false witness. He is a good Protestant. Then why was he taken? Your Majesty might ask. Merely because he had been in the service of the Duke of York who thought highly of him.'

'No one is safe,' murmured the Queen. 'No one is safe.'

She looked at Mary and was ashamed of herself for suspecting her. But the thought had crossed her mind then; how could she be sure who was her friend?

Who was this man Bedloe who had sworn he had seen the body of a murdered man on her backstairs? Had he been here, disguised as one of her servants?

How could she know who were her enemies; how could she know whom she could trust?

*

In the streets they were saying that the Queen's servants were the murderers of the City magistrate; and since these men were the Queen's servants, that meant that it was at the instigation of the Queen that the man had been murdered.

She was alone ... alone in a hostile country. She did not believe now that they merely wished to be rid of her; they wished for her death.

They were going to accuse her of murder, and there was no one to stand between her and her accusers.

The country was feverish with excitement; plot after plot was discovered every day; armed bands walked the streets wearing the sign 'No Popery' in their hats; and they all talked of the Papist Queen who had murdered the Protestant Magistrate.

Titus Oates went about the town in his episcopal gown of silk, in his cassock and great hat with its satin band; he wore a long scarf about his shoulders and shouted to the people that he was the saviour of the nation.

He was ugly in spite of his finery, but none in those fear-ridden streets dared so much as hint that this was so. All who saw him bowed in homage, all called to him that England had been saved by him.

Catherine knew that the misshapen little man was thinking particularly of one victim whom he longed to trap; she knew he was waiting for the right moment, because she was such an important victim that he dared not pounce too soon.

Then suddenly she knew that she was not alone. She knew that she had not been mistaken, for the King came riding into the capital from Windsor.

He had heard of the accusation against the Queen's servants, and he would realize to what this was leading.

He sent for Bedloe. He would have an exact description of what had taken place at Somerset House. Would the man describe the room in which the murder had taken place? Would he give the exact day on which this had happened?

Bedloe was only too willing to oblige. He gave details of the Queen's residence, for he had made sure of being correct on this.

But when he had finished the King faced him squarely. 'It is a strange thing to me,' he said, 'that I should have visited Her Majesty on the day you mention, and that I should have been at Somerset House at the very hour the murder took place.'

'Your Majesty,' began the man, 'this may have been so, but Sir Edmund was lured inside while Your Majesty was with the Queen.'

The King raised his eyebrows. He said lightly: 'Since you and your friends startled my people with your stories of plots, my guards have been most careful of my person. I must tell you that, at the hour when the magistrate was said to have been lured into Somerset House, every possible entry was well guarded because I was there also. Could he have been lured past the guards, think you? And I will add that your tale lacks further conviction, for the passage, in which you say the body of the man lay, is that which leads to the Queen's dining chamber, so that her servants, when bringing her meals, must either have walked over the corpse or not noticed it, which I scarcely think is likely.'

Bedloe was about to speak.

'Take this man away!' roared the King.

And Bedloe was hurried out, lest a command to send him to the Tower might be given. Charles was too shrewd to give such an order. He was aware that, as at the time of the war with the Dutch, revolution was in the air.

He could not stem the stream of accusations against the Queen, but he was there to give her his protection while he could do so.

*

The people continued to believe that the Queen was guilty. Buckingham and Shaftesbury were bent on two things: the exile of the Duke of York and his Duchess; and the ruin of the Queen. The King had declined to rid himself of her by divorce; therefore there was only one other way of ridding the country of her.

Why should she not be accused of plotting against the King's life? Titus Oates had the people ready to believe any lie that fell from his lips. He must now uncover for them a plot more startling than any which he had given them before. It could be proved that the Queen had written to the Pope; she had done this during the first weeks of her arrival in England; she had offered to try to turn the King to Catholicism, in exchange for the Pope's recognition of her brother as King of Portugal. But more should be proved against the Queen.

She had refused to enter a nunnery; perhaps she would prefer the block.

Titus Oates, drunk with power, delighting in his eminence, knew what was expected of him.

He set out to concoct the plot to outshine all plots.

The country waited; those men who had determined on the ruin of the Queen waited. And Catherine also waited.

*

Oates stood before the members of the Privy Council. He had grave matters of which to speak to them. He was a careful man, he reminded them; he was a man who had pretended to become a Jesuit for the sake of unearthing their wicked schemes; he was a brave man, they would realize from that, so he did not hesitate to make an accusation against a person however high that person stood in the land.

'My lords,' he said in his high affected voice, 'there are certain matters which I feel it my duty to disclose to you concerning the Queen.'

'The Queen!'

The members of the Council feigned to be astonished, but Titus was aware of their alert and eager faces.

'Her Majesty has been sending sums of money to the Jesuits. They are always at her elbow ... in secret conclave.'

They were watching his face. Dare I? He wondered. It needed daring. He was uncertain, and this matter concerned no other than the King's own wife.

But Titus was blown up with his own conceit. He was not afraid. Was he not great Titus, the saviour of his country?

He made his plots, and he made them with such care and with such delight that he came to believe in them even as he elaborated and made his sharp little twists and turns to extricate himself from the maze into which his lies often led him.

'I have seen a letter in which the Queen gives her consent to the murder of the King.'

There was a sharp intake of breath as every eye was fixed on that repulsive, almost inhuman face.

'Why did you not report this before?' asked Shaftesbury sharply.

Titus folded his hands. 'A matter concerning so great a lady? I felt I must make sure that that which I feel it my duty to bring to your notice was truth.'

'And you have now made certain of this?'

Titus took a step nearer to the table about which sat the ministers.

'I was at Somerset House. I waited in an antechamber. I heard the Queen say these words: "I will no longer suffer such indignities to my bed. I am content to join in procuring the death of the Black Bastard, and the propagation of the Catholic Faith." '

'This were high treason,' said Buckingham.

'Punishable by death!' declared Shaftesbury.

But they were uneasy.

'Why did you not tell this earlier?' asked one of the ministers.

'I have been turning over in my mind whether I should not first impart it to His Majesty.'

'How can you be sure that it was the Queen who spoke these words?'

'There was no other woman present.'

'So you know the Queen?'

'I have seen her, and I knew her.'

'This is a matter,' said Shaftesbury, 'to which we must all give our closest attention. It may be that the King's life is in imminent danger – in a quarter where he would least expect it.'

*

Titus was elaborating his plot. Poison was to be administered to the King; and when he was dead the Duke of York would reign, and there would be a place of honour in the land for his Catholic sister-in-law.

In Somerset House the Queen was fearful. Rumour reached her. She knew that evil forces were working against her. What if, next time she was accused, the King could not save her?

What would he do then? she asked herself. Would he stand by and leave her to her fate?

*

The climax came on a dark November day. Titus could contain himself no longer. His friend Bedloe had been pardoned for all his offences, as payment for the evidence he had given against the Papists.

Titus, so happy in his episcopal robes, smoothing his long scarf, thinking of the happy days on which he had fallen after all the lean years, hearing the shouts of acclamation when he had been so accustomed to shouts of derision, was called to the bar of the House of Commons to give further evidence of plots he had unearthed.

He stood at the bar, and his voice rang out.

He said those fatal words which were meant to condemn an innocent woman to the block and to bring about the long hoped-for conclusion of unscrupulous statesmen: 'Aye, Taitus Oates, accause Catherine Queen of England of Haigh Treason.'

The words were greeted with a shocked silence.

Buckingham was heard to curse under his breath: 'The fool! It is too soon as yet!'

And then the news was out.

All over London, and soon all over the country, the people of England were calling for the blood of the woman who had sought to poison their King.

*

So this was the end. Catherine sat like a statue, and beside her was the Count Castelmelhor, whose expression of blank misery made it clear that he believed there was nothing more that he could do for her.

There would be a trial, thought Catherine; and her judges

would find her guilty because they had determined to do so.

And Charles?

She understood his case.

His position was an uneasy one. The people were crying out for the blood of Papists, and she was a Papist. Revolution trembled in the air; she was fully aware that there was one day which Charles would never forget – that was a bleak January day when his father had been led to execution.

If he showed any leniency towards the Catholics now, the country would be screaming for his blood too. He knew it, and he had sworn that, at whatever cost, he would never go travelling again.

The people of England were repudiating her. She was a barren Queen; she was a Queen whose dowry had never been paid in full; and she was a Papist. The tall dark man with the melancholy face was no longer ruler of England; that role had fallen to a shuffling man with the most evil of countenances who went by the name of Titus Oates.

There seemed nothing to do but to wait for her doom.

*

Castelmelhor had news for her.

'The King has questioned those who accuse Your Majesty. He has questioned them with the utmost severity, and it is clear to all those who hear him that he is greatly displeased with those who would destroy you.'

A gentle smile illumined Catherine's face. 'Yes, he would be unhappy. That is like him. But he will do nothing. How can he? It would be against the people's wishes. And he must consider them now.'

'He has insisted on a minute description of the room of this Palace in which Oates swears he overheard you plan to poison him; he says a woman would have to shout, for Oates to have heard her say what he declares he heard you say; he has said that you are a low-voiced woman. He is doing everything to prove your accusers liars.'

Catherine smiled, and the tears started to flow gently down her cheeks.

'I shall remember that,' she said. 'When they lead me to the block I shall remember it. He did not pass by on the other side of the road. He stopped to succour me.'

'Your Majesty must not despair. If the King is with you, others will follow. He is still the King. He is very angry that you should be so accused. They are saying now that Sir George Wakeman was to have brought the poison to you, and that you were to administer it to the King when he next visited you. The King has laughed the idea to scorn, and he says he will never suffer an innocent lady to be oppressed.'

'I shall never forget those words,' said Catherine. 'I shall carry them with me to the grave. I know they have determined on my death, but he would have saved me, if he could.'

'You underestimate the power of the King, Madam.'

'My dear Castelmelhor, come to the window.'

She took his hand and drew him there, for he was reluctant to go with her. Already the crowds were gathering. She saw their hats with the bands about them on which were written 'No Popery! No Slavery!' They carried sticks and knives; they were a vicious mob.

They had come to mock and curse her on her journey to the Tower.

*

A barge was on the river. The crowds hurried to its edge.

They have come to take me away, thought Catherine. I shall lie in my prison in the Tower as others have before me. I am guilty of the crime of Queens; I could not bear a son.

This was the end then – the end of that love story which was to have been so perfect, and of which she had dreamed long ago in the Lisbon Palace. She would sail down the river to the grim grey fortress into which she would enter by way of the Traitors' Gate.

It might be that she would never again set eyes on Charles's face. He would not wish to see her. It would distress him too much, for however much he wished to be rid of her, he would never believe her guilty of conspiring to poison him.

She heard the shouts of the people. She could not see the barge, for the crowds on the bank hid it; but now someone had stepped ashore. It was a tall figure, slender, black-clad, the dark curls of his wig falling over his shoulders, his broad-brimmed plumed hat on his head, while those about him were hatless.

Charles!

So he had come to see her. She felt dizzy with her emotion. He had come; and she had never thought he would come. He could have only one purpose in coming to her now.

With him were members of the Court, and his personal guards; he came from the landing stairs to the house with those so well-remembered quick strides of his.

'The King is here!' The words echoed through the house. It was as though the very walls and hangings were trembling with excitement – and hope.

He strode into the room; she tried to approach him, but her limbs trembled so that she could not move. She wanted to sink to her knees and kiss his hand. She merely stood mutely before him, looking up into that lined and well-loved face.

Then he put his hands upon her shoulders and, drawing her towards him, kissed her there before them all.

That kiss was the answer to all who saw it; it was the defiance of two people who were going to stand against all those who were the enemies of the Queen. They had not understood him. They had thought him too facile. They thought that he, being an unfaithful husband, was faithless throughout. They thought that he, finding it so easy to smile and make promises, could never stand firm.

'I have come to take you with me to Whitehall,' he said. 'It is not meet that you and I should live apart in these times.'

Still she could find no words. She felt his hands gripping hers; she saw the tender smile which she remembered from the days of their honeymoon.

'Come,' he said, 'let us go now. I am eager to show them that, whatever comes, the King and Queen stand together.'

Then she could not suppress her emotion.

She threw herself against him and cried, half laughing, half in tears: 'Charles, you do not believe these stories against me? Charles, I love you with all my heart.'

He said: 'I know it.'

'They will seek to prove these terrible things against me.' They will lie and . . . and the people listen to their lies.'

'You are returning with me to Whitehall,' he said, 'whence we shall go to Windsor. We will ride through the countryside together, you and I; for I wish the people to know that in this turmoil there are two who stand side by side in trust and love and confidence: the King and his Queen in whom he puts his trust.'

The crowds were gathering about the house. She could hear their shouts.

'Come,' he said. 'Let us go. Let us leave at once. Are you afraid?'

'No,' she said, putting her hand in his, no longer afraid.

They left the house; the people stood back in a hushed silence; they stepped into the barge; the King was smiling at the Queen, and he kept her hand in his.

They sailed along the river to Whitehall and it was seen that never had the King paid more attention to any woman than he did at that time to his Queen.

Catherine felt then that those dreams which had come to her in the Lisbon Palace had materialized. She knew that it was such moments as this which made all that she had suffered worth while.

All through the years to come she would treasure this moment; she would remember that when she was lonely and afraid, when she was in imminent peril, that man who had come to her and brought her to safety was the one whom she loved.

EPILOGUE

SOME TWENTY-FOUR years after the reign of Charles had ended, Barbara, Duchess of Cleveland, lay in a house in the village of Chiswick; she was dying.

Sixty-eight years of age, an intriguante to the end, she had not ceased to look for lovers. So many of those who had witnessed the days of her glory were long since dead. Even Catherine the Queen, who had lived to an old age, had died four years before, just at the time when Barbara was contracting that most disastrous marriage with a man who had in his day been one of the most handsome rakes in London.

She lay on her bed, swollen to a great size by the dropsy which had attacked her. She felt too old and tired even to abuse her attendants; a sure sign, they felt, that the end was near.

She dozed a little and allowed her mind to slip back to events of the past. It was the only pleasure left to her. The greatest evil which could befall her had come upon her; she was old, no longer beautiful nor desirable; she remembered faintly that some member of the Court, with whom she had quarrelled, had once declared that he hoped to see her come to such a state.

Well, it was upon her now.

She had lost the King's favour to her old enemy the Duchess of Portsmouth; she had had many lovers since then but she had never ceased to regret the loss of Charles. She had schemed to marry her children into the richest and most noble families of England; and only Barbara, her youngest and Churchill's child, had become a nun.

She thought of coming back to England just before Charles's death, with high hopes of returning to his favour. But he remembered too well the tantrums and furies of the past; he was happy with Louise de Kéroualle, his Duchess of Portsmouth, and Nelly the play-girl.

In place of the King she had found an actor lover, a gay adventurer, named Cardonell Goodman. Ah, he had been handsome, and what joy to see him strut across the stage as Alexas in Dryden's *All for Love*, or Julius Caesar, or Alexander the Great. She had paid him well; and he had been grateful, for an actor's pay of six and threepence a day had been inadequate for the needs of such a man. No wonder he had loved her. No wonder he had refused to allow the play to start until his Duchess was in her box, even though the Queen herself had come to see it! He had tried to poison her children. Oh, he was a rogue, but an exciting one, and she had his child to remember him by.

But she was growing old and her body had become over-heavy; and the worst calamity which had befallen her was the death of Roger, for then she had been foolish enough to go through a form of marriage with Robert Feilding, who was known as 'Beau'.

The thought of that villain could rouse her from her torpor even now and bring the tumultuous blood rushing to her head. Be calm! she admonished herself. You do yourself harm by thinking of the rogue!

In Feilding she had found another such as she herself had

been; but, being ten years her junior, he had the whip hand, and he used it. He had dared to dictate to her and, if she did not carry out his wishes, to lay about her with his heavy hands. He had dared to inflict bruises on the Duchess of Cleveland!

But Fate was kinder to her than perhaps she deserved; for she discovered that she was not after all his wife, since he had contracted a marriage with another woman some short while before he had gone through the ceremony with her.

And with Feilding had ended her matrimonial adventures. She had felt only one desire then – to live in seclusion.

So in the village of Chiswick she had come to end her days.

The room was growing dark; she could hear voices but she could no longer see the figures which moved about her.

She closed her eyes, and as her attendants bent over her bed, one murmured: 'Was this then ... this bloated creature ... was she once the most beautiful of women?'

*

It was four years before the death of Barbara when, in the quiet Palace of Lisbon, in that chamber to which no man must be admitted, Catherine of Braganza lay dying.

She was an old woman now, having reached her sixty-seventh year, and it was twenty years since Charles had died.

Now, as she lay in her bed with only Donna Inez Antonia de Tavora to wait on her, she felt life slipping away from her and was not always conscious of the room in which she lay.

It seemed to her that sometimes she was back in the Palace of Whitehall, enduring agonies of jealousy as she saw her husband become deeply enamoured of other women. It had not been the end of jealousy when he had come to Somerset House and saved her from her enemies. He had not changed towards her. He was the same Charles as he had ever been. She had still remained his plain wife who did not attract him, who must be perpetually jealous of the beautiful women with whom he surrounded himself; but she had learned one thing: he would always be there when any dire peril threatened her.

He had saved her; it had been said, during the weeks which followed that journey from Somerset House to Whitehall: 'The King has a new mistress – his wife.'

Yet he had been unable to save her servants; he had been against the bloody executions which had followed, but he had done all he dared in saving his wife.

She recalled those unhappy days when England was ruled by a cruel rogue and wicked perjurer. She remembered the exile of the unhappy Duke of York, and later his defeat by his daughter's husband; she remembered the coming of William of Orange – and her own unhappy treatment at the hands of that sovereign and his wife Mary. She remembered returning to her native land and building this Palace of Bemposta; and she looked back on these last five years of her life as the peaceful years.

But there was one thing she remembered more vividly than anything, and that was the last time she had seen the man she had loved throughout her life. The pain he suffered could not disturb that wry smile; the agony of death could not quench the wit which came so readily to his lips.

She had wept and had begged that he would forgive her for failing him – for failing to bring him the dowry which he had so desired, for failing to bring him the beauty which he had so much admired, for failing to give him a son.

She would treasure his answer to the very end. 'You beg my pardon? Do not, I pray you, for it is I who should beg yours, and this I do with all my heart.'

Now she murmured those words to herself.

'He begged my pardon with all his heart. What need had he to beg my pardon with all his heart, when I loved him with all mine?'

The end was near. The room was now crowded; she was vaguely conscious of the last ceremonies, for it seemed to her that at the last there was one who stood beside her – tall and very dark, with a jest on his lips – who took her hand to lead her; and she was smiling, for thus she was not afraid.